THE LOST ABBOT

The Nineteenth Chronicle of
Matthew Bartholomew

Susanna Gregory

SPHERE

First published in Great Britain in 2013 by Sphere
This paperback edition published in 2014 by Sphere

A CIP catalogue record for this book
is available from the British Library.

ISBN 978-0-7515-4974-4

Typeset in New Baskerville by Palimpsest Book Production Limited,
Falkirk, Stirlingshire
Printed and bound in Great Britain by Clays Ltd, St Ives plc

MIX
Paper from
responsible sources
FSC® C104740

Papers used by Sphere are from well-managed forests
and other responsible sources.

Sphere
An imprint of
Little, Brown Book Group
100 Victoria Embankment
London EC4Y 0DY

An Hachette UK Company
www.hachette.co.uk

www.littlebrown.co.uk

For Sheila Hakin

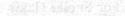

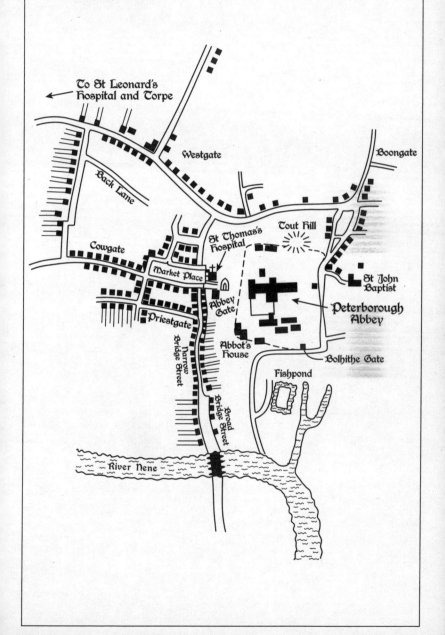

Peterborough in the 1350s

To St Leonard's Hospital and Torpe

Westgate

Boongate

Back Lane

Cowgate

Tout Hill

St Thomas's Hospital

Market Place

St John Baptist

Abbey Gate

Peterborough Abbey

Priestgate

Abbot's House

Bolhithe Gate

Narrow Bridge Street

Fishpond

Broad Bridge Street

River Nene

PROLOGUE

Lawrence de Oxforde did not believe for a moment that he was going to be executed. A pardon would arrive from the King, the hangman would stand down, and Oxforde would live to fight another day. Or, to put it more accurately, he thought with a smirk, to burgle another house, because he had no intention of giving up the life that had turned him from a nameless clerk into the most celebrated outlaw in the region.

It was a grey day, clouds hanging flat and low over the little Fenland town, and the threat of rain was in the air. The scaffold had been erected on the far bank of the River Nene, and it seemed to Oxforde that the entire population of Peterborough had turned out to trail after his cart as it trundled from prison to gibbet. There were toothless ancients, brawny labourers with sun-reddened faces, maidens, children and monks from the abbey. Oxforde allowed himself a small, self-satisfied smile. It was only natural that work should grind to a halt on this of all days. He was famous, so of course everyone would want to see him in the flesh.

As the cart lumbered across the wooden bridge, he glanced behind him. Peterborough was a pretty cluster of red-roofed houses nestled among billowing oaks, all dwarfed by the mighty golden mass of the abbey church.

1

Oxforde's mouth watered – wealthy homes, shops loaded with goods, and a monastery bursting with treasure. It was a burglar's dream, and he would certainly linger there for a few days once he was free to resume his life of crime.

He swaggered as he alighted from the cart, and called brash witticisms to the spectators. He was puzzled when they only glowered at him, and wondered what was wrong. He was a legend, a man who had relieved more rich folk of their ill-gotten gains than any other thief in history. The town's paupers should be all admiration that he had eluded capture for so long.

'Murderer!' howled young Joan Sylle, the abbey's laundress.

Oxforde was stung by the hatred burning in her eyes. 'Only the rich,' he snapped back at her. Surely she understood that he had had to dispatch the odd victim? What robber had not? The occasional slit throat was unavoidable in his line of business.

'The potter was not rich,' shouted Roger Botilbrig, a spotty lad who was never far from Joan's side.

'Neither was his wife,' a deeper voice called out.

'Nor his children,' another added.

A chorus of condemnation rippled through the crowd, and Oxforde slowed his jaunty progress. He had had no choice but to kill the potter and his family – they had stumbled across him as he was poring over his latest haul. Unfortunately, he had been less than thorough, and one had survived long enough to identify him.

'That was different,' he said, less resonantly than before. 'It was hardly my fault they—'

'Keep walking,' interrupted the priest who was behind

him. His name was Kirwell, and lines etched into his thin, pale face suggested that life had been a struggle. He was going blind, too, at which point he would lose his post as parish priest. It would not be easy for a sightless cleric to make ends meet, so Oxforde had decided to help him – and to help himself into the bargain. Kirwell had been unrelenting in his efforts to save Oxforde's soul, and although the robber had scant time for religion, he thought Kirwell deserved some reward for his dogged persistence.

'Do not worry about the future, Father,' he murmured. 'I have plans for you.'

'It is not me you should be thinking about today,' Kirwell whispered back, kindly but dismissively. 'It is your immortal soul. Now ignore the crowd and keep moving. I shall stay at your side, so you will not die alone.'

'I will not die at all,' said Oxforde, loudly indignant. 'My pardon will arrive soon, you will see.'

He spoke with such confidence that some folk exchanged uneasy glances. Oxforde laughed, gratified by their disquiet. Doubtless they were afraid that he might visit them next. Well, perhaps he would, because although he had amassed a huge fortune and hidden it in a place where no one else would ever think to look, there was always room for more.

The Sheriff stepped forward. 'Hurry up,' he ordered the executioner sharply. 'Every extra moment he lives is an insult to God.'

'And an insult to his victims,' added Joan, while those around her nodded agreement.

'Victims!' spat Oxforde. '*I* am the victim here. A man has to make a living, you know.'

'A little contrition would not go amiss,' counselled Kirwell softly. 'It would count for something when your sins are weighed. And they are many – too many to count.'

Oxforde sniffed to indicate that he did not agree. He climbed the steps to the scaffold with jaunty defiance, then turned to the priest, supposing it was as good a time as any to put his plan into action.

'I like you, Kirwell, so I am going to give you something. However, there is a condition: you must never show it to anyone else. If you keep it secret, you will enjoy a long and comfortable life. But if you sell it – or even let another person see it – you will die.'

'I do not want anything from you,' said Kirwell, although not before hope had flashed in his eyes. He was terrified of the grinding poverty that lay ahead of him, a fear that Oxforde fully intended to exploit.

'You will want this,' he crooned enticingly. 'It is the prayer I composed last night – the one thanking God for my pardon. You said it was beautiful, so I wrote it down for you.'

There was no mistaking Kirwell's disappointment, although he accepted the folded parchment graciously enough. 'Thank you.'

'But remember: show it to no one.'

Kirwell nodded, but there were many who would pay handsomely for something scribed by England's most famous thief, and the priest needed money desperately. Of course he would sell the thing. Indeed, Oxforde was counting on it.

'It is time to think of more urgent matters,' the priest said, shoving the parchment into his scrip. 'Death is but moments away and—'

'Rubbish!' declared Oxforde. 'The Sheriff will not execute a legend.'

He continued in this vein until the noose was placed around his neck, then he became uneasy: the King was cutting it rather fine. He started to add something else, but the words never emerged, because the hangman was hauling on the rope.

There was a ragged cheer from the spectators as he jerked and twisted, feet kicking empty air. Kirwell bowed his head to pray, but he was the only one who did: everyone else was too relieved to see the end of the man who had plagued the shire for so many years.

When his struggles were over and the executioner had declared him dead, Oxforde was placed in a coffin. It was thicker and stronger than most caskets, and the hangman's assistants fastened the lid with an inordinate number of nails. Most of the crowd followed as it was toted to the cemetery.

'Are you sure it is right to bury him in St Thomas's churchyard?' the Sheriff asked Kirwell, as they joined the end of the procession. 'He was impenitent to the end, and the Church does not normally let executed criminals lie in consecrated ground.'

Kirwell gestured to the long line of people who walked silently behind the coffin. 'They have a terrible fear that he might return from the dead to haunt them, and there is a belief that only holy soil will keep him in his grave. I think they deserve some peace of mind after living in fear of him all these years.'

The Sheriff nodded his understanding, then gave a wry smile. 'And there is a certain satisfaction in putting him in that particular hole.'

Two months before, a silversmith had been interred in St Thomas's cemetery, amid rumours that he had bought the plot next to it for bits of his favourite jewellery. Oxforde had been digging for them when he had been caught.

So Oxforde was lowered into the pit he himself had made, and the hangman and his lads began to shovel soil on top of him: it landed with a muffled thud. Then there was a different kind of thump, one that caused everyone to start back in alarm. Had it come from inside the coffin?

'Continue,' ordered the Sheriff urgently. 'Quickly now!'

Several onlookers hurried forward to help, flinging great spadefuls of earth down so fast and furiously that even if another sound had emerged, it would not have been heard. They finished by stamping down the mound as hard as they could, and some folk brought heavy stones to pile over the top.

When it was done, the Sheriff breathed a sigh of relief. 'There! That should hold him.'

The next morning was even more grey and dismal, with clouds so thick that it felt like dusk. Kirwell returned to the grave to petition the saints for the dead man's soul, although he suspected he was wasting his time: Oxforde's sins were too great and his victims too many. The prayer was on the table in his house, and he had already been offered a shilling for it. He was inclined to accept, because he did not believe for a moment that selling it would shorten his life.

He dropped to his knees, but his thoughts soon went from his devotions to Oxforde's scribbles. Perhaps someone might be interested in buying them for a higher price. The notion had no sooner crossed his mind when a shaft of sunlight blazed through the clouds and bathed the grave so intensely that it hurt his eyes. He fell backwards with a cry. And then, just as suddenly, the light vanished, leaving the little cemetery as dark and gloomy as before.

'Did Oxforde do that?' asked Botilbrig, running over to help Kirwell to his feet. The youth looked frightened. 'Because you were nice to him?'

'I do not know,' replied Kirwell unsteadily, crossing himself. But one thing was certain. He would not sell the prayer now. Not ever.

Suffolk, Summer 1358

Cambridge and Clare were less than two days' ride apart, but they could not have been more different. Cambridge was flat, busy, dirty and noisy, while Clare nestled amid gently rolling hills and was a tranquil, orderly village. Both possessed castles and priories, although Clare's lacked the bustling urgency of Cambridge's, and were smaller and quieter. But the biggest difference was that Clare had no University – no argumentative, arrogant, opinionated throng that antagonised the locals and was thoroughly resented for it.

Matilde was not sure which of the two she preferred. Clare was her home now, but there were times when she missed Cambridge's vibrancy. She had fled the University town three years before, certain in the belief that the physician she adored there would never ask her to marry him. Since then, she had found a modicum of peace in Clare. She later learned that she had been mistaken about Matt Bartholomew, and that he had actually intended to put the question to her on the very day that she had left. But by then, of course, it was too late.

Or was it?

Her heart had clamoured at her to dash back and hurl herself into his arms, but that would have been selfish, for it would have deprived him of the two things he loved most: his teaching and his impoverished patients. If he married her, he would have to resign his University post, as scholars were not permitted to wed; and providing for a wife would necessitate exchanging needy clients for ones who could pay.

Staying away after she had discovered that he loved her as much as she loved him was not easy, but it had been the right decision – for him, at least, because the occasional report she received suggested that he was content. But then she heard that another woman had entered his life: Julitta Holm, trapped in a barren marriage to the town's new surgeon.

The news that he was ready to look elsewhere came as a shock to Matilde, and gradually she began to view her noble sacrifice as rather silly. This was reinforced when she met a wise-woman named Mother Udela, who informed her bluntly that she was a fool to sit back and watch while the only man she had ever really loved gave his heart to someone else. So Matilde started to consider ways in which she and Matt could be together.

The main stumbling block was money. If they had some, he could continue to physick the poor, which would go some way to consoling him for losing his students. As he was unlikely to acquire any on his own

– he invariably forgot to collect fees that were owing, and was less interested in wealth than any man Matilde had ever met – she saw it was up to her to secure the necessary fortune. She did not know if it was possible, but she was a resolute woman and the prize was her future happiness, so she was determined to try.

She rode north that very day.

CHAPTER 1

Peterborough, August 1358

Everyone was relieved when the towers and pinnacles of the great Benedictine abbey finally came into view. It had not been an easy journey, and misfortune had dogged them every step of the way – lame horses, flooded roads, accidents and a series of raids by robbers. And as none of the party had wanted to leave Cambridge in the first place, the litany of mishaps had done nothing to soothe ragged tempers.

'At last!' breathed Ralph de Langelee. 'I thought we would never arrive.'

'I told you we should not have come,' said Father William, an unsavoury Franciscan who wore a filthy habit and whose thick hair sprouted in oily clumps around an untidy tonsure. 'It is hundreds of miles across dangerous country, and we are lucky to be alive.'

'It is not hundreds of miles,' countered Matthew Bartholomew, gripping the reins of his horse with fierce concentration. He was not a good rider, and had fallen off twice since the journey began; he was determined it would not happen again. 'It is less than forty.'

William only sniffed, declining to acknowledge that he might be wrong. Bartholomew did not blame him for thinking the distance greater than it was, when a journey that should have taken no more than two or three days had extended to almost a fortnight. He glanced at his companions.

Langelee was in charge, not only because he was Master of Michaelhouse, the Cambridge College to which they all belonged, but because he had been a soldier before embarking on an academic career, and so knew what to do in the kinds of crises that had plagued them. Most of the University thought he should have stuck to warfare, because he was patently unsuited to scholarship, and his classes had a tendency to slide off into discussions about camp-ball, his favourite sport. But he was a just and fair leader, and his Fellows were content with his rule. Or they had been before he had decided that some of them should visit Peterborough.

There were seven Fellows in his College, and he had picked three of them to travel with him, while a fourth had been ordered to go by no less a person than the Bishop of Lincoln. As all had hoped to spend the summer recovering from the rigours of an unusually frantic Easter Term, not to mention preparing work for the next academic year, the decision to drag them away had been unpopular, to say the least.

'I do not see why I had to come to this godforsaken place,' grumbled William, glaring at the monastery with dislike. 'I will be unwelcome here – the Black Monks will mock me and make me feel uncomfortable. And they have no right, because everyone knows that the Franciscan Order is the only one God really likes.'

'Is that so?' asked Brother Michael coldly. He was a Benedictine himself, tall, generous of girth and whose 'rough travelling habit' was cut from the finest cloth. He had lank brown hair that was trimmed carefully

11

around a perfectly round tonsure, and expressive green eyes. Besides teaching theology, he was also the University's Senior Proctor, and through the years he had manoeuvred himself into a position of considerable authority. He had not found it easy to surrender his hard-won power to his deputy.

Worse yet, one of the King's favourite ministers was in the process of founding a new College, and Michael was uneasy with the entire venture – the unseemly speed with which matters were being pushed along, the fact that only lawyers would be permitted to enrol there, and the resentment that was brewing in the rest of the University, which felt it was being bulldozed. Michael had promised to write Winwick Hall's charter himself, to prevent the founder from slipping anything sly into it, but if the return journey took as long as the outward one, he would be too late. The resulting strain did not render him an amiable travelling companion.

'Yes,' William flashed back. 'Benedictines are venal and greedy, and everyone knows it. And if you do not believe me, then look at the size and grandeur of this abbey.'

The Franciscan had a point. It had been four hundred years since the Black Monks had arrived in Peterborough, which had given them ample time to build themselves one of the finest monasteries in the country. Michael was disinclined to admit it, though.

'You should not have brought him,' he said testily to Langelee. 'He has been nothing but trouble the entire way.'

'How dare you—' began William hotly.

'I have already explained why he had to come,' interrupted Langelee. 'He upset a lot of people by accusing the Deputy Sheriff of corruption last month, and this jaunt will allow time for tempers to cool.'

'But I was right,' objected William, stung. 'He *is* corrupt.'

'Almost certainly,' agreed Langelee. 'But you should not have made the point in a public sermon. Your remarks almost caused a riot.'

'And me?' asked Clippesby, the last of the four Fellows to be travelling. He was a Dominican, who spoke to animals and claimed they answered back. Most people considered him insane, although Bartholomew often thought that the gentle, compassionate friar was more rational than the rest of the Fellows put together. 'Why did you drag me all the way out here? I made no slurs against deputy sheriffs.'

'No,' agreed Langelee. 'But Thelnetham will be Acting Master while I am away, and he does not like you – it seemed prudent to eliminate a source of discord. Besides, just think of all the new creatures you will meet. It is an opportunity to expand your social life.'

Clippesby shot him a baleful look. He did not usually let his colleagues' opinions of his eccentricities perturb him, but even his serene tolerance had been put to the test on the journey. 'It was inconvenient, Master. I had hoped to complete my theological treatise on rabbits this summer. Now it will remain unfinished until Christmas.'

'A lunatic discourse, full of the heresy that your Order loves,' scoffed William. He harboured a passionate aversion to Dominicans, and it was fortunate that Clippesby usually ignored his bigoted eccentricities or blood would have been spilled.

'Do not waste your time on essays, Clippesby,' advised Langelee. 'I never read anything my fellow philosophers write. Their ramblings are either boring or nonsensical. Or both.'

His Fellows exchanged wry glances.

'And Matt?' asked Clippesby. 'Surely it was unnecessary to force him to come? He is needed at home, where he has huge numbers of patients relying on him.'

'There are two reasons why he could not be left,' replied Langelee crisply. 'Julitta Holm and Gonville Hall.'

Bartholomew felt himself blush. He had believed his affection for Julitta was secret, and had been mortified to learn that half the town knew how he felt. He would have to be more discreet in future, because her friendship meant a lot to him, and he was unwilling to give it up. She was wife to Surgeon Holm, a selfish, arrogant man with a negligible grasp of medicine who was unworthy of her in every way.

'Julitta,' mused William. 'Her husband might prefer the company of men, but he still objects to being cuckolded. And matrimony is a sacred—'

'Gonville Hall is the greater crime,' Langelee cut in disapprovingly. He scowled at Bartholomew. 'You did not have to fail *all* its medical students at their final disputations last month.'

'Yes, I did,' said Bartholomew shortly. 'They could not answer any of my questions. Would *you* want to be treated by them, if you were ill or injured?'

'I am rarely ill, and only poor warriors are injured,' countered Langelee, missing the point.

14

'Besides, if you had wanted me out of Cambridge, why could I not have gone to Clare instead?' Bartholomew went on. 'I have heard many good things about the place, and I had intended to visit it this summer.'

'It is overrated,' declared Michael briskly. 'You will enjoy yourself far more in Peterborough, and I was right to encourage the Master to bring you.' He kicked his horse into a canter before Bartholomew could inform him that he had disliked his plans being hijacked. 'If we hurry, we shall be in time for dinner, and I am famished.'

'He is always famished,' muttered Cynric. The Welsh book-bearer was the sixth and last member of the party. 'And it is hardly natural.'

Cynric was more friend than servant to Bartholomew, but although he was usually eager for adventure, he had not wanted to go to Peterborough either. He had carved a pleasant life for himself in Cambridge, with an agreeable wife, a job that entailed little real work, and like-minded cronies with whom to set the world to rights over jugs of ale of an evening. It was only loyalty to the Fellows that had induced him to make the journey, afraid that unless he was there, they might come to harm. And given the number of attacks they had fended off, his concern had been justified.

Bartholomew was glad to talk about something other than Julitta and his conflict with Gonville Hall. 'There will be scant time for feasting once we arrive in Peterborough. Michael will have to carry out his orders.'

These 'orders' were the real reason they were there: to find out what happened to Abbot Robert, who left his monastery a month before, and had not been seen or heard of since.

The little town of Peterborough was dominated by its abbey. Within its precincts, the church, chapter house and cloisters were the largest structures, but it also boasted a number of other buildings that turned it into a self-contained village – refectory, dormitory, almonry, sacristy, kitchens, bakery, brewery, pantries, stables and lodgings for guests and servants.

Bartholomew had attended the monastery school, and as they rode through the town's outskirts he found some parts reassuringly familiar. Others, he was sure he had never seen before, but that was to be expected; he had been twelve when he had left, which had been more years ago than he cared to remember.

'If Brother Michael had not accepted the honour of being made a canon of Lincoln Cathedral two years ago,' Cynric muttered resentfully in Bartholomew's ear, 'we would not be in this position now. And I do not like Peterborough.'

Bartholomew laughed. Despite his reluctance to leave, the journey had been good for him. The nagging fatigue that had dogged him all term had gone, and while he missed Julitta and worried about his patients, he was fitter and more relaxed than he had been in months.

'You cannot say you do not like it. We have only just arrived.'

Cynric gave him a meaningful look, and clutched one of the amulets he wore around his neck. 'It is a feeling, boy, and I have learned not to ignore those. I sense wickedness here, and there will be evil spirits involved. You can be sure of that.'

There had been a time when Bartholomew would have tried to convince the book-bearer that such a notion was ridiculous, but Cynric had grown more superstitious and opinionated with age, and the physician now knew better than to try.

'Brother Michael's canonisation means that Bishop Gynewell has a hold over him,' Cynric went on sourly. 'He should have held out for one in Ely instead, because then we would not have been sent here to hunt for mysteriously vanished Abbots.'

'Michael is a long way from sainthood yet,' said Bartholomew, although he could see from Cynric's glare that the book-bearer did not want a lecture on ecclesiastical terminology.

'Once the Bishop named him as Commissioner, he had no choice but to come to Peterborough,' Cynric grumbled on. 'But that should not have meant that half of Michaelhouse is forced to travel with him. It is unfair.'

Bartholomew made no reply. He had been regaled with Cynric's displeasure over the venture ever since they had left, and he was tired of discussing it.

'I understand why most of us are here,' the book-bearer continued. 'Brother Michael was ordered to come by the Bishop; you and Father William had to escape awkward situations; Clippesby could not be left with mean old Thelnetham; and I am here to look after you. But what about the Master? I do not believe he is here to see old friends.'

As it happened, Cynric was right to be suspicious of Langelee's motives. Bartholomew was not the only one who disobeyed the University's strictures against women, and the Master's latest conquest was the Deputy Sheriff's wife. The man had discovered the affair the same day that William had accused him of dishonesty, and rather than risk having war declared on Michaelhouse, Langelee had opted for a tactical withdrawal. Bartholomew was the only Fellow entrusted with this information, on the grounds that Langelee did not think the others – all clerics in holy orders – would understand.

'He does have a friend here,' Bartholomew replied, although Langelee had confessed that he had only met Master Spalling once, and the expansive invitation to 'visit any time' had been issued after a night of heavy drinking. In truth, Langelee did not know whether Spalling would remember him, let alone agree to a house guest.

'Well, I am glad he came,' conceded Cynric, albeit reluctantly. 'You and I could not have beaten off those robbers alone – we would have been slaughtered.'

'Yes,' said Bartholomew, wincing when he recalled the delight with which the Master had greeted the opportunity to hone his martial skills. Bartholomew's own talents in that direction were modest, as befitted a man whose profession was healing. Bad timing had put him in Poitiers when a small force led by the Prince of Wales had encountered the French army – which had taught him how to hold his own; but he disliked fighting and avoided it when he could.

'Do you think we will survive the return journey?' asked Cynric uneasily. 'Or shall we be doomed to spend the rest of our lives in this infernal place? My wife will not like that.'

'Neither will my students,' said Bartholomew.

'You had better dismount, Matt,' called Michael, as scattered houses gave way to proper streets. 'We do not want anyone trampled. The resulting fuss might make us late for dinner.'

With Bartholomew, horses sensed who was master and immediately exercised their ascendancy by bucking, prancing or heading off to enjoy the grass. The docile nag he had taken from College had been shot during an ambush, leaving him with a fierce stallion that had a tendency to bolt. He did as Michael suggested and passed him the reins, feeling that the beast needed to be in responsible hands if there were people about.

It was not long before their precautions paid off. The road, which had been wide, narrowed abruptly, and an elderly man stepped in front of them. The stallion reared in shock, and even Michael's superior abilities were tested as he struggled to control it. Bartholomew would have stood no chance, and blood would certainly have been spilled.

'You are not allowed to bring dangerous animals in here,' screeched the man, cringing away as hoofs flailed. He was an ancient specimen, with bandy legs, no teeth and wispy grey hair; he wore the robes of a Benedictine lay brother. 'It is forbidden.'

'I imagine it is forbidden to race out in front of travellers and frighten their mounts, too,' retorted Michael.

'Are you the Bishop's Commissioner?' asked the old man, peering up at him.

'Yes, he is,' said William before the monk could reply for himself. 'And so are we.'

'What, all of you?' asked the old man, startled. He

was not the only one to be surprised: it was also news to Michael, Langelee, Clippesby, Bartholomew and Cynric. 'Why so many?'

'Because the Bishop thought Brother Michael might need us,' replied William loftily.

'I see,' said the old man with a philosophical shrug, as if the workings of a prelate's mind were beyond his ken. 'We expected you ages ago because the Bishop asked you to come at once, but you have taken weeks. Why? Do you not consider our predicament pressing?'

'And who are you, pray?' asked Michael coolly.

'Roger Botilbrig, bedesman of St Leonard's Hospital. That means I have served the abbey all my life – I was their best brewer – and I now live in retirement at abbey expense.'

'I know what a bedesman is,' said Michael, disliking the assumption that he was a fool.

Botilbrig went on as if the monk had not spoken. 'My duties are mostly praying for the hospital's founders, but that is a bit tedious, so I offered to wait for you instead, to escort you to the abbey. Of course, I did not expect to be kept hanging around *this* long.'

'My apologies,' said Michael dryly. 'However, our journey has been fraught with—'

'Apology accepted.' Botilbrig gave a sudden toothless grin. 'Bishop Gynewell told us to expect a very large monk, and he was not exaggerating. You are a princely specimen.'

William sniggered, Langelee and Cynric smothered smiles, and Bartholomew waited for an explosion. Clippesby began murmuring to the wasp that had landed on his sleeve.

'I am not fat,' declared Michael tightly. 'I have big bones. Matt here will confirm it, because he is my personal physician.'

Bartholomew blinked, astonished to learn that he had been awarded such a title.

'A physician?' asked Botilbrig, brightening. 'Good! We do not have one of our own any more, not since Master Pyk disappeared at the same time as Abbot Robert. Most of us have ailments that need tending, so it is thoughtful of you to bring us one. I have a sore—'

'He will be helping *me*,' interrupted Michael. 'He will not have time for patients. However, the fact that more than one man is adrift is news to us. Gynewell said it was just the Abbot.'

'The Abbot and Pyk,' stated Botilbrig. 'They disappeared a month ago, on St Swithin's Day, and have not been seen since. It will not be easy to find them after all this time, but the Bishop says you are good at solving mysteries, so we are all expecting a speedy solution.'

'So no pressure then,' murmured Langelee to Michael.

Botilbrig hobbled along the road, gabbling non-stop as he pointed out features of interest. The physician was the only one who listened. William had turned resentful again, claiming that he should be persecuting heretics in Cambridge, not sent to distant outposts just because he had made a few perfectly justifiable remarks about a devious official. Cynric was nodding agreement; Langelee was trying to recall where Spalling had said he lived; Michael was reflecting unhappily on the task he had been set; and Clippesby had been stung by the wasp.

Eventually, they arrived at the town centre, which

comprised a marketplace bordered by handsome houses on three sides and abbey buildings on the fourth. The square was alive with activity. Wooden stalls with colourful roofs stood in neat rows, selling goods that ranged from cakes and candles to bread and baskets. Bartholomew braced himself, expecting it to smell like the one in Cambridge – a brutal combination of dung, urine, stagnant water and rotting offal – so he was pleasantly surprised when all he could detect was fresh straw and baking bread.

'Here is the Abbey Gate,' said Botilbrig, stopping outside a handsome edifice. With a somewhat proprietary air, he addressed the gaggle of people who had stopped to stare at the newcomers. 'These are the Bishop's Commissioners, and *I* am showing them what's what.'

'They took their time,' muttered one woman. 'We expected them weeks ago.'

'We came as fast as we could,' said William indignantly.

'There is a chapel by the gate; we should go there first, to give thanks for our safe arrival,' said Clippesby, earning himself a murmur of approval from the onlookers for his piety, although that had not been his intention.

'Of course,' said William, unwilling to be seen as less devout than a Dominican. Then he frowned as he peered at it. 'Are there *shops* in its undercroft? There are! Blasphemy!'

'That is St Thomas's Hospital, and there are shops below it because it is run by greedy bedeswomen,' explained Botilbrig. 'The workshop on the corner is owned by Reginald the cutler, who is as foul a villain as ever walked the Earth. He is quite rich, though, so Abbot Robert never minded spending time in his company.'

'Clippesby is right: we should say a prayer,' said Michael, raising mystified eyebrows at Botilbrig's peculiar medley of revelations. 'It has been a difficult journey, after all.'

'Why?' asked Botilbrig. 'What happened to you?'

'Amongst other calamities, we were attacked five times by robbers,' replied William. 'Ones who spoke French – I heard them quite distinctly. They must live in this town, as they only became a serious nuisance during the last few miles.'

'I see,' said Botilbrig. 'Then you should indeed give thanks, but do not do it at St Thomas's. That place pays homage to executed felons and is full of false relics. Come to the Hospital of St Leonard instead.'

'Peterborough has *two* hospitals?' said William, impressed, although Bartholomew had already told him as much. Clearly the friar had not trusted his colleague's memory.

'They were founded for lepers,' explained Botilbrig. 'Although St Leonard's is now used to house bedesmen, like me. St Thomas's still takes lepers, though, which should make you think twice about stepping inside its chapel.'

'There has not been a case of leprosy in this country for years,' countered Bartholomew. 'These unfortunates will have contracted another skin disease, such as—'

'Where is St Leonard's?' asked William, before they could be regaled with a list. The physician was difficult to stop once he started to hold forth about medicine, and not all his discourses made for pleasant listening.

23

'A short walk west of the town,' replied Botilbrig proudly. 'We have a holy well, too, along with a man who is a hundred and forty-three years old. We will let you touch him if you put a few coins in the oblations box.'

'Is that possible, Matthew?' asked William. 'Do people really live to such a great age? I know they did in the Bible, but those were different times.'

'I suppose so,' said Bartholomew, although the doubt was clear in his voice.

Botilbrig regarded him coolly. 'Of course it is possible. Now come along. It is not far – just straight through the town, out the other side and along a—'

'We are not leaving now we have arrived at last,' interrupted Langelee firmly. 'So my clerics will pray in *this* chapel. They can visit St Leonard's another time.'

'They will be sorry,' warned Botilbrig. 'It is a dark and gloomy place, not like pretty St Leonard's. I was saying to Master Spalling only last night that—'

'Spalling?' pounced Langelee. 'Where does he live?'

'In the large house out by the parish church,' replied Botilbrig, regarding him curiously. 'Why? Do you know him? If so, you had better not tell the monks.'

'Why not?' asked Michael.

'Because they hate him.' Botilbrig spoke as if this were something he should know.

'And why do they hate him?' pressed Michael, struggling for patience.

'Because he says it is wrong for abbeys, nobles and merchants to have lots of money when ordinary folk have none,' explained Botilbrig. 'I am loyal to the abbey, of course, but it is difficult to dislike Spalling. He is very popular in the town.'

'Perhaps I will join you at his home, Master,' said Cynric to Langelee. The book-bearer had radical views on social justice, and Spalling sounded like his kind of man.

'And perhaps I will stay in the abbey,' countered Langelee. 'I do not recall Spalling harbouring controversial opinions when I met him in York.'

'You are in luck,' said Botilbrig with a grin. 'Because here he comes now. I shall be able to introduce you.'

The scholars turned to see a man striding towards them. He had an impressive mane of long yellow hair, while his beard was full, bushy and gold. His enormous size, along with the fact that he was wearing a simple tunic in the kind of brown homespun favoured by working men, made him an arresting figure. He was trailed by a host of people, and when he stopped walking, so did they, shuffling to a standstill at his heels.

'Another greedy monk, come to devour the fruits of our labour,' he spat, blue eyes blazing as he glared at Michael. 'I thought our troubles had eased when the Death reduced their number from sixty-four to thirty-two, but they have been increasing since, and will soon be back to their former strength.'

'They lost half their number to plague?' asked Bartholomew with quiet compassion. The disease that had ravaged the country, eliminating entire communities and striking indiscriminately at old, young, rich and poor had been a terrible experience. He could still recall the helplessness that had gripped him when all his remedies and treatments failed, and he had been forced to watch much-loved patients die one after another.

'Yes, and it is a pity it was not more,' declared Spalling uncompromisingly. 'They deserve to rot in Hell for the crimes they commit against the common man.'

Behind him, there was a murmur of approval, although Botilbrig looked uncomfortable, caught between his admiration for a man with attractive opinions and his loyalty to the place that housed and fed him.

'And this is your friend, Master?' asked Michael of Langelee, all frosty hauteur. 'Your taste in companions has always been dubious, but you have excelled yourself this time.'

Spalling frowned at Langelee. 'You are an acquaintance of mine? I do not recognise you.'

'I am Master of Michaelhouse now,' explained Langelee, also struggling to see something familiar in Spalling, and thus indicating that the evening they had enjoyed together had been wilder than he had led his colleagues to believe. 'But we met when I was working for the Archbishop of York.'

'That wily old scoundrel!' snorted Spalling. 'You did the right thing by abandoning him and opting for the life of a poor scholar. You are welcome in my house, sir.'

Langelee regarded him coolly; he had admired and respected his Archbishop. 'Thank you, but I think I must remain with my Fellows. They will only get themselves into trouble without me to supervise them.'

'I approve of the two friars and the pauper.' Spalling flapped a hand towards William, Clippesby and Bartholomew, who looked down at his clothes and supposed he could do with some new ones. 'But not the fat Benedictine. I despise that Order with a passion. Ask anyone in Peterborough.'

26

'Brother Michael is our College's finest theologian,' said Langelee stiffly. 'And—'

'Other than me,' put in William.

'And he also runs the University. Do not let his ample girth deceive you. He eats very little, and his weight is entirely due to his unusually heavy bones. Here is his personal physician, who will support what I say.'

'Very heavy,' obliged Bartholomew, aware that the only reason Langelee considered Michael's appetite modest was because he possessed a gargantuan one of his own. Michael was glowering at him, so he added, 'Lead has nothing on them.'

'Well, in that case, perhaps I shall make an exception,' said Spalling graciously. 'The plump devils in this abbey do nothing but eat, and it is the poor who labour to keep them in bread. Do not glare at me, Botilbrig. You know I am right. They almost worked you into an early grave before I intervened and ordered them to make you a bedesman.'

'They would have let me retire anyway,' objected Botilbrig. 'It was just a question of time. And not all the monks are fat. Brother Henry is skin and bone, while—'

'You will stay with me,' said Spalling to Langelee, although it was more order than invitation, and judging from the Master's face, not one he was keen to follow. 'I want to hear more about this University of yours. The physician can come, too, because his clothes reveal him to be impoverished, and the needy are always welcome in my home.'

'The physician will stay with me in the abbey,' stated Michael. 'You can take the Franciscan, though. He is poor, as you can see from his habit.'

'His habit denotes filth, not destitution,' countered Spalling with commendable astuteness. 'But I cannot stand here arguing all day. I am a busy man – I have a wealthy merchant to berate for his miserliness before dinner, and I aim to shame him into donating enough money for a handsome meal for my faithful followers. So come along, those who wish to see me in action.'

Langelee considered for a moment, then turned to his Fellows. 'I think I will go with him. Michaelhouse's coffers are always empty, and if he really can persuade rich men to part with their gold I should like to learn his secret. Come with me, Cynric. Your sword will not be needed in the monastery, but it may be useful at Spalling's house.'

Cynric looked pleased with the opportunity to spend more time with a man who harboured radical opinions, and he and Langelee joined the straggling line of disciples who followed their golden-headed leader. Michael watched them go.

'I wonder the abbey lets him roam about, spouting that sort of nonsense to visitors.'

'The monks are not happy, and even excommunicated him at one point,' explained Botilbrig. 'But Bishop Gynewell overturned their verdict, on the grounds that it was too harsh.'

'We had better make ourselves known to whoever is in charge before we miss dinner,' said Michael, pushing Spalling from his mind as he turned towards the Abbey Gate. 'Langelee is right: I eat very little, but I feel the need for a morsel now. That man upset me.'

'Ignore him, Brother,' advised Bartholomew. 'He may dress like a peasant, but he does not work like one. His hands were as soft as a lady's, and he had spilled egg custard down his tunic – hardly paupers' fare. I sense a good deal of the hypocrite in Spalling.'

'We shall visit the abbey as soon as we have said our prayers,' said Clippesby, indicating the hospital. 'And if we miss dinner, then so be it.'

Michael looked set to argue, but William and Clippesby were striding towards the door, so he had no choice but to do likewise, unless he wanted to be seen as the cleric who put victuals before his devotions. And after Spalling's remarks he was disinclined to do that.

The hospital chapel was a small, neat building, with a frieze in a panel above the gate depicting the murder of St Thomas Becket in Canterbury Cathedral. It had narrow windows with pointed tops and a thatched roof. Inside, it was dark, especially after the brilliance of the sunlight, and its walls were painted in sombre greens and blues, rendering it gloomy. Bedesman Botilbrig pointedly declined to follow, and confined himself to standing in the porch, muttering disparaging comments about the women who ran it.

For a modestly sized place, it was amply provided with doors – the large one that opened on to the market square, a smaller one that gave access to the abbey, and two tiny ones in the north wall. The first of these led to the adjoining hospital, while the other led to a graveyard – a necessity when inmates were likely to be ailing or elderly.

Bartholomew said a few quick prayers and then prowled, leaving his colleagues to manage the serious devotions. He could not recall being in St Thomas's before, and supposed it had not featured in his youthful explorations. It was surprisingly busy, with one clot of pilgrims at the altar, where Michael, William and Clippesby were obliged to jostle for a place, and a second cluster bustling in and out of the cemetery door.

Curious as to why a graveyard should be so popular, Bartholomew eased his way through the penitents until he emerged in a pretty walled garden with gravelled paths. There were perhaps forty mounds, some recent, but most marked with wooden crosses that were grey and cracked with age. People were congregating around one near the wall, which was all but invisible under a heap of flowers. Supervising the operation was a vast lady in the robes of a lay sister. She saw him hovering and came to greet him.

'This is where Lawrence de Oxforde is buried,' she announced. 'Have you come to see if he will work a miracle for you? He has performed many since his death forty-five years ago.'

Bartholomew was bemused as memories flooded back. 'I remember some folk claiming that wishes had been granted at his grave, but I thought his cult had been suppressed, on the grounds that the Church dislikes executed felons being venerated.'

'It was suppressed, but Abbot Robert turns a blind eye,' confided the woman. 'Of course, I understand why the Church disapproves – Oxforde was a violent thief. Yet miracles do occur here, and it is not for the likes of you and me to question the mysterious workings of God.'

'I suppose not,' conceded Bartholomew cautiously, recalling what he had been told about the infamous

Oxforde when he had been a schoolboy. The man had been a ruthless criminal with an inflated sense of his own worth, who had died astonished that the King had not granted him a pardon. He had murdered at least twenty people, including children, and had burgled himself a fortune, although none of it had ever been recovered.

'Kneel at his grave and ask for anything you like,' invited the woman. 'Being a felon himself, he is very broad-minded. And when you have finished, you may leave your donation with me – Joan Sylle.'

'I have nothing to ask, Sister,' said Bartholomew, backing away.

'Oh, come,' coaxed Joan. 'Surely you yearn for something? Perhaps there is a woman you would like to fall into your arms? That is exactly the kind of favour Oxforde grants.'

Bartholomew's retreat stopped abruptly when two faces flashed into his mind. One was Julitta's and the other belonged to Matilde. It had been more than three years since Matilde had left Cambridge, disappearing so completely that not even months of determined searching had tracked her down. He would not mind either of *them* falling into his arms.

'I have just learned that this chapel owns some genuine relics, Matthew,' came William's excited voice from behind him. Bartholomew supposed he should be grateful for the timely interruption, sure his colleagues would not approve of him petitioning an executed criminal to help with his unsatisfactory love life.

'Of course we do,' said Joan, flashing large teeth in a grin that verged on the predatory. 'Would you like a private viewing? I know you are the Bishop's Commissioners, so I am more than happy to clear the chapel to accommodate you.'

'That would be kind,' said William eagerly. 'What do you have?'

Joan swelled with pride. 'The flagstone where St Thomas Becket was standing when he was murdered, the green tunic he was wearing, and two enormous flasks of his blood.'

Bartholomew was sceptical, knowing that if every drop of 'Becket Blood' was genuine, the man would have had enough to fill a lake. Moreover, he was sure the saint would not have been wearing a green tunic when he was cut down.

'Impressive,' murmured William, pressing a coin into her hand.

'You shall see them at once. Nothing is too much fuss for the Bishop's Commissioners.'

'Good,' said William. 'Because I am very interested in lucrative . . . I mean saintly relics. So is Matthew. He is a physician, who knows the healing value of such objects.'

'A physician?' asked Joan keenly. 'Good! My poor knees have not been the same since Master Pyk disappeared, so you can treat them now he is gone.'

Before Bartholomew could inform her that he would not be in Peterborough long enough to see patients, she began to shoo the pilgrims out of the chapel and the graveyard, driving them before her like sheep. They were dismayed, but she ignored their objections, and it was not long until they were ousted. She was careful to leave Michael and Clippesby alone, though; they continued to kneel quietly, side by side.

'There is the blood,' said Joan, nodding proudly at two ornate vases that stood on the altar. Then she pointed to the reliquary that had been placed in an alcove beneath them. 'And his tunic is in that nice box.'

'Where is the flagstone?' asked William keenly.

'In front of the altar. The lump you see next to the candle is a bit that broke off when we dropped it. If you look carefully, you can see blood on it. It is the martyr's.'

Bartholomew doubted that blood would still be in evidence after almost two hundred years. Fortunately, Joan did not notice his scepticism, because William enthused enough over her treasures for both of them.

'May I touch the tunic?' the friar begged. 'Please?'

Joan gazed pointedly at his grimy hands, but her disapproval dissipated with the appearance of another coin. 'On one condition: that your physician tends one of our inmates. She is in terrible pain, and I do not like to see such suffering.'

'He will oblige you at once,' said William, grabbing the tunic, and lifting it to his lips.

Bartholomew was not happy with William for volunteering his services in so cavalier a manner, but he could not refuse help to someone in need, so he followed Joan through one of the small doors in the north wall. William trailed at his heels, still gushing his delight at being allowed to touch the sainted Becket's clothing. Beyond the door was a short passage, which emerged into a large, bright room that was flooded with sunlight. All three blinked: it was dazzling after the shadowy chapel.

'This is our hall,' explained Joan. 'Where we eat and

hold meetings. We keep the sick and elderly bedes-women in the adjoining chamber.'

There were six beds in the second room. The residents brightened when Joan told them that she had found a physician, and clamoured their ailments at Bartholomew as he passed. Joan grabbed his arm and hauled him on, declaring that Lady Lullington must come first.

'Yes, tend her, poor soul,' called one crone. 'It is unfair that she should endure such torments while her pig of a husband struts around enjoying himself with Abbot Robert. Or he did, before Robert vanished.'

'Lullington does not even visit her,' added another. 'Despite her giving him six children.'

'Shame on him,' declared William, who rarely waited to hear the whole story before passing judgement. 'Where is this hapless woman?'

'Upstairs,' replied Joan. 'In a separate room, on account of her being a lady.'

William and Bartholomew followed her up a spiral stair-case and were shown into another pleasant chamber, this one with pale green walls. It was a soothing, quiet place, although the woman who lay on the bed was grey and shrunken with pain. A priest knelt at her side, his face wet with tears. He was a young man with a mop of unruly brown curls, and his priestly robe was frayed and thin.

'Gentle Trentham,' the sick woman was whispering, forcing a smile as she touched his hand. 'Do not grieve so. You know I am not afraid to die.'

The priest nodded without much conviction. He scrambled to his feet as Joan ushered in the visitors, and gripped Bartholomew's arm roughly when informed that here was a *medicus*.

34

'Please help her,' he said hoarsely. 'It is not fair . . .' He turned and stumbled from the room, choking back another sob.

'He is too soft for his own good, blubbering every time one of us prepares to meet her Maker,' said Joan with a sigh. 'Yet he is a kindly soul, who takes his duties as chaplain seriously. I would not change him for one with a harder heart.'

'Nor would I,' whispered Lady Lullington softly.

The patient had probably not been large when she had been healthy, but illness had turned her skeletal. The hands that lay on the covers were almost translucent, and when she raised one to beckon Bartholomew towards her, he could see it was an effort.

'Master Pyk told me that I would recover, but I am not inclined to believe him. What do you say? Am I dying?'

Bartholomew was all too familiar with the appearance of approaching death, and he could see it in Lady Lullington. 'Yes. I am sorry.'

She smiled, although Joan inhaled sharply at his bluntness. 'Thank you for your honesty. But I have been in agony for weeks now, and I am weary of it. Can you give me something to help, even if only for a little while?'

'I will try. Tell me where it hurts.'

'Everywhere. Please do not ask for details – I do not have the strength to tell you. Just give me the most powerful remedy you own.'

Bartholomew's professional curiosity was piqued but he did not press her. Instead, he measured out a potent pain-dulling potion, using a dose he would never have given a patient who was likely to live. As it was, he wondered whether it might ease her into a sleep from which she would never wake. She took a sip, and evidently knew it too, for she looked at him with eyes that were full of silent gratitude.

'Shall we fetch your husband, Lady Lullington?' asked Joan, when the cup was empty.

The dying woman shook her head. 'He has no place here,' she said rather enigmatically. 'But I would like young Trentham to come back. His presence soothes me.'

When she fell asleep, Bartholomew left, sorry that the lines of suffering in her face had not lessened. William followed him down the stairs, where the other inmates watched them pass in silence. Joan stopped to give a falsely cheerful report of the lady's condition, but it was obvious that none of them believed her.

'Did you have to be so free with the truth?' admonished William, once they were in the chapel again. 'She was a dignified soul, and you should have been kinder.'

Bartholomew had never been very good at misleading patients. 'I doubt she would have thanked me for lying.'

'I disagree, and your bleak prognosis might send her into a fatal decline.'

'I am not sure what is wrong with her, but I do know she will not recover. It is clear that her vital organs have started to fail and—'

'Have you never heard of miracles?' demanded William archly. 'She lies above a chapel that contains holy relics. You should not have been so heartless with her.'

Bartholomew winced. Such cases were never easy, and he wished Michael had been with him instead: the monk never questioned his medical judgement. He was about to explain further when there was a sudden clatter at the back of the chapel. It was Botilbrig, come to find out why his charges were taking so long.

'Cow!' he screeched, making the scholars jump. 'Thieving whore! These visitors are *mine*, and if they give any donations for the shrines, then they are mine, too!'

The Michaelhouse scholars gaped their astonishment at such remarks bawled in a holy place, while Botilbrig stared with undisguised loathing at Joan. The expression was returned in kind, and her meaty fists clenched at her sides.

'You are not welcome here,' she said coldly. 'Leave, before the saint takes umbrage at your evil presence and sends a bolt of lightning to dispatch you.'

'I shall go when it pleases me,' bellowed Botilbrig. 'It is not for a harlot to direct my movements. Besides, St Thomas does not go around striking down innocents.'

'No, but Oxforde might,' flashed Joan. 'Especially after all the rude remarks you have made about him in the past. He is certainly offended.'

'He was no more holy than you are,' snapped Botilbrig. 'How can you take money from desperate pilgrims, pretending that he will answer their prayers? You are a wicked—'

'Please,' interrupted Clippesby quietly. 'It is inappropriate to bandy words here. The spiders do not like it – they have just said so.'

'Spiders?' echoed Botilbrig, startled.

'The friar is right,' said Joan. 'So go away, you horrible little man.' She turned her back on Botilbrig, deliberately provocative.

'You two are not married, are you?' asked William. 'Because you sound like my parents.'

'No, we are not,' spluttered Botilbrig, outraged. 'I might have set my sights on her once, but that was before she grew fat and shrewish. Now I would not look twice at her.'

'He is jealous, because we have Thomas Becket's relics *and* Oxforde's grave,' said Joan, scowling at him. 'Whereas St Leonard's has nothing but a smelly well and an old man who should have died years ago.'

'Our spring does not smell,' objected Botilbrig. 'And Kirwell *is* holy with his great age – a saint in the making. When he dies, he will do much better miracles than Oxforde.'

'We should go,' said Michael to his colleagues, as the quarrel escalated. 'The sooner we complete our business here, the sooner we can leave. And I *must* be home by Saturday week, or Winwick Hall's charter will be drawn up without me, and there will be a riot.'

They left the chapel, blinking as they emerged into the sunlight. Immediately, the ousted pilgrims surged forward, demanding to know when they could resume their petitions. They jerked back when Joan propelled Botilbrig out with an unnecessary degree of force; he would have fallen if Bartholomew had not caught him. She raised a large hand for silence, before announcing haughtily that the shrines would reopen after she had counted the day's takings. She was clearly anticipating a generous donation from the Bishop's Commissioners, although she was going to be disappointed – Bartholomew's had had been modest because he never had much money; Michael considered himself exempt from such obligations; and Clippesby had forgotten. The pilgrims cried their dismay, but Joan's only response was to close the door with a firmly final thump.

'Look,' said William, pointing. 'A fellow Grey Friar browsing among the market stalls. Yet my Order has no convent here.'

His curiosity piqued, he hurried off to interrogate the priest about his business. Disinclined to abandon him in a strange place, Michael sat on a low wall to wait for him, tilting his plump face towards the sun. Bartholomew and Clippesby perched by his side, both grateful for the opportunity to relax before presenting themselves at the abbey.

'I hope finding out what happened to Abbot Robert will not take long,' remarked the monk worriedly. 'Gynewell is unfair to expect me to investigate so long after it happened. And he did not furnish me with much in the way of details, either.'

'What did he tell you exactly?' asked Bartholomew. 'You were so angry at being forced to leave Cambridge that you barely spoke a word all the way here.'

'I would have done, but it was impossible,' said Michael irritably. 'Either we were listening out for robbers, or I was worried that distracting you might make you fall off your horse again. But to answer your question, Gynewell told me virtually nothing – just that the Abbot set out to visit a goldsmith one day and no one has heard from him since. He did not even say whether the case has been investigated by the monks.'

'It must have been, Brother. You do not lose your Abbot and wait for someone else to look into the matter. I wonder why the Bishop did not come in person. The disappearance of Peterborough's most senior monk is a serious matter.'

'His Lincoln Mint has been producing counterfeit coins, and the King is incandescent with rage – no monarch wants his currency debased, as it could destabilise the entire economy. Gynewell has been charged to catch the forger as a matter of urgency.'

'Money,' said Clippesby, shaking his head disapprovingly. 'It seems to take precedence over everything.'

'It certainly seems important here,' said Michael wryly. 'Joan is taking an age to count her takings, and it seems that the two bedeshouses compete as to which can raise the most.'

They sat in companionable silence for a while, until William returned to say that his fellow Grey Friar had come to find out why Robert had failed to reply to his convent's letters.

'The Abbot did not leave anyone with the authority to answer them, apparently,' he said, all smug disdain. 'It is unprofessional, and would never happen in a Franciscan foundation.'

Michael grimaced at the claim, but it was pleasant in the sunshine and he didn't want to quarrel. Absently, he watched a gaggle of bedeswomen enter the chapel; the pilgrims had ignored Joan's injunction to wait, and must have either sneaked in or gone away, because there were far fewer of them than there had been. Botilbrig, loitering by the door, had been joined by several men whose robes identified them as cronies from the same foundation. They called challenging remarks after the women, then hooted derisively when there was no response.

'Lord!' muttered William. 'They are old enough to know better.'

The others nodded agreement, but then a man walked past with a pig on a lead, and the animal, scenting something it did not like about the place where it was being taken, made a sudden bid for freedom. An abrupt right-angled turn saw the rope whipped from its master's hand, and it was off. Pandemonium reigned as it raced among the market stalls, leaving chaos in its wake. It was still running amok when there was a shriek from the chapel. It was followed by a lot of shouting, and one of the bedeswomen hobbled out, wailing in distress. The scholars were torn between watching folk cluster around her and the pig's efforts to lay hold of an apple while simultaneously eluding the hands that endeavoured to grab it.

'Marion says that Joan is dead,' reported Botilbrig, evidently deciding that someone should inform the Bishop's Commissioners what the bedeswoman was howling about. 'In front of the altar.'

The four scholars exchanged bemused glances, and went to join the growing throng outside the chapel door. Marion's sobbing jabber was difficult to understand, so Botilbrig took it upon himself to interpret.

'Stone dead and lying on her face. It must be because Joan argued with me in a holy place.'

'Lies!' howled Marion, launching herself at him. Bartholomew stepped between them, catching her flailing hands before she could do herself or her target any harm. '*He* killed her! He slipped up behind her and brained her with the broken bit of St Thomas's flag-stone!'

'What?' breathed William, shocked. 'He did *what?*'

'I never did!' cried Botilbrig. 'I was out here with you. If Joan has been brained, and Oxforde is not responsible, then St Thomas must have done it.'

'That is blasphemy!' shouted William, incensed. 'And while I saw Joan toss you out, I was not watching you the whole time afterwards. You could easily have slipped back inside again without me noticing.'

Botilbrig turned white. 'I did not kill Joan! I admit that I did not like her, but I do not want her dead.'

'Yes, you do,' wept Marion. 'You have hated her ever since she refused to marry you years ago. You are a spiteful, wicked villain who—'

Bartholomew did not wait to hear more. He strode inside the chapel, Michael, Clippesby and William at his heels. Joan was lying near the altar, the remaining bedeswomen in a sobbing cluster around her, and it did not take him a moment to see that someone had indeed battered out her brains with the broken fragment of stone from the altar.

'Is she really dead?' whispered William, crossing himself.

Bartholomew nodded.

'Then we had better pray for her soul,' said Michael softly.

CHAPTER 2

Everyone was eager to see the body of a woman who had been killed by one of St Thomas's relics, and pilgrims, bedesmen and passers-by had flowed into the chapel on the scholars' heels. There was a collective sigh of disappointment when Bartholomew covered Joan with his cloak, followed by much resentful muttering. Michael sent the fittest-looking bedesman to fetch someone in authority from the abbey, but the fellow kept stopping to share the news with people he knew, and it was clear that it would be some time before help arrived.

'What happened to her, Matt?' Michael asked in a low voice. 'Was she murdered?'

As well as being a physician and teacher of medicine, Bartholomew was the University's Corpse Examiner, the man who gave an official cause of death for any scholar who died. As violence was distressingly frequent in a community that included a lot of feisty young men, he had gained considerable experience in identifying murder victims. However, while Cambridge was used to his grisly work, Peterborough was not, and conducting the necessary examination on Joan was unlikely to be well received. He said so.

'There is nothing to see here,' Michael announced, hoping to get rid of the crowd so the physician could work unobserved. 'You can all go home.'

'You have no authority to make us leave,' declared a

43

burly fellow in fine clothes and expensive jewellery. There were several well-armed henchmen at his back. 'I am Ralph Aurifabro, goldsmith of this town, and *I* decide where I go and when.'

'I also determine my own movements,' added a man with broken teeth and a straggly beard whose clothes were of good quality but food-stained and rumpled. There was an unhealthy redness in his face that made Bartholomew suspect his humours were awry. 'I am Reginald the cutler, and it is not every day that St Thomas kills sinners with his relics, so I demand to see his handiwork.'

Reginald had tried to imitate the goldsmith's haughty arrogance, but his slovenly mien worked against him, along with the fact that he did not possess the required gravitas. Bartholomew had heard the cutler mentioned before, but it took a moment to remember where: Botilbrig had described him as the 'foul villain' who had a shop under the chapel.

'You will not *demand* anything, Reginald.' A powerful voice made everyone look around. It was another bedeswoman, smaller than Joan, but her bristly chin and fierce eyes indicated that she would be just as redoubtable. 'None of you will. So go away.'

'That is Hagar Balfowre,' murmured Botilbrig to the scholars. 'Joan's henchwoman. Not that Joan needed one very often, being an old dragon in her own right.'

'I most certainly shall not,' Reginald was declaring angrily. 'Not until I—'

'Do as you are told,' snapped Hagar. She turned to the goldsmith. 'Put your louts to some use, Aurifabro, and get rid of these oglers. It is not seemly for them to be here.'

Neither Aurifabro nor his men moved to comply, but the threat of forcible eviction by them was enough to cause a concerted surge towards the door. The bedeswomen lingered, careful to stay in the shadows, while Botilbrig took refuge behind a pillar. Aurifabro watched them go, then turned back to the scholars.

'I suppose you are the Bishop's Commissioners, come to investigate what happened to that greedy scoundrel Robert. Well, I had nothing to do with his disappearance, and if you claim otherwise, you will be sorry. *I* am not afraid of corrupt Benedictines.'

Michael inclined his head, unperturbed by the man's hostility. 'Your remarks are noted. However, if you have nothing to hide, you have nothing to fear. I am not easily misled, and I always uncover the truth.'

'Good,' said Aurifabro, although his eyes were wary and Bartholomew wished Michael had held his tongue. If something untoward had befallen the Abbot, the culprit would not appreciate a Commissioner who promised to expose him. And the boast would be common knowledge by the end of the day in a small place like Peterborough.

'The Bishop told me that Robert was visiting a goldsmith when he disappeared,' Michael went on, all polite affability. 'Am I to assume it was you?'

Aurifabro's expression became closed and sullen. 'Yes, but he never arrived. And I have better things to do than be interrogated by monks. Good day to you.'

He spun on his heel and stalked out. Only when he and his henchmen had gone did Botilbrig and the bedeswomen emerge from their hiding places.

'Now that Joan is dead, I am head of St Thomas's

Hospital,' Hagar announced to the other ladies. 'Because I am next in seniority. You may call me Sister Hagar. Or better yet, *Prioress* Hagar.' She grinned. 'Yes! I like the sound of that.'

Bartholomew exchanged a glance with Michael; both wondered whether she liked the sound of it well enough to dispatch her predecessor.

'You might wait until Joan is cold before stepping into her shoes,' said Botilbrig, his voice full of distaste. 'I had no love for her, but what you are doing is not right.'

'Of course it is right,' snapped Hagar. 'Would you have our hospital without a leader? But of course you would! It would make us weak, and St Leonard's could take advantage of it. You and your cronies would do anything to see us—'

'Enough,' ordered Michael sharply. 'Tell me about the fellow who just left.'

'Aurifabro?' asked Botilbrig, pointedly turning away from Hagar. 'He is the richest man in Peterborough, and the mortal enemy of Spalling *and* Abbot Robert – who are enemies themselves, of course. However, no one in the town likes Aurifabro.'

Hagar nodded, although it was clear she disliked having to agree with him. 'He is loathed for his surly manners – almost as much as that villainous Reginald. I cannot imagine why Abbot Robert deigned to spend time with *him*. Or with Sir John Lullington, for that matter, because he is not very nice, either. In fact, the only decent friend Robert had was Master Pyk.'

Bartholomew frowned at the contradiction in their diatribes. 'But if Aurifabro is Robert's "mortal enemy", why was Robert visiting him?'

46

'Because the abbey has commissioned a special paten from him,' explained Hagar. 'And Robert wanted to see how it was coming along. Obviously, he would have preferred someone else to make it, but Aurifabro is the only goldsmith in town, so he had no choice.'

'I do not envy you, Brother,' said Botilbrig rather smugly. '*I* would not want the task of proving that Aurifabro murdered the Abbot.'

'Murder?' echoed Michael sharply. 'You think Robert is dead?'

'Of course he is dead,' said Botilbrig scornfully. 'He would have come home otherwise.'

'I have a bad feeling about what the Bishop has asked you to do here, Brother,' murmured Bartholomew, when Botilbrig, Hagar and their cronies began a spirited debate in a local dialect that made their discussion difficult to follow. 'Aurifabro is obviously an aggressive man, and he is your chief suspect.'

'Suspect?' echoed Michael. 'Now *you* are assuming that Robert is dead.'

'Yes, because Botilbrig is right: no head of house would leave his domain without word for a month. He probably *is* dead. And Aurifabro will not be easy to interrogate.'

'No,' agreed Michael. 'But we shall face that problem when – if – it arises. However, I hope we can resolve the matter quickly. I *must* be home to draw up Winwick Hall's charter, or God only knows what liberties its founder might try to sneak into it.'

'I promised my patients that I would be home by Saturday week, too.' And Julitta was waiting, Bartholomew thought but did not say. He wondered if she missed him as much as he missed her, and whether her despicable husband was behaving himself.

'I would go to the abbey and make a start,' said Michael, 'but we had better wait until the officials arrive. To keep the ghouls away, if nothing else.'

'Hagar is more than capable of doing that. She may be old, but she is far from weak.'

Michael grinned. 'I would not have liked to cross her when she was younger. Indeed, I would not like to cross her now, and I am used to dealing with villains.'

'You think she is a villain?'

'Well, she and her bedeswomen are fleecing pilgrims for the right to pray at the grave of an executed criminal. That hardly makes them angels.'

They both turned as William and Clippesby approached.

'Are you talking about Oxforde?' asked the Franciscan. 'That grimy cutler Reginald just told me that Bishop Gynewell came in person to suppress that particular cult, but the abbey looked the other way when it started up again.'

Michael smothered a smile at the thought that William should remark on someone else's cleanliness. 'Then the Abbot is a fool. Gynewell may be kindly, but he will not tolerate open disobedience.'

'The shrine makes a lot of money and the monks share the revenue,' William went on. 'So of course they want it to thrive. But such greed is to be expected of Benedictines—'

'What happened to Joan, Matt?' interrupted Michael, unwilling to listen to more of the Franciscan's vitriol.

Bartholomew crouched to lift the cloak that covered

the body. Blood stained the flagstones, and he wondered whether they would become relics in time. It was not every day that murders were committed in holy places, and if the abbey was the kind of foundation to take advantage of such incidents, then Joan might well be declared a martyr.

'She was struck from behind,' he said, after a brief examination. 'Almost certainly by the smaller of those two pieces of stone from Canterbury Cathedral. The position of the wound eliminates suicide and accident.'

'Murder, then,' surmised Michael. 'So let us review what we know. Joan ousted all the pilgrims and Botilbrig so that she could show William her relics. She was alone when we left the chapel, and she refused to let anyone back in afterwards, as she wanted to pore over her donations. The pilgrims were vexed, and milled around outside . . .'

'She kept them waiting for so long that I think some had started to creep back in,' said Bartholomew. 'But it will be difficult, if not impossible, to find out who.'

'The bedeswomen were in here for some time before the alarm was raised, too,' added Clippesby. 'Yet perhaps they did not notice the body – it is dark, and they might not have approached the altar immediately.'

'Yes, they are certainly suspects,' agreed Michael. 'Especially Hagar, who assumed command with indecent haste.'

'If she is the killer, it means the other ladies stood by and watched,' mused William. 'I saw them all go in at the same time. But perhaps they *did* turn a blind eye as the formidable Joan was felled.'

'Not necessarily,' said Michael. 'As Clippesby pointed

out, the chapel is dark after the brightness of the sun. Hagar – or anyone else – could have brained Joan by the altar while those in the nave remained blissfully unaware.'

'Well, my favourite suspect is Botilbrig,' said William. 'On account of his unseemly sparring with the victim. He claimed he was outside at the time, but I did not see him.'

'Is he not too frail to brain anyone?' asked Michael doubtfully.

'It does not require much strength to bring down a stone on someone's head,' replied Bartholomew. 'Especially if he was fuelled by rage.'

'But Botilbrig *may* have been outside,' said Clippesby. 'Just because we did not notice him does not mean he was not there.'

'The other bedesmen are suspects, too,' William went on. 'I did not see any of them sneaking into the chapel, but I was watching that escaped pig, and I suspect other folk were, too. It was a perfect diversion.'

'There are other ways into the chapel besides the marketplace,' Bartholomew reminded them. 'There are doors leading from the hospital, the abbey and the graveyard – although that was empty. Of course, its walls are not very high, and someone could easily have climbed over them. In other words, virtually anyone might have come in and killed Joan.'

William sighed. 'Well, let us hope the townsfolk do not decide to blame strangers. It would be easy to point fingers at us.'

'At the Bishop's Commissioners?' asked Michael archly. 'They would not dare.'

'True,' acknowledged William, then added ruefully, 'So let us hope they never find out that you are the only one who actually holds that particular title.'

'They will not,' said Michael grimly. 'Because I am appointing you all as my deputies. It seems I shall be investigating an abbot's death, not his disappearance, so I shall need all the help I can get.'

While they waited for the abbey officials, Michael took the opportunity to question the bedesfolk. The men claimed the women had killed Joan, while the women declared the men responsible, but neither side could prove it. Each asserted that the first he or she had known about the murder was when Marion had raised the alarm. He fared no better with the pilgrims, all of whom denied entering the chapel before Marion's screech, although shifty eyes and shuffling feet told him that some were lying.

'It will be a tough case to solve,' he told his colleagues. 'I am glad it is not my responsibility.'

The abbey dignitaries arrived at that point, a collection of sleek, well-fed men with proud expressions and haughty manners. Bartholomew looked for old classmates among them, but the faces above the elegant habits were unfamiliar.

A portly fellow with enormous eyebrows stepped forward. 'I am Prior Yvo, Abbot Robert's deputy. You must be Brother Michael and his Commissioners. I am sorry your arrival has been tainted by bloodshed. It is hardly the welcome we had hoped to extend.'

'No,' agreed Michael. 'We would rather have had dinner.'

Yvo regarded him uncertainly, unsure whether he was making a joke.

'You have missed it,' said a tall, burly monk with a crooked nose. 'What a pity for you.'

The sneering arrogance gave a sudden jolt to Bartholomew's memory, of his final few weeks at school when two monks, not much older than he, had arrived to teach theology. He had not been interested in the subject, which had caused trouble, the only unpleasantness during an otherwise happy phase of his life. Their names had been Welbyrn and Ramseye, and he had all but forgotten the friction his antipathy had created. Was the bulky monk Welbyrn? If so, the intervening years had not treated him kindly, for he had been a handsome lad with an athletic figure. The monk who stood by the Prior had coarse features, oily hair and a sullenness that was unappealing.

'This is our treasurer, John de Welbyrn,' said Yvo. He flapped his hand in a way that was vaguely insulting, causing anger to flare in Welbyrn's eyes. The flash of temper made Bartholomew wary of stepping forward to introduce himself – for all he knew, Welbyrn would object to being hailed by a rebellious former pupil. Or would Bartholomew even be remembered? Welbyrn must have taught hundreds of boys since then.

'If there is no food here, we shall find a tavern,' said Michael coolly. 'Our journey has been long and difficult, and we need victuals to restore our vigour.'

'The Swan is reputed to be the best,' said Welbyrn, obviously pleased to be spared the expense of a meal. 'It is not far.'

'Our treasurer is always looking for ways to cut costs,'

said Yvo, treating Welbyrn to a smile that was wholly devoid of affection or approval.

'Yes, and it is not easy,' muttered Welbyrn. He turned to glare at a tall, aloof man with perfectly groomed hair and an immaculate habit. 'Especially when *some* brethren dispense alms instead of saving for the uncertainties of the future.'

'Of course I dispense alms,' retorted the suave monk irritably. 'I am the almoner.'

'If people are hungry, they should work,' said Welbyrn sourly. 'And that includes those lazy devils who claim to be ill. A little hard labour would make them forget their afflictions. You know I am right, Ramseye.'

Bartholomew regarded the almoner in surprise. He would never have recognised his second teacher, who had been a spotty youth with buck teeth and gangly limbs.

'Ramseye?' asked Michael. 'Are you kin to Robert Ramseye, the Abbot?'

'My uncle.' Ramseye assumed an expression of sadness that was patently insincere. 'We were very close, and I miss him terribly. It is a great pity he is dead.'

'Dead?' asked Michael blandly. 'I understood he was only missing.'

'Of course he is dead,' said Yvo. 'Why else would he fail to come home?'

'He is alive,' said Welbyrn between gritted teeth, his weary tone suggesting this was a debate that had been aired before. 'He will return in his own time.'

'He has been gone a month,' Ramseye pointed out. 'So it seems unlikely that this particular episode will have a happy ending. I wish it were otherwise, but . . .'

He held out his hands in a gesture of resigned helplessness.

'We are holding an election to replace him next week,' Yvo told Michael. 'And—'

'I still think that is a bad idea,' interrupted Welbyrn. 'He will be livid when he returns to find a usurper on his throne.'

'Welbyrn is fond of Robert,' Yvo explained to the visitors, while Ramseye patted the treasurer's shoulder with artificial sympathy. 'And he believes there is still room for hope, although those of us who are realists know when it is time to move on. I have put myself forward as a contender for the abbacy, and so has his nephew.'

'I see,' said Michael. 'However, my understanding of the rules is that you cannot hold an election until the current incumbent has definitely vacated the post. *Ergo*, you will have to wait for the results of my enquiry before you can legally appoint a successor.'

'Hah!' exclaimed Welbyrn victoriously, while Yvo and Ramseye exchanged a glance that was difficult to interpret. 'That means there will never be an election, because he is still alive.'

'We should not be discussing this when Joan's corpse lies before us,' said Yvo, abruptly changing the subject, presumably to mask his annoyance. 'Where is young Trentham? Did no one summon him? As chaplain, he must be the one to investigate her death.'

'Find him,' ordered Ramseye, snapping imperious fingers at a hovering novice. 'But while we wait, perhaps our visitors will tell us what happened.'

'She was brained by a relic,' supplied William. 'But we had nothing to do with it.'

Yvo's princely eyebrows shot up in surprise at this remark, while startled glances were traded between the other Benedictines.

'We did not imagine that you had,' drawled Ramseye. He turned to Michael. 'I am astonished to find you in company with friars and seculars. Could you not find any Benedictines to act as fellow Commissioners? The death of an abbot is hardly something we should share with other Orders.'

'They are colleagues from Michaelhouse,' explained Michael shortly, resenting being told what to do. 'I trust them implicitly.'

'Of course he does,' said William, preening. 'He often seeks my opinion, especially about theology. There is little I do not know about the King of Sciences.'

'Except its name, apparently,' said Ramseye scathingly. 'It is more usually known as the *Queen* of Sciences.'

'A king is higher than a queen,' retorted William, flushing. 'So I elevated it.'

'I see,' said Ramseye, and Bartholomew's heart sank. It would not take long for the almoner to expose William's intellectual shortcomings, after which the Commission was unlikely to be taken seriously. 'However, it originates from . . . what is *he* doing?'

Everyone looked towards the altar, where Clippesby was muttering to a spider. Worse, he was cocking his head, as if he could hear what it was saying in reply. His face was pale, and his eyes wilder than they had been earlier, indicating that bloody murder committed in a holy place had upset him. Bartholomew's heart sank further still: Clippesby distressed was likely to be odder than usual until the shock wore off.

'He is a saint in the making,' whispered Michael, so the Dominican would not hear and deny it. 'I brought him with me, so that his holiness can touch your foundation, too.'

Bartholomew felt his jaw drop, while William looked set to contradict, outraged that beatification should be bestowed on a member of an Order that was not his own.

'Then we had better make sure he has the best available quarters,' said Welbyrn, gazing at Clippesby with awe. 'We do not want saints vexed with us because of their shabby treatment.'

'As you wish,' said Michael smoothly. 'However, you must ensure his guardians are treated well, too. Quite aside from the fact that we are the Bishop's Commissioners.'

When the abbey officials eventually turned their attention to Joan, the scholars were unimpressed, as none of them did or said anything useful. Michael was on the verge of suggesting that the Sheriff be summoned, on the grounds that someone was needed who would do more than tut and sigh, when Trentham arrived.

'I was upstairs with Lady Lullington,' the young priest explained breathlessly. 'I did not know what had happened until the novice told me. Poor Sister Joan! I can scarcely believe it.'

'Is Lady Lullington dead yet?' asked Welbyrn with distasteful eagerness. 'Do you know what she has left the abbey in her will?'

Angry tears glittered in Trentham's eyes. 'No, I do not, and a deathbed is hardly the place to raise such a subject.'

'On the contrary, there is nowhere better,' countered Welbyrn. He seemed genuinely bemused by Trentham's emotional response, and Bartholomew recalled that he had been insensitive as a youth, too.

Trentham addressed Bartholomew, pointedly ignoring the treasurer. 'She is sleeping very deeply, and her pain seems less. Thank you.'

Yvo smiled in a way that was probably meant to be benign but only served to make him seem vaguely sinister. 'To take your mind off her, Trentham, you can find Joan's killer.'

Trentham went wide-eyed with horror. 'Me? But I would not know where to start!'

'He does not want to accuse his beloved charges,' surmised Welbyrn nastily. 'But we all know who is responsible for this vicious crime: a bedesman. Or a bedeswoman.'

'No,' cried Trentham. 'My old people would never harm Joan.'

'Lord!' exclaimed Yvo suddenly. 'Does it mean Hagar will be in charge now? That is a daunting prospect! Perhaps I shall not run for the abbacy after all, because dealing with her will not be easy.'

There was a fervent murmur of agreement from his brethren.

'So you have your first clue, Trentham.' Ramseye's smile was sardonic. 'No monk would murder Joan, as none of us are equal to managing Hagar. Perhaps the same can be said for the bedesfolk. *Ergo*, the culprit must be a townsman.'

'Or a stranger,' added Welbyrn, looking pointedly at the Michaelhouse men.

'I told you,' muttered William in Bartholomew's ear. 'We are about to be accused.'

'Not these strangers,' countered Yvo, glancing at Clippesby, who had abandoned the spider and had cornered a cat. 'A saint would not keep company with killers.'

'True,' acknowledged Ramseye. 'However, the town is full of possibilities. Spalling—'

'Yes!' interrupted Yvo eagerly. 'Spalling is certainly the kind of man who would invade our most lucrative . . . I mean our holiest chapel and strike an old lady with a relic.'

'He spent the morning accusing us of robbing travellers on the King's highways,' said Ramseye resentfully. 'So the murder of one of our bedesfolk would just be one more instance of the malice he bears us.'

'Accusing the abbey's *defensores*, you mean,' corrected Yvo sourly. 'The band of louts that Robert hired. I wish the Abbot had listened to my advice and refrained from doing that – it does our reputation no good at all to have rough fellows like those on our payroll.'

'They are not louts,' countered Welbyrn irritably. 'They are lay brothers. And we need them, given our unpopularity in the town.'

'I certainly feel safer with the *defensores* to hand,' agreed Ramseye. 'However, Spalling has no right to blame us for those robberies when they are *his* fault. His followers comprise a lot of discontented peasants, all convinced that they have a God-given right to other people's property.'

'We must not forget that Aurifabro's soldiers are hardened mercenaries,' said Welbyrn. 'Personally, I suspect that *he* is responsible for these nasty incidents on the south road.'

'Mercenaries?' echoed Bartholomew, bemused to learn that Peterborough seemed to be home to three separate private armies.

'Foreigners mostly,' explained Yvo. 'He refused to recruit locals, on the grounds that he is at war with us and Spalling's followers, and he was afraid he might hire spies who are actually in the pay of one of his enemies.'

'The south road,' mused William. 'Do you mean the track that runs towards Cambridge? We were ambushed five times on that – it is why we have taken so long to get here. And our attackers spoke French. I heard them.'

'It is disgraceful that honest men cannot travel in safety any longer,' said Yvo, shaking his head sympathetically. 'But I prefer Spalling as a suspect to Aurifabro – for Joan's murder, as well as the robberies. That man has been a thorn in our side for far too long. We should arrest him, and bring an end to his villainy.'

'Unfortunately, if we do, he will tell the Bishop that we are persecuting him on account of our past differences,' said Ramseye, raising a cautionary hand. 'And Gynewell will probably believe him. We need evidence before we clap him in irons.'

Yvo turned to Trentham. 'Then you had better find us some by looking into how he dispatched poor Joan.'

'No,' said Trentham, taking his career in his hands by refusing the order of a senior cleric. 'I do not have the ability to investigate murder. Or the time. With two hospitals and a parish to run, I am far too busy.'

'Two hospitals *and* a parish?' asked Michael. 'That is a heavy burden.'

'Too heavy,' agreed Yvo, although he was scowling at the young priest. 'I have been trying to appoint a

59

second vicar, but Welbyrn says we cannot afford it.'

As the abbey was obviously wealthy, Bartholomew thought Welbyrn was lying, and that the hapless Trentham was paying the price for the treasurer's parsimony.

'Brother Michael can do it, then,' said Ramseye slyly. 'He will be looking into our dead Abbot, and two enquiries are as easy as one.'

'No, they are not,' countered Michael indignantly. 'And I did not come here to solve local crimes. They should be explored by someone familiar with you and your idiosyncrasies.'

'What idiosyncrasies?' demanded Welbyrn.

'I agree with Ramseye,' said Yvo. 'Michael will be impartial, because he has no axe to grind. So you are relieved of the responsibility, Trentham. Go and pray for Joan instead.'

'I cannot oblige you,' said Michael irritably, as the young priest scurried away before the Prior could change his mind. 'I will not be here long enough to—'

'You aim to prove Robert dead before our election next week?' pounced Yvo eagerly. 'Good. We can proceed as we intended, then.'

'No, Father Prior,' snapped Welbyrn immediately. 'He is alive, and you cannot say otherwise just because you itch to step into his shoes. Indeed, Bishop Gynewell had no right to invite monks from Cambridge to pry into our business in the first place.'

'Yet we shall cooperate, because we should like to know what happened to him,' added Ramseye with a gracious smile. 'But this is no place to discuss it. We shall do it in the abbey, while the saint takes his ease.'

*　　*　　*

The sun was beginning to set as the monks filtered out of the chapel. Bartholomew hung back – neither Welbyrn nor Ramseye seemed to have improved with age, and he had no desire to renew the acquaintance. William hovered at his side, because some of the brethren were making a fuss of Clippesby and he could not bear to watch a Dominican so fawningly feted.

'The witches are putting on an act for Trentham's benefit,' whispered Botilbrig, making them jump by speaking behind them. He nodded to where the young priest was kneeling by the body with the bedeswomen clustered around him. 'Some are pretending to cry, but the truth is that none of them liked her.'

'Why not?' asked William. 'I thought she was very nice.'

'She was a tyrant,' explained Botilbrig. He seemed more spry than he had been, and Bartholomew regarded him suspiciously. Was he buoyed up by the success of his crime? Reinvigorated by the death of an enemy? Or simply revitalised now the heat of the day had passed? 'Mind you, Hagar will be worse. She looks kinder, on account of being more petite, but she will be a despot, too. And then it will be *her* brained with a relic.'

'Are you saying that one of the bedeswomen murdered Joan?' asked William.

Botilbrig considered the question carefully, then sighed his regret. 'Actually, no, to tell you the truth. Not because they loved her, but because they would not have used a relic to do it. *I* know it is a fake, of course, but they honestly believe it is genuine.'

'Then who is the culprit?' pressed William.

Botilbrig lowered his voice. 'Most of the monks are decent men, but the Unholy Trinity is another matter. I would not put murder past any of them.'

'What is the Unholy Trinity?' William's expression was dangerous, anticipating heresy.

'The popular name for three of the obedientiaries – men the Abbot appoints to be responsible for a specific aspect of the monastery's functioning, which puts them in authority over the rest of their brethren and confers all sorts of benefits.'

'I know what an obedientiary is,' said William indignantly.

Botilbrig ignored him. 'The Unholy Trinity is Ramseye, Welbyrn and Nonton the cellarer. Ramseye tells the other two what to do, and they are all vile men. He will order them to get him elected Abbot now.'

'Welbyrn will not oblige,' predicted Bartholomew. 'He does not believe the previous incumbent has finished with the post.'

Botilbrig grimaced. 'Welbyrn feels he owes Robert his loyalty, because he made him treasurer, whereas all the other abbots refused him promotion on account of his dim wits. But Ramseye will win him round – he always does. They were ordained together.'

Bartholomew did not say that he already knew. 'Why would this Unholy Trinity want Joan dead?'

'Who knows the workings of their nasty minds?' replied Botilbrig airily. 'I hope Ramseye is not elected Abbot, though. He will be better at it than Yvo, because he is shrewd. But he is not as agreeable.'

'Yvo is agreeable?' asked William doubtfully.

*   *   *

The abbey was beautiful in the red-gold light of the fading day. It was dominated by the vast mass of its church, and Bartholomew stopped for a moment to admire its mighty west front, just as he had done when he had been a child. It soared upwards in a breathtaking array of spires and arches, every niche filled with a carving of a saint, so that it seemed as if the entire population of Heaven was looking down at him. Then William grabbed his arm, and they hurried to catch up with Yvo, who had skirted around the cloisters to a small building with sturdy Norman features.

'This is the guest house,' the Prior was telling Michael and Clippesby. 'I shall leave you to refresh yourselves, and then you must join me and the other obedientiaries for a discussion. Afterwards, the cook will prepare you a small collation.'

'It had better be more than a small one,' grumbled Michael when they were alone. 'After all the travails we have suffered today.'

When Clippesby slumped into a chair, Bartholomew knelt in front of him and peered into his face. The Dominican was definitely less lucid than he had been earlier, and his hair stuck up in clumps where he had clawed at it. Clippesby ignored him, another sign that he was not himself, and all his attention was fixed on a hen that he had managed to snag.

'How will you go about solving Joan's murder, Brother?' asked William, going to the best bed and tossing his cloak on it, to stake his claim.

'I will not,' replied Michael firmly. 'I shall ask enough questions about Robert to fulfil my obligations to Gynewell, and then we are leaving.'

'Good,' said William. 'I do not like it here.'

'Neither do I,' said Michael, slipping behind a screen to change. He was always prudish about anyone seeing him in his nether garments. 'Yvo has offered to lend us a few *defensores* for our return journey. He says it should take no more than three days to get home, because robbers will not attack us if we are well protected, and we will make better time.'

'You need to be back by Saturday week, which means leaving by next Wednesday at the latest,' said William, calculating on his fingers. 'That gives us seven days. Will it be enough?'

'It will have to be, because I am not risking a riot at my University over this.'

'I had misgivings about this venture the moment Langelee ordered me to pack,' said William sourly. 'And now I know why: Peterborough is not a happy place.'

'No,' agreed Michael, 'which is a pity, because it is lovely. Wealthy, too.'

'This bed is certainly costly,' said William, flopping on to it and sighing his appreciation.

Michael emerged from behind the screen and inspected his reflection in the tiny mirror he used for travelling. He evidently liked what he saw, for he smiled. 'Will you stay here and mind our budding saint while I address the obedientiaries, Father?' he asked, carefully adjusting a stray hair.

'What saint?' asked Clippesby, snapping out of his reverie.

'Of course,' replied William, kicking off his boots and closing his eyes. 'I do not feel like dealing with more

Benedictines today anyway. But you should not go alone, Brother. Take Matthew with you.'

'I hardly think that is necessary,' said Bartholomew, loath to be thrust into the company of Ramseye and Welbyrn again. 'These are men of his own Order.'

'Yes, but I shall still need help if we are to leave in a week,' countered Michael. 'So don some tidier clothes, and let us make a start on this wretched business.'

Suspecting it would be futile to argue – and he had worked often enough with the monk to know that his assistance would definitely expedite matters – Bartholomew rummaged in his saddlebag for a clean tunic. Unfortunately, it had suffered from being scrunched into a ball to make room for his medicines, and was sadly creased. There was also a stain down the front, where one of the phials had leaked.

'Wear your academic gown over the top,' advised Michael, when the physician declared himself ready. 'That will conceal some of the . . . deficiencies.'

'That is a polite way of saying you are scruffy, Matthew,' supplied William helpfully. 'You might want to consider grooming yourself a little more carefully in future.'

Feeling that if the likes of William felt compelled to comment on his appearance, it was time he did something about it, Bartholomew followed Michael outside. Before he closed the door, he heard Clippesby telling William what the hen had just confided.

'She says the reason for the antagonism between Peterborough's two hospitals is money – St Thomas's earns far more with its relics and Oxforde's grave than St Leonard's does with its healing well. It is all rather sad. They should learn to get along.'

'Yes, they should,' murmured William drowsily. 'Shame on them.'

As Bartholomew and Michael left the guest house, they were intercepted by a monk who reeked of wine. The yellowness of his eyes and the broken veins in his cheeks and nose suggested an habitual drinker.

'You were taking so long that I was sent to fetch you,' he said curtly.

Michael and Bartholomew exchanged a glance. No one had told them that they were supposed to hurry.

'Are you the cellarer?' asked Bartholomew. It was not easy for monks to drink themselves into ill health in an abbey, where wines and ales were locked away, so there had to be some reason why this man seemed to have managed it.

'Richard de Nonton.' The man bowed. 'Abbot Robert made me cellarer five years ago – he took his claret seriously, and knew that I am of like mind.'

'He drank?' asked Michael.

'Only if the wine reached his exacting standards.' The last member of the Unholy Trinity reflected for a moment. 'I would not mind being Abbot myself, but Ramseye is running, and he stands a better chance of winning than me. He will see me right, though.'

'Have you known Ramseye long?' asked Bartholomew.

'Ten years, although he and Welbyrn were here long before that. Peterborough is a lovely place, you see, and no one leaves once he is here. We often joke that the only way we will depart will be in a coffin.'

'I doubt Robert would find that particular jest amusing,' murmured Michael.

Nonton led them to a pretty house next to the refectory, which had a tiled roof, real glass in the windows, and smoke wafting from its chimney. As it was high summer, a fire to ward off the slight chill of evening was an almost unimaginable extravagance.

'Abbot Robert's home,' explained Nonton. 'He liked to be near the victuals, so he had this place built specially. Prior Yvo lives here now, although he will have to move when he loses the election.'

'You think Ramseye will win, then?' asked Michael.

Nonton flexed his fists, an unpleasant gleam in his eye. 'My brethren will vote for him if they know what is good for them.'

'Tell me about Robert,' invited Michael. 'Was he popular?'

'Not really. I liked him well enough, but most of the other monks did not. Why?'

'Because it might have a bearing on what happened to him.' Michael stopped walking and looked Nonton in the eye. 'If the rumours are true, and Robert and Physician Pyk are found murdered, who are your favourite suspects for the crime?'

'I only have one: Aurifabro,' replied the cellarer promptly. 'He and Robert were always squabbling, and we should not have ordered that gold paten from him.'

'Yet you have just told us that Robert was unpopular,' probed Michael. 'Perhaps one of your brethren has dispatched him.'

'They are all too lily-livered,' said Nonton with a sneer, as if a disinclination to commit murder was something to be despised. 'Besides, not everyone found him objectionable. I thought he was all right, and so did Welbyrn,

67

Ramseye and Precentor Appletre. And that pathetic Henry de Overton, although *he* has a tendency to like everyone.'

'Henry de Overton?' asked Bartholomew, his spirits rising. 'He is still here?'

'Do you know him? That is not surprising: the man has friends everywhere.' Nonton scowled, giving Bartholomew the impression that the same could not be said for him.

'Was Henry friends with Robert?'

'He was not,' replied Nonton curtly. 'Our Abbot had three confidants: Physician Pyk, Sir John Lullington and Reginald the cutler. And that was all.'

'Reginald?' asked Bartholomew. Hagar had also mentioned the association, yet a grimy merchant seemed an odd choice of companion for anyone, but especially a wealthy and influential monastic.

Nonton nodded. 'A sly wretch, who would cheat his own mother. I cannot imagine why Robert tolerated him. The same goes for Lullington, who is an empty-headed ass. Pyk was decent, though. I liked him.'

'It sounds to me as though virtually anyone in Peterborough might have killed Robert,' whispered Bartholomew to Michael, as the cellarer began walking again. 'This will not be an easy case to solve, because I doubt the culprit will confess, and if it happened a month ago, there will be scant physical evidence to find.'

'I was charged to discover where Robert went,' Michael whispered back. 'Gynewell said nothing about solving a murder.'

'Sophistry, Brother. If Robert is dead by unlawful means, Gynewell will order you to catch the killer. He will not want his senior clergy dispatched without

68

recourse to justice, as it might open the floodgates to more "removals".'

'What was Robert like?' asked Michael, addressing the cellarer just in time to see him take a furtive gulp from a flask.

'Medicine,' explained Nonton hastily. 'For my chilblains.'

'Chilblains are not treated with—' began Bartholomew.

'Robert was a fellow who knew what he wanted and how to get it,' interrupted Nonton briskly. 'I admire that in a man – I cannot abide indecision. But we had better go inside, or Prior Yvo will wonder what we are doing out here.'

The Abbot's solar was a beautiful room with tapestries on the wall and a wealth of attractive furniture. An array of treats had been left on a table near the window, along with a jug of wine. Nonton headed straight for it, joining Welbyrn who was already there. The cellarer downed his first cup quickly, and poured himself another.

'I summoned all the obedientiaries,' said Yvo, coming to greet his visitors. 'Along with Sir John Lullington, who is our corrodian and always attends important gatherings.'

'Is he any relation to Lady Lullington?' asked Bartholomew.

'Her husband,' replied Yvo, as an elegant man stepped forward wearing the dress of a knight at ease – an embroidered gipon, fastened with a jewelled girdle. He was considerably younger than the woman in the hospital, suggesting the marriage had probably been one of convenience. Lullington bowed gracefully, producing a distinct waft of perfume.

69

'*Bonsoir*,' he said, fluttering his hand. 'I am delighted to meet you.'

Yvo had been speaking French, as was the custom among the country's aristocratic elite, but he suddenly switched to Latin, leaving Lullington frowning in incomprehension.

'The King has it in his gift to foist members of his household on us when they are no longer of use to him – Peterborough is a royal foundation, you see, so His Majesty has a say in its running. The right is called a corrody, and the recipient is a corrodian.'

'I know,' said Michael, irritated by the assumption that he was a bumpkin with no understanding of how his Order's grander foundations worked.

'So we are obliged to house Lullington and his wife in considerable splendour.' Yvo either did not hear or chose to ignore Michael's response. 'He is also entitled to dine at my . . . at the *Abbot's* table whenever he pleases, and to attend occasions like these.'

'Please use French,' snapped Lullington. 'You know my Latin is poor.'

'Then perhaps you should apply yourself a little more rigorously to learning it.' Yvo gave a smile that might have taken the sting from his words had there been any kindness in it, but it was challenging, and Lullington bristled.

'I shall report you to the King,' threatened the knight. 'I thought you wanted my backing when you stand for Abbot. You will not get it with that attitude.'

Yvo raised his eyebrows. 'Would you prefer Ramseye to be Abbot, then?'

Lullington promptly became oily. 'Let us not quarrel,

70

Father Prior. You know I consider you by far the best choice. I support you without reservation.'

'Of course he does,' said Yvo in Latin. 'He knows Ramseye will manoeuvre him out of the comfortable niche he has carved for himself here, whereas I shall let sleeping dogs lie. As did Robert. Ramseye might be bold enough to challenge the King's right to appoint corrodians, but I am no fool.'

'*French*, Yvo,' said Lullington crossly. 'Or English, if you must. I do not understand why you insist on Latin. Bishop Gynewell, who is a personal friend, speaks French to me.'

'Bishop Gynewell is a personal friend of mine, too,' said Michael. 'And he will not be impressed when he hears that Peterborough's officials are constantly at each other's throats. He will appoint an outsider as Abbot. Indeed, I might put myself forward for the post, and he will certainly choose me, should I express an interest.'

Yvo gaped at him, and so did Bartholomew, while Lullington looked the monk up and down appraisingly, as if deciding whether to shift his allegiance.

'You cannot,' said Bartholomew, eventually finding his voice. 'The University—'

'Will flounder without me,' finished Michael comfortably. 'Yes, I know. But I cannot devote myself to it for ever, and I have always said that my next post will be either an abbacy or a bishopric. Peterborough is not Ely, but it has potential.'

'How is your wife, Sir John?' asked Bartholomew, purely to silence Michael before he went any further. He was not sure Peterborough would be such a plum appointment, given the bitter disputes that were bubbling, and he wanted to tell his friend so before remarks were made that might later be difficult to retract.

'What?' asked Lullington, blinking. 'What about her?'

Bartholomew regarded him uncertainly. 'She is unwell.'

'Oh, yes,' said Lullington. He waved his hand rather carelessly. 'But she will be with God soon, which is good, because the abbey resents the extra mouth to feed.'

'Her death will ease our financial burden,' agreed Welbyrn, overhearing and coming to voice an opinion. Bartholomew regarded them in disbelief, sure the frail figure did not eat much, and probably had not done for weeks. Before he could say so, Yvo clapped his hands.

'Take your seats, please, gentleman. Time is passing.'

Once everyone was sitting around a large table, Yvo began to make introductions. He began with the Unholy Trinity. 'You have met our almoner, treasurer and cellarer.'

Ramseye nodded a polite greeting, but Welbyrn and Nonton did not. Nonton was refilling his goblet again, while Welbyrn, presumably to show the Bishop's Commissioners that he was an important man with heavy responsibilities, was scanning some documents.

'My God!' Ramseye exclaimed suddenly, gaping at Bartholomew. 'I thought there was something familiar about you earlier, but I could not place it. Yet I recognise you now you are in the light and have dressed in marginally more respectable clothes. Welbyrn, look!'

'It is Matt Bartholomew!' breathed Welbyrn, parchments forgotten. 'The lad who declined to learn his theology. I see from his attire that he has not amounted to much.'

'On the contrary,' said Michael, while a number of responses were on the tip of Bartholomew's tongue, none of them polite. 'He is the University's most distinguished *medicus* and has the favour of the Prince of Wales.'

This was misleading. First, there were only two *medici* in the University, and being more distinguished than Doctor Rougham was no great accomplishment. And second, the Prince of Wales had noticed Bartholomew once, after the Battle of Poitiers, when he had ministered to the wounded. The physician was sure he had long since been forgotten.

'I am pleased you realised your ambition to become a healer,' said Ramseye with a sly smile, although Welbyrn's dark, heavy features were full of disbelief at Michael's claims. 'I cannot imagine a better profession for someone like you.'

Bartholomew was not sure what he meant, but was certain it was nothing complimentary. He declined to reply, so Prior Yvo began to introduce the other obedientiaries. As Peterborough was a large foundation, a vast number of monks held official appointments, although Bartholomew was disappointed to note that Henry was not among them. He and Michael nodded politely as sacrist, precentor, cook, succentor, novice-master, pittancer, chamberlain and brewer were presented, along with their various assistants and deputies. The long list of names and faces soon merged into a blur.

'Now, Brother Michael,' said Yvo, when he had finished. 'What do you need to make an end to your investigation? It would be good to have the matter resolved tonight.'

'I think I may need a little longer than that,' said Michael, taken aback. 'But we can certainly make a start. When was the last time you saw Abbot Robert?'

'A month ago,' supplied Yvo. 'On St Swithin's Day. He went to visit Aurifabro, who owns a manor in the nearby village of Torpe. He never arrived.'

Not revealing that he already knew this, Michael merely remarked, 'I thought he and Aurifabro hated each other.'

'They did, but Aurifabro is the town's only goldsmith, and we wanted a new ceremonial paten,' explained Ramseye. 'We had no choice but to use him. My uncle took Pyk to ensure his safety on that fateful journey, but unfortunately it did not work.'

'Pyk?' probed Michael guilelessly.

'The town's physician, who is probably the most popular man in Peterborough,' provided Yvo. 'He disappeared at the same time.'

'A *medicus* seems an odd choice of protector,' said Michael. 'Or was Pyk a warrior?'

There was a general chuckle at this notion. 'Pyk was not a fighting man,' said an apple-cheeked, chubby man, whom Bartholomew thought was the precentor. 'Far from it.'

'Why did Robert not take his *defensores*?' pressed Michael.

'Presumably, because he did not want to insult Aurifabro with a show of force,' replied Ramseye with a shrug. 'But we cannot answer for certain, because my uncle rarely took anyone into his confidence.'

He sounded bitter. Bartholomew looked at him sharply, but could read nothing in the bland face.

'I told him to take a few *defensores*,' put in Welbyrn. 'But he said he would not be in danger, and I am inclined to agree. When he returns—'

'He will not return,' growled Nonton. 'Aurifabro is a murderous bastard, and violence is part of his nature. Robert should have known better.'

'He is *not* dead,' snapped Welbyrn. 'Why must you persist in saying he is?'

'What time did Robert leave the abbey?' asked Michael loudly, cutting into the burgeoning spat.

'After the midday meal,' replied Yvo. 'We had ox kidneys that day, and he was a glutton for those. He ate a large dish of them, and rode off shortly afterwards.'

'And his purpose was to inspect a paten?' asked Michael. 'Did he not delegate that sort of task? To the sacrist, for example, whose duty it is to manage such affairs?'

'As Ramseye has pointed out, Robert did not discuss his decisions with us,' replied Yvo. 'However, the paten was a costly venture, so it is not unreasonable that he was keen to assess its progress himself.'

'Is it finished now?' asked Bartholomew.

'No,' replied Yvo. 'When Robert failed to return, I told Aurifabro that we no longer wanted it. He is livid, but our Abbot died on a visit to his lair, so what does he expect?'

'What about Pyk?' asked Michael. 'Did his family search for him?'

'His patients did,' nodded Yvo. 'As I said, he was popular, and he is sorely missed. Much more than Robert, although it grieves me to say it.'

He did not look particularly grieved, and neither did his colleagues.

'Tell me about Robert as a man,' instructed Michael. 'What was he like?'

Immediately, most of the monks stared at the table, unwilling to catch his eye. Welbyrn scowled and twisted one of the documents in his big hands, while Nonton poured himself another drink. Ramseye looked faintly amused, as if he found his colleagues' behaviour entertaining. It was Prior Yvo who broke the uncomfortable silence.

'He was ambitious, greedy and ruthless. I am not in the habit of speaking ill of the dead, but false eulogies will not help your investigation, Brother.'

'My uncle could be cruel,' acknowledged Ramseye. 'And spiteful, on occasion.'

'He was my friend,' said Lullington. 'But even I am forced to admit that he was difficult.'

Their remarks opened the floodgates, and all the monks began to bombard him with examples of the Abbot's shortcomings. Bartholomew and Michael exchanged a glance: how were they to isolate a single suspect when it seemed that the entire monastery had disliked him?

'So to summarise,' said Michael, when the gush had slowed to a trickle, 'this bullying, greedy, cruel man set out to inspect a paten with Pyk, and neither man has been seen since.'

'Yes,' nodded Yvo. 'However, remember that both were well-dressed and rode fine horses, which was reckless with so many outlaws about. And Robert carried his official seals, which are solid gold.'

'His seals?' asked Michael, startled to learn that they were not safely locked in a chest, as was the custom.

76

'Was he in the habit of taking them out and about with him?'

'Yes,' replied Yvo. 'He never left them here, because he was afraid we might use them without his permission. And as you know, no abbey business can be transacted without them.'

'So he did not trust you,' stated Michael baldly.

There was another uncomfortable silence. Again it was Yvo who broke it.

'No, but that says more about him than us. Hah! There is the bell for vespers.'

There was a collective sigh of relief that the interrogation was over, followed by an immediate scraping of benches on the floor as the monks rose and began to file towards the door.

'Thank you for your time, Brother,' said Yvo with a gracious nod of his head. 'Perhaps we shall resume our discussion tomorrow.'

His tone of voice made it clear he thought it unlikely.

CHAPTER 3

The next day was overcast and threatened rain. Bartholomew had slept badly, despite being tired. It was strange being in Peterborough again after so many years, and he was surprised by how much of it he had forgotten – the abbey precinct was hauntingly familiar, but he barely recalled the town.

He remembered the guest house, though, and had visited it often when school was over and interesting visitors were in residence. Some had told him tales of their journeys, which had fuelled his own eagerness to travel. It was a good place to be, warm in winter and cool in summer, with two large bedrooms on the upper floor and a hall below for eating and relaxing. Its blankets were clean and smelled of lavender, and the windows could be opened for fresh air. It was a healthy environment, and one of which he approved.

'Why did your sister send you here when there was a perfectly good school not two streets from her home?' asked Michael, as he tied his rope cingulum around his waist, fiddling fussily until he was satisfied with the way it fell.

Bartholomew's parents had died when he was young, and it had fallen to Edith, ten years his senior, to raise him. 'I doubt it was her idea.'

'You mean it was your brother-in-law's? I thought he liked you.'

'He does, but he was a young man with a new wife. I imagine he wanted his privacy.'

'Did you not mind being exiled?' asked Michael doubtfully. 'I would have done.'

'I was very happy here, and the school is excellent, with patient, gentle masters. Except for Welbyrn and Ramseye, but they only came in my last few weeks.'

'Ah, yes,' mused Michael. 'The treasurer and the almoner, neither men I liked. Tell me about them. Start with Welbyrn. He struck me as stupid. Is that fair?'

'Not really. It was easy to tie him in logical knots when he was trying to teach, but stupid is too strong a word.'

'You challenged your tutors in the schoolroom?' Michael was unimpressed. 'No wonder they do not seem very kindly disposed towards you!'

'I would not have done it if their lessons had been better prepared.'

Michael raised his eyebrows. 'Remind me to ban you from any classes of mine.' He became thoughtful. 'Perhaps I shall not make a bid for the abbacy after all, because the obedientiaries leave a lot to be desired. Mind you, so did Robert by all accounts.'

Bartholomew was fully aware that Michael was ambitious, and that Cambridge would not hold him for ever, but he was glad the inevitable was to be postponed for a while longer. The monk was his closest friend, and he would miss him if he left.

'This was a happy place when I was young, but now it feels uneasy. Welbyrn stands alone in thinking that Robert is alive; he, Ramseye and Nonton have formed this so-called Unholy Trinity; and the monks are being forced to choose between the clever but unappealing

Ramseye and the marginally more likeable but ineffectual Yvo.'

'Lullington's odious presence cannot help either,' added Michael. 'Appletre the precentor is a decent fellow, though. Do you remember him from the horde we met last night? No? Then I shall introduce you to him later. I do not want you leaving Peterborough under the impression that all Benedictines are quarrelsome and disagreeable.'

'It is not just the Benedictines. There is friction in the town as well. Spalling and Aurifabro hate the abbey and each other, and both have followers.'

Michael nodded. 'Meanwhile, the men of St Leonard's and the women of St Thomas's are at one another's throats, and I am inclined to believe that one of them killed Joan, despite their denials. But today is Thursday and we are leaving in six days, so we had better make a start.'

'What do you want to do first?'

'After attending prime and eating breakfast, we shall ride to Aurifabro's home in Torpe, and inspect the track where Robert disappeared. Who knows, perhaps we shall find him there.'

'I imagine it has been thoroughly searched already.'

'Do you? I suspect it was surveyed cursorily at best, given that most people seem quite happy that the Abbot is missing. *Ergo*, we might well happen across a corpse.'

Bartholomew was relieved when Clippesby seemed calmer after a night's sleep. The wildness had gone from his eyes, and he appeared almost normal again as he knelt to recite his morning prayers. William lay with the blankets hauled over his head, doggedly determined to stay in his comfortable bed for as long as possible.

It was still early, so the bells had not yet rung for prime, and the abbey was peaceful. The only sounds were birdsong and a distant clatter from the bakery as bread was shovelled into the great ovens. Bartholomew was about to go for a walk, to savour the silence before the start of what was likely to be a trying day, when there was a knock on the door. He opened it to see a monk standing there, holding a jug of hot water.

'Henry!' he cried in delight, recognising his old class-mate immediately.

The monk beamed as he was clapped affectionately on the shoulder. He had always been small, but now he verged on the minuscule, and his lame leg gave him a more pronounced limp than when he had been a child. He still possessed a head of thick fair hair, though, and the eyes held the same sweet gentleness that Bartholomew remembered so well.

'Welbyrn told me that you had realised your childhood ambition to become a physician,' he said, smiling. 'Well done, although I cannot imagine how you cope with the gore.'

'He revels in gore,' remarked William from under the bedcovers. 'And I suspect he practised anatomy when he was off studying in foreign schools.'

'I did not,' said Bartholomew quickly. Dissection was not illegal in England, but it was frowned upon, and he did not want Henry to think him a ghoul. And while he had attended anatomical demonstrations when he had visited the medical faculties of Salerno and Padua, he had not performed one himself. Of course, that was not to say he had not wanted to – he was of the opinion that much could be learned from the dead.

'What office do you hold, Brother Henry?' asked Michael politely. 'If you have been here since you were at school, you must be an obedientiary by now. Forgive me if we met last night, but Yvo bombarded us with so many introductions that my head was spinning.'

'I am not an obedientiary, just a plain monk,' replied Henry. 'Like you.'

'I am not a plain monk,' said Michael, affronted. 'I am the University's Senior Proctor.'

'My apologies. I should have guessed there was a reason for your fine habit.'

Michael's eyes narrowed. 'Are you implying—'

'Are you happy here?' interrupted Bartholomew. He recalled that Henry could be scathing about monks who ignored the vows they had taken regarding poverty.

'Yes, I am,' replied Henry serenely. 'I serve God, and that is all I ask of life.'

Michael snorted cynical disbelief at this claim, while an odd sound emerged from the bed containing William, too. Clippesby nodded his understanding, though.

'I was surprised to see Welbyrn and Ramseye,' Bartholomew forged on, before any of them could speak. 'I thought they would have found greener pastures by now.'

'They like it here. And they both improved once they were assigned duties that better suited their abilities. Ramseye is a highly skilled administrator, while Welbyrn grew more gentle. Neither is the tyrant you remember, Matthew.'

'Welbyrn does not seem very gentle to me,' said

Michael, startled. 'Indeed, his remarks and behaviour have revealed him to be spiteful, petty and miserly.'

Henry's face clouded. 'He has changed recently. Robert's disappearance has upset him.'

'He is certainly reluctant to acknowledge the possibility that the Abbot may be dead,' agreed Michael. 'To the point of belligerence.'

'Yes,' acknowledged Henry. 'He has always been . . . vehement in his opinions, yet there is no real harm in him.'

Bartholomew recalled his childhood spats with Welbyrn. Most had been verbal, and they had only come to blows once – an encounter that had ended before more than a few cautious punches had been traded, when Welbyrn had tripped and hurt himself on a table.

'Perhaps you will tell us what happened when Abbot Robert disappeared,' said Michael.

'Poor Robert,' sighed Henry. 'He and Pyk went to visit Aurifabro, but I did not know they had failed to return until Prior Yvo made the announcement the following morning.'

'The following morning?' echoed Michael. 'Robert was not missed before then?'

'The obedientiaries became alarmed that night, but as it was dark, they decided to wait for daylight before sending out a search party. The *defensores* set out at dawn, but came back empty-handed. I was with a group of monks who visited Aurifabro that afternoon, but he said Robert never arrived. He was worried about Pyk, though.'

'He was not worried about Robert?'

'No, he did not like Robert, but he admired Pyk, and

sent his own mercenaries to hunt for them both. They had no more luck than our *defensores*.'

'What else was done to find them?' asked Bartholomew.

'The *defensores* searched other roads, and we still waylay travellers in the hope of news.'

'I find this odd,' mused Michael. 'If a high-ranking scholar went missing, I would organise a hunt immediately. And I would continue that hunt until we found him.'

'It is not for me to question the obedientiaries' decisions, Brother.'

'No,' said Michael. 'But there is a difference between questioning decisions and making your concerns known.'

'Appletre the precentor tried,' said Henry, rather defensively. 'He offered to take the *defensores* out again, but Ramseye said he would be wasting his time and that his uncle would come home when he was ready. But he never has.'

'Do *you* think Robert is dead?'

'Yes, I do. Ramseye and Yvo itch to take his place, and I doubt he would have left his throne unattended for so long, knowing that they circle like vultures.'

'Then who might have killed him? Ramseye or Yvo? One of the monks?'

'No,' said Henry firmly. 'We have all been praying for his safe return. You must look to the town for a culprit.'

'Why? What did he do to Peterborough's citizens to warrant being murdered?'

Henry hesitated, but then replied, although it clearly pained him to do so. 'He set high rents for those who live in our houses and farms, and he was miserly with alms. But that is all I can tell you, Brother. You will have to interrogate someone else if you want to know more.'

The moment Henry had gone, William joined Michael in an assassination of his character. Michael had disliked him on sight, while William had detected an innate slyness that he said would make Henry a prime candidate for murderous behaviour. Bartholomew gaped at them.

'Henry would never harm anyone,' he objected. 'He is a gentle, kindly—'

'You have not met him in years,' interrupted Michael. 'He might have changed.'

'The kitchen mouse does not like him, either,' added Clippesby. 'She said last night that she is unsure of his sincerity.'

'There!' pounced William, who only ever listened to Clippesby when the Dominican said something with which he agreed. 'We all know that mice are never wrong.'

Bartholomew regarded them unhappily. Clippesby was astute, and his assessments were often shrewder than those of his saner colleagues. But then he cast his mind back to when he and Henry had been young, and he was sure they were wrong. Henry had never shown the slightest inclination to hurt anyone, verbally or physically. His lame leg had made him a natural target for bullies, but he had accepted the abuse with a quiet dignity that had eventually won their respect. Welbyrn's hounding had persisted longer than the others', and it had been that which had prompted Bartholomew to fight him.

'Welbyrn is a villain, too,' said Michael. 'You will have to watch yourself around him, Matt, because he bears you a grudge. I could see it in his face last night.'

'Because I broke his nose.' Bartholomew shrugged at

85

his companions' astonishment. 'At least, that is what he will tell you. The truth is that he was trying to hit me, but he lost his balance and fell over.'

'You fought your schoolmasters, as well as exposing their intellectual shortcomings?' asked Michael, wide eyed. 'Lord! I am glad you were never a student of mine.'

The bells were ringing for prime, so the scholars walked to the church. Michael joined his Benedictine brethren in the chancel, while Bartholomew, William and Clippesby stood in the nave. As when he had been young, the physician's eyes were drawn upwards, to the splendour of the painted ceiling, which was a riot of geometrical designs in gold, red and green. It soared above three tiers of sturdy Norman arches, all alive with carvings, statues and murals.

'Things usually seem smaller as an adult than a child,' he remarked. 'But this church is even bigger than I remember it.'

'The mouse said much the same thing,' said Clippesby, nodding.

'We had better keep him away from the Benedictines,' muttered William. 'They might relegate us to meaner quarters if they discover that our "saint" is just a plain old lunatic.'

'Be kind to him, Father,' warned Bartholomew. 'He was upset by Joan's death.'

'So was I,' declared William. 'Therefore, I have decided to catch her killer myself. I shall do it when I am not deciding who murdered Abbot Robert.'

'No!' exclaimed Bartholomew, not liking to imagine what would happen if the grubby Franciscan started throwing his weight around in the abbey. 'Leave it to Michael.'

William looked angry. 'He wants my help. Why do you think he made me a deputy Commissioner yesterday?'

Bartholomew suspected the 'appointment' would be withdrawn if the monk knew that William intended to act on it. He flailed around for a way to deter him, feeling Michael's task was going to be difficult enough without William meddling.

'It might be dangerous,' was all he could manage on the spur of the moment.

William waved a dismissive hand. 'I shall question the abbey's servants – ask what they thought of Joan and Robert. And about some of our suspects, too – Aurifabro, Spalling and the obedientiaries. There can be no danger in that, and I imagine they will be more willing to confide in me – a lowly mendicant – than a lofty and ambitious Benedictine like Michael.'

Bartholomew nodded cautiously, supposing it would keep him occupied – and safely away from anyone Michael would not want offended.

'And I shall interview the abbey's animals,' offered Clippesby. Bartholomew started: he had not known the Dominican was listening. 'I saw a number of geese last night, and the horses will almost certainly have something to say.'

'I am sure they will,' muttered William, eyeing him disparagingly. He turned back to Bartholomew. 'Do you want to know who *I* believe murdered Joan?'

Bartholomew was not surprised that William had already formed an opinion; the friar had always been a man for snap judgements. 'Go on then,' he said warily.

'A Benedictine.' William lowered his voice. 'I do not like the Order, and as you pointed out yesterday, any of them could have gained access to the chapel via the back door. *Ergo*, a Black Monk slipped in and brained her.'

'And his motive?' asked Bartholomew.

'I shall find out from the servants,' vowed William. 'This morning.'

'Then do it discreetly, or you may find yourself relegated to the stables tonight, exchanging confidences with Clippesby's horses.'

A flash of alarm crossed William's face, and Bartholomew hoped self-interest would be enough to keep the questions conciliatory.

'What about Abbot Robert?' the friar asked, after a moment. 'Do you have a theory about him? If not, I do.'

'Yes?' Bartholomew braced himself for more harebrained speculation.

'Robert became ill on the journey, so Physician Pyk gave him medicine. But Pyk dispensed the wrong kind, and rather than face the consequences, he hid the body and fled. That is why both are missing.'

'But the robin told me that Pyk was very good at his trade,' argued Clippesby. 'I doubt he made a mistake. But even if he did, he could just have claimed that Robert had a fatal seizure. No one would have challenged him.'

'Rubbish,' claimed William, although he wore a crest-fallen expression. 'But prime is starting, and I am not in the habit of chatting during sacred offices. Please be quiet now.'

Tactfully refraining from pointing out that it had been William doing most of the talking, Bartholomew and Clippesby bowed their heads.

Prime was a beautiful ceremony in Peterborough. The precentor was an innovative musician, and the monks had been taught to sing in parts rather than traditional plainsong. Bartholomew closed his eyes to listen to the exquisite harmonies, but opened them again when someone joined in who should not have done – a discordant yowl that clashed with the tenors. William was smirking, delighted at this example that not everything the Benedictines did was perfect; Clippesby did not seem to have noticed.

When the service was over, Michael was waiting to say that they had been invited to breakfast in the refectory. He began walking there briskly, as though afraid there might not be anything left if he dawdled.

'Did you hear Prior Yvo caterwauling?' he asked, slightly breathless from the rapid pace he was setting. 'He ruined the *Gloria*.'

'That was him, was it?' asked William, amused. 'Why did no one tell him to desist?'

'We did, but he informed us that there was nothing wrong with his warbling, and that it was our ears that were out of tune.'

'You are talking about Prior Yvo,' came a voice from behind them. They turned to see a plump, round-faced, smiling little man who had been at the gathering of obedientiaries the previous evening. 'He made himself heard this morning, even though I had begged him to stay silent. I had dedicated this morning's music to poor Joan, you see. I was fond of her.'

'This is Thomas Appletre,' said Michael to his colleagues. 'The precentor.'

The monk smiled a welcome. 'Any friends of Bishop Gynewell are friends of mine; I admire him greatly. However, I hope he will appoint a new Abbot for Peterborough and not leave us to elect one of our own. I think an outsider would be a good idea.'

'I am considering taking the post myself,' confided Michael. 'And—'

'Oh, please do!' cried Appletre in delight. 'It would be wonderful to have a man who cares for music – and who might be persuaded to sing the responses on occasion.'

'Well,' said Michael, flattered. He was a talented musician, and it was unfortunate that Michaelhouse had one of the worst choirs in the country. 'That would be pleasant. But there is more to an abbacy than a bit of chanting, you know.'

'Not necessarily. You can do what Robert did – delegate all the tedious business to your obedientiaries and keep the enjoyable duties for yourself.'

'What does being Peterborough's precentor entail?' asked William, while Bartholomew and Michael exchanged a meaningful glance at this latest revelation of the Abbot's shortcomings.

'Organising the music and setting the mortuary roll,' replied Appletre. When the friar frowned his bemusement, he explained, 'Arranging prayers for the dead. Of course, that has put me in an invidious position of late.'

'Has it?' asked William, puzzled. 'Why?'

Appletre looked pained. 'Because I should like to

arrange some for Abbot Robert, but Welbyrn refuses to let me, on the grounds that he thinks he is still in the world of the living.'

'But you believe Robert is dead?' asked Michael.

'Yes, I am afraid I do. He loved his food, you see, and I cannot see him staying away from the abbey's table for a month without good cause. He took his victuals seriously.'

'Tell me what you thought of him as Abbot,' ordered Michael.

Appletre considered carefully before replying. 'He was a strong man. Well, he had to be, because a weak one could not have controlled us obedientiaries – we are opinionated fellows, as you may have noticed. But I think he meant well, on the whole.'

'Hardly resounding praise,' murmured Michael, as they followed the precentor to the refectory. 'But kinder than anything anyone else has said. Unfortunately, I suspect Appletre is one of those who looks for the good in everyone, so I am disinclined to believe him. Abbot Robert was an ugly customer, and that is all there is to it.'

The refectory was a long building near the cloister. There was a high table on a dais for the obedientiaries, and Prior Yvo took the Abbot's chair at its head. Welbyrn and Nonton formed a sullen, formidable presence on his left, while Ramseye sat smiling enigmatically on his right with Appletre. The scent of expensive perfume preceded the arrival of Lullington, who informed the precentor in braying French that he would have to move, as Lullington himself intended to sit near Yvo that morning. Appletre joined the lesser officials at the far end of the table, openly relieved to be away from the centre of power and the tense politics that surged around it.

Like the rest of the abbey, the refectory was well designed and clean, with religious murals placed to inspire the brethren to holy thoughts as they ate. It did not take long for the visitors to see that the artist had wasted his time. The meal was sumptuous, and the monks' attention was fixed entirely on the platters that were starting to arrive.

Bartholomew had never been very interested in fine food, mostly because he was unused to it – a life spent in universities had seen to that – and he had never really understood Michael's devotion to his stomach. He began to appreciate it that day, though, and knew he needed to pace himself, or the rich fare would make him ill. Michael and William showed no such compunction, and fell to with undisguised relish. Bartholomew exchanged a wry smile with Clippesby, who was also inclined to be abstemious.

'Lombard slices!' whooped Michael in delight, making a grab for the plate that was being carried past by a servant. 'My favourite. How very civilised to serve them for breakfast.'

As it was a Lenten day, meat was forbidden, but there were plenty of alternatives in the form of eggs, cheese, and fish. Bartholomew was somewhat startled to note that there were also kidneys, small balls of spiced minced liver and roasted chicken.

'Those are not meat,' explained Michael, his words almost indecipherable through his bulging cheeks. Meals were usually taken in silence, but an exception had been made that day in deference to the presence of the Bishop's Commissioners.

'No?' asked Bartholomew archly. 'What are they then? Vegetables?'

'Of course not. What I meant was they are not meat for the purposes of our diet. The Rule of St Benedict prohibits eating the *flesh-meat of quadrupeds* on Lenten days. Well, chickens are not quadrupeds, and liver and kidneys are not flesh-meat.'

'I see,' said Bartholomew, thinking this a rather liberal interpretation. Offal and chicken were meat as far as he was concerned, and the medical authorities he respected would agree. He watched the brethren tuck in. 'Regardless, it is not healthy to consume so much at breakfast. The Greek physician Galen says—'

'Galen was a miserable old ascetic who probably lived a long but very unhappy life,' interrupted Michael, snatching up an egg and inserting it whole into his mouth, as an act of defiance. 'I would rather die young and happy.'

'Then you are going the right way about it. You will never be an abbot or a bishop if—'

'What are you two discussing down there?' called Prior Yvo affably. The scholars had been allocated places at a table in the body of the hall, but near the dais, a ploy which meant that the obedientiaries loomed over them, symbolically asserting their superiority over mere Bishop's Commissioners.

'Spalling has put about a tale that the executed criminal Oxforde gave all his stolen money to the poor,' replied Clippesby, assuming the remark was addressed to him. He held an enormous grass snake in the air. 'This gentleman has just told me. It explains why none of his hoard has ever been found. Yet I am sceptical: felons are not usually generous.'

There was immediate consternation as the monks, not unreasonably, objected to the presence of a serpent at their breakfast table. Some thought it was an adder and flew into a panic, while others simply did not like creatures that slithered. Clippesby was bewildered by the fuss, as his Michaelhouse colleagues had grown used to him producing animals when the fancy took him, and no longer reacted. Bartholomew watched the commotion thoughtfully, finding the various responses revealing.

Welbyrn and Nonton surged forward with daggers, proclaiming their intention to kill the creature; as monks were supposed to forswear violence, Bartholomew wondered why they had armed themselves, particularly in a refectory. Yvo climbed on the table wailing about the snake crawling up his habit, while Lullington grabbed the sacrist and forcibly placed the man between himself and the source of danger. Appletre and the lesser officials struggled to restore calm, and Henry's head was bowed in prayer. Meanwhile, Ramseye looked on with an expression that was difficult to gauge.

When Nonton seized Clippesby roughly in his determination to reach the snake, Bartholomew intervened. He helped the Dominican carry the now-agitated reptile outside, aware that Welbyrn and Nonton were watching its release with eagle eyes, no doubt with a view to dispatching it later.

'It is a good thing he is holy,' said Yvo, when everyone was back in his place and peace reigned once more.

'Because otherwise I would have to ask you to find other lodgings.'

'He *is* holy,' asserted William, loath to lose the Benedictines' luxurious hospitality quite so soon. 'And his eccentricity is proof of it.'

'I am not—' began Clippesby in alarm.

'There is a barn owl looking for you,' interrupted William quickly. 'Outside. You had better go and see what it wants. Hurry now.'

Clippesby regarded him askance. 'Are you sun-touched, Father? A barn owl would not be looking for me. What a peculiar notion!'

'Oh,' said William, painfully aware that he was now the one who looked addled.

'Not at this time of year and in daylight,' Clippesby went on, to William's profound relief. 'It must have been some other bird. A hawk, perhaps. They often have things to say about excessive gluttony at the breakfast table.'

At an urgent nod from Michael, William took the Dominican's arm and hustled him away before any other remarks about their hosts' lifestyle could be made.

'Your Clippesby is an unusual man,' said Yvo, pursing his lips as he watched them go. 'Our own saint-in-the-making – a fellow named Kirwell – does not commune with serpents.'

'Tell me about the election you plan to hold,' said Michael, partly for information, but mostly to prevent questions being asked about their colleague that could not truthfully be answered. 'Why are you determined to do it so quickly?'

'Because it is not good for an abbey to be without a

leader in this day and age,' replied Yvo. 'And the sooner I am in office . . . I mean the sooner we have a replacement, the better.'

'But why?' pressed Michael. 'Some abbeys manage for years without a titular head.'

'It is a dangerous time for us. Aurifabro is a deadly enemy, while Spalling urges our peasants to rebel. Why do you think Robert told Nonton to recruit the *defensores*?'

'Spalling,' mused Michael. 'You should not allow him to air such radical views. He will have the whole shire ablaze if he continues unchecked.'

'He has always held controversial opinions,' said Yvo unhappily. 'And we did excommunicate him for them, but the Bishop pardoned him. All was calm for a while, but he started up again when Robert vanished. Unfortunately, I cannot excommunicate him a second time – the Bishop would not like it.'

'He would not like his diocese inflamed by rebellion either,' Michael pointed out.

'That will not happen. Nonton and Welbyrn visit Lincoln a lot, and they say the rest of the See is calm. It is only Peterborough that is unsettled.'

'Unfortunately, that is untrue. Cambridge is also full of treasonous talk, especially in the taverns after dark. Matt's book-bearer predicts a national uprising, and I fear he is right.'

'Why did Gynewell pardon Spalling?' asked Bartholomew, unwilling to discuss Cynric's revolutionary politics in a place where they might cause him trouble. 'Bishops do not normally take the side of rabble-rousers against fellow clerics.'

Yvo sighed. 'He said excommunication was an inappropriate punishment, and we should have put him in prison instead. Unfortunately, the common folk now think that Gynewell approves of Spalling, and any attempt to silence him meets with public protest. It is an awkward situation.'

'Awkward indeed,' agreed Michael.

The meal went on much longer than the ones in Michaelhouse for the simple reason that there was far more to eat. Michael grew restless, eager to visit Torpe before more of the day was lost. Sensing his impatience, Appletre came to sit with him, taking his mind off the wasted moments by asking about the Michaelhouse Choir, a subject dear to the monk's heart. Ramseye abandoned his exalted spot on the dais to provide the same service for Bartholomew.

'So you really did become a physician,' the almoner said, indicating that Bartholomew was to make room for him on the bench. 'I thought you would have seen sense and studied law instead. That is where the money lies.'

'And you stayed in Peterborough.' Bartholomew declined to explain that he had never been interested in making himself rich, suspecting that Ramseye would not understand.

Ramseye nodded. 'I have not set foot outside it since you took us fishing in Peakirk that time. Well, I went to Torpe a few weeks back, but that is the sole extent of my travels.'

Bartholomew gaped at him. 'But Torpe is only two miles away!'

'Quite, and I was relieved to get back, I can tell you.

97

The jaunt took an entire morning, and I have never felt so vulnerable in all my life. But why the astonishment? Peterborough has everything I want, and the rest of the world is dirty, sordid and dangerous.'

Bartholomew struggled for something to say that would not reveal how very peculiar he found this to be. It was not uncommon to find labourers who had never left their villages, but senior churchmen tended to be more mobile – to inspect their foundations' far-flung properties, if nothing else.

'What did you think of Torpe?' he managed to ask.

'Terrible! It reeked of cows and the silence was unnerving – no bells, no street vendors, no carts or horses. I went because Robert wanted me to inspect the new paten Aurifabro was making. I tried to pass the duty to someone else, but he was insistent, so I had no choice.'

'Did you like the paten?' Bartholomew was wholly out of his depth in the discussion; even Michael, who hated travelling, was not this insular.

'Oh, yes. It is a fabulous piece, and it is a pity that Yvo cancelled the commission.' Ramseye shuddered. 'The journey was a nightmare, though. It was pouring with rain and freezing cold. I am sure Robert picked a dismal day on purpose, to intensify my misery. As I said yesterday, my uncle could be cruel.'

'You also said that you believe he is dead.'

'I do. Why else would he abandon the comfortable life he had here? Besides, there is Pyk to consider. He is missing, too, which almost certainly means that someone killed them. A natural disaster, such as a fallen tree or a bolting horse, is unlikely to have taken them both and left no trace.'

'Then who is the culprit?'

Ramseye gave the sly smirk Bartholomew remembered so well. 'Well, the obvious choice is those who might benefit from his departure – namely Yvo and me. If you ask our brethren, they will probably tell you that we would do anything to be Abbot.'

'Would it be true?'

'Yes and no. I *do* want the abbacy, not for personal gain, but because I believe I can take Peterborough to new levels of greatness. I am not a murderer, though. However, I cannot say the same for Yvo – there is a ruthless streak beneath that insipid exterior.'

There was a ruthless streak in Ramseye, too, thought Bartholomew, one that looked the other way while Nonton and Welbyrn won votes for him by bullying. 'You think Yvo arranged to have your uncle killed?'

'I did not say that – I merely pointed out that he has a motive. However, he is not the only one. Your gentle Henry was often the butt of Robert's sharp tongue, and the bedesfolk did not like him either, while our tenants hated him for being a harsh landlord.'

'Are there any suspects who stand out above the others?'

'Not really: they all despised him with equal passion. But I can tell you one thing: if Michael intends to provide Gynewell with a killer, he will have his work cut out for him. I doubt this particular mystery will ever be solved.'

Bartholomew was grateful when Yvo eventually stood to intone grace, allowing him to escape. He liked Ramseye no more as a man than he had as a youth, and was sorry the abbey had been obliged to endure his disagreeable presence for so many years. It deserved better.

Outside, he breathed in deeply of air that was rich with the scent of scythed grass and ripening crops. Sheep bleated in the distance, and swallows swooped around the nests they had built under the refectory's eaves. He closed his eyes, but opened them in alarm when something breathed heavily and hotly on the back of his neck. It was his stallion, saddled and ready to go to Torpe. It eyed him challengingly, as if it knew there was about to be another contest of wills, one it fully intended to win.

'Are you going to stand there daydreaming or shall we go?' asked Michael.

He was already astride his own horse, and with him were four of the abbey's *defensores*, dour, unsmiling men wearing an eclectic collection of armour. Yet they did not carry themselves like soldiers, and Bartholomew suspected they had been selected for their savage looks rather than their skill with weapons. Knowing he was being watched, he climbed into the saddle with as much grace as he could muster – not a vast amount, but at least he did not embarrass himself – and followed Michael out of the abbey.

Torpe lay west of the town, along a road that wound pleasantly through woods and farmland and occasionally touched the banks of the meandering River Nene. After a mile, the countryside turned into untamed heath, land that had once been under the plough but that had been abandoned after the plague. It was desolate and unsettling.

'Aurifabro's estates,' explained one *defensor*. 'He

bought it for a pittance when the Death took all the farmers, and says it will make him rich when there is a demand for good pasture in the future.'

'It would be a lonely place to die,' said Michael, looking around uneasily. 'I am not a man for fancy, but even the trees look depressed.'

Bartholomew knew what he meant, especially when they passed a lightning-blasted oak and its dead branches swayed to release a moan that sounded uncannily human. His disquiet transmitted itself to his horse, which promptly began to prance.

'Grip with your knees,' instructed Michael. 'And shorten the reins. Lord, Matt! Do you remember nothing of what I have tried to teach you?'

'We should have walked,' muttered Bartholomew.

Michael was about to argue when the oak groaned with such heart-rending sorrow that the *defensores* crossed themselves and even he felt impelled to spur away from it. Bartholomew was concentrating on keeping his seat, but in the corner of his eye the ivy-swathed tree suddenly took on the shape of a monster with branches like ragged wings. Yet when he gazed directly at it, stomach churning with foolish alarm, the discomfiting image had gone.

The stallion was unsettled and took off like an arrow. Bartholomew let it have its head, hoping a gallop would tire it out. Unfortunately, once it was going it was reluctant to stop, and no amount of rein-shortening or knee-gripping could induce it to slow down. It entered Torpe in a fury of thundering hoofs, scattering chickens and goats, and he was aware of startled villagers stopping to gape.

It raced past a chapel, and Bartholomew was just

wondering whether they might overshoot the village and carry on to the next one, when it veered into a cobbled yard. With nowhere left to run, it came to a standstill, and showed its disdain for its rider by ignoring his attempts to steer it back to the road and ambling towards a hay-filled manger. The physician jumped in alarm when he heard the unmistakable sound of a crossbow being wound.

'Leave,' came a low voice that dripped menace. 'Now.'

Bartholomew twisted around in the saddle to see three of Aurifabro's mercenaries, two of whom had weapons trained on him. Their captain stood with his hands on his hips, his face full of angry indignation.

'I am sorry,' said Bartholomew, pulling hard on the reins in an effort to separate horse from fodder. The animal ignored him and continued to munch. 'Is Aurifabro at home?'

'No,' said the captain shortly. 'And he did not say when he would be back.'

'I will wait.' Bartholomew was keen to dismount and recover from his furious ride.

'You will not. We have orders to repel visitors while he is away, and that is what we shall do. Now get out, before I give orders to shoot you.'

To give emphasis to the threat, one of his cronies released a crossbow bolt, which snapped into the ground by the horse's hoofs. The beast released a frightened whinny, and Bartholomew found himself on the move again. Fortunately, it turned left on leaving the yard, thus retracing its steps; he was vaguely aware of the astonished villagers watching him hurtle past a second time. The stallion slowed when it reached Michael and the *defensores*, its sides heaving and saliva foaming from its mouth.

'Where did you take it?' asked Michael disapprovingly. 'Scotland? You have exhausted the poor creature.'

'The "poor creature" almost got me killed,' said Bartholomew crossly, dismounting while he could. He shoved the reins at Michael. 'Aurifabro is out, his mercenaries are in, and I am *walking* back to Peterborough.'

The monk had no more luck in persuading the soldiers to let him into Aurifabro's house than had Bartholomew, and he was disgruntled when he finally caught up with the physician.

'That was a waste of a morning,' he grumbled. 'I shall mention Aurifabro's lack of cooperation in my report to Gynewell. And you should not have stormed off alone. Two men disappeared on this road, you know.'

'I thought I might find some clues if I travelled on foot,' explained Bartholomew, moving so that the monk was between him and the stallion. The beast was guilelessly docile now it was being led by a man who knew what he was doing.

'You found something?' asked Michael eagerly.

'No. However, if I had to pick somewhere to commit murder, the Torpe road would be high on my list of choices. No one lives on the part Aurifabro owns, large sections are obscured by trees, and there are ditches galore to hide in.'

They continued in silence, past a cluster of buildings that Bartholomew had barely noticed when he had been struggling to stay mounted. It was St Leonard's Hospital, and a familiar figure stood outside its gate.

'It is Botilbrig,' said Michael. 'Does he loiter at every entrance to the town?'

'You are needed,' the bedesman informed Bartholomew.

103

'Lots of people are desperate for medical attention now that Pyk is gone. Some are waiting for you inside.'

'I told them you would pass this way,' said William apologetically, emerging to stand next to him. Clippesby was there, too. 'Their plight moved me, and I thought you would not mind. Besides, they offered to show me their holy well if I helped to secure them a few moments of your time, and I like sacred things.'

'They will need more than a few moments,' murmured Clippesby, who had a piglet under one arm and a duck under the other. 'There are dozens of them.'

'Are you ready?' asked Botilbrig, indicating the hospital with a gnarled hand.

'I cannot refuse, Brother,' said Bartholomew, when he saw Michael's brows draw together in an irritable frown. 'It would be unethical.'

Michael gave a gusty sigh, then lowered his voice so their colleagues would not hear. 'I suppose I can replace you with William for the rest of the day, just this once. Do you mind keeping Clippesby? He should not be left alone.'

'He should not,' agreed Bartholomew. 'He is still upset about Joan's murder and—'

'I am more concerned that he does not do something to show he is no saint,' interrupted Michael. 'Our continued comfort depends on it, so please be careful.'

'You should not have lied about that,' said Bartholomew uneasily. 'The truth is bound to emerge, and when it does, you will have some awkward questions to answer.'

'Then we shall have to ensure it does not,' said Michael, unrepentant.

*   *   *

The Hospital of St Leonard was larger than St Thomas's, although it was Norman rather than Gothic. It boasted a range of picturesque cottages, sheds and stables, but its core comprised a chapel and an adjoining two-storeyed building with a hall on its ground floor and three smaller chambers above.

The hall had once held beds for lepers, but as its days of dealing with incurable diseases were over, it had been converted into a pleasant common room. There was a hearth at one end, in which a fire glowed despite the warmth of the day, and its furniture was simple but elegant. Several bedesmen were clearing a long trestle table of what looked to have been an ample meal, suggesting that Peterborough's monks were not the only ones who knew how to cater to their personal comfort.

A long line of people stood patiently outside the hall, and Bartholomew assumed they were queuing for alms until he noticed that most were too well dressed to be beggars. With a start, he realised they were waiting to see him, and wondered if half of Peterborough had turned out. He jumped in alarm at a sudden shriek.

'I am a bat,' cried an elderly man, flapping his arms. 'Get out of my way, or I shall entangle myself in your hair.'

'Simon the cowherd,' explained Botilbrig. 'He has been without his wits for years now, and is one of us bedesmen. We did our best to make him sleep today, given that he is inclined to be disruptive, but he refused to drink the flagon of wine we tried to feed him.'

'Bats never entangle themselves in hair, Simon,' said Clippesby, addressing the cowherd softly and kindly. 'It is a tale often put about, but it is wholly untrue.'

Simon lowered his arms and regarded the Dominican warily. 'How do you know?'

'They told me so themselves,' replied Clippesby matter-of-factly.

Bartholomew was disconcerted when the remark was repeated in awed murmurs down the line of patients, but no one laughed, and there were further whispers that this was evidence of the Dominican's saintliness. Entirely unwittingly, Clippesby reinforced the belief by favouring Simon with one of his sweetest smiles, an expression that revealed his innate goodness.

'They talk to me, too,' hollered the cowherd, beginning to dance again. 'And so do the pigs and the bumblebees.'

'Then you must tell me what they say.' Clippesby caught his hand and led him to sit by the window; Simon went quietly, like a child.

'That is the calmest he has been in years,' said a tall, silver-haired man wonderingly. 'Clippesby truly *is* holy. We are blessed today, with visits from a saint *and* a physician.'

'I am having a consultation with both,' announced Botilbrig. 'They are only here because they took a liking to me yesterday, so I am within my rights to demand it.'

'They had better tend Kirwell first,' said the silver-haired man. He bowed to Bartholomew. 'My name is Prior Inges, head of this fine hospital.'

'I should have been Prior, rightly speaking,' interposed Botilbrig. 'As I am the eldest resident – other than Kirwell, of course. But Abbot Robert told me I was not clever enough, and appointed Inges instead. It was not very nice, actually.'

Inges ignored him. 'Once you have seen Kirwell, I shall show you the healing well. You can begin seeing patients after that.'

'Can I now?' muttered Bartholomew, resenting the presumption.

'Kirwell is our own saint,' Inges went on, 'whom God has blessed with an especially long life. He is a hundred and forty-three years old.'

'How do you know?' asked Bartholomew curiously.

'Because we have irrefutable evidence – namely that he was born in the year of Magna Carta. He remembers his mother telling him so, you see.'

It was not Bartholomew's idea of 'irrefutable evidence', but he followed Inges up the stairs to where Kirwell had been provided with a bedchamber all to himself. Someone was singing a ballad in a lilting tenor, so beautifully that Bartholomew stopped to listen. Inges had no such compunction, however, and barged in without ceremony.

'Very nice, Appletre,' he said briskly and in a manner that suggested it was time for the precentor to leave. 'It was good of you to come.'

'It is my pleasure,' replied the precentor amiably. 'Although I suspect I did more to send Kirwell to sleep than to entertain him.'

Kirwell lay in bed, wizened, concave-headed and entirely bald. Appletre was right to say that he had fallen asleep, for he snapped into wakefulness at Inges's interruption, revealing rheumy eyes that were almost white. However, Bartholomew thought that while he might well be ninety, or even a hundred, he was certainly no more.

'Here is the physician, Kirwell,' announced Inges. 'We

brought him to you first, so keep him for as long as you like. The rest of us are happy to wait.'

'I will come back later, then,' said a figure who had been sitting quietly in the shadows. It was the young chaplain Trentham. He was blinking drowsily, suggesting that Appletre's singing had had a soporific effect on him, too.

'Please do,' said Inges. 'And then I shall finish telling you about my first day as abbey steward, when I was obliged to confront a vicious killer.'

'On your first day?' asked Appletre, wide-eyed. 'That sounds nasty.'

'It was,' agreed Inges. 'The culprit was a man who discovered his wife in bed with a shepherd. He fastened his hands around her throat and slowly wrung the life out of her.'

'Oh,' gulped Appletre, raising a hand to his own neck. 'I have nightmares about that – someone doing something awful to my throat. Singing is my only skill, and without my voice, I would be useless. In fact, I would rather die than live without music.'

'If someone strangled me, I would want it done vigorously,' confided Inges. 'Not like the man with his wife, which took an age. It is more merciful to grab one's victim and finish him with one brief but powerful squeeze. There would be no pain and—'

'Stop!' cried Appletre, putting his hands over his ears. 'Such a discussion is hardly appropriate in front of saints, physicians and priests – or precentors, for that matter.'

'It is only idle chatter,' shrugged Inges. 'But we should not waste Doctor Bartholomew's time, because he has a lot to do today. Thank you for coming, Appletre. You, too, Trentham. Kirwell enjoys these weekly sessions very much.'

Inges accompanied the priest and the precentor out, leaving Bartholomew alone with the patient. Kirwell turned his opaque eyes in the physician's direction.

'How much longer?' he asked in a low voice.

Bartholomew sat next to him. 'How much longer until what?'

'Until I die,' whispered the old man. 'I am weary of life and want to sleep in my grave.'

'That is not a question I can answer.'

'I am tired of lying here while folk prod and gawp at me. The attention was fun to start with, but now I have had enough. So how much longer?'

'Is there anything I can do to make you more comfortable?'

'Yes, you can give me a potion that will ease me painlessly into death.'

'Other than that,' said Bartholomew.

Kirwell scowled. 'Are you following Inges's orders? Has he instructed you not to rob his hospital of its main source of income?'

'He did not need to – physicians are not in the habit of dispatching people.'

Kirwell went on bitterly. 'He sees me as too valuable to die. But I can barely recite my offices these days – I keep falling asleep halfway through them. I am no kind of priest now.'

Bartholomew regarded him thoughtfully. 'I attended the abbey school here, but I do not recall hearing about you. Yet you would have been ancient then – if you really are a hundred and forty-three, of course.'

'Well, you should have paid more attention,' sniffed Kirwell. 'Because I have been a bedesman ever since Lawrence de Oxforde was hanged, which was long before you would have been learning your letters. Do you not know my story?'

'I am afraid not.'

'It began with his execution. I was praying by his grave the following day when there was a brilliant flash of light. It knocked me clean off my feet, and was declared miraculous by all who saw it.'

'Oh,' said Bartholomew. It did not sound very miraculous to him.

'Afterwards, it was decided that I should live here at abbey expense. I was grateful, because my eyes were failing, and what use is a sightless cleric?'

'What caused the light? The sun?'

Kirwell grimaced. 'You are a practical man who looks for rational explanations of God's mysteries. But you are wrong to be sceptical, because my life changed in that moment. Before, I was a frightened man, lonely, poor and going blind. After, I was a bedesman with every comfort at my fingertips. *That* was a miracle.'

'Right,' said Bartholomew, his mind drifting to the people who were waiting to see him below. What manner of ailments would they present? Would any be new to him? Would the town's apothecary be able to produce the complex remedies he might need to prescribe?

'Oxforde gave me a prayer,' Kirwell was saying. 'One he composed the night before he was executed. I told him it was beautiful in an effort to touch his conscience, although it was actually rather trite. But he believed I was sincere, and he wrote it down for me.'

110

'He could write?' asked Bartholomew, pulling his mind away from medicine. He did not want to offend the old man by being inattentive.

'Like you, he attended the abbey school. He promised that I would live long and happily, provided I never showed it to anyone else. I did not believe him, of course, and planned to sell it – some folk pay good prices for that sort of thing. But then that light flared over his tomb, so I decided to do as I was told. Within an hour, I was awarded my life of luxury.'

'I see,' said Bartholomew, wondering where the story was going.

'But a month ago, I decided that I had had enough, so I told my story to Abbot Robert. He said that if I gave *him* the prayer, I would be released from my wearisome life.'

'Really?' Bartholomew wondered what Robert had been thinking. It was hardly appropriate for an abbot to encourage superstition, especially in a fellow religious.

Kirwell scowled. 'I did as he suggested, but he is the one who is dead, while I still linger. It is not fair!'

'I doubt Oxforde's prayer is responsible for—'

'Of course it is,' declared Kirwell crossly. 'I passed it to Robert two days before his fateful journey to Aurifabro, and now he is gone. But why him? He promised *me* death.'

'I do not know,' replied Bartholomew, when he saw that Kirwell expected an answer.

'Damn you, then,' whispered the old man. 'Damn you to Hell!'

His head dropped forward, and he began to drowse.

Moving carefully, so as not to wake him, Bartholomew left.

Prior Inges was waiting in the hall below. 'Did he bless you? Or touch you in benediction? He has been a bit remiss in that direction of late, but he has always admired physicians.'

Bartholomew did not like to say that he had been cursed. 'Not exactly.'

Inges looked disappointed. 'Perhaps he will oblige you next time. Holy men can be unpredictable, as I am sure you know from your Clippesby.'

'Oh, yes.' Bartholomew gestured towards the door, where the line of people seemed to be longer than ever. 'I should make a start if you want me to see everyone today.'

'Not before you inspect our well,' said Inges. 'We cannot have it said that we provided a Bishop's Commissioner with an inadequate tour. Especially as Joan went to some trouble to show you everything at St Thomas's.'

He grabbed Bartholomew's sleeve and tugged him into the chapel. There were steps in one corner, leading down to a deep, stone-lined pool. The water was green and its surface rippled. Bartholomew put his hand in it, but withdrew it sharply. The spring was icy cold.

'Now to business,' said Inges. 'As this is my hospital, you will give me half the fees you earn today. You will, of course, not charge my bedesmen: they will be seen for nothing. Do not worry about collecting the money – we shall do that before anyone is allowed in.'

'What about those who cannot pay?' asked Bartholomew in distaste.

'They will not be admitted,' replied Inges. 'I cannot abide beggars.'

Bartholomew moved towards the door. 'Then I shall hold court in St Thomas's—'

'All right, all right. But they can only be seen when you have dealt with everyone else.'

'They will be seen in the order in which they arrived.'

Inges considered for a moment, then thrust out his hand. 'Agreed. The hospital will still make plenty of money, which will show those witches at St Thomas's that they are not the only ones who can generate a decent income for the abbey.'

The terms having been negotiated, Bartholomew indicated that the first customer was to be shown in. It was a woman with a rash, and he lost count of how many people came after her, so when the last patient had been seen and sent on his way, he was surprised to see it was nearing dusk. He had been pleasantly impressed by Clippesby, who had proved himself invaluable, both by writing out instructions for the apothecary and by stopping Inges from cheating them.

'Unfortunately, even after giving the apothecary everything we earned today, we still owe him eightpence for those who cannot afford their own remedies,' the Dominican said as they walked through the marketplace, both grateful to stretch their legs after so long indoors. 'Perhaps the abbey will pay. They are supposed to dispense alms, after all.'

'I doubt it,' replied Bartholomew tiredly. 'Welbyrn is tight-fisted with—'

'That woman,' interrupted Clippesby. 'She looks uncannily like Matilde.'

Bartholomew followed the direction of the friar's finger, and felt his stomach lurch. The lady in question was walking away from them, but her natural grace and the cut of her kirtle told him that she *was* Matilde! He stood rooted to the spot for a moment, then ran like fury. He dashed in front of a cart, causing the horse to rear in alarm, and collided with Spalling on the other side.

'Have a care,' the rebel cried, grabbing his arm. 'It is not—'

Bartholomew tore free, but the woman was gone. He raced as fast as he could to the end of the market, looking wildly up the alleys to the sides, but there was no sign of her. He set off up the main road, peering desperately into the open doors of the houses he passed, but was at last forced to concede defeat. He returned to Clippesby.

'We must have been mistaken,' said the Dominican. 'Why would Matilde be here? If she were still . . . in the country, she would have contacted you.'

The hesitation told Bartholomew that Clippesby was one of those who thought she was dead, killed by robbers on England's dangerous highways, because no one could have vanished so completely and still be alive. The physician stubbornly refused to believe it, and liked to think that she had reached wherever she had been going and was living happily there.

'It looked like her,' he said, feeling foolish for haring off so abruptly.

Clippesby smiled. 'It did. But no harm is done, other than frightening that poor horse. I shall have a word with him tomorrow, to ensure that he knows it was not malicious.'

Bartholomew was deeply unsettled. It was not the first time he thought he had seen Matilde since she had disappeared from his life, but it had not happened since he had met Julitta. His mind seething with emotions he could not begin to understand, he followed Clippesby back to the abbey.

CHAPTER 4

It took Bartholomew a long time to fall asleep that night, and when he did, his dreams teemed with confusing visions. He had loved Matilde for so many years that it had been unthinkable that anyone else should take her place, but then he had met Julitta. At first, the attraction had been that she reminded him of Matilde, but he had quickly come to love her for herself. Yet he had desperately wanted the woman he had spotted to be Matilde, so what did that say about the strength of his feelings for Julitta?

He woke long before it was light the following morning and went outside, loath to disturb the others by lighting a candle to read. Although it was still dark, there were signs that it would be a pretty day – the sky was clear, the stars fading to softer pinpricks with the promise of dawn. He inhaled deeply of the scent of damp earth and summer flowers, aware that his agitation was, if anything, even greater than it had been the previous night. He began to wonder whether he would ever recover from the wound Matilde had inflicted.

To take his mind off it, he walked to St Thomas's Hospital, where he found Lady Lullington awake and grey with pain. She smiled gratefully when he prepared more medicine, and he knew she hoped it would stop her from waking again. When she slept, he returned to the guest house, but his colleagues were still asleep, and he did not feel like being inside anyway.

As he leaned against the doorpost, trying not to think about Matilde and Julitta, he saw a shadow edging along the dormitory wall. It was moving in a way that could only be described as furtive, stopping every so often to ensure it was not being followed. When it emerged to cross the open space between the cloisters and the Abbey Gate, its silhouette was clearly visible, and Bartholomew was surprised to recognise Welbyrn's hulking form.

It was none of his business, but Bartholomew followed anyway, curious as to why his old tutor should feel the need to skulk around his own abbey. Welbyrn unbarred the gate and threaded through the silent streets until he reached Westgate, and it did not take Bartholomew long to surmise that he was aiming for St Leonard's Hospital. Once there, the treasurer glanced around carefully before unlocking the door and slinking over the threshold.

As he could hardly pursue Welbyrn inside, Bartholomew continued walking, but he did not go far before retracing his steps – it was hardly sensible to wander along the Torpe road alone, given what had happened to the Abbot and Pyk. He had just drawn level with the hospital again when a shape appeared with an unholy screech that made him leap in fright.

'I am a tiger!' It was Simon the cowherd, hands splayed to look like claws. 'I shall tear you limb from limb.'

'God's teeth!' swore Bartholomew, taking a deep breath to control his thudding heart. He forced a smile. 'It is cold out here, Simon. Let me take you back inside.'

'I will eat your bones,' raved Simon, although he was unresisting as Bartholomew guided him towards the door. 'And suck out your brains. Oxforde knew me as

117

a tiger. I saw him in his golden grave when I was a youth. So did Kirwell.'

'That was a long time ago,' said Bartholomew, speaking softly to calm him. Simon would wake the other bedesmen if he continued to holler.

'It was yesterday,' declared Simon. 'Ask my cattle. Do you know my cattle? They have all gone now, but I still know their names. Daisy, Clover, Nettle . . . I am a *tiger*!'

Bartholomew put his finger to his lips as he guided the cowherd upstairs to an empty bed, where he carefully tucked him in. The old man closed his eyes and was instantly asleep.

'Thank you, Doctor,' said Inges, making Bartholomew start a second time by speaking at his shoulder. 'Welbyrn must have forgotten to lock the door again.'

'How long has Simon been a resident here?' asked Bartholomew, following Inges out of the dormitory and out on to a landing, where they could talk without disturbing the others.

'About ten years, when his madness reached the point where he was no longer able to work. There are those who blame Oxforde for his lunacy, but the truth is that Simon was fey-witted long before he witnessed the blinding light in St Thomas's cemetery.'

'Kirwell was knocked from his feet – or so he said.'

'He was, and a number of folk saw it happen. It was the morning after Oxforde's execution. Can you can cure Simon, by the way? Pyk said it was impossible.'

'Pyk was right. You are doing all that can be done already – treating Simon with kindness, and ensuring that his needs are met.'

'He is no trouble.' Inges led the way down the stairs

to the chapel. 'I like a tiger in the house, anyway – it keeps those damned bedeswomen out. Hey, you!'

The last words were delivered in a stentorian bellow that had the slumbering residents upstairs whimpering in alarm. Welbyrn, who had been in the process of sneaking through the chapel door, stopped dead in his tracks, and Bartholomew did not think he had ever seen a more furtive expression. Inges stalked towards him.

'You damned fool!' the Prior snapped. 'You have done it again.'

'Do not address me in that insolent manner,' snarled Welbyrn, masking his discomfiture with aggression. 'I am Brother Treasurer to you.'

'You left the door unlocked and Simon escaped, *Brother Treasurer*.' Inges's tone was acidic. 'For the *third* time this month.'

'Not me,' claimed Welbyrn, although the guilty flash in his eyes suggested otherwise. 'I saw the door ajar as I was passing and came to investigate. Someone else must have done it.'

'Passing on the way to where?' demanded Inges. 'There is nothing else on this road except Torpe, and I am sure you were not going *there* at this time of day. Simon might have reached the town if Doctor Bartholomew had not stopped him. And the last time that happened, he came home covered in honey and *we* had to pay the bill.'

'How is he?' enquired Welbyrn, transparently changing the subject. 'Any better?'

'No,' said Inges shortly. 'Why do you keep asking? He is incurably insane. Pyk declared him so, and Doctor Bartholomew agrees.'

Welbyrn scowled at the physician. 'What are you doing here? The hospital is closed from dusk until dawn.'

Bartholomew could hardly tell him the truth. 'Just taking the air. And you?'

'That is none of your business,' snarled Welbyrn, clenching his fists angrily.

'You seem unwell,' said Bartholomew gently, noting the dark rings under the treasurer's eyes and the unhealthy blotchiness of his skin. 'Would you like me to—'

'No, I am not,' yelled Welbyrn with explosive fury. 'How dare you!'

Bartholomew stepped back in surprise as spittle flew from Welbyrn's mouth and the treasurer's face turned from pale to mottled red. 'I was only trying to—'

'I am not ill,' Welbyrn screamed. 'And if you ever mention it again – to me or to anyone else – I will thrash you to within an inch of your life. Do you understand?'

Bartholomew watched him stamp away, astonished that his well-meaning concern should have sparked such an outburst. Next to him, Inges was glowering.

'His unholy racket will have woken my bedesmen,' he said, overlooking the fact that it had been his own bellow that had sparked the row. 'And the elderly need their rest.'

'Is Welbyrn often like that?' asked Bartholomew, still bemused.

'He has been of late. Moreover, he never used to be concerned about Simon, but now he asks after him constantly. I have no idea why. However, as you are here, would you see to my bunions again? The potion you smeared on them yesterday afforded me such relief.'

*   *   *

When Bartholomew returned to the guest house, it was to learn that he had been invited to another sumptuous breakfast with the monks. He declined, having no desire to encounter Welbyrn again, but Michael muttered that he needed him there to make observations on the behaviour of potential suspects. Reluctantly, the physician trailed after him to the refectory.

As it was a meat day, the repast included an obscene number of cold cuts from, it seemed, any creature that had had the misfortune to stray into the Benedictines' range – ox, rabbit, hare, duck, venison, quail, capon, lamb, goat and goose. Michael and William chomped through them all, although Clippesby regarded the carnage in dismay.

That morning, the scholars found themselves elevated to the exalted company on the dais, and Bartholomew's heart sank when he was placed between Welbyrn and Ramseye. He glanced into the body of the hall, where Henry shot him a sympathetic smile.

'If you say one word about this morning,' Welbyrn breathed in the physician's ear, under the pretence of passing him the eggs, 'you will be sorry. You may have escaped justice when you broke my nose, but it will not happen a second time.'

Bartholomew regarded him in surprise. Surely Welbyrn was not still vexed over the outcome of their childhood fisticuffs, especially as the mishap had been largely his own fault? If he had not been trying to land such a hard punch, he would not have lost his balance and fallen over.

'It is delightful to see you again after so many years, Matt,' Ramseye was saying on his other side. 'And you have done better than your shabby appearance would have us believe. William tells me that you are now the University's Corpse Examiner. Such a lofty achievement!'

'The University's *what*?' asked Welbyrn, regarding Bartholomew as though he had just sprouted horns. 'What in God's name is a Corpse Examiner?'

'Nothing in *God's* name,' drawled Ramseye. 'I suspect it involves dissection, although William assures me that it is no more than inspired poking and prodding.'

'Well, you had better not try it here or you will spend the rest of your stay in prison,' growled Welbyrn. 'I am not having that sort of thing going on. This is a respectable place.'

'A respectable place that does nothing to find its missing Abbot,' retorted Bartholomew, irritated enough to indulge in a rejoinder. 'Or the town's only physician.'

'We searched,' objected Ramseye, cutting across the more colourful response Welbyrn started to make. 'But there was no sign of them, and with outlaws at large, it would have been irresponsible to keep the *defensores* out any longer. We do not want more deaths at their hands.'

'*More* deaths at their hands?' echoed Bartholomew. 'You think Robert and Pyk might have been killed by outlaws? Why did you not say so before?'

'I did not think it was necessary to state the obvious,' replied Ramseye smoothly. 'Nor to explain that by "outlaw" I mean villains who rob and steal to order – men who are in the pay of rogues like Aurifabro and Spalling.'

'Robert is *not* dead,' said Welbyrn between gritted teeth. 'He will return when he sees fit.'

'Then let us hope it is before Yvo or Ramseye is elected

to take his place,' remarked Bartholomew, unable to help himself. 'I doubt either will relinquish what he has won, and Robert will have a fight on his hands.'

'That is why I support Ramseye,' said Welbyrn tightly. 'He has agreed to step aside when Robert returns, whereas Yvo maintains that any Abbot who abandons his post should be replaced with someone more reliable.'

Ramseye inclined his head, although Bartholomew thought Welbyrn was insane if he believed it. Welbyrn turned his attention to his food, and Bartholomew noted that whatever had been bothering him earlier had not affected his appetite.

'Father William told me yesterday that the villains who ambushed you on your way here spoke French,' said Appletre, who was sitting on Ramseye's other side. 'Aurifabro's men are foreigners . . .'

'What our Brother Precentor is trying to say is that the robbers and the men who murdered Abbot Robert are probably one and the same.' Ramseye spoke in a low voice, so that Welbyrn would not hear. 'He is too tactful to say so outright, but I believe in plain speaking. If I were in your position, I would concentrate my enquiries on Aurifabro. And Spalling.'

'Not Spalling,' argued Appletre. 'I doubt his horde knows anything other than English.'

'The men who attacked us did speak French,' acknowledged Bartholomew. 'But so did we at times, so I am not sure it is significant.'

'William claims that the raids turned what should have been a journey of a couple of days into an ordeal lasting almost a fortnight,' said Appletre. 'What happened, exactly?'

'We lost two horses to arrows,' explained Bartholomew. 'Then William was knocked senseless by a stone that was thrown at us. Not long after, Michael suffered a bruised shoulder, and Clippesby lost his saddlebag. It contained the psalter he was given at his ordination, so we had to go back to look for it. And on top of all that, there were violent rainstorms and flooded streams.'

He did not include the fact that two tumbles from his horse had delayed them as well – once when he had been trampled and had been unable to ride for a day, and another when the animal had bolted and it had taken them hours to find it.

'Nasty!' said Ramseye with a shudder. 'But travelling *is* dangerous, which is why I never do it myself. However, we shall lend you a few *defensores* when you leave. We do not want you to stay longer than necessary because you are too frightened to go.'

'No,' said Bartholomew dryly. 'I imagine you do not.'

Yvo stood to say grace at that point, leaving Bartholomew relieved that the ordeal of his old teachers' company was at an end. They disappeared about their duties without another word, so he went to pass the time of day with Henry. It was not long before they were joined by Michael, Appletre positively dancing at his heels.

'We have a treat in store for you, Henry,' the precentor said, his round cheeks flushed with pleasure. 'I have just persuaded Brother Michael to sing one of our offices later.'

'I thought we would be riding to Torpe again, Brother,' said Bartholomew, surprised. 'In the hope that Aurifabro will be home this morning.'

Michael grimaced. 'I am hoping that will not be necessary – that we will uncover enough clues here to obviate the need to trek out there a second time.'

'You are right to be wary of public highways,' said Henry. 'Especially after what happened to Robert and Pyk. However, if you do go, I shall pray for your safe return.'

'Well, then,' said Michael, 'if we come to harm, I shall know who to blame.'

'I wish everyone would lay aside their differences and live in peace,' sighed Appletre, cutting across the irritable retort Henry started to make. 'I am sure some of Aurifabro's men have lovely voices, and my town choir is currently rather short of basses.'

'You would do better recruiting from among the clergy, Appletre,' said Henry sternly. 'It is not right for seculars to sing in our holy church.'

'I plan to question the monks this morning,' said Michael, while Bartholomew stared at his old friend, surprised to hear such a sentiment from him. 'I shall need your help, Matt.'

'I am afraid you cannot have him,' said Henry with a smile that held a faint trace of triumph. 'There are abbey residents who need his services. They could not see him yesterday, as he was busy with bedesmen and townsfolk, so they would like a consultation today.'

'Then they are going to be disappointed,' objected Michael indignantly. 'He is here to help me find out what happened to Robert, not to play physician for the entire region.'

'We will pay him.' Henry's expression turned a little sly. 'And as he owes the apothecary rather a lot of money, he has little choice in the matter.'

He was right: Bartholomew could not leave Peterborough until he had discharged his debts, and his Michaelhouse colleagues had no spare funds to lend him. Michael opened his mouth to argue, but then a cunning gleam flashed in his eyes.

'Of course he cannot refuse to help the sick,' he said, suddenly all gracious charm. 'I shall help him by collecting the fees he earns – and use the opportunity to ask a few questions at the same time.'

Henry's smile grew stiff when he saw he had been outmanoeuvred, although Appletre beamed happily at the example of compromise and cooperation.

'Incidentally,' the precentor said to Michael, 'I have been thinking about what you asked me yesterday: how Abbot Robert spent the morning before he took his fateful journey to Torpe. And I have remembered something.'

'What?' asked Michael, when Appletre only looked pleased with himself.

'Well, it is not much, but I was standing at the Abbey Gate that day, waiting for a new trumpet to be delivered, when I happened to overhear Robert talking to Aurifabro. The Abbot was insisting on seeing the paten that afternoon, and Aurifabro was trying to put him off.'

'Aurifabro did not want him to visit?' asked Michael keenly. 'Did he say why?'

'Yes, but I did not hear the reason, so I am afraid you will have to ask Aurifabro himself.'

'I have remembered something, too,' added Henry. The serene expression was back in place. 'Abbot Robert also visited Reginald the cutler that morning.'

'Why is that odd?' asked Bartholomew.

'There *is* good in Reginald, no matter what everyone says,' said Henry. 'Yet I always thought his friendship with Robert was curious. They are two very different men.'

'Robert was different from Pyk, too, but no one ever questions *their* friendship,' said Appletre, regarding Henry reproachfully. 'Or Robert's association with Lullington.'

'I suppose not,' said Henry, although his face indicated that he thought otherwise.

It was another brutally exhausting day for Bartholomew, who was convinced that every monk, lay brother and servant in the abbey had contrived to develop aches, fevers, rashes, boils, coughs, stiff joints or pains in the innards for him to treat. Even Ramseye came, complaining of persistent indigestion. Welbyrn was conspicuous by his absence, although Bartholomew felt he might actually have benefited from medical advice.

At noon, when Michael had gone to sing sext in the church, Bartholomew went for a walk around the market-place, a brief respite from the long line of demanding patients. While he was out, he met Cynric, who was with Spalling.

'So, you see,' Spalling was informing the book-bearer, 'it is only a matter of time before the natural order establishes itself at last. There are more poor than rich, so it is only right that their voices should be heard before anyone else's.'

'The rich will not like it,' warned Cynric, although Bartholomew could tell from his bright eyes that he wholly approved of what Spalling was saying.

'No,' agreed Spalling. 'But that should not stop us. I advocate rule by the people, which means men like us, not wealthy barons who are more French than English. Ah, Bartholomew. You have a good man here; you should be proud of him.'

'I am,' said Bartholomew, watching Cynric flush with pleasure at the rebel's praise. 'But it is unwise to discuss this sort of thing in public places. There are—'

'Cynric has decent, noble opinions.' Spalling cut across him. 'Ones that match my own, and I am honoured to call him a friend.'

He strutted away, leaving Cynric staring after him in open admiration, and Bartholomew had to shake the book-bearer's arm to gain his attention.

'It is one thing to share these views with trusted cronies in Cambridge,' he said warningly. 'But another altogether to confide them to strangers. It is dangerous to preach sedition.'

'It is not sedition, it is justice, and it is good to meet a man who sees everything so clearly.' Cynric sighed longingly. 'I wish there was someone who could make speeches like him at home. My friends at the King's Head would love to hear what he has to say.'

'I am sure they would, but his is reckless talk, Cynric.'

'Perhaps so, but that does not mean he is wrong.'

They both turned when someone approached. It was Langelee, who was no more happy with Cynric's burgeoning appreciation of Spalling than was Bartholomew.

'I am all for a man being free to say what he likes,' grumbled the Master. 'But Spalling intends to ignite a rebellion.'

'Would that be so terrible?' asked Cynric. 'Is it not time we had a fairer world?'

'Spalling does not care about fairness,' argued Langelee. 'He just wants the poor to rise up against anyone with money. I feel sorry for Aurifabro, who is the target of most of his vitriol. Spalling even accuses him of hiring the outlaws who attacked us.'

'Perhaps he is right,' said Cynric defensively. 'Aurifabro's mercenaries are French, and we all heard that language spoken when they ambushed us.'

'I am acutely uneasy,' Langelee went on, ignoring him. 'Men gather in Spalling's house every night to talk about the day when the poor will rule. They are all wind and no substance, but they have the capacity to do a great deal of damage, even so.'

Bartholomew escaped from the truculent debate that followed, and returned to his duties in the abbey. Mid-afternoon, William and Clippesby came to report the results of their enquiries to Michael. Other than witnesses who claimed that Welbyrn often visited St Leonard's Hospital at night, neither had unearthed much of significance. Bartholomew turned back to his queue of patients, where his attention was soon snagged by an unusual palsy.

'That was a wasted day,' said Michael in disgust, as the last customer hobbled away. It was dark and they had been working by lamplight for some time. 'And we only have four more full ones left before we must leave. We learned nothing new at all.'

'On the contrary,' said Bartholomew, 'I discovered that quinsy responds well to—'

'I meant nothing to help our enquiry. We already

knew that Robert was unpopular. Confirmation from the common monks is interesting, but hardly helpful.'

'I suppose not,' said Bartholomew, rubbing his eyes tiredly.

'Still, at least I now have a good sense of the man,' Michael went on. 'He was corrupt, greedy and selfish, and there was nothing he would not do for money.'

'You refer to him in the past tense. Do you now believe he is dead, too?'

Michael nodded. 'On that point everyone agrees: he would never have left his domain for so long without an explanation. Moreover, he was going to see Aurifabro – a dangerous enemy with mercenaries at his command.'

'It is odd that he chose Pyk to go with him. Or rather, it is odd that Pyk consented to go. Pyk had lots of friends, and did not have to spend time with the likes of Robert.'

'Yes,' agreed Michael. 'It is not often that one hears nothing bad about a man, but Pyk seems to have been a paragon of virtue – kind, generous and decent.'

'You sound sceptical.'

Michael smiled. 'Even my jaded view of the world acknowledges that such men do exist. However, your friend Henry is not one of them.'

Bartholomew blinked his surprise at the remark out of the blue. 'Henry is—'

'I know you were childhood playmates, but I sense something untoward in that man, and I urge you to be cautious in your dealings with him. Yet he is friends with Appletre . . .'

'Yes?' said Bartholomew a little sharply. 'Why should that make a difference?'

'Because Appletre *is* a decent fellow. He is not overly

endowed with wits, but he cannot help that. Of course, it means he cannot see the evil in Henry, either.'

'Henry is not evil,' objected Bartholomew. 'He has always been gentle, even as a child. Welbyrn and Ramseye bullied him relentlessly, but he never complained.'

'Not to you, perhaps, but no one likes being maltreated. And if you do not believe that men bear grudges, then look at Welbyrn and Ramseye. Even I can see that they have not forgiven you for your disruptive behaviour in their classes.'

'That might be true of them, but not Henry. He—'

'But if the obedientiaries leave much to be desired,' interrupted Michael, unwilling to listen, 'the monks are as fine a body of men as I have ever met – with the obvious exception of Henry, of course. I would not mind ruling them, although I would have to appoint new officers.'

'Do you have anyone in mind?' Bartholomew spoke stiffly, angry with Michael for vilifying someone he liked.

'I would certainly keep Appletre as precentor. He is an excellent musician.'

'He is the only obedientiary the monks seem to like.'

Michael nodded. 'Robert made some bad choices, with Welbyrn and Ramseye being the worst. Incidentally, I had a letter from Gynewell today. Most of it was a rant about these counterfeit coins that hail from his Mint. Do you remember me telling you that they are the reason why he could not come to look into what happened to Robert himself?'

'You said forged pennies are a serious matter, more serious than missing churchmen.'

'The King is furious – no monarch wants his realm

131

flooded with debased coins. I would not like the King angry with *me* over money, and poor Gynewell is frantic with worry.'

'Why did he write, other than to rail about his fiscal crisis?'

'To say that if we find out that Robert has been murdered, he wants a culprit. Moreover, the aide who brought the letter heard about Joan's death, and ordered me to investigate that, too. I shall do my best, but we are leaving on Wednesday regardless. I cannot put my University at risk just to solve Peterborough's troubles.'

Bartholomew and Michael were almost at the guest house when they became aware of a rumpus near St Thomas's Hospital. Someone was attempting to force his way inside, and Prioress Hagar was trying to stop him. The troublemaker was Reginald.

'I demand access to Oxforde's tomb!' the scruffy cutler was bellowing. 'I want to pray.'

'Well, you cannot,' said Hagar, giving him a vigorous shove. 'So go away.'

'You cannot exclude me,' yelled Reginald. 'I have every right to be here.'

'No, you do not,' snapped Hagar. 'The chapel needs to be made holy again after Joan's murder, and we are not letting anyone in at the moment.'

'What is happening?' It was Appletre, his rosy face anxious. Henry was at his heels with a number of singers. Apparently, the fuss had interrupted choir practice.

'This woman is keeping me from my devotions,' snarled Reginald. 'Tell her to desist, so that decent folk can go about their prayers.'

'Decent?' spat Hagar. 'You are not decent! You are the most hated man in Peterborough, and you are a pagan into the bargain!'

'And you are the most hated woman,' Reginald flashed back. 'Even Spalling will not give you the time of day, and he talks to any low villain.'

'Stop!' cried Appletre, as Hagar drew breath to respond. 'Remember where you are.'

'The Brother Precentor is right,' said Henry quietly. 'And you cannot pray here tonight, Reginald, because the chapel needs to be reconsecrated. Come back tomorrow afternoon when it is holy again, and I shall accompany you.' He turned to Hagar. 'You will not object to his presence if I stand surety to his good behaviour, Sister?'

'Prioress,' corrected Hagar. She thought for a moment. 'I suppose that would be acceptable, although it will cost him. I want threepence, or he cannot come in.'

Reginald looked set to argue, but Henry raised his hand warningly and the cutler nodded reluctant agreement. Then Henry regaled Hagar with calming platitudes, while Appletre led Reginald towards the Abbey Gate. The skill with which they separated the combatants suggested it was not the first time they had intervened in spats.

'We need to speak to Reginald,' said Michael, setting off after the cutler and dragging Bartholomew with him. 'I want to know what he and Robert discussed the day Robert vanished. Henry seemed to think it might be significant, so we had better see where it takes us. We shall tackle him in his home – where I will distract him while you have a discreet prowl.'

133

It sounded distinctly unappealing, but the monk's grip was powerful and Bartholomew did not have the energy to fight free. They watched Appletre usher the cutler through the gate and then return to his waiting choristers. Once outside, Reginald scuttled towards his shop, and by the time the two scholars reached it, a rhythmic tapping could be heard from within.

'What?' Reginald shouted in reply to Michael's knock.

'We want to talk to you,' called Michael. 'About Abbot Robert.'

'Well, I do not want to talk to you,' Reginald hollered back, and there was another thud as a hammer came into contact with something. 'Now go away. I am busy.'

'You can spare a few moments for the Bishop's Commissioners. Or do you have something to hide?'

'Of course not, but it is late and I have work to do. Come back another time.'

There came the sound of a heavy bar being placed across the door, which gave the discussion a distinct note of finality. Irritated, Michael rapped again, but all he did was skin his knuckles and eventually Bartholomew pulled him away.

'He is unlikely to be helpful if you force your way in. It is better to wait until he is in a more cooperative frame of mind.'

Michael nodded reluctantly, and they walked back to the abbey. As they approached the gate, Trentham stumbled out, sobbing almost uncontrollably.

'Easy,' said Bartholomew, catching him as he reeled. 'Whatever is the matter?'

'Lady Lullington is dead,' wept the young priest. 'I know it is a blessed release after all her suffering, but she was my friend. Abbot Robert rebuked me for growing too fond of my charges, but I cannot help it. I *liked* her.'

Bartholomew knew how he felt, as he had a tendency to form attachments to patients himself. 'When did she die?' he asked gently.

'I left her when I went to soothe Prioress Hagar after the set-to with Reginald, and she was dead by the time I returned.' Suddenly the young priest pulled away from him, and his face turned dark with bitter anger. 'You could have cured her, but you let her die. You physicians are all the same – useless!'

Trentham's hot words had struck Bartholomew where he had always been vulnerable, and it took him an age to fall asleep that night. He awoke the following morning feeling tired and out of sorts, and was unimpressed when he found himself between Ramseye and Welbyrn again for breakfast. The occasion was no more pleasant than it had been the previous day, although the victuals were still impressively plentiful.

'There is an inn nearby,' he said, when he and his colleagues were back in the guest house. 'I think I shall stay there until you have finished your enquiries.'

'Do not worry – we will not dine in the refectory again,' said Michael. 'We shall be too busy from now on. This is our third day here – our fourth if we count the one we arrived – and we have little to show for our efforts, mostly because you have been too busy to help me. Well, that changes today.'

'Clippesby and I have worked very hard on your behalf,' objected William indignantly. '*We* are not more interested in medicine than in learning who murdered Robert and Joan.'

'No,' conceded Michael. 'And I appreciate your efforts. You have saved me hours of work by speaking to the servants.'

'And the animals,' added Clippesby. 'I only wish they had more to report. But we shall soldier on again today, as I have not interviewed the sheep yet.'

'Right,' said Michael. 'Matt and I will visit St Thomas's Chapel again, to see whether we can glean any new evidence pertaining to Joan's murder.'

'And then we had better go to Torpe,' said Bartholomew. 'Aurifabro claims that Robert never arrived, but we should make an effort to see whether he is telling the truth by speaking to his household. We will have to find a way past the mercenaries, of course.'

'Not today,' said Michael. 'Cynric has offered to go with us tomorrow, and he is a better spy than you or me. His sharp eyes will be useful.'

'Why can he not go this afternoon?'

'Because there is an important meeting he wants to attend with Spalling.' Michael frowned worriedly. 'He has always entertained seditious opinions, but until now it has been nothing but talk. Yet here is Spalling, prepared to act on these beliefs, and Cynric sees a kindred spirit. I hope Spalling does not lead him into trouble.'

Bartholomew hoped so, too. 'Langelee will keep his feet on the ground.'

'Langelee has his hands full with Spalling, especially now I have asked him to assess whether the man might be involved in Robert and Pyk's disappearance.'

'It is a good idea to concentrate on the Abbot.' William nodded approvingly. 'He is more urgent than Joan, given that we cannot leave until we discover what happened to him.'

'Unfortunately, I think his fate and hers are connected.' Michael hastened to explain when William opened his mouth to disagree. 'Yesterday, several monks told me that they were lovers – so her death may well have a bearing on his.'

'Joan and Robert?' asked Bartholomew dubiously, trying to imagine what could have drawn the formidable bedeswoman to the unlovable Abbot, and vice versa.

Michael shrugged. 'It seems they were close for years, which is why we must go to St Thomas's Chapel today, where you will examine her body.'

'But we have no jurisdiction here,' objected Bartholomew. 'I will be arrested. Or worse.'

'Nonsense. We are the Bishop's Commissioners, with authority to do whatever we deem necessary. Do not worry. Gynewell will support you if anyone makes trouble.'

Bartholomew was about to point out that Gynewell was in Lincoln and thus too far away to help if matters turned ugly, but a messenger arrived with a letter before he could speak. Michael's jaw dropped in horror as he read it.

'It is from my Junior Proctor. He says I shall not be needed when Winwick Hall's charter is drawn up, because he plans to do it himself. Is he insane to think that *he* can oversee such a complex matter? Lord! I must be home by Saturday, or the results will be disastrous.'

'Perhaps we should leave now,' said William worriedly.

'I wish we could,' gulped Michael. 'But the Bishop's orders are quite clear: he wants the riddle of Robert's disappearance solved, and we are to stay here until we have answers.'

'Then we had better get on with it,' said William grimly.

The scholars parted outside the guest house. William headed for the kitchens to interview more servants, Clippesby went off towards the water meadows, and Bartholomew followed Michael across the precinct to the Abbey Gate. The area had once been grassed, but hundreds of wheels, feet, claws, hoofs and paws had trampled it bald. They met Henry on the way.

'How are your enquiries coming along?' the monk asked amiably.

'Why?' demanded Michael, making Bartholomew wince at his curt tone.

Henry seemed taken aback by the question. 'Because I should like to know what has befallen poor Abbot Robert. And Physician Pyk, of course.'

'Pyk,' said Michael. 'I am glad you mentioned him. What did you think of the fellow?'

'That he was a saint,' replied Henry sincerely. 'He was kind, patient, gentle and understanding. You would have liked him, Matt.'

'What did he look like?' asked Michael.

Henry smiled fondly. 'He had a great domed head that was too big for his body, and it was bereft of hair except for a curious fringe at the back. He always wore a scarlet cloak, so that people would recognise him. Why?'

'For no reason other than that we might have walked past him and Robert a dozen times and not known it,' replied Michael.

'You would know if you had walked past Robert,' said Henry wryly. 'He was enormous. And unlike you, I do not think he could claim heavy bones.'

Michael scowled as Henry walked away. 'Did he just insult me?'

Bartholomew was disinclined to say, and they resumed their journey to the chapel. When they arrived, Michael opened the door and stepped inside, blinking as his eyes adjusted to the gloom. Nothing happened to him, but two bedeswomen materialised out of nowhere and laid hold of Bartholomew. He could have broken their grip with ease, but he was not in the habit of doing battle with elderly ladies, so he stood still, waiting for an explanation.

'This place is more secure than I thought,' murmured Michael, amused. 'My habit protected me from a mauling, but you did not get far.'

'No one slips past us.' The speaker was Marion, who had raised the alarm when Joan had been killed. She was tall, spindly and possessed unusually long teeth. 'Although we leave the monks alone, because they dislike being manhandled. However, everyone else can expect to be stopped and questioned most vigorously.'

'Most people who enter are blinded for a moment,' added the other, a small, dumpy woman. 'Which gives us time to act. Marion and I take our duties seriously, and we never let anyone in who should not be here.'

Marion peered at Bartholomew before giving a strangled cry and releasing him abruptly, hastening to smooth down his rumpled clothes. 'It is the physician, Elene! Let him go, or he may refuse to tend your veins.'

And then there were two sets of hands brushing Bartholomew down. He tried to escape, objecting to the liberty, but they were insistent.

'When will you see us?' asked Elene, tutting at a frayed hem on his tunic. 'You have physicked the old rascals at St Leonard's *and* the monks, so it must be our turn now.'

'What is wrong with your veins, Sister Marion?' asked Bartholomew, still trying to evade their fussing fingers.

'Elene is the veins,' said Marion. 'I am the impostumes.'

'Her impostumes are famous,' added Elene with pride. 'Master Pyk said he had never seen anything like them, and he often bemoaned the fact that he had no medical colleague here, to share the excitement.'

'No, Matt,' warned Michael, seeing his friend's curiosity piqued. 'There is no time.'

But Bartholomew was not a man to deprive people of his services. 'I will see you after we have . . .' He faltered, aware that 'examined Joan's corpse' was not the best thing to say.

'Paid our respects to your dear departed sister,' supplied Michael. 'Alone, if possible. We have prayers to recite for her soul.'

'That is kind, Brother,' said Marion. 'But you had better wait until the chapel is reconsecrated. Her murder has soiled it, you see, so it must be cleansed. Hagar has asked Prior Yvo to conduct the ceremony, but I do not trust him. I would rather have the Bishop.'

'Why?' asked Michael.

'Because Gynewell is a lovely man,' replied Marion fondly. 'The best prelate in the country.'

'I meant why do you distrust Yvo?'

'Because he is only thinking about himself,' explained Marion. 'Our chapel is a source of revenue for the abbey, but we have refused to let pilgrims in until it is holy again. It means folk cannot leave donations, and Yvo dislikes losing money.'

'So does Welbyrn,' added Elene. 'Even more than the Prior.'

'Anyway, suffice to say that we think Yvo is rushing the reconsecration out of selfishness,' confided Marion. 'So that the shrines can start earning for him again.'

'But as soon as we are cleansed, we shall take you to Joan,' promised Elene. 'It will not be long, because Yvo promised to do it straight after sext.'

'Come to the ceremony, Brother,' begged Marion. 'Yvo would not dare do a half-baked job with the Bishop's Commissioner watching.'

'Very well – if you answer a question,' said Michael. 'Were Joan and the Abbot close?'

'Yes, they were a lovely couple,' smiled Marion fondly. 'And were happy together for years. She always said that she was glad she accepted him as a lover, rather than Botilbrig.'

'Of course, it meant trouble,' confided Elene. 'Botilbrig was insanely jealous, and we have been at war with the bedesmen ever since.'

There was no more to be said, so Bartholomew and Michael left the chapel, declining both the offer of wine while they waited for Yvo and a sneak preview of the impostumes.

'Perhaps Botilbrig is the killer after all,' mused Michael. 'Unrequited love is a good motive for murder, and both Robert and Joan are now dead.'

'It sounded to me as though Joan had made her selection a long time ago,' said Bartholomew. 'I cannot see a crime of passion simmering for quite so many years.'

'I beg to differ. Affairs of the heart can remain painful for a very long time, as you will know from your experiences with Matilde. Even now, three years on, you see her in places where she cannot possibly be – Clippesby told me what happened in the marketplace on Thursday evening.'

'How do you know it was not her?' As it happened, Bartholomew thought Michael was right, but there was something in the monk's remark that was oddly suspicious.

'Because I do,' replied Michael firmly. 'Matilde would not be in Peterborough.'

As soon as they left the chapel, Michael aimed for a nearby tavern named the Swan. The place had changed since Bartholomew had last been in it. Then, it had been insalubrious, with a reputation for catering to drunks and criminals. Now it was smart, with gleaming white walls and pristine woodwork.

'I hope you are not intending to eat again, Brother,' he said, noting the energetic way the monk was signalling to the landlord. 'Not after that gargantuan breakfast.'

'Of course not,' replied Michael blandly. 'I just thought it would be a good place to sit and discuss our investigation until it is time to monitor Yvo's reconsecrating skills.'

The tavern was alive with the buzz of genteel conversation. There were ladies present, which underlined the fact that it had grown respectable – decent women did not venture into rough inns. A group of master masons sat at one table, identifiable by their thick leather aprons and dusty leggings, and Aurifabro was at another, talking animatedly to several men who were almost as richly clad as he.

'Peterborough is a nice town,' said Michael, looking around approvingly. 'It is a pity our ancestors did not found a university here. I could come to like it very much.'

'Are you seriously considering putting yourself forward as Abbot?' asked Bartholomew. 'And if so, is there anything I can do to help?'

'Do you want to be rid of me then? So you can be Senior Proctor and run the University in my stead?'

Bartholomew laughed. 'I doubt it would thrive with me in charge. But you have often expressed a desire for high office, and this may be your chance. I should like to see you happy, even if it does mean being deprived of your company.'

'You would?' An oddly guilty expression flashed across Michael's face. 'I may remind you of that sentiment one day.'

It was a curious thing to say, and Bartholomew was about to demand an explanation when the landlord arrived. Michael told him to bring a sample of his wares, but when food as well as wine began to arrive, Bartholomew regarded him disapprovingly.

Michael shrugged. 'It would be rude to decline, and I do not want him remembering the insult when I am

Abbot.' He raised his voice suddenly, silencing the drone of conversation around them. 'Landlord! This is a splendid repast, but do you have any Lombard slices? I like them best of all pastries.'

'I am afraid not,' replied the landlord apologetically. 'My wife used to bake them, but she died in the Death, and I have never attempted them myself.'

'Oh,' said Michael, and Bartholomew was not sure whether the monk was sorrier to hear about the landlord's loss or the absence of his favourite food. 'My condolences. But the rest looks splendid, and Matt will help me do it justice.'

'Here come Langelee and Cynric,' said Bartholomew, nodding towards the door. 'They can spare me a bout of indigestion.'

Cynric's face was flushed with excitement as he sat at their table. 'That Spalling is a tremendous man,' he enthused. 'He has such hopes for the future!'

'Hopes for a rebellion, more like,' said Langelee sourly. 'I do not understand it at all – he was not like this in York. There, he was rather quiet.'

'He is not quiet now,' said Cynric approvingly. 'He had forty men in his house last night, all listening to a very stirring speech. It was even better than the one made by the Prince of Wales at Poitiers, just before we went into battle. Do you remember that, boy?'

'Vividly,' replied Bartholomew bleakly.

'Here he is,' said Cynric, eyes lighting as his hero strode confidently through the door.

Spalling was wearing a new set of workman's clothes, this time the kind donned by stonemasons, although without the dust. The real craftsmen nodded

144

approvingly, although Bartholomew was no more convinced by the attire than he had been the first time they had met Spalling. He thought the man was a fraud, and hoped Cynric would not be too disillusioned when he eventually came to realise it, too.

'Aurifabro!' Spalling roared in a voice designed to carry. 'So this is where you are skulking. Did you not hear that I have been looking for you?'

Aurifabro regarded him with dislike. 'Yes, but I am not at your beck and call. Piss off.'

'Now watch.' Cynric was full of admiration. 'You are about to see an obscenely wealthy merchant berated for keeping all his money to himself and starving his artisans.'

'Are his artisans the men sitting with him?' asked Bartholomew. Cynric nodded. 'Then they are hardly starving – their clothes suggest they are affluent in their own right. Just because Aurifabro employs them does not mean—'

'He has more money than them,' interrupted Cynric shortly. 'And it is not fair.'

'He is bedazzled by the man,' whispered Langelee in Bartholomew's ear. 'Like a lover. You will not persuade him to see reason. I have tried, but I was wasting my breath.'

'You will listen to me, Aurifabro,' Spalling was bellowing. 'When will you stop making yourself rich at others' expense, and share your ill-gotten gains with the poor?'

The landlord stormed up to him. 'You can take that sort of talk outside. This is a respectable establishment, and we do not want your raving—'

'And you are just as bad, Nicholas Piel,' raged Spalling,

turning on him. 'I know why your tavern is so opulent – because you fleece your customers!'

'My wares are expensive,' acknowledged Piel haughtily. 'But quality costs, and those who want cheap rubbish can go elsewhere. I do not force people to come – they do it because they like what I offer.'

'That is true,' agreed Aurifabro. 'Now sod off, Spalling.'

'I am going nowhere,' declared Spalling. 'Not until I have had my say. I ask you again, Aurifabro: when will you share your money with the downtrodden masses?'

His voice was so loud that people stopped in the street outside to listen. There was an appreciative growl from the paupers, although those who were better off exchanged exasperated glances. Immediately, several rough men in boiled leather jerkins shouldered their way into the tavern: they were Aurifabro's mercenaries.

'When you give up yours, you damned hypocrite,' snapped Aurifabro. 'You inherited a fortune when your father died, and you own a fancy house. Give *your* money to the poor if you feel so strongly about it.'

'I shall,' averred Spalling. 'In time.'

'In time!' jeered the goldsmith. 'You mean never. And how are you feeding all the peasants who flock to hear you rant? I know for a fact that you have not touched your own funds, so where does the money come from?'

'He does keep a lavish table,' murmured Langelee. 'We were entertained royally last night, and so were his forty friends. Indeed, I warrant we fared better than you.'

'I would not bet on it,' Bartholomew muttered back.

'If you cannot silence this braggart, I am leaving,' said

146

Aurifabro to the landlord. 'I came here for a quiet drink, not to be harangued by fools.'

'Out,' ordered Piel, turning angrily to Spalling. 'Before I pick you up and . . .'

Cynric was one of several men who came to stand at Spalling's side, and the landlord faltered. Aurifabro stood and walked towards the door instead, his mercenaries in tow. Piel's face was a mask of dismay when the artisans rose to follow their employer out.

'Leave Aurifabro alone, Spalling,' hissed one as he passed. 'He pays us extremely well, and we have no complaints.'

There was a growl of agreement from the others.

'A word, please, Master Aurifabro,' said Michael, running after the goldsmith, and grabbing his arm just as he reached the street. 'I have been asked—'

One of the mercenaries shot forward and shoved the monk away, fingering his dagger as he did so. His fellows immediately moved to form a protective barrier around Aurifabro, their faces bright with the prospect of violence. Bartholomew hurried to Michael's side, although he was not sure what he would be able to do in the event of trouble. He could hold his own in a brawl with students, but these were experienced warriors.

'It is all right,' Aurifabro told his men. 'This monk is not one of the villains from the abbey. He is the Bishop's man, and I have nothing against Gynewell.'

'Other than the fact that he pardoned Spalling after Robert had excommunicated him,' countered the soldier with the dagger. 'You thought he should have stayed excommunicated.'

'I did,' said Aurifabro, his eyes fixed on Michael. 'It was hard to know who to support in that particular quarrel – the stupid firebrand Spalling, whose so-called principles have only driven him to action recently; or the greedy, unscrupulous Robert, who should not have been placed in charge of a brothel, let alone an abbey.'

'As you know, Gynewell has commissioned us to find out what happened to Robert,' said Michael pleasantly. 'So will you answer some questions?'

'That depends on what you ask.'

'Fair enough. Will you tell me what you thought of him?'

'He was a villain, and I cannot imagine why Pyk put up with him. But Pyk always was an amiable fool, incapable of distinguishing between good men and bad.'

'Can you be more specific? *How* was Robert a villain?'

'He was sly over the paten he asked me to make, for a start. Once I had invested weeks of my time in it, he reduced the price, knowing I had no choice but to agree – it is not something I can offer to another buyer: no one else around here is in the market for expensive religious regalia.'

'Why did you agree to make it in the first place?'

'I should have refused, but it was a big order, and I liked the notion of my work being on display in such a grand setting. Of course, now he is dead, the abbey has refused to honour the agreement I struck with him, so I am landed with the thing after all.'

'Where is it?' asked Michael.

'At home. I wrote to ask if Gynewell would buy it for Lincoln Cathedral, but he said he would prefer to have it donated. And I am not *giving* the Church anything. I like Gynewell, but my religion is the older one.'

'You mean you are a heathen?' asked Michael in distaste.

Aurifabro nodded. 'Ever since the plague. It makes more sense to me than your aloof saints and martyrs, who failed to answer my prayers as my children lay dying. And as for Lawrence of Oxforde . . . I cannot condone any organisation that pays homage to a criminal.'

'Robert,' prompted Michael. 'Tell us what happened the day he went missing.'

'He told me in the morning that he was coming to see the paten. I asked him not to.'

'Why?' asked Michael.

'Because I wanted to visit my mother in Barnack. He threatened to cancel the commission unless I made myself available, so I was forced to change my plans. I waited, but he never arrived. I assumed he was delayed by other business and had not bothered to let me know.'

'What then?' asked Michael.

'A group of monks arrived the next day, and told me that he and Pyk were missing. I admired Pyk, so I sent my men to scour the area for them both, but they found nothing. The abbey, on the other hand, conducted a search that was cursory at best.'

'You think they could have done more?' asked Bartholomew.

'I would, had one of my people gone missing. But, as I said, Robert was a villain, and the abbey is obviously glad to be rid of him.'

'What do you think happened to Robert?' asked Michael.

'There are three possibilities. First, he was murdered, and there is no shortage of suspects, given that he was hated by all. Second, he is in hiding, although that seems unlikely, because he liked his creature comforts. And third, he was killed by robbers.'

'The same robbers who have been causing trouble on the King's highways?'

'Yes. The abbey and Spalling will tell you that my mercenaries are responsible, but you should not believe them. They are liars.'

At that moment, young Trentham shuffled past, his face a mask of misery. He shot Bartholomew a baleful glance, to tell him he was still not forgiven for being unable to save Lady Lullington. The scowl sparked an idea in Bartholomew's mind.

'We have assumed the target was Robert,' he said. 'And Pyk just happened to be with him. But what if it was the other way around? I know from personal experience that people are often angry when physicians cannot cure their loved ones.'

'No one would have taken against Pyk,' said Aurifabro firmly. 'He was not like other *medici* – he was a good man. Even his wife will have to concede that.'

'Pyk was married?' asked Michael.

Aurifabro nodded. 'To a woman named Pernel, although not happily, unfortunately. Of course, there is a fourth possibility: that Robert and Pyk have been kidnapped.'

'Then the culprits would have sent word to the abbey,' said Bartholomew, 'demanding payment and giving details of how to make it.'

'Perhaps they did,' said Aurifabro, 'and the abbey

150

refused to pay. However, if that happened, you will never find out, because it is not the sort of thing they will admit.'

'May we visit you in Torpe tomorrow?' asked Michael. 'I want to retrace their journey.' He did not say that he was also keen to confirm the goldsmith's story with his servants.

'No,' said Aurifabro shortly. 'No Benedictine is welcome on my land, not even one who has been hired by the Bishop.'

CHAPTER 5

Bartholomew could not go with Michael to question Pernel Pyk, because people kept waylaying him to report how they were faring after their consultations with him in St Leonard's Hospital. The monk went alone, but the mistress of the house was out. Eventually, both returned to the chapel, which was now full of people – it was not every day that a sacred building was purified after a murder, and the citizens of Peterborough were keen to see how it was done.

'The whole town is here,' whispered Michael. 'Even Spalling, and he hates the abbey.'

He nodded to where the rebel was standing with a huge contingent of the town's poor. Most were farm labourers, sun-bronzed, sturdy people in smocks and straw hats. None looked particularly downtrodden, and they were healthier and better fed than the ones who worked around Cambridge. Spalling had changed his clothes to match theirs, although his tunic was made from finer wool and his hat was worn at a rakish angle.

'Aurifabro has deigned to appear, too,' murmured Michael, seeing the goldsmith near the altar. 'And he is not even a Christian. We had better keep our distance – we do not want to be singed if he is struck by a thunderbolt.'

'It is a good thing Cynric did not hear you say that,'

remarked Bartholomew. 'He tends to believe those kind of statements.'

'Just as he believes everything that falls from Spalling's lips. No good will come from that association, Matt. Perhaps you should order him home before it lands him in trouble.'

'I will talk to him, but he is a free man and must decide for himself what is right.'

The bedesmen had also turned out. They had brought Kirwell on a litter, although he was fast asleep and seemed oblivious to the hands that reached out to touch him – and to the clink of coins that were collected from those who wanted to avail themselves of the privilege.

'Some of those ancients are suspects for killing Joan,' mused Bartholomew, watching the spectacle. 'Yet none of them look guilty, not even Botilbrig, who is the obvious candidate.'

Michael gestured to the other side of the chapel. 'Nor do the bedeswomen, who also had reason to want Joan dead. But Reginald is standing by the cemetery door. Shall we go to see whether he will answer our questions now?'

'We might as well, I suppose. There is no sign that the ceremony is about to begin.'

They eased their way through the throng towards the cutler, who whipped around in alarm when Michael tapped him on the shoulder.

'I am not talking to you,' he declared, eyes furtive as he glanced around. 'I have nothing to say, and what I do in my workshop is my own affair.'

The last words were delivered in a hissing snarl that

turned his face scarlet and caused the veins to stand out on his neck. Bartholomew was concerned.

'Take some deep breaths,' he advised. 'And try to relax your—'

'Leave me alone,' snapped Reginald, redder than ever. 'I cannot help it if I am obliged to do things that . . . But I am not saying more. You will trap me into admitting . . . And Abbot Robert is not here to protect me.'

'To protect you from what?' asked Bartholomew, bemused by the tirade.

'Trouble,' replied Reginald shortly. He tugged at his tunic, as though the material was too tight around his throat.

'You really should sit down. You will feel better if—'

'I am not staying here to be interrogated.' Reginald began to back away. 'You will pretend to befriend me, but all the time you will be trying to trip me up. Robert warned me about men like you.'

Before either scholar could ask what he meant, Reginald had fled, leaving them staring after him in astonishment.

'Now *that* is a guilty conscience,' said Michael. 'We shall have to tackle him again later, and find out exactly what he has done.'

It was not long before there was a flurry of activity and the Benedictines arrived. The obedientiaries were first, grand in their ceremonial finery, although the monks wore their working clothes; many had muddy hands or sleeves rolled up, having come directly from their labours. When they saw Michael and Bartholomew among the onlookers, Nonton scowled, Welbyrn ignored them, Ramseye's grin was wholly unreadable, and Prior Yvo shot them a glance that was full of panic.

'Poor Yvo,' said Henry, coming to talk to the scholars. Appletre was at his side, and so was Lullington until he saw who Henry was talking to, at which point he muttered an obscenity in French and left. 'It is his first public ceremony as Acting Abbot, so he is under pressure to make a good impression.'

'He will not do it if he looks frightened,' remarked Appletre. 'He will only succeed in unnerving people. But that is a good thing – it will give Ramseye an edge.'

'You want Ramseye to become Abbot?' asked Bartholomew in surprise. 'I thought you hoped that an outsider would be appointed instead.'

'I did – I *do* – but I still have to vote in Thursday's election, and the choice is Ramseye or Yvo,' explained Appletre. 'So I shall support Ramseye, because he promised to let me stay on as precentor. But if Yvo wins, he will take over those duties himself, and his voice is . . .'

'Like a rusty saw,' supplied Michael, when the precentor flailed around for the right words. 'But Ramseye and Yvo cannot be the only candidates from the abbey. What about you, Henry? Do you have no ambitions in that direction?'

Henry seemed shocked. 'Good gracious, no! I would not be a good Abbot. Indeed, I have declined promotion several times, lest it interfere with my service to God.'

He raised his eyes heavenward, and Michael was girding himself up for a tart rejoinder when Inges arrived, asking Bartholomew to sedate Simon. The cowherd had been odder than usual that day and Inges was afraid he would disrupt the ceremony. Bartholomew declined, on the grounds that it was unethical to dose lunatics with soporifics for the convenience of others, and recommended a walk in the water meadows instead.

'Why?' asked Inges, bemused.

'Because taking him to a familiar place might soothe him,' explained Bartholomew. 'Those with disturbed minds often find comfort in places they have known well.'

'Do they?' asked Inges. 'Pyk never said so.'

'So this paragon of the medical profession was fallible after all,' mused Michael. 'Even I knew that. Well, I suppose I learned it because of Clippesby. He likes familiar places when he is deranged.'

'You mean deranged in his sainthood,' said Inges.

'Yes,' agreed Michael hastily. 'That is exactly what I meant.'

'Speaking of troubled minds, Kirwell is upset about Lady Lullington,' Inges went on. 'He feels it is not fair that she should precede him to Heaven when she was only a third of his age. It is Oxforde's doing that he has lived so long, of course – him and his prayer.'

'What prayer?' asked Michael.

'Oxforde composed one the night before he was hanged,' explained Bartholomew. 'And told Kirwell that as long as he kept it secret, he would enjoy a long and comfortable life.'

'But recently, Kirwell has expressed a desire to die.' Inges took up the tale. 'So he gave the prayer to Abbot Robert, expecting to perish immediately. It did not work, and now he fears that he might be cursed with immortality. I hope he is, as the revenues would be—'

156

'*Cursed* with immortality?' interrupted Michael. 'Most people would relish it.'

'Not if they do not have eternal youth to go with it,' replied Inges. 'And poor Kirwell can do nothing but sleep and eat. Now he wishes that God had never bathed him in that miraculous glow at Oxforde's tomb all those years ago.'

'The glow that sounds like a shaft of sunlight?' asked Bartholomew pointedly.

Inges glared. 'It was the Lord pointing at the Earth. Of course, I doubt He meant that particular grave to become a shrine, which is what those greedy bedeswomen made it into. Oxforde was a very nasty criminal, and should not be revered.'

'I heard that Gynewell came here specifically to suppress the cult,' said Michael.

'He did,' nodded Inges. 'But it earns a fortune, so Abbot Robert let it start up again. The monastery is fond of money.'

'So we are beginning to understand,' murmured Michael.

As the monks were still fiddling with their purifying accoutrements, Bartholomew went to ensure that being rousted from his bed had not been too great a strain for Kirwell. It did not take him long to ascertain that the old man was so deeply asleep that he probably did not know that he had been moved. Meanwhile, Michael sidled through the spectators, listening to scraps of conversation and noting who was standing with whom.

'We wanted to wait for the Bishop,' Marion was telling Henry and Appletre. 'But Prioress Hagar said we have a duty to get the chapel back to normal as quickly as possible.'

'Too right,' declared Hagar, overhearing and going to join them. 'Joan caused a lot of disruption by getting herself killed in here. Of course, she did have it coming to her.'

'You think she deserved to be murdered?' asked Henry, shocked. 'Why?'

'Because of her sordid "friendship" with Robert,' explained Hagar, pursing her lips. 'There will be none of that sort of thing now I am Prioress.'

'It was inappropriate,' agreed Henry sanctimoniously, although Appletre's round face showed more under-standing. 'But I liked Joan, regardless.'

Hagar shrugged. 'She was all right, I suppose. But St Thomas's Hospital will be happier and better run under me.'

'It is nicer already in some ways,' acknowledged Marion. 'We are free to carry out our duties without interference – Joan was constantly watching us, to make sure we were not shirking.'

'I plan on doing very little supervision,' said Hagar airily. 'I shall have more important matters to occupy my time.'

'Yet I wish we could wait for the Bishop,' said Marion unhappily. 'Yvo says *he* is ecclesiastically equipped to perform this sort of ceremony, too, but we only have his word for it.'

'He does possess the necessary authority,' Appletre assured her. 'And—'

'Well, our pilgrims will be glad when we are open for business again.' Hagar cut across him rudely. 'They all love Oxforde. They love St Thomas's relics, too, but not as much.'

'Speaking of relics, where is the stone that killed Joan?' asked Appletre, his blue eyes wide in his chubby, red-cheeked face. He crossed himself.

'Back on the altar,' replied Hagar. 'I wiped some of the blood off it, but the rest we shall leave. People will assume it is St Thomas's.'

'That would be dishonest,' said Henry sternly.

'Only if they find out,' interrupted Hagar with a predatory grin. 'But I cannot stand here chattering. As Prioress, I have a great deal to do.'

She sailed off, head held high, and Michael followed. When Bartholomew came to stand next to him, the monk was watching her berate Lullington for prising a crucifix off the wall when he had come to collect his wife's personal effects. It belonged to the hospital, and she wanted it back.

'She might have murdered Joan,' Michael said in a low voice, watching her poke the knight in the chest when he started to argue. 'There is a chilling ruthlessness in her.'

'The same can be said about a lot of the people we have met since arriving here,' replied Bartholomew soberly.

As the ceremony still showed no signs of beginning, Bartholomew and Michael went to find out why. The reason soon became clear: Ramseye was asking questions that had Yvo reaching anxiously for his prayer book to assure himself that he knew what he was doing. Welbyrn was with them, smirking at the Prior's increasing discomfiture.

'Ramseye is undermining his confidence,' murmured Michael. 'So *he* will appear the better candidate when the election comes. A sly tactic, but an effective one.'

Yvo's voice was shrill with agitation as he responded to Ramseye's latest query. 'But I *cannot* stamp my Writ of Cleansing with the abbey's seal, because I do not have it. Robert took it with him, if you recall.'

'So he did,' sighed Ramseye. 'Never mind. People will probably accept the writ without it. Just state that you *do* hold the Bishop's authority, and I am sure they will believe you.'

The tone of his voice made it abundantly clear that he thought they would not.

'Are you sure there is not another purple cope in the vestments chest?' asked Welbyrn before Yvo could respond. 'I thought we had one that fitted you.'

'This one will suffice,' said Ramseye with a patently false smile, as the Prior looked down at himself in dismay. 'Just remember not to turn your back on the congregation.'

Bartholomew had no particular liking for the Prior, but he thought that what Ramseye and Welbyrn were doing was cruel. He was about to say so to Michael when Welbyrn spotted him. The treasurer's thick features creased into an ugly scowl.

'Bartholomew! You will leave before the ceremony begins. I do not want you here.'

Ramseye started at his crony's outburst. 'He can stay if he likes.'

'No! He will criticise our theology, just as he did years ago.'

'Nonsense! We are obedientiaries now, while he is just a physician.'

'A physician with opinions about me,' spat Welbyrn angrily. 'He—'

'We should make sure there are enough candles,' interrupted Ramseye briskly. 'I do not trust Trentham to do it, as his distress over Lady Lullington means he is not very reliable at the moment. Come, Brother.'

He hustled Welbyrn away before the treasurer could say anything else, leaving Bartholomew perplexed by the depth of his old tutor's dislike.

'He is bellicose with everyone these days, so do not take him amiss,' said Yvo, watching them go with a sullen expression. 'I suspect he finds the post of treasurer too onerous. I shall relieve him of it when I am Abbot, so that he can become a simple monk again. But never mind him. Help me with this cope.'

It was a fine vestment, and its exquisite quality was another indication of the abbey's wealth. Unfortunately, Welbyrn had been right to remark that it did not fit: it was far too big, and trailed rather ridiculously on the floor. From its ample size, Bartholomew assumed it had been made for Robert.

'I wish I had not consented to do this,' said Yvo wretchedly, clearly aware that he did not cut as majestic a figure as his predecessor. 'I know we are losing pilgrim-money while the chapel is out of action, but I would sooner have waited for the Bishop.'

'So why did you agree?' asked Michael.

Yvo's misery intensified. 'Prioress Hagar is a very persuasive woman.'

He shuffled away despondently, and Bartholomew wondered whether it would be the absurdly oversized cope or his painful nervousness that would underline

161

the fact that Yvo was wholly incapable of filling Robert's shoes.

'Hagar has her arm around Trentham,' remarked Michael, 'but whatever she is whispering in his ear is of no comfort, because he has started to cry again. We had better intervene. He has important duties to perform in a moment.'

'I have just informed him that Joan's will stipulates she is to be buried next to Oxforde,' explained Hagar. 'Indeed, it says we cannot have any of her belongings unless this wish is carried out. However, we cannot have common workmen rooting about near our shrine, so I have just told Trentham that he must dig her grave. He is our chaplain, after all.'

'But I do not know how,' sobbed Trentham. 'I am a priest, not a sexton.'

'We shall bury her on Thursday,' said Hagar breezily, 'so you have five days to master the skill. I am sure you will not let us down.'

And with that she bustled off to her next prey, leaving Trentham staring after her tearfully. Gratefully, he accepted the scrap of clean linen that Bartholomew offered, to wipe his face and blow his nose.

'I am sorry for what I said,' he snuffled. 'About you failing to help Lady Lullington. I know it was not your fault, but I was upset. She was my friend, you see.'

'You can make up for your unkind words by answering a few questions,' said Michael, before Bartholomew could say he understood. 'Start by telling us what you thought of Robert.'

'He was not very nice,' obliged Trentham, dabbing at his eyes. 'Lady Lullington asked him to visit shortly after she was taken ill, but he never bothered. And he was horrible to Henry – he taunted him about being lame and the amount of time he likes to pray.'

'What had Henry done to attract his ire?' asked Michael, while Bartholomew groaned, suspecting this 'evidence' would be used to promote his old classmate as a suspect for murder.

'He is pious, which made Robert look irreligious,' explained Trentham. 'But I miss Pyk much more than the Abbot. He was kind to my old people, and he often "forgot" to charge the paupers in my parish for his services. He was a wonderful man.'

'He was not friends with Spalling, was he?' asked Michael wryly.

'Spalling is right to draw attention to the plight of the poor,' said Trentham with youthful intensity. 'A family of beggars live near my church, and they suffered horribly last winter. It should not have happened when the abbey drips with riches.'

'Then why did you not make Robert aware of their plight?'

'I did, several times, and he said he would arrange for alms, but they never came. I do not know whether it slipped his mind or if he instructed Ramseye not to pay. Regardless, his heartlessness did not endear him to me or to my parishioners.'

'Are these beggars the kind to bear a grudge?' asked Michael keenly. 'Or can you name anyone else who might have wanted to make an end of Robert?'

Trentham shook his head. 'None of my flock are killers. Personally, I think the culprit was the enormous meal Robert devoured before he left. Pyk could not save

163

him, so he rolled him in a ditch and fled before he could be accused of malpractice.'

'No,' said Bartholomew firmly. 'Physicians are not—'

'I do not blame him,' interrupted Trentham. 'Indeed, if you are ever in a similar situation, I recommend you do it yourself. The abbey can be viciously vengeful.'

The reconsecration ceremony did not last long. Yvo gabbled through it so fast that even William was impressed – and he was famous for the brevity of his offices. Bartholomew could only assume that Yvo thought a speedy service would not give his critics time to pick holes in his performance. All the while, he sprayed holy water around with such unrestrained generosity that those standing at the front were dripping by the time he had finished.

The rite ended with a procession around the chapel, but when Yvo reached the door that led to the abbey, he kept on going, leaving the congregation to stand uncertainly, sure there must be more to come. Once they realised there was not, Hagar announced that applications could now be made for visiting Oxforde's shrine. The bedeswomen were on hand to collect donations, and those who did not offer enough were invited to return another day.

Some of the monks, including Henry and the Unholy Trinity, lingered to exchange polite greetings with the townsfolk, while Bartholomew and Michael listened to Langelee carping about Spalling's rabble-rousing. Then Appletre joined them, babbling amiably about how he was torn between disappointment that the ceremony had been devoid of music and relief that Yvo had not

164

tried to sing. Langelee waited impatiently for him to finish so he could resume his diatribe, gazing absently at the other obedientiaries as he did so. Then he frowned and his finger came up to point.

'I know you! You lived in York once.'

The remark was aimed at Nonton the cellarer, whose bleary eyes and red face suggested that he had been assiduous in checking the quality of his supplies that day.

'Rubbish,' retorted Nonton loudly, his brusque reply causing a number of people to turn and look at him. 'I have never been there.'

'Yes, you have, Brother Cellarer,' countered Henry. 'You went for a year, because we had to send an envoy to the Archbishop's court, and Robert said you were the most easily spared.'

'I knew it!' cried Langelee, pleased with himself, although Nonton scowled furiously, and Bartholomew suspected that Henry would have been wiser to hold his tongue. 'We met when the Archbishop's new Mint opened, and there was a party afterwards. It was you who drank that whole jug of fermented honey and then did an impression of—'

'Not me,' interrupted Nonton, flushing crimson. 'As cellarer, I am obliged to be abstemious, so it must have been someone else.'

Bartholomew and Michael were not the only ones to exchange amused glances at this claim. Nonton's anger deepened when he saw people were laughing at him.

'It is true!' he declared. 'Any wine I consume is purely medicinal, for my chilblains. And I dislike being away from Peterborough, so I always expunge such journeys

165

from my mind. If I was ever in York, I will have forgotten about it, so please do not attempt to discuss it with me again. You will be wasting your breath.'

'If you hate leaving us so much, why do you always volunteer to go with Welbyrn when he visits Lincoln?' asked Henry. His smile was innocently curious.

'Because it is good for the soul to undertake unpleasant duties occasionally,' snapped Nonton, ice in his voice. He turned away, to indicate the discussion was over.

'It *was* him in York,' whispered Langelee to Bartholomew and Michael. 'I could never forget such entertainment as he provided that night. However, I understand why he is reluctant to confess – half the town is listening.'

Clippesby and William came to join them, Cynric at their heels, and together they watched the chapel begin to empty of spectators. Lullington was among those who lingered. He stood at the altar, and stared so long and hard at the stone that had been used to kill Joan that the scholars' interest was piqued. They moved towards him, and Michael sneezed when they were met by a potent waft of perfume.

'He smells like a whore,' muttered William in disgust.

'A costly whore,' whispered Langelee. 'The Deputy Sheriff's lady uses that scent, and a pot of it would keep Michaelhouse in victuals for a month. Lullington has expensive tastes. That tunic is new, too. I wonder if he has been spending his wife's money.'

'Our condolences, Sir John,' said Michael to the knight. 'We were sorry to hear of your loss.'

'What loss?' demanded Lullington, whipping around to glower at him.

'Your wife,' replied Michael, taken aback by the peculiar response. 'She died.'

'Oh,' replied Lullington. 'Yes. I shall miss her.'

Trentham was trimming the altar candles, but he turned when he heard the knight's remark. 'In that case, you should pay your last respects. You were not with her when she passed away, so saying a prayer over her body is the least you can do now.'

Lullington pulled a face. 'I have seen more than my share of corpses in the battles I have fought. Must I be subjected to more of them in the evening of my life?'

'What battles?' asked Langelee keenly, while Bartholomew thought the knight's life was more mid-afternoon than evening, and wondered how he had persuaded the King to let him retire so early. 'I was a soldier myself before I took to scholarship and know a thing or two about warfare. And Cynric and Bartholomew were at Poitiers.'

'I cannot recall,' hedged Lullington. 'I played significant roles in so many that they merge together in my mind.'

'Well, never mind, because you can oblige me in another way,' said Langelee, rubbing his hands together in happy anticipation. 'I have not had the opportunity to hone my swordplay since arriving here, so we shall spar together. I can promise you a very good—'

'No!' cried Lullington in alarm. 'I am too old.'

'Nonsense! You are in your prime.'

'Perhaps he will challenge you to a game of chess instead, Master,' said Cynric acidly. 'I imagine that is *his* preferred form of combat.'

'Yes,' said Lullington, missing the sarcasm in the

suggestion. 'I shall be happy to defeat you at chess, Langelee. I am rather good at that.'

'Your wife, Sir John,' said Trentham impatiently. 'If you really have seen so many corpses, then one more will make no difference. And it is not as if you were close. You could not even recall her name when I asked you for it last night, to put in my register.'

'You do not know your own wife's name?' echoed Langelee in disbelief.

'I always called her Lady Lullington,' said the knight stiffly. 'Besides, I was away fighting for most of our married life, so we rarely met.'

'You were wed to her for thirty years.' Trentham was obviously unimpressed. 'And you met her often enough to sire six children.'

'Yes,' acknowledged Lullington. 'All fine, healthy lads who are favourites with the King.'

'Will you see her?' pressed Trentham, becoming exasperated. 'She is upstairs, keeping company with poor Joan. I will come with you if you cannot bear to go alone.'

'So will I,' said Michael, seeing a way to gain access to Joan without waiting for Marion and Elene. 'And Matt will be on hand to answer any medical questions you might have.'

'Very well,' said Lullington with a resigned sigh, seeing he was trapped. 'Lead on.'

Lady Lullington lay in the chamber where she had died, and an involuntary sob caught in Trentham's throat when he saw her. Bartholomew laid a sympathetic hand on his shoulder.

'I know it is hard,' he said gently. 'But Abbot Robert

was right when he said you must learn to keep your distance. You will make yourself ill if you become distressed over every parishioner you lose.'

'Lady Lullington was different,' gulped Trentham. 'She listened to me. How many people listen to priests? They expect us to help them when they suffer, but they never appreciate that we might need patience and understanding, too.'

'Wait outside,' suggested Bartholomew. 'I will stay with Lullington.'

The priest disappeared with alacrity, leaving Bartholomew to lift the gauzy sheet that had been placed across Lady Lullington's face. Her husband approached tentatively, then released a yell that made Bartholomew leap in alarm.

'She is so pale!' he gasped, the colour draining from his own face. 'And thin.'

Bartholomew could only suppose it had been some time since he had seen her. The knight turned away quickly, and indicated with an agitatedly flapping hand that she should be covered again. Bartholomew obliged, then escorted him outside, where Trentham was waiting. When he saw Lullington's distress, the priest immediately hastened towards him, leading him away to be calmed with quiet words.

'Trentham is a good man,' Bartholomew remarked. 'He deplores the way Lullington has neglected his wife, yet he is prepared to set aside his personal feelings to offer him comfort.'

Michael nodded. 'I shall reduce his duties when I am Abbot. It is unreasonable to give him two hospitals and a parish. It is too much, especially for someone so young.'

'Lullington's reaction to his wife's body was odd,' said Bartholomew thoughtfully.

'Not really. He was clearly lying about his military expertise, and hers may be the first corpse he has ever seen. And if she looks very different from when she was hale and hearty, then his shock is understandable.'

'Perhaps. Or there could be another reason.' Bartholomew led the way back to the body and pointed to the bruises on the dead woman's throat. 'She has been strangled, Brother.'

Michael gaped at him, then started to ask some of the questions that clamoured in his mind, but he stopped himself and went to the door instead.

'We do not have much time. Inspect her quickly, then look at Joan. I will stand guard, and if I cough, it means that someone is coming, so drop to your knees and pretend to pray.'

It was sordid and Bartholomew did not like it, but he did as he was told. The marks on Lady Lullington's throat were livid, but although they were obvious to him, he understood why they had been missed by others. The victim had been afflicted with blotchy skin – a side effect of whatever ailment had killed her – which meant they were fairly well disguised.

He touched the bruises lightly. It was impossible to tell whether they had been made by a man or a woman, but he was sure of one thing: whoever had committed the crime had used a massive degree of force. The killer had gripped her throat so hard that Bartholomew could feel damage to the bones underneath. He stared at her with quiet compassion, wondering what sort of monster would strangle a dying lady.

At a sharp hiss from Michael, he pulled himself from his reverie and inspected Joan, but there was nothing to learn from her, except for the fact that the murder weapon was definitely the broken piece of flagstone – he could see that its corner would match precisely the dent in her skull. He put all to rights and escaped from the room with relief.

'Perhaps she viewed the arrival of the Bishop's Commissioners as the final chapter in Robert's life,' suggested Michael, watching Bartholomew close the door. 'That us being here meant he was dead for certain. Grief may have directed her hand – she brained herself.'

'Impossible,' said Bartholomew, watching the hope of an easy solution fade from the monk's eyes. 'I am afraid you *are* looking for a murderer. Probably more than one, because we cannot assume that whoever struck her also strangled Lady Lullington and . . . did whatever happened to Robert and Pyk.'

'I am inclined to keep Lady Lullington's fate to ourselves, lest the Bishop orders us to solve that crime, too. What do you think?'

'I agree – we should confide in our Michaelhouse colleagues, but no one else. Not for the reason you suggest, but because anyone ruthless enough to throttle a sick woman is not someone we want annoyed with us.'

'True,' acknowledged Michael soberly.

Lullington had gone by the time Bartholomew and Michael returned to the chapel, although Trentham was on his knees at the altar, his head bent in prayer. He jumped when Michael tapped his shoulder, but made the sign of the cross and stood to lead them to the back of the building, where they could talk in private. Hagar came to join them uninvited.

'It is good to have our shrines back,' she said, beaming at the penitents who clustered around the relics. Most were staring at the stone that had killed Joan, and Bartholomew suspected it was ghoulish curiosity, not reverence, that had brought them there. Hagar brandished a heavy purse. 'I have collected all this since we opened our doors.'

Trentham looked pained. 'I do not condone this obsession with wealth, Prioress. It is unseemly.'

Hagar shrugged. 'I will confess this evening and you can absolve me. You usually do.'

'Yes, but it would be better if you were genuinely contrite,' argued Trentham. 'I have told you this before.'

'I will be contrite this evening,' offered Hagar blithely. 'Genuinely, if you demand it.'

Michael brought the subject around to the one he wanted to discuss before Trentham could take issue with Hagar's breezy attitude towards sin. 'Poor Lady Lullington. Matt says she had been ill for some time.'

'With a wasting sickness,' nodded Hagar. 'It came on her one night about a month ago, and she had been going steadily downhill ever since. Death was a tremendous relief.'

'It happened suddenly?' asked Bartholomew, surprised. 'That is odd. Did she—'

'I would rather not discuss it,' interrupted Hagar sharply, casting a meaningful look towards Trentham, whose eyes had filled with tears again. 'Her illness was a terrible thing, distressing for all concerned. We should not dwell on its details.'

172

'Very well,' said Michael before Bartholomew could argue. 'We shall talk about her life instead then. Did she have any particular friends? I think we can discount her husband as a caring companion.'

'He never visited her when she was ill,' said Trentham bitterly. 'They were married for thirty years, so you would think he would have shown some concern.'

'Actually, he came yesterday,' said Hagar. 'Just for a few moments.'

Bartholomew glanced at Michael, and saw the monk was asking himself the same questions. Had Lullington stayed long enough to dispatch the spouse he had never loved? But why bother when she would have been dead soon anyway?

'Did he know she was nearing the end?' he asked.

Hagar nodded. 'But his visit was so fleeting that I cannot be certain that he even entered her room. Perhaps he reached the door and his courage failed him.'

'Why would he need courage to face someone he did not care about?' asked Michael, his harsh tone telling Bartholomew that he had a suspect for the crime.

'Perhaps it was guilt,' suggested Trentham. 'He treated her with rank disdain even before she was unwell, although she never gave him cause, poor soul. She did not want to come to Peterborough. She was happy in London, where she could visit her sons.'

'Who was with her when she died?' asked Bartholomew.

'She passed away shortly after Reginald tried to force his way in here,' replied Trentham. 'God forgive me, but I went to offer calming words to Hagar instead of staying at my post. Lady Lullington was alive when I left and dead when I returned.' His face contorted with remorse. 'She died alone.'

'Alone?' probed Michael. 'Surely bedeswomen were on hand to see to the patients' needs?'

'Unfortunately, Reginald caused such a kerfuffle that he claimed every ounce of *my* attention,' replied Hagar. 'I cannot be sure who was where. Marion! Elene! Come here!'

The last was delivered in a stentorian bellow that had the named sisters dashing forward in alarm. Hagar repeated Michael's question.

'We both hurried downstairs when Reginald started yelling,' explained Marion; Elene nodded at her side. 'We were worried that he might damage the chapel. I think all the other sisters were here as well, but I cannot be sure.'

'Who has access to the infirmary, other than you bedeswomen?' asked Michael.

'Why?' demanded Hagar, regarding him suspiciously.

'The Bishop's Commissioner is nothing if not thorough,' replied Michael, smoothly reminding her of his authority.

Hagar sighed. 'Very well. Most of our patients have friends and family in the town, and those folk have leave to visit whenever they please.'

'In other words, anyone could have slipped into Lady Lullington's room to sit with her,' said Trentham. 'However, I imagine they would have said something to me if they had – no one sees a good woman breathe her last and forgets to mention it to her priest.'

'No,' agreed Michael. 'But let us move on to Joan.'

'I would not like to be in her killer's shoes come

174

Judgement Day,' said Trentham bleakly. 'The saints do not look kindly on sacred relics being used to kill people. Whoever committed that atrocity will be damned for eternity.'

'Oh, come, Father,' said Hagar. She had turned pale, while Marion and Elene crossed themselves vigorously. 'Surely it depends on whether there were extenuating circumstances?'

Trentham frowned. 'Extenuating circumstances?'

'Joan could be fierce,' explained Hagar. 'She might have darted at someone, who snatched up the stone to protect herself. Or the culprit might have been inspecting it and swiped accidentally when Joan startled her.'

'Do you encourage people to touch the relics, then?' asked Michael, catching Bartholomew's eye again. Neither of them had missed Hagar's choice of pronoun.

'Not as a rule,' replied Hagar. 'But they cannot always be dissuaded.'

'If you had to point a finger at a suspect, who would it be?' asked the monk.

'One of the men from St Leonard's, of course,' replied Hagar. 'They are all villains. You should arrest the lot of them and close down their nasty chapel.'

'What about you, Trentham?'

'I did not kill Joan!' exclaimed Trentham, shocked.

'I meant who are your suspects,' said Michael irritably.

Trentham calmed himself. 'I doubt it was anyone she knew – they would not have dared. Of course, she was as gentle as a lamb really, or Robert would not have stayed with her all those years. *Ergo*, it must have been a stranger, someone who did not know her.'

'Yes,' said Hagar eagerly. 'A stranger – one of the

many pilgrims who visit. Of course, he will be long gone now, so I would not waste time looking if I were you. But we have wasted enough time today, and we have sick bedeswomen waiting. Are you ready to tend us, Doctor?'

'Which would you like first?' asked Elene sweetly. 'My veins or Marion's impostumes?'

'What a decision!' muttered Michael. 'I am glad it is not incumbent on *me* to choose.'

CHAPTER 6

'We still have no idea what happened to Robert,' said Michael gloomily as he and Bartholomew sat in the Swan Inn that evening. Outside, day was fading to dusk earlier than usual, because it was raining. 'Moreover, we now have two murders to complicate matters.'

'Hagar's reactions to our questions made me wonder again whether she might have killed Joan,' said Bartholomew. 'So she could be Prioress herself.'

Michael agreed. 'And if Joan, then why not Lady Lullington, whose nursing would have been a drain on her foundation's resources?'

But Bartholomew shook his head at that suggestion. 'There is a big difference between knocking someone on the head and choking the life out of her with such vigour that bones were crushed. One suggests opportunism, the other a furious rage. Lady Lullington's husband is *my* prime suspect for the strangling. He ignored her for weeks, but the one time he deigned to visit is the day she was killed.'

'But why bother? She was no trouble, dying quietly with the bedeswomen to take care of her. It is not as if he was obliged to tend her himself.'

'People disapproved of the way he treated her. Perhaps he wanted an early end to it.'

'Perhaps,' said Michael, although with scant conviction. He turned to another suspect. 'We should not

177

overlook Trentham either – he spends a lot of time in the chapel where the murders were committed. I like the boy, but something dark and nasty is unfolding, and until we discover what it is, I am unwilling to exclude anyone from our list of suspects.'

'I doubt he killed Lady Lullington. He was fond of her and I think his distress is genuine. And as for Joan, he was very vocal in his certainty that her murderer is destined for Hell. I cannot see him making that sort of remark if he were the culprit.'

'He might,' countered Michael. 'To throw us off the scent. It depends how clever he is, which is something I do not feel sufficiently qualified to determine.'

'Regardless, we should speak to Reginald tomorrow, because he was the one who caused the trouble during which Lady Lullington was killed.'

Michael regarded him sharply. 'Are you saying it was a deliberate diversion?'

'Yes – and if we can persuade him to reveal who told him to make the fuss, we shall have our villain. Is there any wine left, Brother?'

'It was heavily watered,' said Michael defensively. 'And I was parched.'

'You said you would try again to see Pyk's wife while I was busy with the bedeswomen this afternoon,' said Bartholomew, once his cup had been filled. He thought the brew rather powerful, and was sure water had been nowhere near it. 'Did you?'

'I tried, but she was still out.' Michael sighed. 'It is a pity the taint of murder will hang over Peterborough because of a disagreeable character like Robert. This is a *good* place, and I would enjoy being Abbot here. The food alone would make it worthwhile – I have not eaten so well since we visited my brethren at Ely four years ago.'

'Matilde was still in Cambridge then,' sighed Bartholomew, for whom the episode of two nights before was still vivid. 'I should have been married by now.'

'Then by now you would have been living in a hovel, surrounded by squalling brats, and burdened with a wife who resents the fact that you have dragged her into poverty. Paupers would be demanding free medicine, and you would have to choose between providing it or letting your family starve.'

Bartholomew blinked, startled by the bleak image the monk had painted. Michael had never said anything like it before. 'Matilde is a wealthy woman—'

'Not wealthy enough to support numerous offspring and a husband with an unprofitable practice,' countered Michael. 'Besides, I imagine she lost anything of value to highway thieves – a lone woman would have presented an attractive target to outlaws. She would have been poor, and you would both have been miserable.'

'But if she had not left Cambridge, there would have been no highway thieves,' Bartholomew pointed out, bemused by the monk's remarks. 'We would have—'

'She has gone, Matt,' said Michael shortly. 'So put her from your mind and set your sights on some other lady. And I do not mean Julitta Holm. Her husband may not love her, but that still does not make her available to you.'

'I am not sure there are any women for me, other than them,' said Bartholomew, wondering why they were discussing it. The monk had not so much as mentioned

Matilde in months, while he usually maintained a tactful silence about Julitta.

'There is something wrong with these leeks.' Michael abruptly changed the subject. 'They taste disgusting. You have them, while I concentrate on the meat.'

'That is considerate, Brother.'

'You are used to greenery. Your constitution copes with it better than mine.'

'They are very salty,' said Bartholomew, wincing.

'Salt is good for you,' declared Michael, grabbing the platter of chicken before Bartholomew could take any. 'It keeps the blood healthy.'

'Does it indeed?' Bartholomew began to eat. He was not hungry, but the leeks were there, and it was something to do. 'And on whose authority do you make this claim?'

'My own. I have a lot of experience where victuals are concerned, and you should listen to me because you would learn a great deal.'

Bartholomew did not doubt it, and was equally sure that most of it would be total nonsense. He reached for the wine jug, and shot the monk an irritable glance when he saw it had been drained a second time.

'The chicken is salty, too,' said Michael, unrepentant.

They were about to leave the Swan when Langelee arrived with Cynric and Spalling, the latter still wearing his farmer's smock and hat. The Master slid on to the bench next to Michael, his face sombre, although Cynric remained with his new friend, pausing only to give the briefest of smiles to his old ones. The book-bearer and Spalling joined a group of carpenters at a table by the fire.

'Peterborough is full of rebels,' Langelee whispered. 'Word that Spalling is fomenting unrest has reached the surrounding villages and farms, and people are flocking to join his little army. They are not soldiers, of course, but they already vastly outnumber Aurifabro's mercenaries and the abbey's *defensores*.'

'Is this the beginning of the country-wide uprising that Cynric has been talking about ever since the plague?' asked Michael. 'And if so, does it pose a danger to my University?'

'Possibly, although Spalling is concentrating his ire on the merchants at the moment. Specifically Aurifabro, who is sitting in the corner: look.'

Bartholomew had not noticed the goldsmith while they had been talking, although Aurifabro had evidently noticed them, because he was scowling in their direction.

'He has been glaring at us ever since we arrived,' said Michael loudly. 'I ignored him, as I do not allow other patrons' bad manners to interfere with the important business of eating.'

'Yes, I have been watching you,' Aurifabro called back. Two mercenaries sat with him, while more lurked in the shadows leading to the kitchen. 'You intend to blame me for Robert's murder, and I will not have it.'

The buzz of conversation in the tavern faded as people turned to see what was happening.

'If you are innocent, you have nothing to fear,' said Michael coolly.

'I *am* innocent,' growled Aurifabro. 'Forget it at your peril.'

He stood up and stalked towards the door, his

henchmen at his heels. Unfortunately, the path he chose took him past Spalling, who stretched out a burly arm to stop him.

'My home is full of hungry men, women and children,' the rebel declared in a voice like a trumpet. 'The food has been taken from their mouths by the rich.'

The mercenaries surged forward to push him away, and Cynric leapt to his feet with a dagger in his hand. Instinctively, Bartholomew started to go to the book-bearer's aid, but Michael grabbed his shoulder and jerked him back. Then Landlord Piel arrived to interpose himself between the two factions.

'Enjoy a quiet drink, if you will, Spalling,' he said angrily, 'but I will not have you haranguing my other customers. So either shut up or get out.'

'I shall harangue whoever I like,' declared Spalling indignantly. 'It is not for you to still the voice of the oppressed. And if you try, I shall order your tavern burned to the ground when the time comes to redress this wicked imbalance between the classes—'

He got no further, for the mercenaries seized his arms and marched him towards the door. He was a large man, but they were used to dealing with people who did not like where they were being taken, and his struggles, while determined, were futile. Bartholomew twisted away from Michael and hurried to prevent Cynric from going to Spalling's rescue, but Cynric was no fool – he knew his chances of defeating so many professional soldiers were slim and he made no attempt to intervene.

'You see, Brother?' asked Langelee. 'Spalling makes remarks like that wherever he goes – churches, taverns, the market. I hope to God he never learns that our

University has more wealth than is decent. Cynric has said nothing so far, but he is so enamoured of the fellow that I fear trouble in the future.'

'How dangerous is Spalling, exactly?' asked Michael uneasily.

Langelee shrugged. 'Well, my Archbishop would not have liked him operating in *his* domain, and would have sent me to take care of the matter.'

Michael winced. None of the Fellows were comfortable with what the Master had done for a living before he had decided that an academic career would be more rewarding. 'I shall warn Gynewell. He must have the wherewithal to deal with this sort of situation.'

He spoke just as Bartholomew returned to the table with Cynric, who frowned when he heard the last remark.

'Spalling is a great leader,' the book-bearer declared. 'With vision. The Bishop will not want him silenced, because Gynewell is a decent man, too.'

'As far as I can tell, most of Spalling's "vision" revolves around how to transfer other people's money to the poor – with him as their banker,' countered Langelee acidly.

Cynric shook his head earnestly. 'You misunderstand him, Master. He sees the injustice of a situation where most of us work for a pittance while a minority grows fat from our labours, and he has solutions.'

'What are they?' asked Bartholomew.

'To remove excess wealth from those with too much, and give it to those who have nothing,' explained Cynric. 'It is simple, but fair.'

'Do you want a pay rise, then?' asked Langelee tiredly. 'I suppose we can manage one, although it will put the College in—'

'No, you have always been generous.' Cynric smiled, and continued. 'But Spalling predicts great changes, ones that will result in a more equitable world. I am inclined to help him in his struggle.'

Bartholomew stared at him. 'Is this your way of telling us that you want to leave Michaelhouse? But what about your wife?'

'She will understand, and it will not be for ever – just until this revolution has come to pass. Spalling needs men like me, who are handy with a sword.'

'You mean he plans to fight for this paradise?' Bartholomew was dismayed.

'Only if the wealthy resist,' replied Cynric. 'But they will not, because they will see that surrendering their riches is the proper thing to do.'

'You know better than that, Cynric,' said Bartholomew, wondering whether Spalling had dosed the book-bearer with some substance that had addled his wits. 'No one parts with money willingly. Especially people who have a lot of it.'

'They will when they see how many people are on our side. Please do not try to stop me, boy. You know I have felt strongly about this for a very long time.'

'I will not stand by while you do something so manifestly reckless,' said Bartholomew. 'You are my friend. I will not see you hanged as an insurgent when—'

'I am doing what I think is right.' Cynric gripped the physician's arm in a rare and shy gesture of affection. 'Just as you have always encouraged me to do. But I should take Spalling home now. We have had enough speeches for tonight.'

He nodded a farewell and left, stopping only to mutter

a few soft words to the carpenters at whose table he had been sitting. As one, they stood and followed him out. Bartholomew stared after them unhappily.

'I will keep trying to talk sense into him,' promised Langelee, although his grim expression suggested that he did not think he would succeed. 'How much longer will you be here, Brother? In other words, how long do I have?'

'Three full days,' said Michael soberly. 'Plus a little of Wednesday. After which we shall leave whether we have Robert's killer or not. Oh, look – Lombard slices! When did they arrive? I thought the landlord said he did not have any.'

'Perhaps he ordered them because you declared them your favourites the last time you were here,' said Langelee. 'Word has spread that you might be the next Abbot, so he doubtless aims to win your favour. But I had better go and try again to reason with Cynric.'

'I will come with you,' said Bartholomew. He stood, but was obliged to rest a hand on the wall to steady himself: the salty leeks had encouraged him to drink too much of Piel's powerful wine. Michael, who had imbibed twice as much, was perfectly sober, of course.

'The best thing you can do is help find the Abbot,' said Langelee. 'But do not worry about Cynric – he will come home with us, even if I have to tie him in a sack and carry him there.'

It was a measure of Michael's concern for the book-bearer that he did not even look at the Lombard slices as he left the tavern. Bartholomew took one and ate it as he followed, hoping it would mop up some of the wine sloshing around in his stomach.

Outside, it was a cloudy night with no moon, which

made walking difficult, especially along unfamiliar streets and – for Bartholomew – on legs that were embarrassingly wobbly. At one point, he reeled into a wall, scraping his elbow painfully. Then Michael gave a sharp hiss of alarm before grabbing the physician's arm and hauling him towards the abbey.

'What are you doing?' slurred Bartholomew, trying to free himself.

'Someone is muttering in French,' replied the monk, hammering urgently on the door to be let in. 'Just like the robbers who ambushed us on our way here.'

Bartholomew had heard no muttering in French, but even so, he was relieved when they were inside the monastery with the gate closed behind them. He jumped when a figure materialised suddenly out of the gloom. It was Yvo, with Lullington and Henry behind him. He peered at them warily, wondering why they should be so far from their beds at such an hour of the night, particularly as they seemed unlikely companions.

'Is anything wrong, Brother Michael?' asked the Prior.

'Yes – someone was about to attack us,' declared Michael, fear turning to anger now he was safe. 'I saw shadows milling about, and I heard them speaking French.'

Yvo regarded him askance. 'Peterborough is a busy place, Brother, and shadows "mill about" all the time. Moreover, many folk speak French. Indeed, we are using it now.'

'So we are,' said Michael pointedly. 'And there would have been enough time for you to reach the monastery before us – just.'

'I assure you, no one from the abbey—' Yvo's angry denial was interrupted by a rap on the door. The guard opened it, and the Unholy Trinity walked in, four *defensores* at their heels. All were armed.

'I have been looking for you three all evening,' snapped the Prior, promptly turning his back on the two scholars. 'I did not give you permission to go out.'

Welbyrn shrugged with calculated insolence. 'We went to visit the town's merchants, to discuss the problem that Spalling has become. It was Ramseye's idea – and a good one, too.'

'I know how *I* would deal with the man, left to my own devices,' muttered Nonton darkly.

'Why did you want us, Father Prior?' asked Ramseye. He smiled unpleasantly. 'To help you prepare for your next public appearance, given that the last one was less than impressive?'

'No, he wanted Welbyrn to unlock the treasury for me.' Lullington spoke before the Prior could defend himself. 'My wife kept her jewellery there, and I intend to sell it tomorrow.'

'But not before I have selected a piece for the abbey, as stipulated in her will,' interposed Yvo sharply, treating him to a scowl. 'Henry is going to choose it, given that he has the best eye for such things.'

'Does he?' Bartholomew was astonished that his principled friend should possess such a worldly talent.

'You are thinking of hawking your wife's possessions already, Sir John?' asked Ramseye in distaste, sparing Henry the need to reply. 'She is barely cold.'

'I need the money,' said Lullington stiffly. 'Her jewels should have been mine years ago, rightfully speaking,

187

but her sly father slipped a clause into our marriage contract, which kept them in her hands all these years. Well, that changes now.'

'He has been making purchases since her death,' explained Yvo. 'And we do not want it said that abbey residents decline to pay their bills.' He addressed Welbyrn. 'So are you going to open the treasury, or do we stand here all night?'

Still sniping at each other, the monastics and Lullington moved away, although Henry paused long enough to shoot Bartholomew an amiable smile. The physician watched them go, aware of two things: that Yvo had avoided returning to Michael's accusation, and that the Unholy Trinity had been very heavily armed for a meeting with merchants. Meanwhile, Michael was angrily indignant that his claim of ambushers had been so summarily dismissed. He stalked to the guest house, where he told Clippesby and William what had happened.

'But no one actually assaulted you?' asked William. 'You just saw people lurking and heard them speak French?'

'I could read their intentions,' snapped Michael, annoyed that even his own colleagues seemed to be doubting his word. 'They would have been on us had we not fled. And look at Matt's arm – we did not escape unscathed from the affair.'

'Does it hurt?' asked Clippesby sympathetically.

'I do not trust any of them,' Michael stormed on before Bartholomew could say that his stumble against a wall could hardly be blamed on someone else. 'Welbyrn, Nonton, Ramseye, Lullington, Yvo and Henry. All six are on my list of suspects for dispatching Robert.'

'Not Henry,' said Bartholomew doggedly. 'Besides, his lame leg means he is unlikely to have reached the abbey before us.'

Michael ignored him. 'Then we must remember that the incident took place near St Thomas's Chapel, where the bedeswomen live and where Reginald has his shop. Meanwhile, Aurifabro and Spalling cannot have gone far.'

He continued in this vein while Bartholomew, still queasy from the wine and salty leeks, went to lie down. The physician sat on the bed and was about to sink back and close his eyes when there was a knock on the door. He stood hastily when the Unholy Trinity trooped in.

'Yvo has just told us what happened to you,' declared Ramseye, all righteous indignation. 'And while *he* may not be interested in attacks on the Bishop's Commissioners, we are appalled.'

'We are,' said Welbyrn. It was impossible to tell whether he was sincere. 'Especially as he mentioned that you thought the culprits might hail from the abbey.'

'I hope you do not think our *defensores* are to blame,' said Nonton, going to the table for wine. 'Did we not lend you some when you went to Torpe the other day? If they had meant you harm, they would have assaulted you then – on a lonely road, miles from help.'

'Those *defensores* could not have assaulted anyone,' William murmured to his colleagues. 'Nonton detailed the most feeble ones to protect you, and kept the best ones back for himself. He spent the day putting them through various training exercises.'

'Of course, tonight's affair was your own fault,' said

Welbyrn, frowning as he tried to hear what the Franciscan was muttering. 'You should not have been out after dark.'

'We were on official business,' retorted Michael. 'For the Bishop.'

'In a tavern?' smirked Ramseye. 'I shall have to remember that one!'

'We shall discuss it in the morning,' said Clippesby, as Michael drew breath to make a scathing rejoinder. 'It is late, and we are all tired.'

'There speaks the saint,' jeered Welbyrn. 'We had better do as he suggests, Brothers, because we do not want to be struck down. He might—'

'Leave him alone,' warned Bartholomew, seeing Clippesby's confusion. He was loath for the Dominican to discover that night what had been claimed about him, as he did not feel equal to soothing the dismay that would certainly follow.

'Or what?' challenged Welbyrn. 'You have no authority here. You are nothing but a physician with a sinister interest in corpses.'

'You might find yourself the object of his attentions if you do not shut up,' snarled William. 'And Clippesby is right: we shall discuss this matter tomorrow, when you have regained your wits and accept that it is not politic to insult the Bishop's—'

'Who are you calling witless?' shrieked Welbyrn with such sudden fury that even the other two members of the Unholy Trinity reacted with shock; Ramseye jerked away from him, and Nonton's hand went to the knife he carried in his belt. 'How dare you! It—'

'Come, Welbyrn,' ordered Ramseye sharply, stepping forward to lay a wary hand on the treasurer's arm. When

Welbyrn resisted, Nonton came to help, and together, almoner and cellarer bundled him out of the guest house and into the darkness beyond.

Bartholomew watched William bar the door behind them, thinking that Welbyrn's face had been abnormally flushed. Was something wrong with him? But he did not feel like pondering medical matters that night. He lay on the bed, but the moment he was comfortable, he realised that he was still very thirsty. Wearily, he started to rise, but William waved him back down and went to pour him some watered wine.

'I heard and saw nothing out there, Brother,' Bartholomew said, watching the friar fiddle with jugs and goblets and wondering what was taking so long. He felt his eyes begin to close: the Benedictine's beds really were extremely luxurious, and he wished the ones at Michaelhouse were half as soft. 'Are you sure you—'

'Of course I did,' snapped Michael. 'And so would you, if you had not been drunk. It is fortunate that I remained sober, or we both might be dead.'

'Right.' Bartholomew was disinclined to argue, although it occurred to him that since Michael had downed a lot more wine than he had, the monk was probably not a reliable witness either. William finally presented him with a brimming beaker, and he was thirsty enough to drain the lot in a single draught. 'Is there any more?'

'Yes, but you cannot have any,' said William, regarding the empty goblet in alarm. 'It is unwise to gulp claret – even watered – after a serious injury, especially for a man who is usually abstemious.'

Michael began to hold forth again before Bartholomew could inform William that a graze did not constitute a serious injury. Piqued by the friar's presumptions, Bartholomew considered going to get a drink himself but was not sure he could manage it without reeling, and he was reluctant to let the others see him totter – he would never hear the end of it. He closed his eyes again.

'It might have been anyone,' the monk was fuming. 'Aurifabro's mercenaries, Spalling and his rabble, the obedientiaries and their *defensores*, the bedesfolk, Reginald . . .'

'Lullington,' added William. 'The abbey servants say he only pretended to be Robert's friend, in order to accumulate privileges as corrodian. And I saw armour under his gipon tonight.'

'What did you mean when you said the *defensores* Nonton lent us were feeble, Father?' asked Michael, reining in his temper with difficulty. 'How do you know?'

'The servants again,' replied William. 'Apparently, Nonton has recruited two kinds of soldier: ones who know how to fight, and ones who look fierce but who actually possess no martial skills whatsoever and who are probably cowards. He supplied you with the latter kind.'

Bartholomew began to drowse. Then he supposed he should pay at least some attention to the conversation, so he forced himself to open his eyes. It was not easy, and when he finally managed it the room undulated alarmingly. He wanted to rub his damaged elbow, but his hand was suddenly too heavy to move. What was wrong with him? He tried to speak, but no words came, and when his eyes closed again, a crushing sense of darkness rushed in to meet him.

'Matt?' came Clippesby's anxious voice. 'Are you ill?'

He sensed his colleagues clustering around him, but it was as if they were speaking from a great distance. He felt himself drift further away, and the last thing he heard before he gave himself to the blackness was Michael's horrified declaration.

'The leeks. They were poisoned!'

Bartholomew knew it was Sunday, because he could hear the jubilant jangle of bells, and he also knew he should rouse himself and go to church. Someone else thought so, too, because he could feel his shoulder being shaken with irritating persistence. But he was still tired, and the bed was very comfortable. He closed his eyes and went back to sleep.

'I am right: the leeks *were* poisoned,' said Michael worriedly, when increasingly strenuous efforts on his part did nothing to jostle the physician awake.

'It was not the leeks, Brother.' William's face was sober. 'It was the Lombard slices. Clippesby and I visited the Swan as soon as we woke up this morning, and we quizzed Landlord Piel. He denied providing you with any – he has not sold cakes since his wife died. *Ergo*, someone else left them for you.'

'You said you were too anxious about your investigation to eat any,' Clippesby reminded Michael. 'But that Matt took one on his way out.'

Michael was horrified. 'They are my favourites, and I said so in both the Swan and the abbey. Anyone might have heard me . . .'

'Quite,' nodded William. 'I searched the place thoroughly while I was there, but the cakes had disappeared. In other words, the culprit has slyly reclaimed the evidence.'

'Or someone ate them after we left,' Michael pointed out.

'It is not that kind of establishment,' said William. 'Its wares are expensive, and the folk who patronise it are wealthy – they do not need to scavenge leftovers from other tables.'

Michael scrubbed at his face. 'Matt ate one Lombard slice and it has sent him into a stupor. What would have happened to me had I sampled the entire plate?'

'You would be dead,' replied William baldly. 'So we had better ensure we do not touch any food that does not come from a communal pot from now on. Pity – I was growing used to being properly fed; it makes a pleasant change from Michaelhouse.'

Michael's expression was bleak. 'Are you *sure* the Lombard slices were to blame? I tried one of those leeks, and it tasted very odd.'

'Yes, because while William was looking for the cakes, I interviewed the tavern's pig,' said Clippesby. 'She told me that Piel had over-salted his vegetables by mistake – she overheard him laughing about it with his potboys. The leftovers were in her slops, which did not please her, but she ate them anyway with no ill effects.'

'So there you are, Brother,' concluded William. 'The leeks tasted nasty because there was too much salt, and the poison was in the Lombard slices – the pastries that Piel denies providing, and that have now mysteriously vanished.'

194

'Do you think that whoever provided the cakes also ordered you ambushed when you did not eat them?' asked Clippesby.

'I hope so,' said Michael softly. 'Because I should not like to think there are two lots of people eager to kill me.'

Aware that the stakes had now been raised, and that the time was fast approaching when they would have to return to Cambridge, Michael became businesslike. He sent Clippesby to tell Langelee all they had reasoned, with orders to warn the Master to be on his guard, and told William to watch over Bartholomew.

'What will you be doing?' asked the Franciscan.

'Visiting suspects,' replied Michael harshly. 'For trying to dispatch me *and* for murdering Robert, Pyk, Joan and Lady Lullington.'

'Perhaps we should leave today,' said William anxiously. 'Gynewell cannot expect us to stay when we are in fear of our lives, and we can hire a cart to carry Matthew – he would be safer in one than on horseback, anyway.'

'I am not in the habit of fleeing from villains,' said Michael haughtily. 'And Peterborough deserves answers. We will catch this killer and then we shall see him hang.'

Inspired by his own defiant words, Michael stalked out of the abbey, stopping only to inform a waiting Henry that visitors to the guest house would not be welcome that day. His first port of call was Reginald's workshop, where a rhythmic hammering told him that the cutler was in. He tried to open the door but it was barred, so he knocked, courteously at first, and then with increasing irritation when there was no answer. Eventually, a grille was snapped open.

'What do you want?' barked Reginald.

'To buy a knife,' lied Michael. 'You sell them, do you not?'

'Yes, but not today. I am busy.'

Michael frowned suspiciously. 'I am a customer. You cannot be too busy for those.'

'Well, I am,' declared Reginald. 'And I do not do business with bishops' commissioners, anyway. You have no right to poke your nose into Abbot Robert's affairs.'

'I am trying to learn what happened to him,' replied Michael indignantly, aware that their hollered discussion was attracting amused glances from passers-by. 'I am told he is probably dead, but there is also a possibility that he is in trouble and requires help. And as one of his friends, you should be doing all you can to assist me.'

'He will not be in trouble,' Reginald shouted back. 'He has probably found a hovel somewhere, and is enjoying the peace and quiet. I would not blame him. His monks are a pious crowd, and I would not want to live among them.'

'He is an abbot – such men *like* living among pious monks. And what about Pyk? Will he also be in this mud hut while the whole town mourns his loss?'

'No, but he might have seized the opportunity to escape from his dreadful wife,' Reginald shot back. 'But I am not talking to you any more, because you will try to trick me. Now go away. I do not have any knives to sell you.'

Michael became aware of a presence behind him. It

was Botilbrig, standing brazenly close to ensure he did not miss anything.

'You should not buy one of his blades, anyway,' he said, not at all discomfited by the monk's annoyed glare. 'They are all below standard, and he will cheat you.'

'I heard that,' yelled Reginald angrily. 'There is nothing wrong with my cutlery.'

'Then show me some,' challenged Michael. 'And at the same time, you can tell me why you think I might trick you. You should not be concerned if you have nothing to hide.'

'He *will* have something to hide,' whispered Botilbrig. 'If there is anything untoward happening in Peterborough, you can be sure that Reginald will be at the heart of it. How else could a mere cutler afford a nice shop and such lovely clothes? There are rumours that he has discovered Oxforde's treasure, you know.'

'What treasure?' asked Michael, forbearing to mention that the shop was squalid and the cutler's clothes were a long way from being sartorial.

'The things that Oxforde stole during his life of crime,' explained Botilbrig impatiently. 'He amassed a fortune, but he never told anyone where he hid it.'

Michael recalled what Clippesby's grass snake was alleged to have said. 'Spalling maintains that Oxforde gave it all to the poor.'

Botilbrig spat. 'Spalling never met Oxforde, or he would not make such a ridiculous claim. Oxforde was ruthless and greedy, and would no more have given his ill-gotten gains away than he would have flown to the moon.'

197

'Some people believe it, or Oxforde's shrine would not be so popular.'

'Fools,' sneered Botilbrig. 'All misled by the witches at St Thomas's Hospital, who have seized on Spalling's remarks and used them to encourage even more folk to pray at his tomb.'

'What are you saying out there, Botilbrig?' demanded Reginald. 'You had better not be telling him that stupid tale about me finding Oxforde's treasure. It is a lie – I was not even born when he was hanged. Now go away, both of you, before I come out with my sharpest knife and hack you both to pieces.'

'We had better do as he says,' gulped Botilbrig, pulling on the monk's arm. 'He went after Master Pyk with a dagger once, just for asking concerned questions about Reginald's wife. She vanished, you see.'

'Vanished?'

'We all suspect he killed her, but that was five years ago, shortly after Robert became Abbot, so you will not get him to admit it now. Too much time has passed. However, it means I do not want him after me with pointed implements.'

Michael turned his attention back to Reginald. It was frustrating, knowing the man might have information to help his enquiries, and he heartily wished he had a pack of beadles at his command, as he did in Cambridge. Beadles made short work of inconvenient doors.

'How is your friend?'

Michael had been so engrossed in his thoughts that he had not seen Lullington approach. The knight was wearing a magnificent new cloak, although a light mail tunic could be seen underneath it, which led the monk to wonder what the man had done to warrant such precautions.

'Still insensible,' Michael replied shortly. 'And if he fails to wake, I will not leave Peterborough until I catch the villain who poisoned him.'

'Do not take that tone with me,' objected Lullington. 'I had nothing to do with it.'

'Then who do you think might have done it?'

A sly expression flitted across Lullington's face. 'Where to start? Aurifabro is a vicious rogue. Then there is Ramseye, who is as cunning and duplicitous a fellow as I have ever met. Yvo will be innocent, though.'

As Michael knew that Yvo represented Lullington's best chance of continued luxury, he was inclined to dismiss the last claim.

'Trentham is also a villain,' the knight went on. 'Do not let that look of innocent youth deceive you, because he is a rascal. How dare he tell me how to treat my wife!'

The abbey's cook, sacrist and brewer were also vilified, and it quickly became apparent that Lullington's list of suspects just comprised people who had crossed him. Unwilling to waste more time listening to it, Michael went on the offensive.

'I find it odd that you happened to be by the gate when we returned last night. What—'

'Yvo has already explained what we were doing,' snapped Lullington. 'Waiting to get my wife's . . . *my* jewellery from the treasury. If Welbyrn had not gone out without his Prior's permission, we would not have been obliged to hang around waiting for him to come back.'

Michael moved to another subject. 'I understand you

199

and Robert were friends. Yet I am told he could be . . . difficult.'

'He probably should not have taken the cowl,' acknowledged Lullington. 'He would have done better at court, for he had the wit and cunning to best any politician.'

'What did you do when you learned he was missing? You, Pyk and Reginald were his particular friends, but Pyk is also lost and Reginald is not a caring man. That leaves you.'

'What could I do, Brother?' asked Lullington, spreading his hands. 'I am a poor corrodian with very little money. Well, that has changed now my wife is dead—'

'You could have gone to look for him. Did you?'

Lullington was decidedly furtive. 'No, I left the search to the *defensores*. It would have been impolite to launch one of my own, and I am not a man to make a nuisance of myself.'

He strode away, leaving the monk staring after him thoughtfully.

Michael spent the rest of the day asking questions about Robert, Pyk, Lady Lullington and Joan, but learned nothing new. He attended vespers as the brash sun of afternoon faded to the softer tones of evening, where the exquisite harmonies of Appletre's choir went some way to calming his troubled mind – until Yvo joined in and spoiled it with his discordant bray. When the office was over, Henry was waiting to conduct him to the chapter house, where the obedientiaries had assembled to hear a report on his progress.

The chapter house was a large building, designed to hold upwards of eighty monks. Like the church, it combined Norman strength with Gothic elegance, and the stained-glass windows were among the finest Michael had ever seen. A fire had been lit, despite the mild weather, and cushions prevented black-robed posteriors from becoming chilled on the stone seats. Michael sat on the bench that had been placed ready for him, and studied his interrogators.

Prior Yvo had claimed the Abbot's throne-like chair, but his meagre frame did not fill it, which served to underline the fact that he was a lesser man than his predecessor. Ramseye, inscrutable as always, sat on his right, scribbling on a piece of parchment, while Welbyrn was scowling at the fire as though he might leap up and kick it. Nonton had turned away, pretending to cough while he took a gulp from the flask hidden in his sleeve, and Appletre hummed under his breath, fingers tapping out the rhythm of a new composition.

Somewhat irregularly – seculars were not normally permitted in the chapter house – Lullington was there, preening like a peacock in a handsome tunic bought with his dead wife's jewels. He wore a sword in his belt, although he should not have been permitted to do so in an abbey, and it occurred to Michael that the obedientiaries aimed to intimidate the Bishop's Commissioner by inviting an armed knight to the proceedings. Indignation at such tactics turned him testy and confrontational.

'Why did you not search for Robert when he first failed to return home?' he demanded.

'We did,' objected Yvo, startled by the anger in

Michael's voice. 'I ordered the *defensores* to look for him, and Henry took a group of monks to speak to Aurifabro. I do not see what else could have been done.'

'That was the following day. I want to know why you did nothing *that night*. For all you knew, he might have had an accident or been robbed. He might have been lying bleeding, waiting for help.'

'He knew how to look after himself,' said Ramseye. 'Besides, Pyk was with him.'

'I hardly think a physician counts as a bodyguard. They are trained to heal, not fight.'

'But Pyk's presence would have deterred robbers,' explained Appletre, openly dismayed by Michael's hostility. 'He was popular, and soldiers are not always the best form of defence.'

He had a point, although Michael did not acknowledge it. 'None of you went to inspect the road yourselves, to look for clues regarding his murder. Why not?'

'Because he is not dead,' snapped Welbyrn, while his colleagues exchanged weary glances behind his back. 'Besides, none of us know how to do that sort of thing. We are monastics, not spies.'

'That is why you are here, is it not?' asked Ramseye silkily. 'To poke around in ditches and bushes, and deduce answers from what you discover? Gynewell said you have unique talents. Of course, we have yet to see them.'

'All you have done so far is ask impertinent questions and allow one of your number to be poisoned,' said Nonton, taking over the attack. 'Moreover, Joan was killed the moment after you arrived. It is damned suspicious, if you ask me.'

'Hear, hear,' crowed Welbyrn, eyes flashing with spite. 'Before her, there had not been a suspicious death in Peterborough since Oxforde went on the rampage forty-five years ago.'

'That is true,' agreed Yvo. 'Ours is a safe, law-abiding town.'

'Really?' asked Michael acidly. 'Then what about Reginald the cutler's wife, who disappeared five years ago?'

'She ran away from her brutish husband,' said Yvo. 'There is no mystery there. Personally, I cannot imagine why our Abbot made friends with Reginald. I find him a most objectionable fellow.'

'Perhaps Robert was trying to save Reginald's soul,' said Ramseye. The expression on his face was bland, although amusement flashed briefly in his eyes at the notion.

Welbyrn turned on Michael again. 'From your questions, I assume you have discovered nothing since you arrived – not about Robert and Pyk, and not about Joan either. Moreover, I do not believe Clippesby is a saint. He seems more lunatic than holy to me – not that I am qualified to judge insanity, of course. We do not have madmen in Peterborough.'

'Simon the cowherd is rational, is he?' asked Michael coolly.

'Simon is none of your damned business,' yelled Welbyrn, so loudly and abruptly that everyone jumped. 'How dare you pass judgement on him!'

'He was only defending Clippesby,' objected Appletre, hand to his chest to indicate the fright he had been given. 'And your response is—'

He got no further, as Welbyrn surged forward and

grabbed him by the front of his habit. Appletre's rosy cheeks blanched in alarm.

'You are a damned fool!' raged Welbyrn, shaking the precentor like a dog with a rat. 'Robert is not dead and Simon will be cured. You wait and see.'

He shoved Appletre away with such force that the smaller man staggered backwards and ended up in Nonton's lap. Then Welbyrn stormed out, slamming the door behind him so hard that the sound reverberated like a thunderclap.

'Does he often explode so?' asked Michael, in the shocked silence that followed.

'Just over the last few weeks,' said Yvo, watching Appletre scramble off the cellarer's knees. 'It must be the strain of continuing to believe that Robert is alive when it is obvious that he is dead. Appletre can sing to him later – that should soothe his ragged nerves.'

'I suspect that might be beyond my modest skills, Father Prior,' said Appletre, his anxious eyes suggesting he was loath to be manhandled again.

'Well, try,' snapped Yvo. 'I do not like it when he is fierce. To be frank, he frightens me.'

'Very well,' gulped Appletre. 'As soon as I have said a prayer for Matthew in the church. Henry is there now, and has been much of the day. He is worried about his old friend.'

Michael narrowed his eyes, pondering the possibility that guilt might have led Henry to spend so many hours on his knees. He bowed a curt farewell to his brethren and returned to the guest house, where he found that Bartholomew was not the only one fast asleep. So was William. The friar stirred when the door opened, and

Michael noted with relief that Bartholomew did, too: the effects of whatever he had been fed were wearing off. As he wanted time alone, to think, the monk suggested that William attend compline.

He had not been pondering long when Clippesby arrived. He had a visitor with him, swathed in a cloak with a hood. Uninvited, the person stepped into the room and let the hood fall away, so that her face was visible in the candlelight.

'Matilde!' exclaimed Michael.

The love of Bartholomew's life glided towards the bed, and Michael thought it was a pity the physician was not awake to see her. Then it occurred to him that perhaps it was for the best, given his recent fondness for Julitta Holm.

'I heard some of the bedeswomen talking,' whispered Matilde, her lovely face anxious. 'They said the visiting *medicus* had been poisoned, so I waited outside the abbey, hoping for news. Then I saw Clippesby, who smuggled me inside.'

'Let us hope he can smuggle you out again,' said Michael, glaring at the Dominican. 'Women are not allowed in here, and breaking that particular rule would see us ousted for certain. Then I would never solve the Abbot's murder.'

Matilde waved an irritable hand to indicate her disregard for what she deemed foolish regulations. 'What about Matt? How serious is this poison?'

'It was delivered in Lombard slices,' explained Michael. 'An unpardonable sacrilege, which makes me even more determined to catch the culprit. Fortunately, Matt only ate one, and I imagine we could wake him now if we shook him hard enough.'

'No,' said Matilde hastily. 'Let him rest.'

'When he told me that he had seen you, I assumed he had imagined it.' Michael's expression was reproachful. 'As used to happen several times a week when you first left.'

Matilde winced. 'I am travelling north. It is bad luck that put us together now.'

'He will be glad to have you back,' said Clippesby warmly. 'He was never the same after you left.'

'That is not why I am here,' said Matilde. 'Michael understands – I explained it to him when we met in Clare last summer.'

Clippesby gaped at the monk. 'You knew where she was, but did not tell Matt? I hope you had a good reason, because that is not the act of a friend. Indeed, not even a goat would do it, and they are notoriously unromantic.'

'He did it because I asked him to,' explained Matilde, when Michael made no attempt to defend himself. 'If I had married Matt, he would have lost his University post. I have no money of my own – I lost every penny to thieves shortly after leaving Cambridge – so he would have had to give up his poorer patients, too. He would have been unhappy, and would have grown to hate his life. And perhaps hate me, too, for bringing him to it.'

'You put me in an impossible situation,' said Michael softly. 'I have been obliged to pass remarks about you that must have made him think I was losing my wits.'

'I am sorry,' said Matilde. 'But it was for the best.'

'I beg to differ,' argued Michael. 'He does not care

206

about money, and would be happier with you regardless.' Then a vision of Julitta flashed into his mind. 'Probably.'

'On reflection, I am not so sure,' said Clippesby, making Michael regard him sharply. 'He *would* hate turning paupers away in favour of calculating horoscopes for the wealthy. He spends all his stipend on them, and I have recently learned how expensive medicines can be. He would certainly baulk at not being able to practise in what he sees as an ethical manner.'

'You see, Brother?' murmured Matilde. 'I always said Clippesby was the wisest of Michaelhouse's Fellows.'

'But you must talk to him before you go,' Clippesby continued. 'Explain your reasons. You may cajole Michael into lying for you again, but you will not persuade me.'

'Nor me, not this time,' asserted Michael. 'It was one of the most unpleasant things I have ever had to do, and that includes once abstaining from meat for the whole of Lent.'

Matilde shook her head. 'That would be too painful for both of us. But I will dictate a letter, if you will write it for me.'

'That depends on what you plan to say,' replied Michael suspiciously.

'I shall ask him not to come after me, because I will not be found,' said Matilde. 'However, I shall also say that I have decided to do something about my impoverished circumstances, and that if I succeed, I shall return to Cambridge to see whether he might be interested in . . . in a resumption of our friendship.'

'How will you succeed?' asked Michael curiously. 'By taking up burglary?'

'That would be one way, I suppose,' said Matilde with the wry smile he remembered so well. 'But I am hoping to work through more legitimate channels. An old friend has agreed to help me, and I am astute with finances. I shall do my best to acquire the fortune that will keep Matt's paupers in salves and potions.'

Michael looked sceptical, but Clippesby grinned.

'If anyone can do it, you can,' the Dominican said.

CHAPTER 7

When Bartholomew woke the following day, he found it difficult to rally his thoughts. He was lethargic, and had backache from lying in one position too long. Even so, he did not possess the energy to move, so he stared at the ceiling, watching the first tendrils of light creep across it as dawn broke. Only when he heard his colleagues stir did he sit up.

'At last!' exclaimed Michael in relief. 'I am glad to have you back, because I shall need your help today. Not to mention the fact that we have been worried. In future, perhaps you would stay away from poison.'

'Poison,' murmured Bartholomew, as events filtered slowly back into his mind.

'We have not caught the culprit yet,' said William. 'But last night was eventful, even so. First, we had news that Spalling has made Cynric his official deputy. Then Inges arrived to say that Welbyrn had died in St Leonard's well. But before either of those, Matilde came and . . .'

He trailed off, horrified with himself for the inadvertent slip. Michael glowered, Clippesby rolled his eyes, and Bartholomew wondered whether he had misheard.

'I was going to tell you after breakfast, Matt,' said the monk wearily. 'You must be hungry after lying about for so long without so much as a crumb to eat.'

Clippesby took William's arm. 'Come, Father. There

is a sparrow you should meet, one who might be able to tutor you in the art of discretion.'

'No, I want to know what—' But when William saw the dark expression on Michael's face, he left the room in what could best be described as a scurry.

When the door had closed, Michael turned warily to Bartholomew. 'Are you well enough for this? I do not think I could stand the strain of a relapse.'

Bartholomew was experiencing an awful churning in his stomach, and could tell from Michael's face that he was about to be told something he would not like.

'A drink or some food must have been laced with a soporific,' he said, aware that his speech was slurred – his tongue could not seem to form the words properly. 'But now I am awake, the effects will soon dissipate. There will be no relapse.'

'A soporific?' echoed Michael in alarm. 'Lord! I have been going around telling everyone that you were poisoned!'

'Soporifics can be toxic in the wrong hands.'

'William and Clippesby deduced that it was in the Lombard slices. I blamed the leeks, but Piel's pig ate the rest of those with no ill effects . . .'

'The leeks came from a communal pot, but the pastries appeared out of nowhere – and you left the tavern without eating any.' Bartholomew wished his wits were sharper, for he knew that Michael had managed to side-track him, but he was not alert enough to stop it.

'I learned nothing to help our investigation while you were asleep,' the monk went on. 'And the situation is now desperate, because we leave the day after tomorrow.'

'Was Matilde really here?' asked Bartholomew.

Michael ignored the question. 'Seeing what one cake did to you, I dread to imagine what would have happened had we finished the plate. We both had a very narrow escape.'

'Brother,' said Bartholomew quietly. 'Please.'

'As William said, a lot happened last night.' Michael was determined to postpone the inevitable. 'Spalling held a rally of his supporters and declared Cynric his lieutenant. According to Langelee, the announcement took Cynric by surprise, but it is a cause dear to his heart, and Langelee said he responded with delight. He intends to stay here after we leave.'

'I am sure he does. But what did Matilde—'

'Then Lullington accused you of murdering Welbyrn – your ancient feud is common knowledge, and Lullington made much of the fact that you once broke Welbyrn's nose. Ramseye defended you, though, pointing out that you were insensible at the time.'

'Ramseye did?' Bartholomew was struggling to follow the gabbled tale.

'He said you could not have walked to the door, let alone gone all the way to St Leonard's, and he argued so convincingly that I did not have to defend you myself. Of course, now everyone is flailing around for another suspect, and the usual names have been aired – Spalling, Aurifabro, Reginald, the bedesfolk . . .'

'*Has* Welbyrn been murdered?'

'I hope you will be able to tell me that when you examine his body. I ordered everything left as it was found, in the hope that there will be clues as to what happened.'

'Matilde,' prompted Bartholomew, feeling they had

211

skated around the issue quite long enough. 'What did William mean when he said she came?'

Michael took a moment to compose himself, then began, starting with how he had met her in Clare the previous year, and the vow she had extracted from him never to mention it. He finished by handing over the letter she had dictated. After he had read it, Bartholomew was silent for a very long time.

'You did not have to make that promise,' he said eventually. 'You could have refused.'

'She was very insistent.'

'You have resisted more powerful people than her.'

'I was not happy about it, believe me. So what will you do? Leave the University and set up a practice of wealthy people, so she will know she means more to you than your paupers? Wait for her to earn her own fortune? Or has she been superseded in your affections by Julitta?'

Bartholomew chose to ignore the last question. 'The Matilde I remember would not have left a letter when she could have spoken to me directly. She was never a coward.'

'She said it would have been too painful to meet in person.'

'Perhaps.' Bartholomew was silent again, before saying in a low voice, 'But I did not think *you* would keep such a thing from me.'

Michael winced. 'I told her it was a mistake, but she persuaded me that it was in your best interests – in the best interests of both of you.'

Bartholomew nodded, but made no reply, and Michael suspected, with a pang, that while Bartholomew might have lost the love of his life for the second time and perhaps permanently, he himself had just lost the trust of a friend.

The effects of whatever Bartholomew had swallowed lingered in the form of a persistent lethargy, even after he had eaten a breakfast that William assured him was safe, followed by copious amounts of his favourite cure-all – boiled barley water. He struggled to think about the news he had been given, but it was not easy when all he wanted to do was sleep, so he went for a walk, hoping fresh air would revive him. He left the abbey and turned south, but did not have the energy to go far. He stopped on the rough wooden bridge that spanned the river.

It was quiet there, with only the occasional cart rumbling past to intrude on his thoughts. A heron strutted and stabbed in the shallows, and two crows cawed in a nearby elm. The fields were full of crops that were turning gold under the summer sun, and the air was rich with the scent of warm earth and scythed grass.

He leaned on the railing and stared down at the sluggish water, wondering when he had last been beset by such a bewildering gamut of emotions. Uppermost was relief that Matilde had not been killed on the King's highways, as most of his colleagues had believed. The rest were far more complicated, and involved a confusing combination of hope, hurt, exasperation, resentment and unease.

Should he be angry with Michael for keeping a secret of such magnitude from him; a betrayal, in fact, of their friendship? The monk, more than anyone, knew the depth of his feelings for Matilde and the lengths to which he had gone to find her after she had left.

As he pondered, peculiarities in the monk's past behaviour began to make sense. The first time Michael had been to Clare he had returned sullen and snappish, and had spent the next twelve months informing Bartholomew that the place was not worth seeing. Encouraging Langelee to bring him to Peterborough had been yet another way to prevent him from going there, although it could not have misfired more badly. And finally, there was his recent uncharacteristically whimsical remark that he enjoyed Bartholomew's company – clearly he had been anticipating the day when the truth would come out.

But Michael had not asked to be placed in such an invidious position, and it would be unfair to blame him for what had happened. Although Bartholomew was exasperated with him – and disappointed that he had allowed himself to be browbeaten by Matilde – he bore him no malice, and supposed he had better say so lest the incident drove a wedge between them. Michaelhouse was too small for two of its Fellows to be at loggerheads, and when all was said and done, Michael had been a good friend in the past.

He watched a leaf undulate under the bridge. Should he abandon his University, patients and students a second time, and try to find Matilde, despite the plea in her letter that begged him not to? Should he resign his Fellowship and start recruiting wealthy patients so that she knew he would produce horoscopes for the rich if it meant her return? Or should he put her from his mind, on the grounds that the woman he had loved would not have been afraid to face him, and that time and experience might have turned her into a different person?

Her letter had outlined a complex plan that involved borrowing money and making certain investments. She seemed confident that it would work – the only question being the time it would take – and she would then return to Cambridge. As money had never been important to him, it seemed inconceivable that it should be the thing that stood between him and happiness, but he was not so naïve as to believe that everyone felt that way. And Matilde was a woman of refined tastes.

But what about Julitta? Her arrival in his life had reminded him that Matilde was not the only woman in the world. Did that mean his love for Matilde had diminished, and he should refuse her if she arrived back with a fortune in her purse? His relationship with Julitta was still fairly new, but he knew he could come to love her just as deeply in time. Of course, she was already married, and so would never be fully available to him, unless something fatal happened to Surgeon Holm. But what if—

'I thought I might find you here.'

He whipped around to see Cynric standing beside him. He had not heard the book-bearer approach, and the Welshman's eyes gleamed in the knowledge that he had not lost the ability to creep up behind his master and startle him out of his wits.

'I came to tell you that she has gone,' said Cynric. 'Matilde, I mean. Last night, Father William came to tell me what had happened, so we went to see if we could persuade her to stay. We managed to locate the inn where she had been lodging, but she had already left.'

'Did the taverner know where she might be going?'

'She was careful to let nothing slip. I spent the rest of the night searching the roads, but she left no trace of her passing.' Cynric's dark face was grudgingly impressed. 'I can track most people, as you know, but she eluded me. She might have gone in any direction, and I doubt you will catch her. But if you want to try, I will go with you.'

'I thought you had been made Spalling's deputy.'

Cynric nodded proudly. 'But I am willing to leave him for a while, to help you with Matilde.'

'Perhaps I should accept. It would keep you out of trouble.'

'You mean with Spalling? But he is right, boy. The poor have been poor long enough, and it is time to put matters right. You will join us eventually – you are not a man to sit by while injustices are done. I would not have stayed with you so long if you were.'

'There is a difference between wanting justice and insurgency, Cynric. Besides, Spalling does not seem entirely rational to me.'

'Only because you are poisoned and your wits are awry. But here he is, come to collect me. We are off to Aurifabro's shop again, to berate him for suppressing his workers.'

'You mean the workers who say he is a generous employer?' Bartholomew held up his hands in surrender when he saw Cynric ready to argue; he did not feel equal to debating the morality of England's social order that morning, and wished he had held his tongue.

Spalling had taken care with his dress that day, and had donned an outfit reminiscent of a ploughboy's, although his fine calfskin boots had never been anywhere near a field.

'Want to come, physician?' he asked amiably. 'You will enjoy watching that villain Aurifabro denounced for his greed and miserliness.'

'No, thank you,' said Bartholomew coolly.

'You prefer to let me tackle him on your behalf,' nodded Spalling, although without rancour. 'I heard Oxforde was the same. Did you know that he stole from the rich in order to ease the lives of Peterborough's peasants?'

'I think you will find he stole from the rich in order to benefit himself,' countered Bartholomew, disinclined to listen to such fanciful nonsense.

'That is a tale put about by his detractors,' argued Spalling. 'And if he was not a saint, then why have there been miracles at his tomb?'

He flung an arm across Cynric's shoulders and they strode away together, leaving the physician wondering how Spalling could have drawn such wild conclusions about Oxforde, whose ruthless brutality was a matter of record. With a sigh, he supposed it was a case of a man changing history to suit himself.

Although Michael had promised that Bartholomew would be spared more meals in the refectory, he insisted that they attend the one that was to be held mid-morning, because Yvo was going to make an announcement about Welbyrn, and he wanted all his Michaelhouse colleagues there as observers. It was a sombre affair.

Welbyrn's seat was ominously empty, and everyone kept glancing at it, stunned by what had happened. Appletre wept copiously, but Yvo informed the scholars *sotto voce* that he always cried when someone died, so they should ignore him. Henry sat next to the sobbing precentor, murmuring comforting words.

Bartholomew was reluctant to eat, partly because Matilde had robbed him of his appetite, but mostly because he did not fancy being poisoned a second time. He took some bread and cheese, but only after the obedientiaries had sampled them first. He was aware of Michael, William and Clippesby doing the same, although such restraint was clearly difficult for the portly Senior Proctor.

'Welbyrn's accident comes as a great shock to us all,' Yvo proclaimed at the end of the meal. 'Yet perhaps it is a blessed release. He has not been himself these last few weeks.'

'No,' agreed Ramseye. 'As exemplified by his insistence that the Abbot is still alive.'

'And his short temper,' added Appletre, hand to the front of his habit, where the treasurer had laid hold of it during his explosion in the chapter house.

'How did he die, Father Prior?' called someone from the body of the hall. 'Only there have been rumours . . .'

'I am sure there have,' said Yvo curtly. 'But the truth is this: Welbyrn went to St Leonard's well in the dark, but the steps are slippery, and he fell. A tragic mishap.'

'And I would remind you all that idle gossip is a sin and should be beneath you,' added Nonton sternly, casting a cool but bleary eye around the gathering that had more than one monk blushing in shame.

'Welbyrn will be missed,' declared Yvo, scowling at the cellarer for voicing something he wished he had said himself. 'God rest his soul.'

'What about his replacement?' asked Ramseye.

Bartholomew was surprised by the almoner's dispassionate response to the death of a man he had known all his life – and who had been backing his bid to be Abbot into the bargain. Henry shook his head in silent disapproval at the question, and there were raised eyebrows and grimaces from the other monks, although it was impossible to tell whether they thought like Henry, or felt relief that a more stable man could now be appointed to the post.

'Appletre will be treasurer,' announced Yvo. 'He can start today.'

He glanced at Lullington, who nodded encouragingly. The knight was resplendent in another set of new clothes, and had doused himself so liberally with perfume that he had attracted flies. Meanwhile, Appletre was gazing at the Prior in horror.

'But I do not know anything about money,' he objected. 'There must be a better choice than me. For example, Henry, who is—'

'I have made my decision,' interrupted Yvo. 'You will be our new treasurer, and I shall take over the precentor's duties myself, concurrently with being Prior.'

'But you cannot sing!' cried Appletre, appalled.

'Nonsense,' snapped Yvo. 'I have a beautiful voice, and it is time it was heard.'

'No!' Appletre was becoming tearful again. 'I cannot, not so soon after Welbyrn. It is not right. Please! Let us have time to mourn.'

219

'We will mourn,' said Yvo coolly. 'However, an abbey's finances wait for no man, so you will assume your duties with immediate effect.'

'Do as he says, Appletre,' advised Ramseye. 'It will only be for three days, because the new Abbot *will* rescind this decision.'

Appletre smiled gratefully in response to his meaningful look, and Bartholomew supposed it was one way of securing a vote. Not everyone was impressed, however.

'You intend the election to go ahead?' asked Henry, for once forgetting himself and speaking without due deference. 'Even though two high-ranking officers now lie dead? Surely it is now even more important to wait for the Bishop's Commissioners to—'

'Welbyrn's death is irrelevant to who becomes Abbot,' interrupted Lullington.

'But Father Prior,' objected Henry, standing up and glancing at his fellow monks as he did so. All were nodding their support. 'I do not feel this is right.'

He had ignored the corrodian, but it was Lullington who replied anyway. 'These are uncertain times, and we need an *abbot* to lead us. A prior does not carry the same authority, and we cannot afford to be perceived as weak.'

'That is right,' agreed Yvo. 'Now sit down, Henry, before I make you spend the rest of the year in the vegetable garden.'

Henry sat abruptly.

'We had better inspect Welbyrn's body,' said Michael, in the silence that followed. 'The Bishop will want to know exactly what happened to him. Did you leave everything as you found it, as I asked, so I may draw upon the expertise of my Corpse Examiner?'

'We did,' said Ramseye in distaste. 'Although I cannot see why such unpleasantness is necessary. Must Bartholomew be given licence to paw Welbyrn's mortal remains?'

'He will be able to tell whether there has been foul play,' said Michael coldly. 'I cannot begin to count the number of killers we have caught with his skills and my wits. No wicked villain has ever gained the better of us. And none ever will.'

His words echoed around the refectory like a challenge, and Bartholomew closed his eyes. Such hubris was asking for someone to make another assault on their lives.

'You will find nothing amiss,' growled Nonton irritably. 'As Prior Yvo just told you, it was an accident.'

'If so, then Matt will confirm it,' said Michael, kicking Bartholomew under the table when the physician started to say that he might be able to do nothing of the kind.

'Very well,' said Ramseye. 'Shall we go now? The bedesmen are eager to open their chapel to pilgrims, but they cannot do it with a corpse bobbing in their healing well.'

'You left Welbyrn *in* the water?' Bartholomew was shocked.

'Michael said nothing should be moved,' replied Ramseye blandly. 'So nothing was. Far be it from us to disobey the Bishop's Commissioner.'

Michael glared at him. 'You know I did not mean you to leave Welbyrn soaking! It was the rest of the chapel that I wanted left as it was found.'

'Then you should have made yourself clear. We did exactly as you ordered.'

'We did,' smirked Lullington. 'After all, *we* do not want to be accused of murder.'

'As you accused Matt?' asked Michael archly. 'Even though he was insensible at the time, and incapable of doing anything?'

'He was an obvious suspect, given their past antipathies,' argued Lullington.

'Welbyrn was far more likely to have murdered Matthew than the other way around,' said Ramseye. '*He* was the one who bore the grudge. It is a pity you can no longer ask him whether he acted on it by sending a gift of poison.'

A sizeable deputation accompanied the two scholars to St Leonard's Hospital. Michael led the way, Yvo and Lullington hard on his heels, both regaling him with theories about how Welbyrn might have come to fall. The monk's face was expressionless, but he was wondering why they were so determined that Welbyrn's demise should be deemed an accident.

Bartholomew was next, with Ramseye, Henry and Appletre. Nonton was behind them, stopping occasionally to take a swig from the flask he had hidden in his sleeve. A flock of monks, lay brethren and townsfolk followed, while the bedeswomen brought up the rear, gleeful that they were not the only ones to suffer the inconvenience of a corpse in their holy places.

Bartholomew was now marginally more alert, although his spirits were low – a combination of hurt that Matilde had not waited to speak to him, a residual vexation with Michael that he suspected would take a while to wear off, and sadness that Cynric would no longer play such a large role in his life.

'Are you sure you are recovered, Matt?' asked Henry kindly. 'You are oddly quiet.'

'Just tired.' Bartholomew knew Henry would be a sympathetic confidant, but his feelings were too raw to be shared with anyone else just yet.

'I do not want to be treasurer,' said Appletre miserably. 'I am a musician, not a financier. I shall have the abbey in debt within a month.'

'You only need do it for three days,' Ramseye reminded him. 'At which point, the new Abbot will appoint someone else. It is high time we had a treasurer who knew what he was doing, anyway. Welbyrn did his best, but he was out of his depth.'

'Do not speak ill of the dead,' said Henry sharply, not seeming to care that he was berating a superior. 'He was meticulous and honest.'

'And mean,' added Ramseye. 'Which is what he will be remembered for.'

Henry opened his mouth to argue, but apparently could think of nothing to refute the remark, so he closed it again without speaking.

'He was unquestionably loyal to Robert, though,' said Appletre.

'Yes,' acknowledged Ramseye with a weary sigh. 'Including his ridiculous assertion that my uncle is still in the land of the living.'

'Perhaps he is,' sniffed Appletre. 'I cannot believe

that God would deprive us of treasurer, Abbot *and* physician within a few weeks. Maybe Robert and Pyk are kidnapped, not dead.'

'If that were true, a ransom demand would have been received by now,' said Ramseye. 'Or perhaps one was, but someone decided not to pay it.'

Appletre regarded him in horror. 'Then we must search for them at once! I will—'

'Search the Fens?' Ramseye's voice was scathing. 'How do you propose we do that?'

'But who would do such a wicked thing?' asked Henry doubtfully. 'If the letter is not acknowledged, the kidnappers may harm their victims. Or even kill them.'

'Quite,' said Ramseye pointedly. 'Which brings me back to my original contention – that my uncle is dead. We need another abbot in post as quickly as possible, and the sooner I am elected, the sooner I can begin to put things right.'

'Do you really think you will win?' asked Henry wonderingly.

Ramseye regarded him haughtily. 'When the alternative is Yvo? Of course! He has been Acting Abbot since Robert disappeared, but look at what has happened during his reign: a bedeswoman murdered, our treasurer dead in a sacred well, and the Bishop's Commissioners probing our affairs. May I count on your support?'

'Yes,' nodded Appletre eagerly. 'So I can be precentor again.'

'And you shall be my almoner, Henry,' said Ramseye when the other monk remained silent. 'Just think of how much you could do for hungry beggars if you held such a post.'

Bartholomew was appalled, sure Ramseye was saying that the poor might suffer if Henry did not do as he was told. Appletre changed the subject, and Henry shot him a grateful glance that he would not be pressed for an answer there and then.

'Inges has been telling everyone that Welbyrn was murdered.' The precentor shook his head slowly. 'But I cannot believe it. Who would want to kill Welbyrn?'

'A great many people,' replied Ramseye. 'He had become something of a bully recently, so there are many who will be pleased that he is no longer with us.'

'Including you?' asked Bartholomew, before he could stop himself.

Ramseye raised his eyebrows. 'Me? I wanted him alive. He and Nonton were going to help me win the election, and his death is a blow to my cause. I am deeply sorry he is gone.'

But there was something in his voice that set alarm bells ringing in Bartholomew's mind. He stared at his old tutor, struggling to read his bland expression, but then Appletre started to talk about the music he thought would be suitable for Welbyrn's requiem mass, and the moment was gone.

There was a delay before the deputation could enter St Leonard's, because the bedesmen called out that they were praying. Hagar snorted in disbelief, but Yvo declared that such an activity could not possibly be interrupted, grinning his triumph when several monks nodded approval of his pious decision. While they waited for the bedesmen to finish their devotions – although clunks and scrapes from inside suggested rather that a hasty spring-clean was in progress – Yvo began to inform the onlookers that he had always admired the bedesfolk's dedication to their religious duties. Ramseye did not demean himself with brazen electioneering, though he did not object when Nonton did it for him.

Bartholomew had no wish to listen, so he went to stare along the road that led to Torpe, wondering what had happened to the two men who had ridden along it on St Swithin's Day. His thoughts were still annoyingly sluggish, and he took several deep breaths in an effort to clear them. He stifled a groan when Ramseye came to stand next to him.

'If your work as a Corpse Examiner entails dissections, you might be wise to restrain yourself while you are here,' the almoner warned. 'The townsfolk are unlikely to be very understanding of such practices, and you may find yourself decried as a warlock.'

Bartholomew's immediate assumption was that an uneasy conscience had prompted the advice – that Ramseye was worried about what clues might have been left on Welbyrn's body.

'I am not an anatomist,' he said, then smiled, aiming to disconcert. 'But such techniques are rarely necessary, because the evidence is usually obvious.'

'Is it?' Ramseye's expression was closed, and Bartholomew could read nothing in it. 'The things you know, Matthew! It has certainly been an experience meeting you again.'

'And you,' said Bartholomew, a little deflated that his ploy had not worked.

'You sound tired.' Ramseye studied him closely. 'Not

fully recovered from your brush with death. I never touch cakes, personally. I have always held them to be dangerous.'

Bartholomew glanced sharply at him. Had *he* poisoned the Lombard slices? Ramseye regarded him with a hurt expression, guessing exactly what he was thinking.

'I have nothing to fear from the Bishop's Commissioners, and nor do I have any desire to see them dead. However, if you will accept perilous missions, like investigating missing abbots, then you must expect attempts on your life.'

Bartholomew frowned. Had he and his colleagues just been threatened? This time, if Ramseye knew what he was thinking, he did not acknowledge it.

'You owe me your thanks, by the way,' the almoner said with a smile. 'When fingers started pointing in your direction blaming you for Welbyrn's demise, it was I who defended you.'

'Yes, I heard.' Bartholomew forced himself to sound grateful, although in reality the discussion was reminding him of why he had so detested Ramseye's classes and had done his best to disrupt them. 'Thank you.'

Ramseye shrugged. 'It was the truth. None of you left the guest house last night.'

Bartholomew was puzzled. 'Were you watching us? Why?'

'Honestly? Because I was worried that your fat friend might accuse me if you succumbed to that toxin – I imagine you told him that I was a less than kindly tutor. Of course, it was a long time ago, and I am a different man now.'

Not so different, thought Bartholomew, taking in the sly eyes and silkily cajoling voice. 'And Welbyrn? Had he changed as well?'

Ramseye shrugged. 'I really cannot say. We had very little to do with each other outside the routine course of our duties, and rarely spoke socially.'

'You just told me that he supported you in your aim to be Abbot,' Bartholomew pointed out. 'Along with Nonton.'

'The Unholy Trinity, as everyone likes to call us,' sighed Ramseye. 'I do not associate with them from choice, but because it is expedient. Yvo would be a disastrous ruler, whereas I will be just, generous and enlightened.'

Bartholomew could think of nothing to say to such a claim, and they stood in silence for a while. A gentle breeze ruffled the crops in the fields, and distant rain scented the air.

'Poor Welbyrn,' said Ramseye eventually. 'Even with the limited contact we shared, I could see he was an unhappy man. I imagine it was because he knew he fell short as a monk – as sanctimonious men like Henry were always ready to remind him.'

'Henry would never do that,' objected Bartholomew.

'Perhaps not in words, but glances can say a great deal. Henry was very vocal in his silence, and Welbyrn knew exactly what he thought of him.'

'Then why did Welbyrn not try to rectify the matter? Become a better man?'

'That is easier said than done. Could you change your nature so easily? Give up what you are, in order to become something others want you to be?'

Bartholomew supposed he might find out if Matilde returned to Cambridge with a fortune at her disposal.

228

CHAPTER 8

When the Bishop's Commissioners and their unofficial entourage of monastics and townsfolk were eventually admitted to the hospital, it was to find it spotlessly clean. Freshly cut rushes had been scattered on the floor, the furniture had been dusted and little pots of fragrant summer flowers sat on the windowsills. The residents had also benefited from an overhaul. Hair had been brushed, beards trimmed and robes sponged. Even Simon the cowherd had been groomed; he sat in a corner whispering to himself.

'Welcome to our domain,' said Inges, haughty and proud in his finery. 'We have done as you asked: the chapel has been shut ever since we made our terrible discovery.'

'Good,' said Lullington, sailing inside on a wave of expensive perfume that made the older man sneeze. 'Will you show us the body?'

'I thought he had an aversion to corpses,' murmured Michael to Bartholomew.

'Just his wife's, it would seem,' Bartholomew muttered back.

'You had better tell us what happened, Inges,' said Michael, stepping into the hall and closing the door before anyone other than Bartholomew, Yvo and Ramseye could follow. There was a collective sigh of disappointment from the excluded spectators.

'It was me who found him,' said Botilbrig excitedly. 'I came to fetch a flask of holy water for Kirwell just after compline last night, and there was Welbyrn floating in the well. I raised the alarm, and Prior Inges sent word to the abbey—'

'And I locked the chapel when a messenger arrived to say that we should leave everything as it was discovered,' finished Inges. 'However, I want that corpse out of our spring, Father Prior, and then I want St Leonard's resanctified, like you did for the bedeswomen.'

'Today, if possible,' added Botilbrig. 'Kirwell is still waiting for his drink, and we have had to turn three pilgrims away already this morning – folk who would have left donations.'

'That depends on Brother Michael,' replied Yvo. 'But he is a practical man who understands the importance of revenue. He will not waste time.'

'You consider investigating Welbyrn's death wasting time?' asked Michael coolly.

'Of course not,' sighed Yvo irritably. 'But running a large abbey is expensive, and we cannot afford to lose money, as Welbyrn himself would have said had he not been . . . Besides, you have less than two days before you must leave, so you are not in a position to dawdle.'

Michael turned his back on him, not bothering to mask his distaste. 'I have been told that Welbyrn was in the habit of coming here late at night. Is it true?'

'I suppose I can be honest with you now that he is not in a position to punch my teeth out,' replied the bedesman. 'Which he threatened to do if I ever mentioned his visits to anyone else. You see, he had an affliction, and claimed our healing waters eased his discomfort.'

'What kind of affliction?' asked Bartholomew curiously.

'I think it had something to do with his intellectuals.' Inges sniggered unpleasantly. 'Maybe he feared he was losing them – and he did not have many to start with, no matter how much he liked to pretend otherwise.'

There was a chorus of wry agreement from the other bedesmen.

'You may be right, Inges,' said Ramseye thoughtfully. 'About a month ago, he mentioned that he was struggling to remember certain things. Perhaps his mind *was* beginning to fail.'

'Matt will identify the problem when he examines him,' stated Michael.

Bartholomew blinked. 'How am I supposed to deduce such a thing from a corpse? Even the dissectors at Salerno and Padua failed to—'

'Dissectors?' pounced Ramseye. 'I thought you said you were not an anatomist.'

'I am not,' said Bartholomew, wishing his wits were sharper, because he would never have made such a slip had he been himself. 'However, I have seen them at work, and there are no obvious changes in the brain that can be associated with—'

'You *watched* a coven of ghouls chop up someone's head?' asked Ramseye in horror. 'But that is the Devil's work!'

There was a murmur of consternation from the bedesmen and monks, who promptly began to ease away. So did Lullington, his face pale. Bartholomew looked at Ramseye and saw malice behind the façade of disquiet.

'We did not come here to listen to your views on dissection,' snapped Michael, intervening quickly before the situation became any worse. 'We came to investigate what happened to Welbyrn, which, as I am sure you will agree, is a far more pressing matter. Now, who let him in last night?'

'No one – he had his own key,' replied Inges, although his wary glance was fixed on Bartholomew. 'He liked to visit at night, you see, when the place was empty. I refused to let him have one at first, but he threatened to raise our taxes, so I gave in. That was about two months ago. Since then, he has come several times a week.'

'I saw him once, Brother,' said Bartholomew. 'He left the door ajar, and Simon escaped. He was oddly furtive the whole time, and threatened to thrash me if I suggested to anyone that he might be ill.'

'So he arrived unannounced and began . . . doing what?' asked Michael of the bedesmen. 'Bathing in the well? Drinking the water? Praying?'

'He usually got down on his knees and scooped a few handfuls of water over his head,' supplied Botilbrig. He shrugged when Inges regarded him in surprise. 'I was interested, and decided to find out what was wrong, but I never did manage to overhear his prayers.' He sounded indignant, as if he thought Welbyrn had made spying difficult on purpose.

'Did any of you hear him arrive last night?' asked Michael.

There were a lot of shaken heads.

'He only came when he was sure he would have the place to himself,' said Inges. 'He might have gone undiscovered until this morning had Kirwell not asked for some water.'

232

'Poor Welbyrn,' said Ramseye flatly. 'Whatever did he think he was doing?'

Michael was keen for Bartholomew to examine the body so that they could leave, but the young priest Trentham appeared from upstairs and said that Kirwell needed a physician. With an irritable sigh, Michael indicated that Bartholomew should see what the old man wanted. Bartholomew obliged, disconcerted when everyone followed him up the stairs and crowded into the old man's bedchamber on his heels, jostling him and each other as they vied for a place inside.

'He may dispense a blessing, you see,' explained Inges. 'And he has been rather niggardly with those since Abbot Robert went missing. We cannot afford to miss out – it is his saintly benedictions that keep us all hale and hearty, after all.'

'Be careful, Kirwell,' called Ramseye from the back of the room. 'This physician has watched anatomists chop off other people's heads.'

'We will not let him have yours, Kirwell, do not worry,' said Inges comfortingly. Then he lowered his voice and gripped Bartholomew's arm with surprising strength. 'If you harm him, I will see you burned alive in the market-place.'

Bartholomew could see he was serious, and was half tempted to leave, just in case Kirwell chose that particular day to give up the ghost. But he had sworn oaths to help those in need, and was unwilling to break them. He stepped forward, and so did everyone else.

'I am not blessing anyone, so you can all go away,'

snapped Kirwell. 'Trentham may stay, but the rest can clear out. Go on! You, too, Inges.'

There were resentful mutters, but the onlookers did as they were told, and it was not long before Bartholomew, Trentham and Kirwell were alone. At a gesture from the old man, Trentham closed the door, which was followed by the distinct sound of Botilbrig hissing his annoyance that he was to be deprived of an opportunity to eavesdrop.

'How much longer?' whispered Kirwell, when Bartholomew went to stand next to his bed. 'How much longer must I live?'

'I do not know,' replied Bartholomew shortly. 'Is there anything else I can do for you?'

'You could prescribe a remedy for his knee,' suggested Trentham. 'It pains him badly.'

Bartholomew inspected the inflamed joint, then began to rub a cooling salve into it. Trentham held Kirwell's hand while he worked, a liberty Bartholomew would never have taken with such a curmudgeonly fellow. It was clear that the priest possessed a rare way with his elderly charges, and had won their irascible hearts with his gentle compassion.

'I wish I had never seen that light over Oxforde's grave,' said Kirwell bitterly, his expression distant as he reflected on events from long ago.

'Hush,' said Trentham softly. 'You were honoured to witness such a miracle, and—'

'It was not a miracle,' interrupted Kirwell harshly. 'Although I have let everyone think it was. It was just sunlight, as Doctor Bartholomew said when he first came to see me. And now I am being punished for my deception with this terrible, lingering life.'

'No,' said Trentham kindly. 'I do not believe you would—'

'Even then, I was almost blind,' Kirwell went on. 'And I was frightened for my future. I lied about what had happened because I wanted a place in this hospital.'

'But there were other miracles afterwards,' argued Trentham. 'It was not just the shaft of brilliance on an otherwise gloomy day. It was the first wondrous event of many.'

'All of which can be explained by wishful thinking or happenstance,' countered Kirwell. 'Headaches cured, a lost purse found, a long-absent soldier returned, a promotion granted. There is nothing holy about Oxforde, and there never was.'

'Then tell the Bishop,' suggested Bartholomew. He had encountered other shrines that had grown out of lies or misunderstandings, and so was not surprised to learn that Oxforde's was no different, although he was aware of Trentham's growing dismay at the revelations. 'He does not want the cult to thrive, and if you denounce it, his task will be made easier.'

'Yes,' said Kirwell softly. 'I think I must. Oxforde was the most evil man who ever lived, and it is a travesty that he should be venerated.'

'But this happened forty-five years ago,' Trentham pointed out, stunned. 'Why wait until now to tell the truth?'

Kirwell scowled. 'I did not wait until now – I have been saying it for the last decade, but no one has listened. Bring your writing equipment the next time you come, lad, and I shall dictate a letter to Gynewell – it would be a burden lifted. However, you cannot send it until I die. I cannot afford to be thrown out of St Leonard's at this stage of my life.'

Trentham nodded, although Bartholomew thought the old man could not be very sorry for his years of deceit if he was unwilling to accept the consequences. But Bartholomew was not a priest, and it was Trentham's duty to lecture him about contrition. Trentham, however, was more interested in hearing about Oxforde, pressing the old man for details with a guileless curiosity that reminded them both that he was still very young.

'You accompanied him right to the scaffold?' he asked, eyes alight with interest.

Kirwell nodded. 'Yes, and he showed not a whit of remorse. He thought he would be reprieved right up until the noose tightened around his neck. I have never known such arrogance before or since. Did you hear how he came to be caught?'

'No.' Trentham was spellbound.

'A wealthy silversmith had died a few weeks earlier, and there were rumours that the fellow had bought the plot next to his grave for some of his favourite jewels. Oxforde was in the process of digging for them when the Sheriff himself happened across him.'

'Was there a fight?'

'Not really. Oxforde was so convinced that the King would pardon him, that he saw no need to risk himself with the Sheriff's blade. Anyway, I decided that he should be buried in the hole he himself had dug, because there was a fear that the Devil would raise him up if he was put in unconsecrated soil like other executed felons.'

'I had forgotten that,' said Bartholomew. The threat that Oxforde would come for them if they misbehaved

236

was one that had been used to keep the abbey schoolboys in check.

'He would have been furious if he could have seen how the abbey has benefited from his death,' Kirwell went on with a distinctly impious smirk. 'Making money hand over fist from donations to his shrine. He hated the Church.'

'Are any of his victims still alive?' Trentham's eyes were like saucers.

'He usually killed witnesses to his crimes, which is why he remained free for so long. God alone knows how many lives he took. I have long been amazed that those who lived through his reign of terror should have forgotten his true character.'

'You mean bedeswomen like Hagar, who tell pilgrims that he was holy?' asked Trentham. 'The bedes*men* say he was wicked, though, and I have always wondered who was right.'

Kirwell waved a dismissive hand. 'The men denounce Oxforde solely to annoy the women, and if his tomb was moved to St Leonard's they would be delighted to exploit him there. But never mind this. I am so tired, Doctor. Surely there is something you can do for me? It is not right that a man should live for so long.'

'It is beyond my control,' replied Bartholomew. 'And you are not in serious discomfort. Not like poor Lady Lullington.'

'No,' acknowledged Kirwell. 'She used to visit me, and tell me stories about her clever sons. She was a good woman, and I was sorry when I heard she was ill. Pyk never did discover what was wrong with her. She was struck down very suddenly.'

'Illnesses often do that.'

'Not like this, according to Pyk.'

'It is true.' Trentham's boyish enthusiasm for Kirwell's tales had gone, replaced by sadness as he contemplated his dead friend. 'She became ill shortly after Robert went missing, and I always wondered if her husband did something to her. I told Yvo, but he said nothing could be proved one way or the other.'

'She is at peace now, poor soul,' said Kirwell. 'As I should be. Are you sure you—'

'Yes,' said Bartholomew firmly.

When Bartholomew returned to the hall he found Michael engaged in a futile effort to reduce the number of people who intended to watch a Corpse Examiner at work.

'We bedesmen have a right to be here,' Inges was declaring indignantly. 'It is our chapel, and we should be allowed to watch what happens in it.'

'Actually, it is the *abbey's* chapel,' countered Yvo. 'And Welbyrn was our treasurer, so I should be here to ensure that justice is done for him.'

'No, that honour should fall to me,' argued Nonton. He had availed himself of the bedesmen's wine, and was unsteady on his feet. 'Welbyrn was my friend.'

'We shall *all* watch,' determined Ramseye. 'Although Lullington claims he has an aversion to corpses, so perhaps he should wait outside.'

Lullington adopted a martyred expression. 'It cannot be worse than seeing my poor wife. I shall stay. It is the least I can do to repay my debt of gratitude to the abbey for its care of me.'

'So you are stuck with us all, Brother,' said Ramseye with a victorious smile. 'But we shall stand well back – for our own safety as much as the Corpse Examiner's convenience.'

'Too right,' muttered Botilbrig. 'This robe was clean on this morning.'

Bartholomew wondered what they were expecting him to do. 'It will only—'

'Do not try to explain, Matt,' advised Michael in a low voice. 'You will make matters worse, and it is easier just to let them observe. Unless you plan on doing something macabre, in which case I had better use the Bishop's authority to oust them.'

'Of course not,' said Bartholomew irritably.

'You cannot blame me for asking.' Michael raised his hands defensively. 'You have done some perfectly dreadful things to corpses in the past, things that have shocked me.'

Without further ado, Inges led the way to the well. No one spoke and the chapel was eerily silent, the only sounds being the lap of water and the scrape of feet on flagstones.

The treasurer lay face down, arms floating out to his sides. The angle of his head made it appear that he was looking for something he had lost on the bottom. Bartholomew set about fishing him out. Unfortunately, the stones at the pool's edge were slick, and the listlessness that had afflicted him since dawn made him careless. He was on his knees, leaning forward to grab Welbyrn's sleeve, when he lost his balance.

Michael reacted with commendable speed and caught him before more than his head had dipped below the surface. The water was shockingly cold, yet if it was unpleasant, it did dispel the sluggishness that still lingered from the soporific.

'I could have told you it was slippery,' said Ramseye, exchanging a smirk with Nonton, while Lullington brayed his mirth out loud, a jeering, mocking, inappropriate sound that echoed harshly around the chapel's ancient stone arches.

'So could Welbyrn,' muttered Yvo.

Wordlessly, Botilbrig handed Bartholomew a frayed piece of sacking. As there was a pile of similar scraps on a nearby bench, the physician could only assume that such accidents occurred on a fairly regular basis. He wiped his face, then watched as Nonton helped Michael to retrieve Welbyrn and lay him by the side of the pool.

When they stepped away, he knelt and pressed on Welbyrn's chest. Foam emerged from the nose and mouth, which meant that water had mixed with air in the lungs – in other words, the treasurer had been alive when he had gone into the water, and the cause of death was almost certainly drowning.

Ignoring the exclamations of disgust from his audience, he inspected Welbyrn's body for other marks or abrasions. Ramseye was particularly vocal, although Bartholomew was only looking and feeling – nothing that should have horrified anyone. He hesitated before opening Welbyrn's mouth, but then did it anyway, feeling it would be wrong to perform an incomplete examination just because the onlookers were squeamish.

At last, he sat back. 'There is only one unusual mark,' he said, pointing to a faint bruise on Welbyrn's forehead.

It was long and straight. 'This suggests that he may have hit his head on the side of the well. I have just demonstrated how easy it is to fall, and he came at night, when it was dark.'

'An accident,' declared Yvo with satisfaction. 'Just as I told you.'

Ramseye peered over Bartholomew's shoulder. 'Do you mean that tiny blemish? But it is almost invisible! I seriously doubt *that* had any bearing on his demise.'

'On the contrary, it would have been enough to stun him,' said Bartholomew shortly, disliking the almoner contradicting him on a matter that lay well outside the fellow's area of expertise. 'And remember, it does not take long to drown. However, he may also have been pushed.'

'It is more likely to have been suicide,' stated Botilbrig. 'He tossed himself in the well deliberately, because he was alarmed by the fact that he was losing his intellectuals.'

'Oh, I imagine he was pushed,' said Inges. 'No one liked him, and this is the kind of thing that happens to unpopular people.'

'Lord!' exclaimed Michael suddenly, recoiling in distaste. He was examining the dead man's clothes, which Bartholomew had removed and passed to him, and he had just reached Welbyrn's scrip.

What spilled out when he had upended it was a sticky bundle wrapped in cloth, to which adhered an assortment of coins, some illegible documents and the hospital key. Michael wiped his fingers fastidiously on a piece of linen, and indicated that Bartholomew was to separate the mess. The physician obliged only because refusing would have prolonged their stay – and he was oppressed by the shadowy chapel and was eager to leave. He poked at the goo with one of his surgical blades, uninterestedly at first, but with increasing urgency when he realised its significance. He looked up at Michael.

'It is a packet of Lombard slices.'

Ducking his head in cold water had not only expunged the lingering effects of the soporific, it had imbued Bartholomew with new energy. Matilde was a sharply gnawing pain in his heart, but although it was more acute than usual, it was one that had been with him ever since she had left Cambridge and he was used to it. And as he was disinclined to examine his feelings about her, the best way to avoid this was to turn his mind to other matters.

'Where first?' he asked briskly, after he and Michael had pushed through the inquisitive throng that still clustered around the hospital door and were walking back to the town.

'To see Pyk's wife. I have tried several times, but she is always out.' Michael shot him a sidelong glance. 'Perhaps Inges is right to claim his well has healing properties: you seem much happier now than you were an hour ago. Or has mauling the corpse of an old adversary put you in a better mood?'

Bartholomew winced, and hoped no one else would think so. 'The water was unusually cold – like ice – so a dousing will always be invigorating. However, I am not sure it has *healing* properties as such and—'

'I am having second thoughts about being Abbot here,' interrupted Michael, sensing a lecture on medicine in the offing and hastening to avert it. 'The monastery is wealthy, attractive and influential, but there are too many disagreeable residents. Of course, unless we find answers soon, we might lose a few more to mysterious circumstances. So tell me what you discovered back there: what really happened to Welbyrn?'

As it transpired, the germ of a solution *had* started to form at the back of Bartholomew's mind. He was silent for a moment, struggling to piece it together from what he had observed and learned during his encounters with his old tutor.

'Welbyrn was unwell. He grew angry when it was mentioned and denied it vigorously, but the fact that he availed himself of St Leonard's curative waters indicates that he knew something was wrong.'

'He did not look healthy. What ailed him? Did your examination reveal it?'

'No. I would need to look inside him for—'

'Then we shall never know, because I am not condoning that sort of activity. At least, not here, where our every move is being carefully monitored.'

'I was not suggesting it as an option; I was pointing out that I cannot give you answers with the kind of examination I *am* allowed to conduct. However, there were no obvious external symptoms, no disturbance to his appetite and no indication that he was in pain.'

'So what are you saying? That he was *not* ill?'

'It is possible. However, he certainly thought he was.'

Michael regarded him balefully. 'I have no idea what you are trying to tell me.'

'He was ashamed of whatever he believed was wrong with him – he visited the hospital at night, when the place was empty, and he threatened violence to anyone he feared might reveal his secret. Inges said he had taken to asking after Simon the cowherd recently, demanding to know whether there was any improvement in his condition.'

'And?' Michael was growing exasperated. 'What of it?'

'I suspect he was terrified that he might be going the same way.'

'So what Inges said in jest was right – Welbyrn *was* losing his intellectuals?'

'He told Ramseye that he kept forgetting things, but although Ramseye does not seem to have paid it much heed, I think Welbyrn actually disclosed something that was a genuine cause of concern to him.'

'So *was* he going mad?'

'The fact that he thought he was is probably an indication that he was not – the genuinely deranged do not see anything amiss with their behaviour, which is part of the problem. But Welbyrn, being proud and stubborn, refused to seek help. His fear gnawed at him, making him more aggressive.'

'Yes – we have been told that his belligerence had escalated recently.'

'We will never be able to prove any of this now he is dead. However, if it is true, then I am sorry. No one deserves to think that he is losing his mind.'

'No,' conceded Michael. 'However, he was sane enough to leave the Bishop's Commissioners a plate of toxic Lombard slices, and then retrieve the evidence. He was not completely witless.'

'I am surprised he was the culprit,' said Bartholomew unhappily. 'I would not have predicted that he would resort to a sly weapon like poison.'

'Perhaps he had help,' suggested Michael. 'From the other members of the Unholy Trinity, for example, who may then have decided to shove him in the well before he gave them away. Men on the verge of insanity do not make for reliable accomplices.'

'We do not know he was murdered. It may have been an accident. Or suicide.'

'He was murdered all right,' stated Michael grimly. 'Of that I am certain.'

Pyk had occupied an attractive house on the market-place. Its window shutters were freshly painted, its timbers scrubbed, and it had a clean, wholesome look about it. Bartholomew felt instinctively that he would have been at home there, and wished he had known his fellow *medicus*.

The door was opened by a maid, who recognised Michael from his previous attempts to interview her mistress. She smiled, said Pernel was in at last, and led them to a solar. Lying on a couch like an indolent Roman emperor was a very fat woman in middle years, whose jaws worked furiously as she finished what appeared to have been a sizeable plate of cakes.

'You are here about my husband Hugh,' she said, indicating that they should sit. 'Aurifabro sent soldiers to hunt for him, but they had no more luck than the abbey's men.'

'What about you?' asked Bartholomew. 'Did you search, too?'

'Me?' Pernel regarded him askance. 'How could I succeed where mercenaries and *defensores* had failed? I am not some bloodhound, trained to sniff out prey.'

'I meant did you hire people to look on your behalf?' explained Bartholomew.

'No, it would have been a waste of money. Besides, these things happen, and there is no point crying over spilt milk.'

Bartholomew frowned. 'You do not seem very concerned.'

Her eyes were small and hard in her doughy face. 'Is that a crime? I never wanted to marry a *medicus*. They are an unpleasant breed, with their urine flasks and astrological charts and boring lectures about diet.'

'But he was your—' began Bartholomew.

'My eating is none of his business. It is *my* body, and I shall put what I please inside it.'

'Quite right, too,' interjected Michael.

'But he thought that a healer's wife should set a good example, and he ordered me to lose weight. It was entirely unreasonable.'

'Indeed it was,' agreed Michael sincerely. 'Completely unfair.'

'You *would* take his side.' Pernel rounded angrily on Bartholomew, even though he had not spoken. 'You are one of them – a physician!' She spat the last word, as if she wanted it out of her mouth. 'Of course, he did not interfere with cadavers, which is a point in his favour.'

'I do not—' began Bartholomew, not liking the connotations of 'interfere'.

'But my dietary regimen is *my* affair, and none of his,' Pernel concluded firmly. She glared at Bartholomew. 'And none of yours, either.'

Bartholomew was beginning to feel considerable sympathy for Pyk.

'I quite understand,' said Michael. 'I suffer similar intrusions myself. But that is not why we are here. We wanted to ask about your husband's—'

'The poor will miss him,' said Pernel rather spitefully. 'He saw a number of them free of charge, although I did my best to put an end to such nonsense.'

'What do you think happened to him and Robert?' Michael was forced to speak quickly, to get the question out before he was interrupted again.

'Thieves killed them, of course. He and the Abbot would have made an attractive target, because it threatened rain that day and they were both wearing nice cloaks. Hugh's was scarlet, shot through with gold thread, while Robert's was trimmed with ermine.'

'An attractive target indeed,' murmured Michael.

'Many townsfolk believe these so-called outlaws are actually Aurifabro's mercenaries, but I do not. He would not have sent them to look for Hugh if that had been the case.'

'He might,' countered Michael. 'To forestall accusations.'

Pernel shook her head, making her chins swing from side to side. 'Hugh was one of the few people Aurifabro liked. I think my husband's disappearance can be laid at *Spalling's* door. Spalling encourages the poor to think they have a right to the property of the rich, so is it any surprise that they then go out and put this philosophy into action?'

'Do you have proof that Spalling's followers are responsible?' asked Bartholomew.

Pernel shot him a haughty glance. 'I do not need proof. It is what I think.'

'What I do not understand is why Pyk agreed to accompany Robert in the first place,' said Michael. 'I know they were friends, but it seems an unlikely association – a popular physician and a universally despised Abbot.'

'Oh, that is easily explained. I encouraged the relationship, on the grounds that a high-ranking churchman was better company than his vile paupers – we have our social standing to consider, you know. Hugh liked everyone, so he had no trouble tolerating Robert.'

'They arranged to ride to Torpe together on the day they disappeared?'

Pernel nodded. 'Hugh had patients to see there, and Robert thought Hugh's popularity with low-born villains would prevent him from being robbed. So much for that notion!'

'I do not suppose you have received a ransom note, have you?' asked Michael, more in desperation than hope – the interview had told them nothing new.

Pernel shook her head. 'And I would not pay if I had. I do not believe in negotiating with extortionists. It only encourages them to try again.'

'Surely you would have made an exception for your husband?' Bartholomew did not try to mask his distaste for her icy pragmatism.

'I would not,' she said firmly. 'But I am famished! Would you care to join me in a—'

'No,' said Bartholomew curtly, eager to be away from her objectionable company. 'We have taken enough of your time.'

*   *   *

248

'Poor Pyk,' he said, as they walked towards Reginald's shop. Michael had decided that it was time to force the cutler to tell them what he knew, and had already devised a list of threats that would compel him to open his door. 'Perhaps he disappeared in order to escape from her.'

'Taking Robert with him?' asked Michael. 'I doubt that.'

'Did you believe her when she said she had forced Pyk to make friends with Robert? I cannot imagine following that sort of order – not for anyone.'

'Fortunately for you, neither Matilde nor Julitta are the kind of women to demand that sort of obedience. But perhaps we have not been told the whole truth about Pyk – maybe he was not the saintly healer we have been led to believe.'

Bartholomew disagreed. 'People have had no compunction about denigrating the Abbot, and if Pyk had had faults, they would have been listed, too. However, despite what Pernel claimed, I still think that Robert and Pyk were unlikely friends.'

'People probably say the same about us: the man who will be the next prelate of Peterborough, and his sinister, anatomy-loving companion.'

Bartholomew regarded him sharply. 'You said not an hour ago that you had decided not to try for the abbacy, on the grounds that there are too many disagreeable residents.'

'There are, but I shall have the authority to oust most of them once I am invested. Yvo, Nonton, Ramseye and Henry can be exiled to distant outposts, while the threat of excommunication will keep Spalling in check.'

'Do you think you will win an election?'

'I would not demean myself by becoming involved in one of those! I shall tell Gynewell to appoint me, and he will oblige because he will be grateful to have me in his See. And who can blame him? I will be an excellent Abbot.'

But Bartholomew's attention had wandered. 'Something is happening near the fishmonger's shop. A crowd has gathered outside it.'

They hurried forward, and Michael released a cry of dismay when he saw the cutler on the ground in the throes of an apoplectic attack. Bartholomew thrust his way through the onlookers and dropped to his knees next to the stricken man. Abruptly, Reginald went limp. Bartholomew put his ear to the cutler's chest, then began compressing it.

'What is he doing?' whispered Hagar, watching in fascinated horror.

'Perhaps it is anatomy,' suggested long-toothed Marion.

Bartholomew would have reassured them that it was not, but he was concentrating on the task in hand and had no breath for explanations.

'It is Corpse Examining,' declared Botilbrig with great authority. 'I just saw him doing similar things to Welbyrn.'

'Excuse me,' said someone, trying to push Bartholomew out of the way. The physician glanced up to see Spalling, clad in the simple attire of a fisherman, although the apron was conspicuously devoid of blood and scales. 'Would you mind moving aside?'

'I am busy,' snapped Bartholomew, still trying to restart Reginald's heart.

'So I see,' said Spalling. 'But I need some fish. I am

holding another meeting tonight, and people expect to be fed.'

He shoved hard enough to knock Bartholomew off balance and disappeared into the shop. Bartholomew gaped, astonished that anyone should consider shopping more important than a man's life, but then his attention was taken by a faint thud beneath his fingers: Reginald's heart was beating again. The cutler opened his eyes, but his lips were blue, and Bartholomew could see he had only delayed the inevitable.

'He needs last rites, Brother,' he said urgently. 'Hurry!'

Although monks were not priests, Michael had been granted dispensation to hear confessions during the plague and had continued the practice since. He crouched down obligingly, fumbling for the chrism he carried for such occasions, while Bartholomew stepped back to give them privacy. Everyone else craned forward, then shuffled back sheepishly when Michael favoured them with a black glare. Reginald grasped the monk's hand and started to whisper, but it was not long before he went limp again.

'You could not save him then?' asked Spalling conversationally, emerging from the shop with a parcel under his arm. Silvery heads poked from one end, tails from another.

'No,' replied Bartholomew shortly.

'What happened?' Spalling regarded the body dispassionately. 'Apoplexy?'

'Possibly,' replied Bartholomew. 'Why?'

'He had two attacks last year, and Master Pyk warned him that he would have another unless he stopped drinking a pint of melted butter with his custard every night. It is a pity Pyk is not here to see Reginald dead. He liked being right.'

'Did he?' pounced Michael. 'Was he arrogant, then?'

'No, he just took pride in his art. We shall have to ask the new Abbot to arrange for a replacement, because Peterborough should not be without a *medicus*. Of course, we will be lucky to get another man like Pyk. Not many physicians tend the poor free of charge.'

'Did you tell Spalling the truth, Matt?' asked Michael in a low voice, when the rebel had moved away to nod friendly greetings to the more disreputable members of the crowd. 'Did Reginald really die of apoplexy?'

'It seems the most likely explanation. Why?'

'Because he just told me he was poisoned.'

CHAPTER 9

Had Reginald been poisoned? As Bartholomew had come close to suffering a similar fate himself, he gave his undivided attention to finding out what had happened to the cutler. Still in the doorway to the fishmonger's shop, he inspected the dead man's hands and lips. He saw nothing amiss, so he opened the mouth and tipped back the head to look down the throat. Only when there was a collective exclamation of disgust did it occur to him that he should have insisted on working somewhere less public.

'Perhaps being examined so pitilessly serves him right,' said Botilbrig. 'He was a very evil villain, and I have not forgotten how his wife disappeared so suddenly.'

'Yes, within days of Abbot Robert's arrival,' recalled Spalling, still with the fish under his arm. 'Maybe *he* seduced her and encouraged her to leave, just as he seduced Joan. I would not put such unsavoury antics past a Benedictine, especially that one.'

'Well, Matt?' Michael moved closer to the physician, so they could speak without being overheard. Fortunately, the spectators were more interested in discussing whether Mistress Cutler had been Robert's kind of woman.

'There is no evidence of poison that I can see, although that proves nothing, given that most are undetectable. However, if Reginald really did drink melted butter every night and had suffered similar attacks in the past . . .'

Michael was silent for a moment. 'He refused the sacrament of confession, saying that he preferred pagan deities, so I suppose I can tell you what he confided. He admitted to creating a diversion when Lady Lullington was killed – he was paid for it, apparently. Unfortunately, he died before I could ask by whom. His last words were that the purse would tell us all we need to know.'

'What did he mean by that?'

'I have no idea, but we should look in his shop for it. A clue that tells us "all we need to know" would be very useful.'

Bartholomew agreed, so they left the body in the fishmonger's reluctant care, and walked to Reginald's domain beneath the Chapel of St Thomas – a workshop at the front and living quarters behind. Bartholomew looked around in distaste, wondering if the cutler had grown so slovenly after he had no wife to care for him. The workshop was a chaotic mess, broken tools vying for space with scraps of discarded metal and sticky pools of grease, but the living room was worse. The table was thick with dirt, the blankets filthy and the plates stained with the remnants of past meals. Bartholomew retreated to the shop, leaving Michael to tackle the rest.

'This is odd,' he called, when they had been searching for a while. He went to the adjoining door, weighing something in his hand. 'It looks like a—'

'Matt, please,' Michael was trying to summon the courage to peer beneath Reginald's flea-infested mattress. 'Just look for the purse.' Bartholomew stared down at what he had found, and was not surprised the monk

254

was uninterested – it was just a metal cylinder in two parts, one fitting inside the other. But it looked like a coining die – a press for making money – although he supposed that was unlikely. Such items were very carefully guarded, and all old ones were destroyed to prevent counterfeiting. He put it back where he had found it, then opened a dirty wooden box that contained pewter spoons. A few had been daubed with gold leaf in a sly attempt to make them appear as though they were made from solid gold.

'Look,' Batholomew went to the door a second time, to show them to Michael.

The monk grimaced. 'I imagine Reginald *was* up to no good in here, given that he declined to open the door, but those spoons can have no bearing on Robert's fate – or on who hired him to make a fuss so that Lady Lullington could be murdered. So find the purse, because I shall be sick if I am obliged to stay in here much longer.'

Bartholomew did as he was told, listening with half an ear to the discussion taking place outside the door, as people gathered there to cluck and gossip about the dead man. Predictably, Spalling was denouncing him for having money that should have been shared with the poor; Botilbrig recited a list of the crimes he was known to have committed; and Lullington had arrived to assert that Reginald had dabbled in witchery.

'How do you know?' asked Hagar. She sounded uneasy: his shop was under her chapel.

'My wife told me,' replied Lullington. 'She knew about that kind of thing.'

'She never did!' snapped Hagar angrily. 'She was a

255

saintly soul. Will she be going in our cemetery, by the way? Trentham is digging a pit for Joan, so I am sure he would not mind excavating one for her as well. We can put her on Oxforde's other side.'

'She can go in the parish churchyard,' came the callous reply. 'I am not paying for anything special.'

'It would not cost much,' insisted Hagar. 'Indeed, Trentham would probably waive his fee, because he liked her. Shall we ask him now? He is digging at this very moment, and I am sure he will be grateful for a respite while we negotiate.'

'No.' Lullington's next words came from a distance. 'I do not want my wife anywhere near where I plan to be buried myself.'

'He is a heartless pig,' declared Hagar to whoever was listening. 'And if anyone is worthy of a special grave, it is Lady Lullington. She deserves one even more than Joan.'

'Joan does not deserve it,' countered Botilbrig. His voice became wistful. 'Although she was a lovely lass when she was young. It is a pity she turned out the way she did.'

'She always said the same about you,' said Hagar.

Back in Reginald's home, Bartholomew and Michael were having no luck. The monk had moved to the cooking pots, screwing up his face in revulsion as he peered inside each one. Bartholomew had finished rummaging through the cutler's tools, and had just dropped to his knees to look under a bench when the door opened to reveal Henry.

'I am afraid you must leave,' the monk said. 'At once.'

'Why?' demanded Michael, bemused.

'Because now Reginald is dead, these premises belong to the abbey.'

'I imagine they belong to his family,' countered Michael. 'The abbey is—'

'There is a will,' interrupted Henry. 'The obedientiaries are studying it as I speak, and it says the abbey inherits everything.'

'They wasted no time,' said Bartholomew, disgusted.

Henry grimaced. 'Reginald could not read, and while Robert *should* have been trusted to write what his friend dictated . . . well, suffice to say that the will is likely to be contested by Reginald's sons. Thus the property must be sealed, and you must leave. I am sorry – I am only carrying out orders.'

'Whose orders?' demanded Michael. 'Yvo's?'

'Yes, I suppose so. Now please do as I ask. I do not want trouble.'

'But we are looking for information that may throw light on your Abbot's disappearance,' objected Michael. 'Do you not want him found?'

'Yes, of course. However, I doubt Reginald had anything to do with Robert's murder.'

'His *murder*?' pounced Michael.

'A slip of the tongue,' said Henry, crossing himself. 'Pray God it is not true. But you will find no clues to Robert's whereabouts here, I am quite sure of that.'

'Are you indeed?' muttered Michael, shoving past him to the street.

Yvo was bemused when Michael stormed into the Abbot's House, and he claimed to know nothing about an order to seal it up. The other obedientiaries said likewise, so

Henry was summoned. The monk raised his hands in a shrug, and said the instruction had been given to him by a lay brother named Raundes.

'Raundes?' Yvo turned to Nonton. 'He is a *defensor*, is he not?'

The cellarer nodded. 'But he has gone to Lincoln. Welbyrn was supposed to travel there tomorrow, so I thought I had better notify Gynewell that he would not be coming.'

'Raundes spoke to me before he left,' explained Henry.

'Convenient,' murmured Yvo. He spoke a little more loudly. 'However, whoever issued these instructions was right: we cannot let anyone paw through Reginald's belongings until the issue of ownership has been decided.'

'I was not *pawing*, I was looking for clues that might explain what had happened to your Abbot,' said Michael coldly. 'And I insist that I be allowed to continue.'

'What manner of clues?' asked Yvo. He sighed in sudden irritation. 'For God's sake, Appletre! *Must* you blubber every time someone dies? It is not as if Reginald was a good man.'

'He was a fine bass,' sobbed Appletre. 'And he made lovely forks.'

'You have something nice to say about everyone,' accused Ramseye. 'And it is an aggravating habit. Take him to the kitchens for wine, Henry. He is as white as a sheet.'

Bartholomew seized the opportunity to leave with them, preferring their company to that of the remaining obedientiaries and Michael in a temper. Once outside, Henry began to apologise again for ousting him from

258

Reginald's lair, pointing out that it was not for a mere monk to question orders that were alleged to have come from obedientiaries. Bartholomew was more concerned with Appletre, who was indeed pale.

'It is the thought of Welbyrn and Reginald in Purgatory,' explained the precentor tearfully. 'Welbyrn will rise to Heaven eventually, I suppose, but Reginald will not – not only was he a heathen, but he committed many terrible sins.'

'Then we shall help by praying for their souls,' said Henry kindly. 'You are as bad as young Trentham with your soft heart! Did you see him as he dug Joan's grave? He was sobbing fit to break his heart. You are both too sensitive for your own good.'

The pair went to the kitchen before beginning their vigil. Bartholomew accompanied them, but although he was hungry, he declined the cook's offer of some apple pie. Appletre sipped a cup of wine, and the colour gradually seeped back into his cheeks, while the cook, a portly, smiling man named Walter, chatted amiably.

'Raundes galloped away in a great rush. I suppose he is keen to put himself out of range of Aurifabro's robbers before nightfall. Or are they Spalling's, do you think?'

'Aurifabro's, probably,' replied Appletre. 'Those mercenaries are very rough men.'

'Yet Spalling *has* been inciting violence of late,' said Henry thoughtfully. 'He always did hold controversial opinions, but he has been much more vocal recently. Much more active, too, with his rallies and meetings.'

'He only developed those ideas to annoy his rich father,' said Walter. 'If they had been genuine, he would not have accepted a princely inheritance when the old man died. Aurifabro told me that Spalling is spending none of his own money on this revolution.'

'You have been talking to Aurifabro?' asked Henry, startled. 'The abbey's enemy?'

'Just in passing,' replied Walter, a little cagily. He hastened on with his gossip before Henry could question him further. 'He says that Spalling's riches are safely invested with the town's jewellers, and thinks that someone is paying him to foment discontent.'

'Come now, Brother Cook,' chided Henry. 'I do not believe that and nor should you.'

'Do you think Bishop Gynewell will come when he hears there has been a second death in the abbey?' asked Walter, ignoring the admonition and ranging off on another subject. 'First our Abbot and now our treasurer.'

Appletre shook his head. 'He has his hands too full with his own troubles. Doubtless he will order Brother Michael to look into Welbyrn's death, too.'

'I do not envy Michael his duties,' said the cook soberly. 'I doubt he will find answers, and he has been wasting his time from the start.'

Bartholomew felt the need to defend his friend. 'He is very good at what he does.'

'Maybe so,' said Walter. 'But Peterborough excels at keeping its secrets, and it will take a much sharper mind than his to make it yield them.'

The cook's smug prediction made Bartholomew want to prove him wrong, so he spent the rest of the day in a determined effort to discover what Peterborough might be hiding. He questioned Cynric about Spalling's finances, interviewed a lot of monks about Welbyrn, and visited taverns to ask about Reginald, Pyk, Joan, Robert and Lady Lullington.

He learned nothing, and was dispirited when he returned to the abbey, the energy that had surged through him after his icy dip in the well at St Leonard's gone. Moreover, despite his resolve not to dwell on Matilde, she kept entering his thoughts, and his stomach lurched several times when he thought he saw her. He was still recovering from one such start when his arm was grabbed and he was spun around roughly.

'I was talking to you,' snapped Aurifabro. 'Or is a Bishop's Commissioner too grand to pass the time of day with a lowly goldsmith?'

'Of course not,' said Bartholomew wearily. 'How may I help you?'

The phrase was one he used on patients, and had emerged instinctively rather than from any desire to be polite, but Aurifabro softened when he heard it.

'I want to know who will be the next Abbot, and I thought you might give me a more honest answer than those damned Benedictines.'

'Why are you curious about that?'

'I am tired of sparring with the Church, and hiring mercenaries is expensive. I should like to make my peace with Robert's successor. With luck, he might even buy that wretched paten. It is the best piece I have ever crafted, and it would be a pity to melt it down – and my own religion has no use for that sort of thing.'

'Yvo plans to hold an election on Thursday. You will find out then whether the monks have chosen him or Ramseye.' Bartholomew was disinclined to add that the result might be irrelevant if Michael persuaded Gynewell to appoint him instead.

Aurifabro grimaced. 'Neither is likely to agree to a truce.' He was silent for a moment, reflecting gloomily, then seemed to pull himself together. 'The other thing I want to know is whether you have caught the villain who murdered the villainous Robert.'

'Not yet.'

'Pity, but I am not surprised. The only people who cared about him were Pyk, Reginald and Welbyrn, and now they are all dead, too.'

'Lullington liked him,' Bartholomew pointed out.

Aurifabro spat. 'Lullington is incapable of liking anyone but himself.'

Bartholomew suspected that was true. He studied the goldsmith thoughtfully, and decided it was time he also spoke his mind. 'If you really want the culprit found, you would not have told your mercenaries to prevent us from asking questions in Torpe.'

Aurifabro regarded him with an expression that was difficult to read. 'Then come again, and I shall order them to admit you. However, think very carefully before you do. It would be wiser and safer simply to tell Bishop Gynewell that the case will never be solved.'

And with those enigmatic words, he strode away.

When Bartholomew arrived at the guest house, he found that Michael, William and Clippesby had been entertaining Langelee.

'I had better go,' said the Master, setting his goblet on the table. 'Spalling is holding another of his revolutionary rallies tonight.'

'So?' asked Michael waspishly. 'Surely you cannot enjoy that sort of nonsense?'

'No, but it is an opportunity to learn his plans, so I can pass them to the Sheriff. Spalling *must* be stopped. I will keep Cynric's name out of my dispatches if I can.'

'And if you cannot?' asked Bartholomew, alarmed. 'He might hang!'

'Yes, but the alternative is to stand by while England erupts into open rebellion. The situation is bigger than any of us, and I am morally obliged to do whatever is necessary to nip it in the bud before it spreads.'

'But—' objected Bartholomew.

'I have told Cynric what I plan to do,' Langelee went on. 'Which shows a good deal of trust on my part, because Spalling would certainly kill me if he thought I was a spy.'

'Spalling is all wind,' said William dismissively. 'The abbey servants tell me that he does not give his own money to his cause, and that he will run away if there are signs that his fiery words are working.'

'They may be right.' Langelee turned to Michael. 'However, the reason I came here tonight was to tell you something I overheard – a discussion between Spalling and some of his rabble. They plan to attack Aurifabro soon, in the hope that he can be driven off his lands. Unfortunately, Aurifabro has enough mercenaries to fight back.'

'But Aurifabro's mercenaries are skilled warriors,' said Bartholomew in horror. 'Spalling's peasants will be cut to pieces. Can you do nothing to stop them?'

Langelee shook his head. 'Spalling believes that Aurifabro is responsible for the Abbot's disappearance, and thinks an invasion of his manor will force the matter into the open.'

'What do you think?' asked Michael. 'Is Aurifabro the culprit?'

Langelee considered the question carefully. 'Well, I am suspicious of the fact that Robert and Pyk were riding to *his* home when they vanished. Moreover, two days before, Spalling heard Robert yell at Aurifabro over the paten he was making.'

'Walter the cook also heard a fierce argument,' agreed William, 'in which the Abbot accused Aurifabro of using substandard gold. Needless to say Aurifabro was offended, because he takes pride in his craft.'

Langelee stood. 'I had better go before I am missed. I have offered to distribute fish stew to Spalling's audience before his speech – which will take a while because a veritable horde is massing outside his house. If they all join his cause, he will command a significant army.'

'Something the abbey already has, and so does Aurifabro,' said Michael gloomily. 'We are the only ones on our own.'

Once Langelee had gone, Clippesby and William began to tell Michael what they had learned during the course of the day.

'I spent part of it with Prior Yvo,' said Clippesby. He frowned in consternation. 'He seems to be labouring under the misapprehension that I am a saint. I kept assuring him that I am not, but he would not listen.'

'We discussed this,' said William irritably. 'We agreed that you would ignore him if he mentioned that particular fantasy. The poor man is sun-touched, and the best

264

way to deal with his sad condition is by going along with everything he says.'

'He took no notice of my denials anyway. Then he told me to kneel at the prie-dieu in his solar, and petition God to appoint *him* as Abbot. I told him I would petition God to choose the most worthy candidate.'

'Thank you, Clippesby,' said Michael. 'I shall remember your support.'

Clippesby regarded him in incomprehension, then went on. 'When I had finished, I met a chaffinch who told me that Robert had enjoyed reading Oxforde's prayer. Apparently, Kirwell gave it to him in the expectation of immediate death. But Kirwell still lives.'

'How did the chaffinch know about the prayer?' asked Bartholomew, who had been under the impression that Kirwell had kept that particular matter close to his chest, and that while Inges and the bedesmen might know the tale, it was not general knowledge.

'She overheard Robert telling Nonton the cellarer about it.'

'He means a monk overheard the discussion and confided it to him,' translated William scathingly. 'However, what *I* learned is a lot more important.'

'What?' asked Michael impatiently, when the friar paused for dramatic effect.

'That Welbyrn asked the cook to bake him a batch of Lombard slices the day Matthew became ill,' replied William triumphantly. '*Ergo*, Welbyrn was the poisoner. I showed Walter the soggy ones that had been in the villain's purse, and he recognised them at once. He also said there was nothing toxic about them when they left his kitchen.'

'Then the soporific was added later,' surmised Michael. 'Sprinkled on, perhaps, as a coating.'

'Do you think Welbyrn tried to kill you, then tossed himself in the well when he failed?' asked William.

'It is possible,' replied Bartholomew. 'But leaving the cakes in his scrip was tantamount to an admission of guilt, and I am not sure he would have risked embarrassing his monastery so. Even if he had been losing his mind, I think he still would have known he should dispose of the incriminating evidence before killing himself.'

'Then perhaps this "admission of guilt" was intended for his brethren's eyes only,' suggested William. 'He was not to know his corpse would be examined by you.'

'He was not a total fool,' averred Michael. 'Even in lunacy, he would have anticipated that his death would interest the Bishop's Commissioners. And I do not believe it was suicide anyway. He was murdered – I feel it in my bones.'

They were silent for a while, straining for answers that would not come.

'I also found out that Robert had some sort of hold over Reginald,' William went on eventually. 'The servants did not know what, but they said that Reginald did everything Robert asked, not out of friendship, but because he had no choice.'

'And I have been regaled with tale after tale about Oxforde's treasure,' added Clippesby. 'Some folk say it was never found; others claim he gave it all to the poor, or that it is funding Spalling's rebellion; and the rest believe that Reginald dug it up and spent it all on himself. Regardless of the truth, the foxes say it is worth a fortune.'

William patted his hand patronisingly. 'Well, if these

foxes ever learn where it is, make sure you come to me first. Michaelhouse's coffers are always empty.'

While his colleagues debated how much gold would be needed to solve the College's ongoing financial problems, Bartholomew sat in the window. He tried to review what he had discovered about Robert, Pyk, Joan, Lady Lullington and Welbyrn, but tiredness meant he was less effective at locking Matilde from his thoughts than he had been earlier, and it was not long before he gave up and let her fill his mind.

What would he do if she appeared in Cambridge one day? Had too much time passed for them to be happy together? How much had she changed? And he knew she had, because the old Matilde would not have been afraid to speak to him. Of course, he had changed, too – he was more sober and reflective now, and it was possible that she might not like it.

And what about Julitta? Would he forget about her if Matilde appeared laden down with riches and offered to be his wife? Yet how could he abandon Julitta to a man who did not love her, and who might even do her harm? He thought about her silky brown hair and mischievous smile, and his stomach lurched.

He yelped in alarm when there was a soft tap on the window, and he saw a face staring in at him. They were on the upper floor, so no one should have been outside.

'Sorry, boy,' said Cynric, climbing in off the ivy that grew up the wall. 'I did not want anyone to see me visiting. The men who support Spalling are nervous about spies, see.'

'I imagine they are,' muttered Michael. 'So what have you got for me?'

'Nothing,' replied Cynric in disgust. 'I walked very slowly along the Torpe road today, but it has been too long since Robert and Pyk were there. If they were killed by robbers, then there are no clues to tell us the identity of the culprits.'

'How did you manage to escape from Spalling?' asked William curiously.

'I told him I was going out. He is too busy to object.'

'So, let us summarise what we know of Robert's final journey,' said Michael with a weary sigh. 'He went to inspect the paten that Aurifabro was making, Pyk at his side. Aurifabro claims they never arrived. So, the first possibility is that they *did* arrive and Aurifabro killed them. It is common knowledge that they disliked each other, and we know they argued over the paten.'

'But Aurifabro did not dislike Pyk,' Bartholomew pointed out.

'Yes, but if Pyk saw Robert murdered, Aurifabro would have had no choice but to kill him, too,' put in William. 'From what I have heard, Pyk was not a man to turn a blind eye.'

'The second possibility is that they fell foul of outlaws,' Michael went on.

'For which there is no evidence,' Cynric reminded him.

'And the third possibility is that they were dispatched by someone they knew,' Michael finished. 'God knows, Robert had enough enemies.'

'There is no evidence for that, either,' said Cynric.

Michael thumped the table in frustration. 'We are no further forward than we were when we first arrived. Meanwhile, we have four more suspicious deaths to solve, and we must leave the day after tomorrow.'

'It is odd that Reginald should die just as we were going to talk to him,' said Bartholomew. 'Then there is his peculiar guilty behaviour, and the fact that we were removed from his shop before we could search it properly – via a message from a *defensor* who is conveniently unavailable to tell us who issued the order.'

'It is odd,' agreed William. 'But I think *Lullington* paid Reginald to create the diversion that allowed his wife to be strangled. It explains why he could not bear to look at her corpse.'

'But she would have been dead soon anyway,' argued Bartholomew. 'And Lullington is not the kind of man to squander money. Your conclusion is illogical.'

'Do you have a better one, then?' demanded William.

Bartholomew did not.

It had been an exhausting day, and Bartholomew was beginning to pay the price for his earlier vigour. He wanted to go to bed, but Prior Yvo had other ideas.

'We always have a little fun on the second Monday of every month,' he said. 'I was tempted to cancel, but that would have been the last thing Welbyrn would have wanted. He loved Entertainment Night.'

'Entertainment Night?' asked Michael warily.

'When members of our community show off their talents,' replied Yvo, eyes blazing rather fanatically. 'I shall sing, and you will see others with equally impressive skills. And at the end, we vote for the best performance. You will attend.'

'Not me,' said Bartholomew. 'I am too tired for—'

'Nonsense,' declared Yvo. 'Entertainment Night will make you feel like a new man. Even Kirwell rouses himself for the occasion, and he always enjoys himself.'

It sounded distinctly unappealing, but the four scholars trailed obediently across the yard to the refectory, where there was a buzz of excited anticipation as the monks and lay brothers converged. They were joined not only by the men of St Leonard's Hospital, but by their female counterparts from St Thomas's. Lullington and Trentham had also been invited, and stood with Nonton, whose red face suggested he had been sampling the wines that were to be served later. The scholars entered the crush, and Bartholomew found himself next to Lullington. The knight began to make polite conversation in his aristocratic French.

'I saw you talking to Aurifabro earlier. I hope he was not denigrating dear Abbot Robert.'

'We discussed the paten,' said Bartholomew, not entirely truthfully.

'A paltry piece that would have been a waste of money.' Lullington grimaced. 'Burying my wife next to Oxforde would have been a waste of money as well, because if anyone is going to claim that hallowed spot, it will be me. But not for many years, of course.'

'Of course. Why did you never visit her when she was ill?'

'I was busy,' replied Lullington stiffly. 'Not that it is any of your business. Besides, I started to walk into her room the day she died, but my courage failed when I smelled sickness and urine. However, I am shattered by her death – my grief knows no bounds.'

'Yes, you seem heartbroken.'

Lullington scowled as he brushed invisible specks from another handsome new gipon. 'I am a knight – we do

270

not display unmanly emotions in public. She loved me for it, of course. I know, because she was loyal.'

Bartholomew was bemused by the last remark and started to ask what it meant, but Lullington had spotted Yvo and hurried away to corner him, making no effort to disguise the fact that he considered the Prior a more worthy recipient of his attentions. Bartholomew was about to go after him when Trentham approached. The priest had donned a clean robe, brushed his hair and shaved. His cheeks were pink and very youthful, but there was a sadness in his eyes that was older than his years.

'I buried Lady Lullington this afternoon,' he began miserably. 'In the parish churchyard, beneath my favourite tree. I did not want her near Oxforde, not after what Kirwell said.'

'Unlike poor Joan,' said Michael, overhearing as he came to join them, 'who will keep the villain company for eternity. Have you finished digging her hole yet?'

Trentham shook his head. 'I am not very good at it, so it is taking an age.'

'Perhaps one of the monks will help you,' suggested Bartholomew.

Trentham grinned suddenly, an expression that made him look more boyish than ever. 'A monk! Why did I not think of that? Perhaps Henry will oblige; he is a good man. So is Appletre, although I doubt the other obedientiaries will offer. They are too grand.'

'Entertainment Night should have been cancelled.' It was Henry speaking, his expression troubled. 'We should not be making merry when we have an abbot missing and a treasurer dead.'

271

'I disagree,' said Appletre, who was with him. 'Music will make everyone feel better, and Robert and Welbyrn would have agreed.'

'Poor Welbyrn,' said Trentham with a sorrowful sigh. 'Still, I suppose we should not be surprised. His father was the same.'

'The same as what?' asked Michael.

'He also lost his wits,' explained Trentham. 'In the end, he tossed himself in the river, a tormented and lost soul. My grandfather told me about it. Perhaps it was terror of insanity that made the younger Welbyrn such an angry, unhappy man.'

'It is certainly what drove him to take his own life,' said Henry. 'Because we all know that is what really happened, despite Yvo's efforts to make us believe it was an accident. It is a pity, but these things happen, and all we can do is pray for his soul.'

Michael watched him, Appletre and Trentham walk away together. 'Henry is very eager for everyone to view Welbyrn's death as suicide. Does he *want* his old teacher to roast in the fires of Hell for committing a mortal sin? Or is there another reason for his insistence?'

'Henry is not a killer,' said Bartholomew, tired of Michael's irrational dislike of his old classmate.

'So you keep saying.'

Yvo cut through the babble of conversation in the refectory by clapping his hands. There was immediate silence, although Bartholomew sensed it was more from eager anticipation than obedience. The Prior stood on the dais and beamed, eyebrows waving genially.

'Welcome to Entertainment Night. We shall dedicate

tonight's proceedings to Welbyrn, who will certainly be looking down on us from Heaven.'

A number of monks glanced upwards at this claim, their uncomfortable expressions suggesting that their enjoyment of the occasion had just been curtailed.

'Most of you know what to expect,' Yvo went on. 'But for the benefit of our guests, the evening works as follows: there will be ten different acts, after which the audience will vote for the one it liked best. The winner will receive a carp.'

'A carp,' murmured Michael, green eyes dancing with amusement. 'The stakes are high, then.'

'We shall dispense with the serious stuff first,' Yvo proclaimed. 'So let us have your poem, Henry.'

Henry's piece was a prayer, beautiful in its simplicity, and the gathering was more sober after hearing it. Appletre was in tears again, and when he was asked for his own contribution, it took three false starts and a lot of throat-clearing before he was able to sing. But when he did, his poignant *Lacrimosa* had more than one listener dabbing at his eyes.

Hagar was next. She marched towards the dais with Marion and Elene at her heels, and announced defiantly that their act was for Joan, not Welbyrn. They each produced three coloured wooden balls, and began to juggle. The performance started simply enough, but worked up to a finale that was an impressive blur of flying orbs. The other bedeswomen whooped and applauded when it was finished, as did many monks, although the gentlemen of St Leonard's Hospital remained pointedly silent.

Lullington recited a lively French poem about fighting

a dragon, accompanied by cuts and thrusts from an imaginary sword, which revealed that he would have no idea how to use a real one. Bartholomew glanced around for Cynric, knowing he would be laughing, before realising with a pang that the book-bearer was off fomenting rebellion with Spalling. The knight made no reference to dedicating his performance to his wife, although he nodded testy agreement when Trentham surged to his feet and did it for him.

The cellarer was next, with some tediously uninspired strumming on a rebec. When he announced that he was only halfway through his repertoire, and had plenty more with which to thrill his audience, Yvo strode on to the dais and confiscated the instrument. Everyone roared their approval, but Nonton shot the Prior a look of such glowering hatred that the cheering trailed away to an uncomfortable murmur.

Ramseye's contribution was an impression of the Pope, complete with thick French accent and a bizarre interpretation of his monastic reforms that had the brothers howling appreciative laughter, although most of the allusions passed over Bartholomew's head.

'That was very clever,' said Michael, wiping tears of mirth from his eyes. 'He caught the fellow perfectly. I am voting for him.'

Then there was a break, during which Nonton served mulled ale. He spilled some in Yvo's lap, and his expression was gleefully vindictive when the hot liquid caused the Prior to screech. He provided a separate jug for the Michaelhouse men, murmuring that it was better quality than that provided for the rabble. Bartholomew took it outside and discreetly emptied it down the nearest drain.

He returned to find that Kirwell's litter had been moved to the door, because the old man had expressed a desire for some fresh air.

'How much longer?' he whispered when he saw Bartholomew. 'Abbot Robert promised faithfully that I would die if I gave him Oxforde's prayer, so why am I still here?'

'Do you remember any of this prayer?' asked Bartholomew, more to prevent another request for a nudge towards the grave than because he was interested.

Kirwell glared peevishly at him. 'I only heard it once, and that was forty-five years ago. So no, I cannot recall the words.'

'Presumably, that is why he wrote them down – to remind you.'

'Yes, but my eyes were dim, even then. You had better take your seat now, because Inges is on next and you do not want to be standing up when he starts. You might topple over with the shock of it. I did, when he treated me to a preview.'

'What do you mean?'

The old man gave the ghost of a smile. 'You will see.'

Inges's contribution was a startling and very energetic *pas seul* in the style of a Turkish dancer. Bartholomew laughed heartily, but glares from Botilbrig and his cronies made him realise it was not meant to be funny. William gaped at the spectacle, while Clippesby closed his eyes and began whispering to the cat he had managed to smuggle in.

'Are we permitted to vote for ingenuity?' Michael whispered in Bartholomew's ear. 'Because I have never seen anything quite like *that*.'

275

Two more acts followed, culminating with Yvo, who had saved himself for last, clearly in the belief that he would win more votes by being the most recent. It was a tactical error, for his singing comprised an off-key dirge that was wholly unrecognisable as Tunsted's *Gloria*; he might have done better if the audience had been given a chance to forget that a sizeable part of it had been painful to the ears.

The ballot was taken, with Nonton scowling at some monks until they raised their hands and Yvo doing likewise. Ramseye did not resort to such tactics, although Bartholomew had noticed him moving among the audience when the wine was being served, smiling at those he considered worth wooing. However, many resisted the obedientiaries' efforts and voted for Inges, who won by a narrow margin, much to his competitors' disgust.

'If this shameful bullying happens at the election on Thursday,' said Michael, watching in distaste, 'then Gynewell will appoint me for certain, just to restore peace and unity.'

'That might be beyond even your abilities, Brother,' said Bartholomew.

CHAPTER 10

Although dawn the next day was clear and blue, clouds were massing in the south-west, and a stiff wind indicated that it would not be long before rain swept across the countryside. Bartholomew regarded Michael with a distinct lack of enthusiasm when the monk suggested it was time they interviewed Aurifabro's household in Torpe.

'We have today and a few hours tomorrow before we must leave,' said Michael. 'This villain is *not* going to be the first killer to best me, and it would be a pity for my abbacy to begin with a sinister mystery surrounding the fate of my predecessor. Besides, Aurifabro virtually invited you.'

'Yes, and he followed it by saying it would be safer and wiser to tell Bishop Gynewell that the case will never be solved. If it was an invitation, it was one cloaked in menace.'

'Nonsense,' declared Michael. Then he relented. 'We have no choice, Matt. We have questioned everyone in the abbey, plus a huge number of townsfolk, but answers have been in frustratingly short supply. Aurifabro's servants are our last hope.'

Bartholomew made no reply, because Michael was right.

'If you must go, then William and I will escort you,' offered Clippesby. 'There is a huge discrepancy in the quality of the *defensores*, and the ones Nonton plans to lend you today are hefty men who look mean, but who barely know one end of a weapon from another.'

Michael narrowed his eyes. 'How do you know?'

'One of the chaffinches saw them at drill. I doubt these "warriors" will be much use.'

'I told you the same,' William reminded him. 'Only I had it from the abbey's servants, who are more reliable than birds. But Clippesby is right about one thing, Brother – you will be safer with him and me at your side.'

'I need you to continue your enquiries here.' Michael was loath to point out that neither was very useful in a fight. 'But to deter thieves, I shall borrow an old habit from the abbey, while anyone looking at Matt will know that he is not worth robbing.'

'You may have mine,' said William generously, beginning to untie the oily cingulum that cinched it around his waist. 'No villain would dare attack a Franciscan.'

'No, thank you.' Michael was unable to suppress a shudder at the thought of that particular garment next to his skin. He turned to Bartholomew. 'Saddle the horses while I beg a robe from Yvo. It will be far too big, of course, but a belt should help.'

'Horses?' gulped Bartholomew, sufficiently alarmed that he did not even smirk at the notion of the bulky Michael fitting into anything owned by the little Prior. 'If we are pretending to be poor, it would be better to walk.'

'We shall ride,' declared Michael. 'For three reasons. First, it will be faster, and we cannot afford to waste time. Second, it will allow us to escape if outlaws do appear.

And third, it is too far to travel on foot.' He softened. 'You will not fall off if you grip with your knees and hold the reins as I have taught you.'

Bartholomew was not so sure, but he went to the stable and began the perplexing business of working out which strap went where. Michael appeared long before he had finished, clad in an old brown robe, and promptly began making adjustments to the physician's handiwork. Then he led his horse outside, sprang into the saddle and started a series of fancy manoeuvres that showed him to be an equestrian *par excellence.*

Bartholomew muttered resentfully as he tried to keep Clippesby's gentle mare from shifting about while he fastened the last buckle. He had rejected the black stallion the moment the two of them had made eye contact and he had read what was there.

'Let me do it,' said Cynric, making Bartholomew jump by appearing silently at his side. 'And wait while I saddle mine, too.'

'You are coming with us?' asked Bartholomew, standing back in relief.

'I had intended to ride with you on Sunday, but you were ill then, so I shall do it now instead. Spalling is vexed, but it cannot be helped – you will only get into trouble without me to look after you. Besides, there is a witch in Torpe who sells charms against danger and demons.'

'Do you think you are in need of them, then?' asked Bartholomew, concerned for him.

'They are for you. Danger, because someone poisoned you; and demons, because I do not like what is happening with Oxforde.'

'Oxforde?'

Cynric pursed his lips. 'He was an evil rogue, who was buried in the chapel cemetery to prevent him rising from the dead and resuming his reign of terror. But Trentham is digging a hole right next to him, so it is only a matter of time before he escapes.'

Bartholomew knew better than to argue with Cynric on matters of superstition, but he could not help himself. 'Men who have been dead for forty-five years cannot—'

'Yes, they can,' interrupted Cynric with absolute conviction. 'It is Kirwell's fault – he encouraged people to pray at this so-called shrine, and Oxforde's wicked soul is awake and waiting. No wonder Kirwell has been cursed with such a long life! God is furious with him.'

'I do not think—'

'You do not understand these things, boy,' said Cynric darkly. 'But I will protect you, so do not worry.'

He soon had the horses ready, and once Bartholomew was mounted – no mean feat when even Clippesby's docile nag knew who was in charge and let the physician know it – they set off towards Torpe. They were accompanied by the same four *defensores* who had gone with them the last time, although Cynric's solid presence was far more reassuring to the scholars.

They soon reached the desolate land that Aurifabro had bought after the plague. Its silence was oppressive, the air was heavy with the threat of rain, and there was not so much as a tweet from a bird or a hiss of wind in the trees. Michael was uncommunicative, using the time to ponder the few clues he had gathered, and Cynric was also disinclined to chat. Reluctant to be alone with his thoughts, all of which revolved around Matilde and

Julitta, Bartholomew dismounted, better to inspect the side of the road as he went.

'I have already done that,' said Cynric immediately.

'So have I,' replied Bartholomew. 'But there is no harm in doing it again.'

'Just be ready to leap back on if I yell,' warned Cynric. 'It means robbers are coming and we need to escape. And do not take as long as you did earlier, or we will all die.'

Michael and Bartholomew arrived at Aurifabro's house to find mercenaries still on guard, but this time the soldiers stepped aside and indicated that the visitors were to ride into the yard. The captain then informed them, in thickly accented English, that the goldsmith was out.

'We shall wait for him to come back,' determined Michael, dismounting. 'And while we do, you can tell me what *you* know about the Abbot's disappearance.'

'Me?' asked the captain in alarm. 'Why? The first I heard about it was when Master Aurifabro ordered us to look for Robert and Pyk the following day – when we found nothing.'

Michael smiled wolfishly, more than happy to hone his interrogative skills on the goldsmith's men. He plumped himself down on a bench, and beckoned the captain towards him. The man advanced warily.

'I shall have a bit of a scout around, boy,' whispered Cynric in the physician's ear. 'But you will have to distract the servants who are watching us from the kitchen window.'

'How am I supposed to do that?' asked Bartholomew,

turning to see at least twenty faces looking at them with undisguised curiosity.

'With free medical consultations,' replied Cynric promptly.

Bartholomew baulked, feeling it was underhand, but Cynric was already striding towards the house and had made the offer before he could be stopped. The physician was about to withdraw it when he noticed that one of the servants had an interesting case of rhagades. Telling himself that the deception was defensible if he learned something about the condition to help others, he allowed himself to be led into a large, pleasant room that was spotlessly clean and smelled of fresh bread. He was a little disconcerted when two dozen retainers crowded in behind him with the clear intention of watching him work.

'Perhaps I might use the scullery?' he suggested, not liking the notion of an audience while people described what might be embarrassing ailments. It would be unfortunate if he prescribed the wrong treatment because half the symptoms had been deliberately omitted.

'Why?' asked the steward, a thickset man named Sylle, who had already mentioned that he had been cousin to the formidable Joan. He sounded bemused. 'We will be crushed in there, and those at the back may not be able to see.'

'He seeks to spare our blushes,' explained an old woman called Mother Udela. She was small and frail, but the others treated her with a reverence verging on awe, not least because she had once travelled to Suffolk, a journey deep into the unknown as far as they were concerned. Bartholomew supposed she was the witch that Cynric had mentioned, and made a mental note to stay away from any discussions of religion.

'There is no need for sculleries, Doctor,' said Sylle. 'We all know each other's secrets.'

Bartholomew was not entirely happy, but those who lined up to secure his expertise did not seem to mind, and he was soon lost in his work. Most of the ailments were routine, but he took his time with each, not sure how long Cynric would need.

'It is a pity Fletone is not here,' said Udela, watching him lance a boil. 'He loved this kind of entertainment, and always said he was happiest when Pyk was visiting.'

Bartholomew had never thought of his work as 'entertainment' before. 'Who is Fletone?'

'A shepherd who died a month ago,' replied Udela sadly. 'The day after the Feast of St Swithin.'

Bartholomew frowned. 'Abbot Robert disappeared on the Feast of St Swithin.'

'Yes, coming here to inspect our master's paten.' Udela turned to one of the maids. 'Fetch it, Mary. Doctor Bartholomew will appreciate its fine craftsmanship, and Master Aurifabro is too modest for his own good. His work *should* be touted about for all to admire.'

'How did Fletone die?' asked Bartholomew, more interested in that than the paten.

'Mountain fever.'

Bartholomew blinked. 'Here? In the Fens?'

'It is a serious condition,' averred Udela, while the rest of the household nodded sagely. 'I did my best, but he was beyond my skills. He needed a man like you.'

'I have no experience with mountain fever. It is not very common in Cambridge.'

283

'It is not very common here, either,' said Sylle. 'But Fletone always thought he would die of something unusual, and he was right. He made the diagnosis himself.'

'I see,' said Bartholomew, thinking that a little knowledge was a dangerous thing in his profession.

'Of course, he was raving by the time Sylle found him,' Udela went on. 'He kept claiming that he had seen Pyk die.'

Bartholomew's pulse quickened. 'Did he say where?'

It was Sylle who replied. 'Near that dead oak – the one we call the Dragon Tree – on the Peterborough road, which is where I found Fletone himself. But Pyk did not die there, of course, so it was his ghost that Fletone saw.'

'How do you know Pyk did not die there?' asked Bartholomew, aware that every onlooker was clutching some sort of amulet and murmuring incantations. It was, he thought sourly, like being in an entire room full of Cynrics.

'For two reasons,' replied Sylle. 'First, because there was no Pyk when I found Fletone, dead or otherwise. And second, because Fletone's sickness struck long after Pyk would have ridden past with Abbot Robert. Thus Fletone could not have seen Pyk die.'

'Did Fletone tell you when he became ill, then?'

'No, but that is the nature of mountain fever,' said Udela with total confidence. 'It strikes hard and fast. If Fletone had already been ill when Pyk and Robert went missing, he would have been dead long before Sylle discovered him the following day. It is a matter of logic.'

'That's right,' nodded Sylle. 'He was crawling around

284

on the road when I happened across him, and did not survive long after I brought him home.'

'Perhaps it was for the best,' said Udela sadly. 'He lived for Pyk's visits, and would have hated being without a physician to consult.'

'What do you think happened to Pyk and Robert?' asked Bartholomew, not sure what to make of their tale.

'Outlaws, most likely,' replied Sylle. 'One thing is sure, though: they are definitely dead. Robert would never have abandoned his abbey, and Pyk would never have abandoned us.'

'Pyk was a good man.' Udela smiled fondly. 'He was even nice to Reginald.'

'That scoundrel!' spat Sylle, while Bartholomew glanced sharply at Udela, wondering why she should have singled out the cutler for such a remark. 'He has been up to no good of late, hammering away in his workshop at peculiar hours. And I warrant he is not making knives, either.'

Udela's bright gaze was on Bartholomew. 'You started when I spoke Reginald's name. Why? Do you know something about him that the rest of us do not?'

'Only that he is dead.'

'From apoplexy?' Udela nodded sagely. 'We always knew he would succumb to that, because Pyk warned him time and again not to drink melted butter, but he refused to listen.'

'He was a greedy devil,' said Sylle. 'And thought of nothing but money. It served him right that there was a rumour saying that he had found Oxforde's hoard.'

Bartholomew studied him closely, 'I do not suppose that tale originated in Torpe, did it?'

Sylle's expression was sly, but the physician could read the truth behind it. 'Who can say? However, it annoyed him, which was satisfying.'

Bartholomew turned the conversation back to Robert. 'Did you like the Abbot?'

'No,' replied Udela shortly. 'We do not like any of the monastery's officers – Welbyrn, Ramseye, Nonton, Yvo, Appletre. We like the common monks though, especially Henry.'

'My cousin Joan used to tell us such tales about the obedientiaries,' added Sylle, shaking his head and pursing his lips. 'Almoners who refuse to feed the poor, cellarers who drink their own wines, treasurers who creep around the town after dark on evil business . . .'

'Welbyrn was ill,' said Bartholomew, feeling the need to protect his old tutor from unfair gossip. 'He went to St Leonard's for the healing waters.'

'Joan never saw him doing *that*,' said Sylle. 'But she did see him meet Reginald at the witching hour, so I think we can safely assume that whatever Reginald was doing in his workshop involved the abbey's loutish treasurer.'

'Welbyrn is dead as well,' said Bartholomew, feeling like a harbinger of doom.

'I am not surprised,' sighed Udela. 'He came to me in a terrible state not long ago, and asked if self-murder was in his stars. It was not and I told him so. However, there were signs that he would not die naturally, although I kept that from him – he was suffering enough already.'

'Suffering from what?'

'He thought he was going insane because he kept forgetting things. His father took his own life because *he* lost his wits, and Welbyrn was afraid that the affliction had passed to him. Pyk told him his fears were groundless and so did I, but he did not believe us.'

No one had any more to add, so Bartholomew worked in silence for a while, tending two earaches, one indigestion and a case of gout. His every move was watched minutely by his audience, and the only sounds were the occasional approving murmur and – once – spontaneous applause. It made a pleasant change from the yawns of bored students.

'Joan is going to be buried next to Oxforde,' said Sylle eventually. 'It was in her will.'

'I know,' said Udela disapprovingly. 'I told her to change it. A good woman like her deserves better than to be near that vile wretch.'

'But Oxforde is a saint,' objected Sylle. 'Miracles have occurred at his grave.'

'Miracles!' spat Udela. 'There were never any miracles. Kirwell lied about that blinding light, just to get a place in the hospital. And he has done well out of it, because it is his life of leisure that has allowed him to live so long, not his purported saintliness.'

'Abbot Robert always said that Kirwell was holy,' argued Sylle. 'So does Prior Yvo.'

'Because they like the money pilgrims pay to touch him,' scoffed Udela. 'But the practice is deceitful, and I hope the new Abbot will put an end to it.'

'Who will win the post?' asked Sylle eagerly. 'Have you consulted the stars?'

Udela inclined her head. 'Yes, I have, but all I can say is that it will not be Yvo or Ramseye.' She became thoughtful, then addressed Bartholomew. 'Your portly

287

friend would be worthy of the post. He has natural dignity, a clever mind and he is honourable.'

'I am sure he would be the first to agree,' said Bartholomew.

For the next hour, Bartholomew concentrated on medicine. He was vaguely aware of Cynric sidling in at the back of the room, and when the book-bearer caught his eye and gave a slight shake of the head, it took him a moment to understand what it meant. But the last patient was thanking him for his time, so he began packing away his implements, salves and bandages.

'And now you may see the paten,' said Sylle, as though Bartholomew had allowed himself to be besieged by patients just for that end. He handed the physician a large golden plate. It was a magnificent piece, one of the finest Bartholomew had ever seen, and he understood exactly why the goldsmith was reluctant to melt it down.

'Master Aurifabro made it himself,' Udela was explaining. 'He did not delegate to a lesser craftsman, as others might have done. Of course, now he does not know what to do with it, because our gods – the older ones – have no use for this sort of thing.'

'Why did he take such trouble for a foundation he despises?' asked Bartholomew.

'Oh, he likes the abbey,' said Sylle. 'It is the obedientiaries he loathes. He was terribly disappointed when Yvo cancelled the commission. This paten would have been in the abbey's treasury long after we are in our graves, and was his path to immortality.'

'Would *you* like a consultation, Doctor?' asked Udela suddenly. 'I will do it for free.'

Bartholomew regarded her blankly. 'A consultation?'

'An interview with the spirits,' elaborated Udela, a little impatiently. 'What other kind is there? And they will certainly answer today, because they have taken a shine to you.'

'They have?' asked Bartholomew uneasily.

'They appreciate your generosity to us. It is not every physician who waives his fees in the name of human kindness.'

Bartholomew stood hastily. 'It is good of you, but—'

'Sit,' commanded Udela, reaching into a pouch at her side and removing a handful of shiny stones. 'Let us see what they have to say.'

'No,' said Bartholomew, still on his feet. He saw Cynric frantically signalling for him to show her proper respect. 'It would not be—'

'There is nothing to be afraid of,' said Udela irritably. 'And I am trying to help.'

Before he could argue further, she had tossed the stones on the table, and firm hands were pushing him back into the chair. He could have tried to fight his way clear, but he had the sense that he would not get very far. Judging by the awed looks that had been exchanged when Udela had made the offer, free consultations were not granted often, and her flock was determined to ensure that this one was received with appropriate appreciation.

Udela peered at the pebbles and nodded knowingly. 'There is evil associated with the disappearance of Robert and Pyk. A terrible deed . . .'

'Yes,' said Bartholomew, feeling he could have told her that himself.

'But Pyk is innocent,' said Udela, looking hard at him. 'It is in your mind that *he* might have dispatched Robert, but it would not be true. The stones do not tell me this: my instinct does. Pyk was not a killer.'

'I hope you are right,' said Bartholomew sincerely. He liked the sound of Pyk, and it would do his profession scant good for the arch-villain to be a *medicus*.

'There is nothing more specific, though,' said Udela, inspecting the pebbles again, then shaking her head apologetically. 'The spirits are frightened, which tells me that the wickedness is very strong. All I can say is that death and danger lie ahead for you.'

Bartholomew did not doubt it. Death was his daily companion, given that few of his remedies for serious diseases were effective, while he still had to make the return journey to Cambridge, which was likely to be every bit as perilous as the outward one. But despite his natural pragmatism, her words sent a shiver down his spine.

'And a terrible monster with flailing claws,' added Udela matter-of-factly. 'It will stand over you screaming its fury, and its left hand is more lethal than its right.'

Wryly, Bartholomew supposed he would just have to make sure he avoided left-handed fiends for a while. He nodded his thanks to Udela, hoping she would not read in his face that he considered her prophecies a lot of nonsense.

'There is one more thing.' She smiled suddenly and sweetly. 'And on this, the spirits are crystal clear. You *will* find love one day. I cannot say when, but it will come.'

Bartholomew stared at her, while the listening female

servants issued a chorus of happy coos and Sylle nudged him in the ribs with a manly wink.

'And that,' said Udela, gathering up her stones, 'is all I can tell you.'

Eventually, there was a rattle of hoofs outside as Aurifabro arrived home, more of his mercenaries at his heels. Watching the cavalcade, Bartholomew asked whether the goldsmith had always felt the need for such an elaborate personal guard.

'He recruited these men a year ago,' explained Udela, 'to prevent the abbey from encroaching on his land by moving fences, diverting streams and that sort of thing.'

'But they have accompanied him out and about since Robert disappeared,' added Sylle. 'I hate to say anything nice about Robert, but he did keep good order. Now he is dead, thieves abound and the roads are not safe for wealthy goldsmiths.'

'Why do you think Master Aurifabro hopes a reasonable man will be appointed as the next Abbot?' asked Udela. 'Because he wants to make peace. It is expensive to keep these foreign soldiers, and *we* do not like them. They are louts.'

'I have been told that the roads are more dangerous now Spalling spouts incendiary messages,' said Bartholomew, more to gauge their reactions than because he believed it.

'Spalling used to be such a nice boy,' said Udela sadly. 'Not like his father, who was a tyrant. I cannot imagine what has encouraged him to take so violently against our master. It is wholly undeserved – we are very generous with alms.'

'Spalling does encourage the poor to strike at Aurifabro in particular,' muttered Cynric in Bartholomew's ear. 'Indeed, sometimes I wonder whether Peterborough only has one wealthy merchant, because he rarely mentions anyone else by name.'

Bartholomew was about to leave the kitchen and rejoin Michael when the goldsmith appeared at the door. Aurifabro's expression was simultaneously wary and suspicious.

'What is going on?' he demanded. 'Why is no work being done?'

'Doctor Bartholomew has been tending our ailments,' explained Udela, without a trace of servitude. 'For free. I feel better already.'

'You do not want him touching you,' said Aurifabro. 'He is a Corpse Examiner.'

'It makes no difference,' said Udela, cutting short the murmur of unease that began to ripple through the staff. 'No evil aura hangs around him, or I would have seen it. He is as pure as the driven snow.'

'Is he?' asked Aurifabro doubtfully, while Bartholomew also regarded her askance.

'Yes,' said Udela, meeting her master's eyes. 'You have nothing to fear from him.'

Bartholomew was tempted to take her back to Cambridge with him – he could do with someone who spoke with such conviction on his behalf. Aurifabro nodded what might have been an apology and left. Bartholomew started to follow, but was waylaid by people who wanted to thank him for what he had done, so it was some time before he was able to escape.

'There was nothing to find,' Cynric murmured, as he

followed the physician towards a smart solar in the main part of the house. 'I had hoped that Robert and Pyk were being held prisoner, so I could rescue them, but I am fairly sure they were never here.'

'So am I,' said Bartholomew. 'Udela and the servants might have agreed to stay silent if Robert was locked up, but not Pyk. They like him too much.'

Cynric clapped him on the shoulder. 'I will ask her a few more questions when I go for my private consultation. But be careful with Aurifabro. I do not trust him.'

Apparently, Aurifabro did not trust the scholars either, because his henchmen were ranged behind him as he lounged in a chair near the hearth.

'I have nothing to say to you,' he was telling Michael, who was sitting opposite. 'I want you to leave.'

'Now, now,' said Michael, stretching out his legs and looking so relaxed that Aurifabro might have been forgiven for thinking that he was settling down for a nap. 'That is no way to address the man who might be Peterborough's next Abbot.'

Aurifabro stared at him. 'You? But how will you defeat Yvo and Ramseye? The monks will be too frightened of the retribution that will follow if they vote for you.'

'You think it will be decided by election, do you?' said Michael, smugly condescending. 'The Bishop will make his own selection, and I am his favourite canon.'

'I see.' Aurifabro stared at the floor for a moment, and seemed to reach a decision. He indicated with a snap of his fingers that refreshments were to be served, and tried for a conciliatory smile, an expression that did not quite work on his dour features. 'As I told your physician last night, I am tired of my dispute with the abbey. I want peace.'

'I do not see why that cannot be arranged,' said Michael, accepting a goblet of wine and nodding his appreciation at its quality. 'Of course, it depends on your cooperation in answering questions about Robert.'

'Ask then, but please be brief. I am a busy man.'

'Business is good, then, is it?' probed Michael. 'Spalling is right to claim you are one of the wealthiest merchants in the region?'

'Yes, but I am also generous, and I do not understand why he singles me out for censure. Most merchants never donate a penny to the poor.'

'How many times did Robert visit you?' asked Michael, abruptly changing the subject.

'A lot,' growled the goldsmith. 'He was a nuisance, and I was beginning to wish he had commissioned someone else to make his paten. He wanted to inspect it every few days, to see how it was coming along. And now the abbey refuses to buy it. Of course, I imagine a discerning man like you will be keen to have it on his high altar.'

'I might. Did he come here just to inspect your craftsmanship?'

'No, he tried to foist his oily friendship on me as well, although I was having none of it and I told him so.'

'How did Robert take your rejections?'

'Badly – he told me I would rot in Hell. But I care nothing for his curses or his religion. I am a son of the older faith, which is why I keep a witch in my home.'

'Do you indeed?' murmured Michael.

'Udela is a great seer, and your physician should be

grateful that she has my respect, because otherwise I would have trounced him for distracting my entire household from their duties. No one has done a stroke of work in hours.'

'Tell me what happened the day Robert was due to visit you.' Michael refused to be intimidated by the man's bluster.

'What, again?' groaned Aurifabro.

'Yes, again,' snapped Michael. 'You may not care about Robert, but Pyk was with him, and he seemed a decent soul.'

'Yes, he was,' acknowledged Aurifabro. 'Very well then. Robert approached me that morning and said he was coming to see the paten. I told him I was going to visit my mother, but he threatened to cancel the commission unless I stayed in. He said he planned to leave the abbey after his noonday meal – God forbid that he should miss that – and ride to me in the afternoon.'

'And Pyk? Why did he come?'

'To tend my servants. He often travelled with Robert, as he was one of few who could tolerate the fellow's company.' Aurifabro's habitual glower softened. 'Everyone liked Pyk, and the sight of his great domed head and scarlet cloak lifted the spirits of all who saw them.'

'Why did Robert come here to inspect the paten? Surely you have a workshop in town?'

'Of course, but I was making this particular piece at home. However, Robert's visits were such a trial that I was on the verge of taking it to Peterborough, just to avoid them.'

'What do you say to the people who lay Robert's disappearance at your door?'

'That they are wrong,' snapped Aurifabro. 'I had reasons to dislike the man – lots of them. But I am not in the habit of dispatching powerful churchmen. Or physicians.'

'I am glad to hear it,' said Michael dryly. 'But are you sure you know nothing – even something which may seem unimportant – that might explain what happened?'

Aurifabro closed his eyes and sat still for so long that Michael exchanged a bemused glance with Bartholomew, both wondering whether he had fallen asleep.

'Just one thing,' said the goldsmith at last. 'Robert always took his seals with him when he left the abbey. It suggests he distrusted his obedientiaries – that he was afraid they might use them fraudulently.'

'Clearly. So what are you suggesting?'

'That if he thought them capable of forgery, why not other crimes, too – such as killing him and Pyk on a lonely road?'

Unwilling to be blamed for the disappearance of a second important churchman, Aurifabro instructed some of his mercenaries to escort the scholars safely away from Torpe. Michael demurred but the goldsmith was insistent, and six burly warriors kept them close and rather menacing company for a while, then turned without a word and rode back the way they had come. Both scholars and *defensores* were relieved when they had gone.

'What do you think?' Michael allowed his horse to settle into a more comfortable pace. 'Did Aurifabro do away with Robert and Pyk, as half the town, most monks and Spalling believe?'

'Robert, maybe,' said Bartholomew. 'But not Pyk. Besides, Aurifabro had a point about the seals – it does suggest that Robert distrusted his own house.'

'Yes, but who in particular? Henry?'

'No.' Bartholomew was tired of arguing the point. 'He is a good man – Udela said so.'

'You mean the witch?' asked Michael archly. 'That is meant to impress me, is it?'

'There is nothing wrong with witches, Brother,' put in Cynric. 'But this one was wrong if she said Henry is good, because he is not. Nor are Ramseye and Yvo. They would certainly commit murder to become Abbot, and neither would hesitate to sacrifice Pyk in the process.'

'Appletre admires Henry,' Bartholomew pointed out. 'He—'

'Appletre is like you in that respect,' interrupted Michael acidly. 'Unable to tell the villains from the decent men.'

There was no point arguing with such rigidly held convictions, and Bartholomew did not try. Behind them, the *defensores* began muttering that they would not be in Peterborough until midnight if the men they were guarding insisted on ambling along at such a leisurely pace. Although Bartholomew did not see Michael do anything with reins or knees, the monk's horse immediately slowed further still.

'Could Aurifabro's mercenaries have killed Robert and Pyk without their master's knowledge?' asked Cynric. 'They are ruthless brutes. Moreover, I heard them speaking French, and the outlaws who kept ambushing us on our way here spoke French.'

'It is possible.' Michael sighed irritably. 'Our visit to

297

Torpe was a waste of time, and we must go home tomorrow. You being poisoned did not help, Matt. We lost a whole day over that.'

'My apologies. However, I am not the only one who has fallen foul of a toxic substance recently. So did a shepherd called Fletone, who died the day after Robert and Pyk disappeared.'

'What?' asked Michael in alarm.

'His friends say he contracted mountain fever, which I think you will agree is unlikely around here. He diagnosed himself, being interested in medical matters, but he was raving by the time he was found, and I doubt he was rational.'

'Neither are you, if you conclude from this that he was poisoned. There must be all manner of horrible diseases that could have carried him off.'

'There are, but it is odd that Fletone should have contracted one on this particular road and on that particular day. Moreover, Reginald claimed that *he* had been poisoned—'

'But you said Reginald died of apoplexy,' interrupted Michael. 'On account of his unhealthy diet and the fact that he had suffered previous attacks.'

'Yes, he probably did. However, it is what he *believed* that is important. He must have had a reason for making such a remark – such as knowing what had happened to Fletone.'

Michael stared at him. 'Are you sure you are fully recovered? Because that is wildly illogical! How could Reginald have "known" that Fletone was poisoned, when Fletone himself – and the people who knew him – thought he had mountain fever?'

'Reginald would have known the truth if he had been involved in Fletone's demise. Perhaps that is what made him act so suspiciously whenever we tried to talk to him.'

'No,' said Michael impatiently. 'You are reading too much into the situation.'

The monk continued to pour scorn on the theory, but Bartholomew was not listening because they had reached the lightning-blasted oak where Sylle had found the dying Fletone. He reined in to look at it, understanding exactly why the villagers had named it the Dragon Tree. Its ivy-coated trunk looked like a body, two branches on its 'back' had the appearance of wings, and two more at the front formed arms with claws. It had a head, too, with gaping jaws that appeared to be baying at the sky. It had unnerved him when he had travelled to Torpe the first time, he recalled, by groaning so eerily that his horse had bolted.

He dismounted and began to poke around it with a stick, while Cynric and Michael watched in weary resignation, and the *defensores* complained in sullen voices about the delay. It had started to drizzle, and they wanted to be home.

'There will be nothing to see now,' said Cynric irritably. 'Mother Udela told me that Fletone did not die here, anyway. Sylle carried him home and he breathed his last in Torpe. Besides, I have already explored the area around that tree. Twice.'

Bartholomew sniffed the air. 'I can smell something unpleasant . . .'

'There is a dead sheep nearby. One of Fletone's, probably, which died when he was not around to look after it.'

Bartholomew found the animal and crouched next to it, putting his sleeve over his nose in an effort to filter out the stench. But even taking the mild weather into account, he did not think it had been dead for a month. He said so.

Michael was dismissive. 'You usually tell me that time of death is impossible to estimate, but now you claim to be able to do it with sheep?'

'The thing looked fairly fresh when I came across it last Thursday,' put in Cynric, earning himself a scowl from the monk. 'He is probably right.'

Bartholomew began to prod again. There was a ditch behind the Dragon Tree, which had widened to form a natural pond. He watched a blackbird hop along the edge, dipping its beak towards it every so often, but it did not drink, and eventually it flew away. He scooped some of the water into his hand and sniffed carefully. There was a faint odour of decay.

'Something is buried near here,' he said, standing up and looking around. 'And putrefaction is leaking into the pond. That is what killed the sheep, and that is why the bird declined to drink.'

'Sheep know to avoid bad water, boy,' said Cynric, although he slid to the ground and began to make the kind of inspection at which he was skilled. The *defensores*' grumbling grew louder, and Michael rolled his eyes.

'Perhaps this one made a mistake.' Bartholomew expanded his search to the left of the tree. 'Or was too thirsty to care. However, there are no obvious injuries on it, and—'

'Here!' exclaimed Cynric suddenly. 'Quick!'

Bartholomew hurried towards him. The book-bearer

was kneeling by a particularly deep part of the ditch, which was overgrown with weeds and the roots of trees. Underneath them, a patch of red cloth was visible. It was costly stuff, shot through with gold thread.

'Pyk had a cloak sewn from material like this,' said Cynric soberly.

CHAPTER 11

Bartholomew pulled the vegetation away, and it was not long before he had exposed the body hidden beneath. It was almost completely underwater, and might have lain undiscovered for ever if the dead sheep had not alerted him to the fact that something was wrong.

It was not pleasant inspecting what remained, because the water had caused the soft tissues to rot and swell – Pyk would be unrecognisable to anyone who had known him. Bartholomew did what he could, causing Michael to gaze studiously in the opposite direction and Cynric to move away under the pretext of hunting for Robert. The *defensores* huddled inside their cloaks against the rain, and also kept their distance.

'I am fairly sure it is him,' said Bartholomew eventually, sitting back on his heels. 'Henry mentioned his domed head, and so did Aurifabro. Then there is his distinctive cloak . . .'

'How did he die?' asked Michael.

'Probably bludgeoned, but I will look more closely when we get him back to Peterborough.'

'Is there any sign of Robert? If so, it is almost an anticlimax. I was sure some terrible plot was brewing, but here we are with two men set upon on a deserted stretch of road, murdered and rolled into a ditch. It is rather banal.'

'The ditch is clear in both directions,' reported Cynric,

coming back when he saw Bartholomew's grisly examination was over. 'Does it mean Robert is still alive?'

'Pyk's fate makes that unlikely,' replied Michael soberly. 'He is dead, and it is just a case of locating his body. We shall return to Peterborough, and order a thorough search in the morning. It is too late to start now – it will be dark soon.'

Bartholomew started to roll Pyk in his cloak, but then had second thoughts. The body was in such a poor state that they could not toss it over the back of a horse, or they would lose bits of it en route. However, if it was left unattended by the pool while they fetched a bier it would attract scavengers, and he doubted the *defensores* would agree to guard it. Gently, he eased it back into the ditch, supposing it could rest there for a little longer.

He was just climbing back into the saddle when the attack came. Suddenly, the air was full of screaming voices and an arrow narrowly missed his face. He heard Cynric yelling for him to mount up fast, while Michael brandished the stave he had looped into his saddle. The *defensores* were a distant cluster of thundering hoofs as they galloped away from the danger. Terrified, Bartholomew's horse ripped away from him and joined them.

Bartholomew had no weapons with which to defend himself, so he grabbed a stick from the ground. He managed to score a swipe that sent one ambusher reeling away, but a second man came, and a third, and he was forced to give ground until he was backed up against the bole of the dead oak. He ducked as a cudgel swung at his head, and it smacked into the mat of ivy behind him. Immediately, a wrenching groan made him and his assailants glance upwards in alarm. The wood was rotten, and the weight of the ivy had rendered it unstable. The hefty swipe was enough to make one of the dragon's 'arms' begin to fall.

Udela's words filled Bartholomew's mind – of a monster whose left hand was more deadly than its right. Reacting instinctively, he flung himself towards the weaker one. His opponents howled in horror as the branch crashed among them, and one went silent when it caught him on the top of the head.

Then Cynric was among them, wielding his sword like a demon and howling in Welsh. The surviving attackers turned and fled.

It felt like an age before Bartholomew, riding pillion behind Cynric, saw the lights of Peterborough twinkling in the distance. They arrived to find a huge crowd had gathered at the Abbey Gate, where the *defensores* were telling their story. Voices were raised in shock and recrimination, but Prior Yvo was wholly incapable of imposing order. Ramseye stood to one side, arms folded, as he watched his rival struggle for some semblance of control.

The safe arrival of the Bishop's Commissioners was met with a variety of reactions. Clippesby, William and the common monks surged forward with a delighted cheer; Appletre sang a hymn of thanksgiving; Lullington shrugged; Ramseye's face wore its usual mask of inscrutability; and Nonton raised a flask and took a gulp from it. Henry and Yvo exchanged a brief glance, then joined those who were clamouring their relief.

'The *defensores* claimed you were dead,' said Henry,

crossing himself. 'That they narrowly escaped after their efforts to protect you had failed.'

Bartholomew gave the soldiers a hard stare. They glowered back defiantly, making it clear that they would vigorously deny any accusations of cowardice.

'I am glad to see you unscathed,' said Yvo, although he spoke without warmth. 'I was just arranging for Nonton to collect your corpses. And Pyk's.' He turned to the cellarer, who was in the process of draining whatever was in his flask. 'Are you ready? The sooner you set out, the sooner you can return.'

Nonton frowned his bemusement. 'You still want me to go?'

'Of course! It would be improper to leave Pyk in a ditch another night.'

'Besides, we do not want to lose him again,' added Ramseye with a look that was impossible to interpret.

'True,' nodded Henry. 'Obviously, the rogues who attacked Matt and Michael are the same as the ones who killed Pyk. They may try to dispose of the evidence.'

'Are you sure Nonton and his men will be safe out there with outlaws lurking?' asked Appletre worriedly. 'Perhaps we should wait until tomorrow. I am sure Pyk would not—'

'Our brave *defensores* will not be defeated a second time,' said Yvo. It was difficult to tell whether he was being ironic. 'This is the sort of thing we hired them for, after all.'

'To collect murder victims in the middle of the night?' asked Michael.

Lullington stepped forward, all bristling self-importance. 'You cannot be sure that Pyk was murdered. He probably died of natural causes.'

'And then hid himself in a ditch?' retorted Michael. 'Besides, my Corpse Examiner says he was murdered, and that is good enough for me.'

'The Corpse Examiner,' muttered Lullington, giving Bartholomew a glance that was far from friendly. 'I might have known.'

Appletre addressed Yvo, his face sombre. 'I want it on record that I do not believe this is a good idea. The living are more important than retrieving a man who has been dead for a month. Nonton may be marching into danger.'

'Appletre is right,' agreed Henry. 'These villains will be vengeful and angry after their failure to kill the Bishop's Commissioners, and—'

'All the more reason to collect Pyk tonight, then,' interrupted Yvo, waving away their concerns with an impatient flick of his hand. 'Lest they vent their spleen on his body. And while Nonton is out, he can look for Robert. It is high time we proved him dead.'

'In the dark?' Nonton's voice dripped contempt. 'Pyk was so well concealed that he evaded all our previous daylight searches, so how can we expect to find Robert when we cannot see?'

'Well, try,' snapped Yvo. 'That is an order, and I am in charge here. You and your louts will take no more orders from Ramseye until after the election. Is that clear?'

Nonton's dark, angry expression said it was, although Ramseye's only reaction was a small and rather secretive smile. Bartholomew noticed that the *defensores* who had been detailed to accompany the cellarer were more of the burly ones, said to be lesser warriors than their smaller counterparts, and he could only suppose that

Nonton favoured brawn over military competence for this particular mission as well.

'Nonton can collect the robber who died, too,' said Michael. 'Then we shall—'

'You killed one?' cried Henry in horror. 'But you are a monk!'

'I am aware of that,' snapped Michael, treating him to a look that had subdued many a recalcitrant student. Henry, however, only stared back with accusing eyes. 'But it was an accident – part of a tree fell on him.'

'Who was he?' asked Ramseye. 'Did you recognise him?'

'No,' replied Michael shortly. 'We removed his face-scarf, but he was unfamiliar. Of course, that means nothing – we do not know many people in Peterborough.'

'I shall ride with Nonton,' announced Appletre suddenly. He swallowed so hard that it sounded like a gulp. 'I am better at negotiating than him.'

'Negotiating?' asked Nonton in confusion. 'Why would we want to do that?'

'To avoid violence,' explained Appletre, his usually rosy cheeks devoid of colour in the flickering torchlight. 'I have a better chance of persuading these villains to stand down than a man who looks ready for a spat.'

'But I *am* ready for a spat,' declared Nonton belligerently. 'And how will you negotiate, exactly? By singing to them?'

'Better that than knocking them senseless with wine fumes,' muttered Walter the cook. Lullington sniggered, and Yvo's eyes flashed briefly with amusement.

'You cannot go, Appletre,' whispered Henry, appalled. 'You will be . . . let *me* do it.'

'No,' said Appletre with quiet dignity. 'I appreciate the dangers, believe me – I am not a brave man. But I am treasurer now, not just a precentor, and I know my duty.'

'Good,' said Yvo, with a speed that made Bartholomew wonder whether the Prior wanted to be rid of the man he had so recently promoted. Could it be because Appletre intended to vote for Ramseye in the looming election? 'Off you go then.'

'Perhaps you should accompany them as well, Sir John,' suggested Ramseye slyly. 'I am sure our men would appreciate having a knight among their number.'

'No,' said Lullington quickly, while the expressions of the *defensores* also suggested they would be happier without whatever the corrodian could provide. 'It is better that I stay here, and coordinate the operation.'

Before anyone could ask him what was to be coordinated, Nonton slurred a command and his men set off, one or two riding, but most on foot. Cynric offered to go with them, to guide them to the body, but was curtly informed that they knew where the Dragon Tree was and did not need a visitor to tell them.

'It is a pity the abbey was not so assiduous when Robert went missing,' remarked Michael. 'Because then the Bishop would never have needed to appoint Commissioners.'

Once Nonton, Appletre and the *defensores* had gone, Yvo ordered his monks to bed. They went reluctantly, giving the impression that they would rather have waited for their people to return. Henry was one of the last to go, gazing anxiously at the gate, as if he thought he might conjure them back through it if he stared long enough. He asked Yvo for permission to keep a vigil, and his expression became piously exultant as he aimed for the church.

Meanwhile, Lullington was muttering to Yvo, although he slunk away when he saw the scholars watching. Ramseye had also lingered, and Yvo issued a curt order for him to retire to the dormitory immediately. An expression of such dark fury flashed across the almoner's face that Bartholomew recoiled, but the look disappeared so fast that he wondered if it had been his imagination or the torches casting strange shadows.

'I recommend you rest now,' said Yvo, coming to address the scholars. It was more command than suggestion. 'We shall talk in the morning. Goodnight.'

Given no choice, Michael led the way to the guest house, where lamps shed a welcoming glow into the night. Bread, cheese and wine had been left, but none of the scholars took any, although Michael shot them a longing glance. Lest the monk allowed hunger to triumph over common sense, Bartholomew tipped the wine out of the window and Cynric parcelled up the food in a cloth, ready to discard on his way to Spalling's house.

'Yvo was right, you know,' said William. 'Pyk's body *is* evidence that he was murdered, and by the time Nonton reaches that Dragon Tree the outlaws may have spirited it away.'

'What would be the point?' asked Michael. 'We have seen it now, and reported it.'

'Yes, but people do not believe or trust us.' William glanced at Bartholomew. 'Especially now they know one of us holds the disturbing title of Corpse Examiner.'

Michael winced. 'Perhaps we should devise a more innocuous one when we go home, because it does have a sinister ring. Lord! My legs are like jelly. We were lucky the branch chose that particular moment to fall, or we might have joined Pyk in the ditch.'

'There would not have been room,' said Cynric absently. 'Especially for you.'

'Meaning what, pray?' asked Michael, a little dangerously.

'Someone with heavy bones,' supplied Bartholomew. 'But Cynric makes a valid point, Brother: Robert was large, whereas Pyk was small. Perhaps Robert would not fit in the ditch, which explains why he is not there – he had to be taken elsewhere.'

'Almost certainly,' agreed Cynric. 'Shall I look tomorrow?'

'No, let the abbey do it,' said Bartholomew. 'It is too dangerous for you.'

Cynric gave him a look that expressed his disdain for that sentiment, then stood, the parcel of food under his arm. 'I had better go. Spalling is making a speech tonight in one of the taverns, and I would hate to miss it. Would you like to come?'

'No, thank you,' replied Michael in distaste. 'But it was good of you to break off your campaign to help us today. There is no question that we would have been killed without you.'

'And without Udela's warning,' added Cynric. He smiled at Bartholomew. 'She told me what she had seen when she rolled her stones for you – the monster with the left-handed claw. It was the Dragon Tree, and the south-pointing branch fell down.'

310

Bartholomew was unwilling to discuss such matters with the fanatical William in the room. However, although he was trying to ignore it, a voice in his head kept whispering that if Udela had been right about the oak, then perhaps she would also be right about him finding love. He shook himself impatiently. What was he thinking? The old woman had no more idea of what the future held than he did.

'Lord!' he breathed, as something occurred to him. He stared at Cynric. 'Could it mean Udela *knew*, rather than predicted, that ambushers were waiting there? That people from Aurifabro's household were responsible? The assault did occur after the mercenaries had left us – perhaps they donned disguises and doubled back.'

'If they had been the culprits, we would be dead,' replied Cynric soberly. 'They are professionals.'

'Then who?' asked Michael. 'Spalling's rabble? They might have been fended off by a monk, a physician, a book-bearer and a tree.'

'It was not them, either,' said Cynric sharply. 'They will be in the tavern, waiting for Spalling's address and the free ale that will follow.'

'You are right to doubt Spalling's efficacy as a warrior, though, Brother,' said Clippesby. 'The man is a coward, who will flee at the first sign of trouble. I am surprised his followers cannot see through his wordy bluster.'

'Could the other *defensores* have attacked us?' asked Bartholomew, after a short pause during which everyone stared at the Dominican in astonishment. He rarely disparaged anyone, and it was odd to hear such a bald denouncement coming from him – so odd that Cynric

311

was too startled to defend his hero. 'It would explain why ours vanished with such indecent speed.'

'But we rode hard after the attack,' said the book-bearer, belatedly shooting Clippesby a cross glance. 'We would have caught up with them.'

'Not necessarily,' argued Bartholomew. 'We spent some time inspecting the man who was killed. Perhaps there is a good reason why so many of them went out on foot just now – their horses are winded from what would have been a furious gallop.'

'That is certainly possible,' agreed Clippesby. 'Some of them were wearing armour *before* Yvo issued the order to go and collect Pyk. Of course, they are soldiers, so perhaps they dress like that all the time.'

They exchanged an uneasy glance at the notion that they were about to spend the night in a place where other residents might want them dead. Cynric offered to stay and stand guard, and Bartholomew was inclined to accept – to keep him away from Spalling, but William offered to do it instead. When the book-bearer started to argue, a coin was tossed to decide the matter.

'What now?' sighed Michael, when Cynric had gone. 'I do not feel like sleeping, but there is nothing we can do tonight.'

'We can return to Reginald's shop,' said Bartholomew. 'I am sure the answers to some of our mysteries lie there.'

'Perhaps, but the place has been sealed, and I doubt if Yvo will agree to let us in.'

'I am not suggesting we ask permission.'

Michael was shocked. 'You mean burgle it? Break in like common thieves?'

Bartholomew nodded. 'Unless you have a better idea.'

'Very well.' Michael's abrupt capitulation revealed the depth of his desperation. 'We shall go after nocturns. It is the darkest part of the night, when all innocent folk should be abed. Hopefully, we can commit our crime with no one any the wiser.'

'Then let us pray that you find answers,' said William grimly. 'Because it is Wednesday tomorrow, when we must leave. And do not suggest staying another day, Brother, because the University will riot if you are not back in time to write Winwick Hall's charter. We cannot risk Michaelhouse's safety to save Peterborough.'

'No,' agreed Michael determinedly. 'We cannot.'

Bartholomew estimated that they had roughly four hours before embarking on their nocturnal expedition, but was too tense even to think about sleeping. Not only was he nervous about doing something that would land them in trouble if they were caught, but his thoughts were a bewildering jumble of questions – about their mysteries, Udela's unnerving predictions, and Matilde and Julitta. He was glad when William announced that he and Clippesby had information to impart, as it represented a distraction.

'Me first,' the Franciscan said, giving Clippesby a shove. He addressed Michael. 'Trentham is still struggling to dig Joan's grave – people keep coming to talk to him, so his progress is slow. To help, I offered to save him some time by hearing the bedeswomen's confessions. And I learned something about Joan.'

'Then you cannot tell us,' said Michael sharply. 'The Seal of Confession is sacred.'

'I was not going to repeat anything from those,' said William indignantly. 'Although you would be bored senseless if I did – I have never encountered such a dull catalogue of sins. What I learned was in their hall afterwards, when they were thanking me with ale and cakes.'

'Well?' asked Michael, when the Franciscan paused.

'You will recall that Joan was acting as a guard on the day she was murdered, minding Becket's relics and Oxforde's tomb. Well, that was highly unusual, because she never undertook such lowly duties as a rule – it is Marion and Elene's responsibility. But she did it that day to impress us, the Bishop's Commissioners.'

'What are you saying?' asked Michael, bemused. 'That her sudden change in behaviour afforded someone the opportunity to dispatch her?'

'No, I am just reporting a fact – it is for you to interpret its significance.' William dropped his haranguing manner and grimaced. 'Actually, I do not know what it means, Brother, but I thought it might be important.'

'It might,' said Michael, nodding. 'Thank you. What have you found out, Clippesby?'

'Something about Welbyrn. I spent some time with the granary mice today, and they overheard Henry and Ramseye reminiscing about their schooldays – specifically the time when Matt and Welbyrn fought, and Welbyrn fell over and broke his nose.'

Bartholomew groaned. 'Is it not time that incident was forgotten?'

Clippesby ignored him. 'Apparently, Welbyrn was not himself when he provoked that brawl. He had just received some terrible news: that his father had drowned himself.'

'Really?' Bartholomew closed his eyes. 'Damn!'

Clippesby patted his hand. 'I am not trying to make you feel guilty, Matt, but to explain something about his character. Henry remembered the older Welbyrn telling his wife that he was made of lead, and that if he ever fell in water, he would sink like a stone. *Ergo*, he knew he would die when he jumped in the river – there was no clearer case of suicide.'

'So he was a lunatic,' surmised William. 'No wonder our Welbyrn was frightened when he thought he might be losing his wits. He believed he would end like his sire.'

'Henry and Ramseye were discussing how the death had influenced our Welbyrn's views on self-murder,' Clippesby continued. 'He considered it the gravest of all sins, and would never have contemplated it, no matter how terrified he was of going mad.'

'So they believe someone else killed him?' asked Michael. Clippesby nodded. 'But why were they talking about it in a granary? Surely that is odd?'

'I thought so,' said Clippesby. 'As did the mice.'

A few moments later, there was a knock on the door. It was Ramseye, who shot inside the moment William answered it and indicated with an urgent gesture that it was to be closed behind him. Then he went to the window and cracked open the shutter to peer outside.

'What are you doing?' asked Michael, watching the almoner's antics suspiciously.

'Being careful,' replied Ramseye. 'Men and women have been dying far too frequently since you arrived, and I do not intend to join them. I came to bring you this.'

He handed the monk a purse. It was little more than rags, and had clearly belonged to someone poor. Its greasy sheen suggested it was ancient, too.

Michael held it between thumb and forefinger in distaste. 'What is it?'

'A purse,' replied Ramseye impatiently. 'It was found in Reginald's workshop and brought here, along with everything else that was considered valuable or curious.'

'I thought the place was supposed to be sealed until his will is proved.'

Ramseye nodded. 'Yes, but before the door was locked, Yvo sent Lullington to bring anything readily portable to the Abbot's House. I argued against it, but he over-ruled me.'

'I imagine he thought it would be safer,' said Bartholomew, suspecting that Ramseye would have done the same had he been Acting Abbot. 'Empty properties attract thieves.'

'Perhaps.' Ramseye cast a disdainful glance at Bartholomew before turning back to Michael. 'Yvo has been pawing through everything all day, ostensibly to find out why Reginald died, but in reality to assess how much it might be worth.'

Michael held up the purse. 'And why do you think I might be interested in this nasty thing?'

'Because Reginald said that a purse would tell you all you needed to know.'

Michael's eyes narrowed. 'How do you know? Reginald was whispering, and no one else was close enough to hear.'

'You told your colleagues,' explained Ramseye, 'who mentioned it when they were questioning our servants today. It is now common knowledge.'

'I was trying to help,' said William, flushing a deep red. 'Time is short, and we are due to leave tomorrow.'

'Are you?' asked Ramseye hopefully.

'It depends on the state of my investigation,' lied Michael. He stared at the tatty item in his hand. 'But Reginald was a cutler. Surely he owned a better purse than this?'

'Yes, he did, and it is in Yvo's solar, full of silver.' Ramseye nodded to the other. 'But that was also among his belongings, and it struck me as odd. So I decided to bring it to you.'

'Why?' asked Michael charily.

'Because I was horrified when William's questions implied that Lady Lullington was murdered, and that Reginald might have been complicit in the crime. And because I have a terrible feeling that the culprit is one of us – a Benedictine. In fact, I think it may be Henry, because he has been on his knees constantly since she died.'

'He cares for her soul,' said Bartholomew coldly. 'And if you were any kind of monk, you would understand that prayers are acts of compassion, not signs of a guilty conscience.'

The physician could not recall if he had ever received a blacker look than the one directed at him by the almoner. Michael saw it, and stepped between them.

'If you suspect Henry of such a terrible crime, why were you discussing Welbyrn with him in the granary?'

Ramseye gaped. 'How do you— no, it does not matter. Bishops' Commissioners have spies, we all know that. But to answer your question, Henry said it was somewhere that he and I could talk undisturbed.'

'That does not explain why you were discussing Welbyrn,' Michael pointed out.

'When I first heard what had happened in St Leonard's, I believed Yvo's contention that it was an accident. Henry thought it was suicide, and took me to the granary to say so. But as we debated, we began to realise that we were both wrong. The truth is that he was murdered.'

'By whom?'

'We do not know. We spent an age discussing possible candidates, as your informant no doubt told you, but no one stood out above the others. Please do not glower at me, Brother. I did not come here to be interrogated like a common criminal. I came to help.'

'Thank you,' said Michael. 'Although you will forgive me for being cautious.'

Ramseye gave one of his unreadable smiles. 'Why, when my motive is obvious? I want you gone. You are a disruptive influence on my . . . on the abbey, and if helping you with your enquiries expedites your departure, then nothing is too much trouble.'

'You may be seeing more of me in future,' warned Michael. 'The Bishop is a great admirer of my talents, and I like it here. The abbacy would suit me very well.'

The blood drained from Ramseye's face, and he turned and left without a word. Bartholomew went to the window, and watched him break into a run the moment he was outside. There was no pretence at stealth this time – he did not care who saw him. The physician experienced a surge of unease, and wished Michael had held his tongue.

'There is no money in this purse,' said William. Michael had set it on the table and was wiping his fingers on a piece of scented linen, but the friar had no qualms about touching it, being used to grimy things. 'Just a scrap of parchment.'

Bartholomew took it from him, but the writing was so tiny that he could only make out some of the words. William and Michael declared it illegible, and even Clippesby, who had the keenest eyesight, struggled.

'It is a pardon for sins committed this year,' said the Dominican eventually. 'And there is a cross drawn at the bottom. How curious!'

'I rarely dispense pardons these days,' said William, blithely ignoring the fact that the Church frowned on such practices. 'Well, not unless the petitioner is willing to pay a hefty fee.'

Bartholomew stared at him, then snatched the little document from Clippesby. The cross indicated that a cleric had written it, and suddenly the answer to the mystery surrounding Lady Lullington was as clear as day.

'It is Reginald's reward – his payment – for creating the diversion when she was strangled!' he exclaimed. 'He was right: the purse *has* told us all we need to know. Well, all we need to know about Lady Lullington's death, at least.'

'It is not much of a clue,' grumbled Michael. 'Because I do not understand it. Moreover, sin can only be pardoned through proper penitence, not because someone scrawls a few words on a bit of parchment.'

'Theology is irrelevant here,' said Bartholomew impatiently. 'The point is that it comes from a man who could not pay coins for the favour he wanted, so another commodity was provided instead. And as Reginald was involved in something unsavoury, the offer was accepted.'

'But Reginald was not a Christian,' argued Michael. 'He refused absolution. Why should he want a pardon from the Church?'

'Perhaps he was persuaded that it would ease his troubled conscience,' suggested Bartholomew with a shrug. 'We will probably never know why he accepted it. However, the more I think about this, the more I am sure I am right.'

'I agree – you are,' said Clippesby. 'And the fact that Reginald mentioned the purse – with the clue it contained – as he lay dying suggests that he wanted to expose the culprit. I suspect it was because he had not known *why* he was ordered to make a fuss in the chapel, and when he found out, he was horrified and angry that he had been tricked into helping a killer.'

'A monk?' asked William, frowning as he sifted through likely suspects.

'Monks cannot grant pardons,' said Bartholomew impatiently. 'Only priests can.'

'Trentham?' asked Michael, wide-eyed with shock. 'A poor cleric who has no money of his own? *He* is the killer? I do not believe it! He is a good, decent lad, and his grief for Lady Lullington has been profound.'

'He must have been acting,' said William in distaste. 'What a scoundrel!'

'No,' said Bartholomew. 'I think he was driven by compassion, not malice. He was sorry when she woke after the strong medicine I gave her, and so was she. They had become close, and her suffering distressed him deeply.'

'But you said she had been throttled with unusual ferocity,' Michael pointed out. 'That does not sound compassionate to me.'

Bartholomew knew the reason for that, too. 'Inges told a tale about strangulation when I was with Kirwell, and Trentham heard it. Apparently, it is more merciful to do it vigorously. Clearly Trentham did exactly that in the hope of sparing her more pain. I imagine he will confess when you confront him, Brother. But do it gently.'

Michael sighed unhappily. 'Come with me, Clippesby. You can grant him absolution, because I do not have the stomach for it.'

'Leave him to me,' said William grimly. 'I will be far better than a Dominican at informing him that murder leads straight to the fiery pits of Hell.'

Michael was unwilling to let William loose on a grieving and conflicted young man. 'I know, but whoever confronts Trentham will be busy for hours, and I need you here.'

'Why?' asked William suspiciously.

'To prevent anyone from coming in and noticing that Matt and I are missing.'

'Why would you be missing? There is no point in burgling Reginald's shop now that Yvo has removed everything of value.'

'Lullington was only ordered to collect easily portable items from Reginald's home,' explained Bartholomew, 'so it *is* still worth exploring.'

'I sincerely hope we find something,' said Michael unhappily. 'Because if we fail, we will have to invade the Abbot's House instead. But I shall live there myself soon, and I would rather my enjoyment of its luxury was *not* tainted by the memory of a crime.'

* * *

Trentham lived in a small house next to the parish church, and Bartholomew, Clippesby and Michael walked there in silence. A glimmer of light under the shutters showed that the priest was awake, as did the sound of weeping, which was distinctly audible as they approached. Michael opened the door without knocking, and stepped inside.

The house comprised a single room containing a few sticks of furniture and some utensils for cooking. Other than a wooden cross that had been nailed to the wall, there were no decorations. It was clean, though, and the ancient blankets had been carefully darned. Trentham was kneeling at a prie-dieu, his youthful face wet with tears.

'I cannot pray,' he said brokenly. He did not seem surprised to see the Bishop's Commissioners in his home. 'I have not been able to pray since . . .'

'Since you strangled Lady Lullington,' finished Michael baldly.

Trentham made no attempt to deny the accusation. 'She begged me to do it, and it seemed right at the time. She was in such agony, and had been for weeks. But now I wish I had stolen Doctor Bartholomew's bag, and used some of his potions instead. It would have been . . .'

'Tell us what happened,' said Michael, sitting on the bed. His voice was kind, and Clippesby stepped towards the priest, to lay a comforting hand on his shoulder.

'Abbot Robert always said that I was unsuitable for this post, and he was right – it hurts me to see people suffering. Especially Lady Lullington, who was so virtuous and good. Her husband treated her abominably, but she never once complained. She was a saint.'

'But then she became ill,' said Michael, encouraging him.

'Shortly after the Abbot vanished.' Trentham looked at Bartholomew. 'On Saturday, you seemed surprised when you heard that her illness had occurred suddenly. I wanted to ask why, but Hagar was talking too much. Will you tell me now?'

'I can think of any number of ailments that bring about a lingering death, but none with the symptoms I could see in Lady Lullington – including an abrupt onset. She declined to let me examine her and would not answer questions . . .'

'But you suspected something odd,' surmised Trentham bitterly. 'Well, you are right. Her illness struck her down after a meal in the abbey.'

'You think a monk did her harm?' asked Michael uneasily.

'No,' replied Trentham shortly. 'Not them.'

'Lullington,' said Bartholomew. 'Her loving husband. What happened? Did he try to poison her but fail to do it properly?'

'She would never accuse him, but I believe so. She became violently ill that night – purging blood and the like. I think whatever substance he fed her did irreparable harm, but instead of killing her quickly, it sentenced her to a slow and lingering death.'

'It would explain why he never visited,' said Clippesby softly. 'He did not have the courage to look his victim in the eye.'

'So you took matters into your own hands,' said Michael, regarding the youth sternly. 'You throttled her, using a massive degree of force because of a certain discussion you heard between Inges and others in Kirwell's room.'

Trentham nodded, and his eyes filled with tears again. 'He said a brief but powerful squeeze would see it all over in an instant. He was right: something snapped in her neck immediately, and I do not believe she experienced more than a momentary flash of pain. Nothing compared to what she had borne already.'

'It is still murder,' said Michael.

'I know,' sobbed Trentham. 'God help me.'

'Make your confession to Clippesby,' said Michael tiredly. 'The Bishop will decide what happens to you.'

He beckoned Bartholomew outside, where the sky was clear and splattered with stars, all sparkling in the black velvet of night. They stood in silence for a while.

'What a horrible business,' Michael said eventually. 'I cannot find it in my heart to condemn the lad, yet what he did . . . Of course, it was unkind of Lady Lullington to ask it of him.'

'People often beg the same of me, and I understand why he yielded. What do you think Gynewell will do with him?'

'He has benefit of clergy, so he will not hang. A life of atonement, perhaps?'

'Then it might be a good idea to suggest that he does not do it in another hospital, lest he feels inclined to meddle with nature a second time.'

'I doubt that will happen; he has learned his lesson. However, now we have another killer to confront, one who is a lot more ruthless than Trentham.'

'It will not be easy,' warned Bartholomew. 'Lullington is not the sort of man who will confess willingly, and our

324

only "evidence" is Trentham's suspicions. The opinion of a self-confessed strangler will not count for much, and Lullington will know it.'

'And he will doubtless use the fact that his wife would not have wanted him charged with her death,' sighed Michael. 'Trentham's testimony suggests she knew exactly what he had done to her, but she elected to say silent about it.'

'Yes, and I suspect Lullington knew that, too, because of something he said at Entertainment Night – about her "loyalty" to him. I thought at the time that it was an odd thing to say, and I have been mulling over the possibility that he had harmed her ever since. But why would she let him get away with such a monstrous thing?'

'Because of her sons, lest the shame of murder blight their careers – they are attached to the King's court, where that sort of thing matters. I suggest we tackle him now, Matt, when he will be befuddled with sleep and may let something slip. We will not have time tomorrow, and I should like to present the Bishop with one killer before we leave.'

'Perhaps we should stay another day, Brother – at least until a proper search has been made for Robert's body. After all, Gynewell is unlikely to make you Abbot if you leave before exposing the culprit.'

'A difficult choice,' mused Michael. 'My present responsibilities to the University or my future ones to the abbey.'

Despite the late hour, the knight was not in his quarters when Michael stormed in without knocking. A brief glance around showed that Lullington had secured himself some of the best lodgings in the monastery. There was a little pantry at one end of his elegant solar, which was well stocked with exotic treats – all recently purchased, suggesting that his wife's jewels had been put to good use. Its top shelf was invisible from ground level, and as Lullington was a stupid, unimaginative man, Bartholomew was willing to wager that the knight considered it a cunning hiding place. He stood on a stool and groped around.

The phial was hidden behind some pots of preserved fruit. It was not easy to reach, for it had been shoved as far back as possible, but he managed to hook it forward eventually. He opened it and took a cautious sniff.

'Well?' asked Michael.

'It will have to be tested, of course, but it smells like a substance I encountered in Padua. An anatomist fed some to a dog, and when the body was opened, it was full of lesions. There is no reason – no *legitimate* reason – for Lullington to have this in his possession.'

'Is it the same as the toxin in the Lombard slices?' asked Michael.

Bartholomew shook his head. 'I would not have recovered from a dose of this. But I have been thinking about the stuff that was used on me. It made me sleep for hours, which means I swallowed a significant measure. But how could it have all gone into a single cake without me tasting something amiss? It—'

'Give the phial to me,' interrupted Michael, unwilling to listen to a lecture on the subject. 'We shall confront Lullington with it later.'

'There is something else up here, too,' said Bartholomew, standing on tiptoe and supposing his

326

conclusions about what had happened to him would have to wait until a more opportune moment. 'Hand me the candle, Brother. I cannot see.'

The item transpired to be a pouch, pushed so far into the shadows that the physician had to use Lullington's spare sword to reach it and drag it towards him. It was heavy for its size.

'It has not been there long,' said Michael. 'Or it would be dustier. And the leather is new.'

He shook its contents out on to the table. There were two seals, several large jewels and a bar of gold that was the size of a small book and considerably weightier.

'The gold alone must be worth a fortune,' mused Bartholomew. 'Not to mention the diamonds. Or are they sapphires? Regardless, it tells us that Lullington is a rich man in his own right, and he had no need to plunder his dead wife's possessions.'

'These do not belong to him. The seals are an abbot's – his personal one, with an image of him reading his bible; and the monastery's, with St Peter holding the keys to Heaven.'

'I thought Robert took them with him when he went to visit Aurifabro.'

Michael nodded. 'And as I doubt he surrendered them willingly, we must conclude that they were acquired by force. Or after he was dead. No wonder Lullington showed a marked lack of concern for his missing "friend". The villain is involved in whatever happened to him!'

'What about the precious stones and the gold?'

'I suspect they represent a large chunk of the monastery's portable wealth.'

'Shall I put them back?'

'No! When he learns his game is up, Lullington might manage to sneak back and make off with them, leaving the monastery penniless.'

Outside, a bell chimed for nocturns, which meant it was roughly two o'clock. After a moment, monks began to process from their dormitory to the church, a silent line of men in hoods and swinging habits, sandals whispering on the flagstones.

'Should we ask them to help us find Lullington?' asked Bartholomew. 'We cannot do it alone – the abbey is too big.'

'If we do, we shall have to tell them why, and the tale will be all over Peterborough tomorrow. It is better to deal with the matter quietly and discreetly.'

Bartholomew was not sure he agreed, but he deferred to his friend's judgement. However, he wished he had objected when a search of the refectory, chapter house, kitchens and various other buildings met with no success. Lullington was not there.

'Perhaps he fled because he knew we were closing in on him,' suggested Michael.

'How? We have not spoken to anyone except Trentham, and he is hardly in a position to gossip. Besides, I do not see Lullington abandoning his comfortable existence without a fight.'

'True,' agreed Michael. Then he regarded the physician in alarm. 'Lord! I hope *he* is not dead, because we cannot investigate another murder.'

CHAPTER 12

It was not long before Michael decided they were wasting their time hunting for Lullington: the abbey had far too many hiding places, and they had no idea where to look for him outside. Moreover, the opportunity to search Reginald's home might not arise again – it had to be done that night. When he had hidden the poison, seals, gold and jewels in the guest house, the monk took a deep breath and indicated that Bartholomew was to follow him to the Abbey Gate.

They arrived to find it patrolled by a *defensor*, but the little Bolhithe Gate in the south wall was secured by no more than a bar; it was a simple matter to remove it and walk to the marketplace. The streets were very dark, although lights gleamed here and there. A baby was awake in one house, wailing insistently, while from another came the sound of laughter as friends whiled away the small hours together. A dog's claws clicked as it trotted purposefully across the cobbles, and an owl hooted in the distance.

'Are you sure we should be doing this?' whispered Michael anxiously. 'What if we are seen? It will not look good for the Bishop's Commissioners to be caught raiding the homes of wealthy townsfolk.'

'Then we shall have to be careful,' said Bartholomew with more confidence than he felt. 'Although if you have an idea that does not involve us breaking in, I am all ears.'

'I do not,' said Michael, after a moment during which Bartholomew could almost hear the monk's mind working. 'But I am not climbing through any windows. I am not built for that sort of thing. You do it, while I stand guard.'

'I had a feeling that might be the plan.'

When they reached the cutler's shop, Bartholomew led the way to the back, knowing it was what Cynric would do – the book-bearer possessed an unsavoury but useful talent for entering places uninvited. He looked at the house rather helplessly at first, but then saw that one of the windows had a defective shutter. He tugged on it, but nothing happened, so he pulled harder. Michael squawked in alarm when it dropped to the ground with a clatter.

'It came off in my hand,' whispered Bartholomew.

Michael shot him a reproachful glare. 'In you go, and please hurry. If you are caught, I shall be mortified.'

Resisting the urge to point out that his capture would give them a lot more to worry about than mere mortification, Bartholomew clambered through the window. He had had the foresight to bring a tinderbox, so he lit one of the cutler's lamps and headed for the workshop. He started by the door, and worked systematically until he arrived back where he had started, and then did the same in the filthy bedchamber. It was easier and quicker now that Lullington had removed much of the clutter, but despite his efforts, Bartholomew found nothing that might have a bearing on what had happened to Robert and Pyk.

The only unusual thing was that several silver pennies had fallen between the floorboards, and Reginald had neglected to retrieve them. As most people tended to be careful with money, Bartholomew prised one out. It was new and shiny, and came from Bishop Gynewell's Mint in Lincoln, but that was not surprising – it was the one closest to Peterborough.

'Nothing,' he reported, climbing back through the window and promptly stumbling over a pile of discarded tiles. One slipped off the heap and landed with a loud crack. Michael cringed away in alarm.

'My nerves!' the monk complained. 'They are not built for this kind of thing.'

'Nor mine,' retorted Bartholomew. His heart was pounding from tension. 'You can burgle the Abbot's House on your own, because I am not doing this again. Can we go now?'

'I have something to show you first. While you were inside, I lit a candle and prodded about in that mound of grass you can see over there.'

'The one that looks like a grave?' asked Bartholomew uneasily.

Michael's reply was to relight his candle and lead the way to the shallow hole he had excavated. Bartholomew crouched down to see a skeletal human hand. It was not very big, although the state of the joints told him it had belonged to an adult.

'Reginald's wife? So the rumours were right – he did kill her?'

'It looks that way, and think of the implications. The murder of a spouse is a powerful secret, and we know she disappeared shortly after Robert's arrival. Do you recall what the gossiping servants told William about the Abbot's relationship with Reginald?'

'That Robert had some kind of hold over him – they were not friends, but something less pleasant. So can we assume that Robert discovered what Reginald had done, and used it to blackmail him?'

'It makes sense to me, and we have been told countless times that Robert was not a good man – extortion might be just another of his failings. Yet how would he have found out?'

'Perhaps he saw this grave-shaped heap and drew his own conclusions. Or perhaps Robert was less than principled with what he heard in the confessional – which may have been why Reginald turned pagan. However, what we should be asking is: what did Robert force Reginald to do that resulted in him wanting Trentham's pardon?'

It was a question neither could answer, so Bartholomew scraped the soil back over the sad remains and turned to leave, eager to be away. Michael fell into step at his side.

'I did some serious thinking while you were in Reginald's house. I *know* Welbyrn was murdered – someone shoved him so he cracked his head on the side of the pool and left him to drown – and I am sorry, Matt, but my suspicions keep returning to Henry.'

'Why would Henry turn from devout monk to ruthless murderer?' demanded Bartholomew, speaking loudly enough to set a dog barking in the house they were passing.

Michael made an urgent gesture for him to lower his voice. 'Perhaps because Welbyrn tried to poison you, his old friend. You did battle with Welbyrn once to protect him, so he may have thought it incumbent on him to return the favour.'

'Hah!' Bartholomew stopped walking to regard Michael triumphantly. 'Then your theory has just collapsed, because Henry did not poison me – William did.'

Michael gaped at the physician. The baby was still howling in the house they had passed earlier, and an owl glided silently along the lane, death on wings as it hunted rodents among the rubbish. The same clicking-clawed dog trotted past, this time going in the opposite direction. There was a faint hint of colour in the eastern sky; dawn would break soon.

'William might be a bigoted old fool, but he would never harm you,' said Michael, once he had recovered from his shock. 'Or anyone else from Michaelhouse.'

'Not deliberately,' agreed Bartholomew. 'He was trying to help, but he actually did something very dangerous. You see, he was with me when I physicked Lady Lullington. She was in agony, so I gave her a huge dose of an extremely powerful medicine.'

'So he did the same for you? He thought you were in pain because you had scraped your elbow on the wall, so he decided to dose you with something to make you feel better?'

'Precisely. Unfortunately, he failed to appreciate that I keep this particular potion for the terminally ill; I would never give it to anyone who might live.'

'To help them towards the grave?' asked Michael, round eyed. 'Like Trentham—'

'No, of course not! I mean it contains a potentially toxic combination of ingredients that should only be used in extreme cases, when relief of pain is the only recourse. I would never give it to someone for a graze.'

'I remember William passing you a large beaker of

333

watered wine,' said Michael. 'And I also recall you gulping it down quickly enough to alarm him.'

Bartholomew smiled ruefully. 'I was thirsty because I had eaten those salty leeks.'

'But Lady Lullington did not sleep for two nights and a day.'

'She would have developed a tolerance for strong medicines during the weeks she was ill, and I suspect William dosed me with rather more than I gave her, on the grounds that she was small and frail and I am not. Moreover, I was drunk from the claret in the Swan, and combining wine and poppy syrup is never a good idea.'

'Could he have killed you?' asked Michael uneasily.

'Yes, quite possibly.'

'So the Lombard slices were harmless?'

Bartholomew nodded. 'I have been thinking about those, too. We know Welbyrn provided them, but I think they were meant to be a peace offering. He was terrified of what he thought was happening to him, and I believe he may have been sufficiently desperate to solicit my help.'

'Do you think so?' asked Michael doubtfully. 'I would have said you were the last person he would have turned to.'

'What choice did he have? Pyk was not here, and there is no other *medicus* in Peterborough. And he must have been aware that his visits to St Leonard's were not helping.'

'Very well,' conceded Michael. 'But then what? *I* know you are too honourable to allow personal animosity to interfere with your dealings with patients, but he probably judged people by his own shabby standards . . .'

'Quite, so he decided to see if a gift would make us

regard him in a more favourable light. He asked the cook to bake him some Lombard slices, because you had declared a liking for them. Unfortunately, William fed me the soporific, and you declared me poisoned . . .'

'So he retrieved them from the Swan, lest the anonymously donated Lombard slices were blamed for your condition, which explains why they were in his scrip when he died.'

'He was innocent of any wrongdoing, but it would have been a difficult charge to disprove, given his very public hostility towards us. And he would not have wanted to tell the truth, because that would have meant revealing that he might be losing his wits.'

'When did you reason all this out?'

'Earlier – I started to tell you in Lullington's quarters, but you interrupted.'

'It was hardly the right place.' Michael shook his head. 'But William! How could he?'

'He is not a clever man, Brother. He will have no idea what he has done.'

Michael rubbed his hand across his eyes. 'So where does this leave us? I am so tired that I can barely think straight and—'

He stopped speaking when a torch flashed across the street. Moments later, there was another, and when one started to bob towards them, Bartholomew grabbed Michael's sleeve and pulled him into a doorway. Both scholars held their breath as a number of people trotted past, their footsteps beating an urgent tattoo on the cobbles. At the very end of what was a sizeable mob was a familiar figure. Bartholomew stepped forward to intercept it.

'What are you doing out at this time of night?' demanded Langelee. He wore his boiled leather jerkin under his academic tabard, and his sword was at his waist.

'Breaking into houses,' replied Michael shortly. 'What is happening? I can tell just by looking that these folk are up to no good.'

'I told you earlier, Brother – Spalling aims to attack Aurifabro's house.'

'I did not realise it would be tonight,' said Michael in alarm.

'Nor did I,' said Langelee grimly. 'He just made a speech in a tavern, and suddenly his army was on the move.'

'Then Aurifabro's mercenaries will earn their keep today.' Michael nodded at the eclectic array of hoes, scythes and kitchen knives that were being carried.

'These people are no match for professional warriors.' Bartholomew was horrified. 'Moreover, they will run into Nonton and his *defensores*, who are still on the Torpe road looking for Robert's body.'

'I tried to dissuade them, so did Cynric,' said Langelee, but their blood is up and we were lucky not to have been lynched. You must go to the abbey at once, and tell Prior Yvo to stop them.'

'He will not help,' predicted Michael. 'Why would he, when a battle between Aurifabro and Spalling will injure two of the abbey's enemies? And do not say he will want to save the *defensores*, because he would not mind being rid of them, either – Nonton intends to use them to intimidate the monks into voting for Ramseye in the election.'

'So what do we do?' asked Bartholomew, appalled. 'We cannot stand by while people are slaughtered. There are children in Spalling's throng!'

'We had better follow them and see what opportunities arise.' Langelee's expression hardened as he fingered his sword. 'And if not, then we had better be ready to fight.'

'Yes,' said Michael soberly. 'But on whose side?'

The night was not as black as it had been, and the eastern sky was streaked with silver, although it would be another hour before the sun made its appearance. It was not easy to see where they were going, and Bartholomew, Michael and Langelee stumbled over ruts and potholes as they hurried through the market and along the Torpe road.

They heard Spalling's raiders before they saw them: they were singing a revolutionary song that allowed them to march in time with the music. The result was a little disjointed, as the scholars were not the only ones who could not see where they were putting their feet, and the bobbing torches allocated to a chosen few were insufficient to light everyone's way.

Bartholomew was horrified by the number of people who had rallied to Spalling's call. Some were feisty young men fuelled by ale and a belief that the world owed them something, but most were folk who should not have allowed themselves to be cajoled into such reckless foolery – grandmothers, men with young families, pregnant women and youngsters who should have been in bed.

It was not long before the scholars reached the stragglers, which comprised old folk who could not walk fast enough to keep up with the main column and those who had imbibed their leader's ale too liberally. The elderly insurgents hobbled along gamely, exchanging tales about the inconvenience of ageing bladders.

'They will be massacred,' breathed Bartholomew, torn between exasperation and despair. 'They are making such a racket with their singing, stamping and chattering that Aurifabro's men will hear them coming a mile away.'

'I told Spalling that his only chance of success would be to launch a surprise attack, but he refused to listen.' Langelee's voice was thick with disgust. 'The man is an ass!'

'Where is Cynric? Surely he can see that this madness will end in disaster?'

'Of course, but Spalling has everyone convinced that God is with them, so Cynric's warnings have gone unheeded.'

'Something is happening ahead,' said Michael urgently. 'By the Dragon Tree. Everyone has stopped walking.'

They broke into a run, and caught up with the vanguard just as Spalling was launching into one of his speeches. He was dressed as a foot-soldier, although there was nothing common about the quality of his jerkin and helmet – they had been made to protect their wearer well. He was railing at Nonton, whose *defensores* had drawn their weapons. Appletre hovered behind the cellarer, white-faced and frightened.

'The poor have been downtrodden long enough,' Spalling was bawling. 'And tonight we shall redress the balance. It is the first step towards a fairer society.'

'Stop, please!' shouted Appletre. 'Stay here and help us look for corpses instead. We have found Pyk, although he is sadly rotted, and now we must hunt for the Abbot. There is a deep pond nearby that looks promising. I am sure he will be in it, and we shall need assistance to haul him out, if Pyk is anything to go by.'

Not surprisingly, this invitation was met with scant enthusiasm.

'Bold *defensores*,' said Spalling, addressing the abbey's soldiers. 'Will you join us? We shall loot Aurifabro's house before we burn it, and it would be a pity for you to miss out.'

The greedy glances exchanged between the *defensores* suggested they thought so, too.

'No,' said Michael firmly. 'Aurifabro will fight to protect his property, and you will die. Moreover, if the scent of rebellion carries, it may ignite—'

'I hope so,' declared Spalling hotly. 'It is what we have been working towards.'

'Bloodshed and mayhem?' demanded Michael. 'Is that what you itch to see?'

'If that is what it takes to set the poor free, then yes.' Spalling raised his voice. 'The brave men of Peterborough are not afraid of Aurifabro's louts. Are they?'

There was a resounding denial, louder and rougher than the previous chorus, because the *defensores* had joined in.

'Wait!' cried Appletre. He swallowed hard when everyone looked at him. 'I heard you singing when you arrived, but you were out of tune. Stay with me, and I shall teach you how to—'

'Are you ready?' roared Spalling, shooting Appletre

a disdainful look. 'Are you willing to take what is right-fully yours, my good people?'

A wild cheer said they were. Spalling shouldered the scholars out of the way and resumed his march, while the *defensores* tossed their tools aside and followed. Appletre scurried after them, pleading with them to see reason.

'Why did you not order your men to stay here, Nonton?' demanded Michael angrily, seeing the cellarer watching silently from the side of the road. 'You must see that the abbey cannot be involved in this.'

'Involved in what?' asked Nonton. 'Ridding Peterborough of a villain who has made nasty accusations against our foundation – a heretic who keeps a witch in his house? The Bishop will applaud our decision to stand with the townsfolk.'

'He will not,' snapped Michael. 'Especially if this rebellion spreads to other parts of his diocese. Can you not see the damage it may do?'

Nonton snorted his disdain, and turned to follow his men: the *defensores* were not the only ones whose imagination had been fired by talk of plunder. Helplessly, the scholars watched him leave. Then Appletre came racing back.

'Spalling threatened to punch me when I tried to reason with him,' he said, close to tears in his agitation. 'But he will lead everyone to destruction! What are we going to do? We *must* stop them before blood is spilled.'

'How?' asked Michael, exasperated. '*We* have no army.'

'I shall fetch Prior Yvo,' said Appletre with sudden determination. 'Nonton will have no choice but to obey him, and once the *defensores* turn back, the others may follow.'

He was trotting back towards the town, short legs pumping furiously, before Michael could tell him he was wasting his time.

'This is all wrong,' came a quiet voice from behind them. It was Cynric, staring unhappily at the receding torches. 'The redistribution of property is a noble goal, but Spalling is talking about looting, which is not the same thing at all. And what about the witch?'

'What about her?' asked Michael warily.

'She will not be pleased if she is killed,' explained Cynric worriedly. 'She might curse us. It will be a—'

He was interrupted by a sudden scream from the road ahead. It was followed by more cries, some of pain, others of fear.

'It has started,' said Langelee grimly. 'I guessed correctly – Aurifabro has pre-empted Spalling and has launched a counterattack.'

They raced towards the commotion. Dawn was approaching rapidly now, and it was light enough to see that the road was blocked by a wall of mounted, well-armed men, some carrying bows. Langelee's bleak prediction was right.

Spalling's people milled in terror as arrows rained down among them. They outnumbered the mercenaries ten to one, but hoes and pitchforks were no match for real weapons, and they lacked the skill to know how to press their advantage. Nonton and his *defensores*, who might have evened the odds, were suddenly nowhere to be seen.

From the rear, Spalling screamed at his troops to advance, but bewildered and frightened, they simply cowered. Then Aurifabro appeared, sitting astride a massive warhorse. He wore a helmet, armour and carried a sword, but although Bartholomew could tell he was uncomfortably unfamiliar with them, he appeared distressingly invincible to Spalling's peasants. They issued a collective moan of despair.

'I have had enough of your nonsense, Spalling,' the goldsmith announced in a ringing voice. The townsfolk went silent. 'You want a fight? Then let us have one and resolve our differences once and for all.'

'Very well,' Spalling yelled back, careful to keep plenty of people between him and the mercenaries' bows. 'And when you are defeated, all your riches will belong to me . . . I mean to the poor. God stands with us today, because not only do you crush peasants with your greed, but you murdered Abbot Robert and poor Pyk.'

'*You* murdered them,' Aurifabro snarled. 'Just as you have been attacking other travellers on our roads. It makes sense to me now: you have not been using your own money to provoke unrest – these robberies have funded it.'

'Rubbish!' bellowed Spalling, outraged. 'How dare you accuse us of being criminals. We are doing God's work, whereas you are an evil pagan who lives with a witch.'

'There is nothing evil about my religion,' spat Aurifabro. 'Yours is the one that pays homage to executed criminals.' He turned to someone who was standing behind him. 'Bless us, Mother Udela, and let us see whose deity is stronger.'

'Lord!' gulped Cynric at Bartholomew's side. 'I cannot fight a witch!'

'Stop this madness,' ordered Michael, striding forward and interposing himself between the two sides. 'It is not—'

'Prepare to advance!' shouted Aurifabro to his men. 'On my mark.'

There were a number of metallic clangs as the townsfolk in the vanguard dropped their tools and turned to flee. They collided with those who clustered behind them, causing chaos and panic. Unable to escape, some fell to their knees and began to beg for mercy. The savage expressions on the mercenaries' faces suggested it was unlikely to be given.

Appalled, Bartholomew shouldered his way through Spalling's rabble to stand at Michael's side. Langelee followed, and so did Cynric. Bartholomew knew their frail barrier of four men was unlikely to survive Aurifabro's charge, although Langelee's white-fisted grip on his sword suggested that *he* would not go down easily.

'We are the Bishop's Commissioners,' declared Michael, drawing himself up to his full, considerable height and using the voice that had quelled riots in Cambridge. 'And we order you all, in Gynewell's name, to turn around and go home. There will be no battle today.'

Aurifabro laughed, a shrill, mocking sound that made Cynric clutch anxiously at one of his amulets. At that moment, a rogue gust of wind blew and the grass at the side of the road gave a sharp hiss, as if in anger. More of Spalling's people downed weapons and ran.

'Did you hear that?' cried Spalling. He sounded desperate. 'It is the Devil talking to Aurifabro. Fight, my valiant people. Prove that Peterborough men do not bow to Satan.'

Far from inspiring his troops, Spalling's words served to eliminate any residual resolve they might have possessed, as taking on the Prince of Darkness was not what they had had in mind when they set out to put the world to rights. More slunk away or fell to their knees.

'Steady!' howled Aurifabro to his soldiers. He raised his sword, although it was heavy and not designed to be waved with one hand, so it wobbled precariously. 'Cha—'

'Wait!' came a high, wavering voice from behind Spalling. It was feeble, but still piercing enough to make the goldsmith falter. 'Stop! In the name of all that is holy.'

For a moment, nothing happened, but then Spalling's rabble parted to allow some people through. It was the bedesfolk – men and women – clad in their ceremonial finery. They might have been an imposing sight if they had not been panting, hobbling and wheezing after what had obviously been a rapid dash.

Some carried a litter bearing Kirwell, who was scowling his displeasure at being hauled from his comfortable bed and spirited around the countryside. Behind them, Botilbrig and Inges staggered under the weight of a flagstone, while Hagar and Marion held the vases containing St Thomas Becket's blood. Appletre was with them, and Bartholomew could only suppose that he had met them on the road and had urged them to hurry.

'Retreat,' ordered Aurifabro angrily, obviously disconcerted by the fact that he would have to plough through a lot of old folk in order to reach his quarry. 'Or you will die, too.'

'We have brought our relics,' announced Hagar, although no one needed to be told. 'We command you,

344

in the name of St Thomas Becket and St Leonard, to go home. All of you.'

'You cannot kill defenceless elders, Aurifabro,' said Michael quickly. 'Neither the King nor the Bishop will condone that. You must stand down.'

Aurifabro stared at him, eyes glittering. 'I will take my chances.'

'Then if you will not listen to us,' said Appletre, 'listen to *him*.'

From the bedesfolk's midst, someone was ushered forward. His substantial girth and haughty bearing showed he was a man of some importance, although his silver hair was unkempt and his robes were stained with mud. He was scowling furiously, and jerked away from the propelling hands as if their touch was an outrage.

'It is Abbot Robert,' declared Hagar in a ringing voice. 'Come home at last.'

CHAPTER 13

For a moment, no one spoke, then Spalling's followers surged towards the angry Abbot, begging him to order Aurifabro and his mercenaries home. Robert regarded them with an arrogant disdain, which suggested that there was a good reason why he had been unpopular.

'I was sure he was dead,' murmured Michael, staring in astonishment as Robert began to dispense blessings, which he did sparingly, as though he did not want to expend what was a limited supply. 'I wonder where he has been.'

'Nowhere pleasant,' whispered Cynric. 'Look at the state of him.'

'God be praised!' bawled Spalling, silencing the hubbub and reclaiming the attention at the same time. 'Aurifabro has released the poor Abbot at last. It is a sign that God is on our side, so let us trounce his mercenaries and—'

'I never had him,' objected Aurifabro indignantly. 'And anyone who says otherwise is a liar.'

'I was seized by brigands,' declared Robert in a strong, steady voice. 'I do not know yet on whose orders. But I escaped. However, I did not expect to find my domain in a state of war. What is going on? And where are my *defensores*? Surely they should be on hand to prevent this sort of thing?'

'They slunk away when they saw me,' said Aurifabro,

346

not bothering to hide his contempt for the abbey's unreliable troops. 'As did Nonton.'

'We found Robert walking down the road,' explained Hagar, obviously proud to be part of the company who had arrived to save the day. 'He wanted to return to his abbey, to let his monks know he is safe, but we persuaded him to turn around and deal with this situation first.'

'It is a pity we did not meet him sooner,' muttered Inges, wiping sweat from his brow with the back of his hand. 'Because then we would not have had to tote these heavy relics and Kirwell all the way out here.'

'A pity indeed,' came Kirwell's querulous voice. 'Will I never be left in peace?'

Appletre stepped forward, beaming. 'We are delighted to see you safe, Father Abbot. But where have you been?'

'Imprisoned in a hut somewhere to the north of here,' replied Robert frostily. He gave a fastidious shudder. 'But I refuse to discuss it until I have bathed and changed.'

'You had better call a truce first,' said Langelee, nodding towards the onlookers.

'Why should I?' demanded Robert, eyeing the gold-smith coldly. 'I have no love for Aurifabro, and I do not care what happens to him today.'

'What will happen is that he will win a victory which will make him impossible to govern in the future,' hissed Langelee. 'So unless you want trouble with him for the rest of your reign, you would be wise to do as we say. After all, we *are* the Bishop's Commissioners.'

Robert regarded him icily, and it seemed he would refuse, but then he turned to Aurifabro and spoke, albeit with obvious reluctance.

'I apologise if the abbey or the town has caused you offence in my absence, but there will be no fighting today. We shall all go home and thank our respective gods that we live to see another day.'

'Speak for yourself,' muttered Kirwell.

'I agree,' said Spalling, determined to keep his status as leader. He turned to his people. 'We could have bested these louts if the *defensores* had stood firm, but their cowardly retreat has weakened us, so we shall do as the Abbot suggests for now.'

'But you claimed we could take Aurifabro on our own,' said a baker accusingly. 'You told us we were so strong that the mercenaries would run when they saw us coming.'

'And what about the money that you promised would be ours?' called someone else. 'Our rightful part of Aurifabro's wealth?'

The goldsmith released a sharp bark of laughter. 'I am disinclined to share it with you – you are not poor, just greedy. And I shall accept Robert's apology on one condition: that he buys my paten. If not, we shall do battle here and now, because I am tired of Spalling and his ridiculous lies. I am not intimidated by him, his army or these "holy" relics.'

'Maybe not, but your mercenaries are,' said Michael quietly, nodding to where several of them were eyeing the blood, stones and Kirwell uncomfortably. 'And the abbey *will* buy the paten. Do not argue, Abbot Robert. I speak with the Bishop's voice. The abbey will honour the arrangement it made with Aurifabro.'

'Very well,' said Robert, although the furious flash in his eyes suggested he resented the interference, and that the matter was far from over.

'Good,' said Langelee in relief. He glared at Spalling. 'I told you this was a bad idea, and you should have listened. Half these people might have been dead by now if the ancients had not intervened.'

'Here, who are you calling ancient?' demanded Botilbrig. He jabbed a gnarled finger at Kirwell. '*He* is ancient. We are in our prime.'

There was no more to be said, so the townsfolk began to shuffle back towards the town, rather less defiantly than when they had left it. Inges and Hagar, arm in arm in a rare display of unity, led the way. Robert was next, slapping angrily at the grateful hands that reached out to touch him, but Spalling was nowhere to be seen.

'Slithered away with his tail between his legs,' said Langelee in disgust. 'He should be here, assuring his troops that there is no shame in refusing an encounter they could not have won. The man is no kind of leader.'

Aurifabro watched in silence, and Bartholomew took the opportunity to put a question to him. The goldsmith regarded him suspiciously at first, but Udela indicated with a nod that he should reply. He obliged, then turned away to snap orders for the road to be guarded day and night until it was certain that the trouble was over.

'What did you say to him?' asked Michael, as Bartholomew took a corner of Kirwell's litter. The bedesmen were incapable of lugging it home, and the townsfolk were too shamefaced to approach a man they considered holy, so the task had fallen to the scholars. Kirwell muttered venomously at the inadvertent jostling.

'I asked if he had been charged to melt gold into a

bar recently – like the one we found in Lullington's quarters. He told me that Robert had paid him to consolidate a number of rings and bracelets last spring – gifts made to the shrines by pilgrims. It is common practice, apparently.'

'It is,' nodded Langelee. 'My Archbishop often did it, as ingots are portable and more easily stored than handfuls of lumpy jewellery.'

'Be careful!' snapped Kirwell, when the Master shifted his grip, and the whole litter tilted.

'I am eager for Robert to tell us about Lullington's role in his abduction,' said Michael. 'I would ask him now, but an open road is no place for such a discussion, so we shall have it in his solar, where we can enjoy a restorative cup of wine.'

'He will need it,' smirked Langelee. 'Spalling's throng and the bedesfolk are pawing him relentlessly, and I doubt he is used to such liberties.'

'He should try being me,' muttered Kirwell bitterly. 'Then he would know.'

Ahead, the Abbot was indeed the subject of intense attention. People grabbed his clothes, patted his hair, and poked his limbs to see whether he had been injured. He assured them that he was not, but they were indignant on his behalf and muttered all manner of revenge against the culprits.

'I thought no one liked him,' remarked Cynric. 'Yet here he is, being fawned over.'

'Because he is dishevelled,' explained Michael. 'They feel sorry for him. They would have been less sympathetic if he had appeared sleek and groomed.'

'I wonder how many of his monks will be pleased to

350

see him,' mused Bartholomew. 'I know two who will not: Ramseye and Yvo.'

'What about you, Brother?' asked Cynric. 'Are you horribly disappointed?'

'No,' replied Michael. 'On reflection, I think I would rather be a bishop than an abbot.'

'Gynewell had better watch himself, then,' grinned Langelee.

Bartholomew was still thinking about Robert. 'So who kidnapped him, given that neither Spalling nor Aurifabro claim responsibility? Unless the *defensores* did it – which I think you will agree is unlikely – it means there is yet another band on the loose.'

'Can we walk a little faster?' Michael picked up the pace. 'There are a lot of questions still to be answered, and time is short. We leave Peterborough today – now Robert is home, my duty to Gynewell is discharged. I am sorry we have not exposed the rogue who killed Joan and Welbyrn, but we can stay no longer.'

They walked in silence the rest of the way, concentrating on the balance between speed and not joggling the litter. When they reached St Leonard's, Botilbrig was waiting to say there had been a change of plan: Kirwell was to be taken to St Thomas's instead.

'I am not a pack animal,' grumbled Michael. 'And besides, I thought you were at war with St Thomas's. Why would you want him carted there?'

'Because the women are going to hold a feast to celebrate our victory,' explained Botilbrig. 'Us bedesmen are invited, including him.'

'A feast?' asked Kirwell with eager greed. 'Very well, then, but tell these Commissioners to be careful with me. Being carried by them is akin to lying on a bucking stallion.'

'We do not have time for this,' Michael fretted. 'We still have Lullington to confront and the Abbot to question – and I had hoped to be riding home by now.'

The town was oddly deserted as they approached, and the few market stalls that were open drew scant trade. Bartholomew could only suppose that people were either sleeping off their night of rebellion, or were telling the tale to those who had not taken part.

While the others waited, Michael none too patiently, Bartholomew carried Kirwell into St Thomas's. Once inside, he saw that Botilbrig had not been exaggerating when he had said that the women intended to celebrate: the hall adjoining the chapel was packed, not only with bedesfolk, but with Benedictines and abbey servants. The place reeked of ale, and despite the early hour, more than one face was already flushed with over-indulgence.

'Inges has gone to fetch the rest of the monks,' said Hagar, revelling in her role as one of those who had averted a crisis.

'I doubt they will come,' cautioned Bartholomew. 'They will be too busy with Robert.'

'They will be grateful for an opportunity to elude him,' countered Hagar. She turned as the door opened. 'See? Here they are now. Besides, Robert will be more concerned with putting his own affairs in order than with his flock today.'

From what he had been told about the Abbot, Bartholomew suspected she was right. He left Kirwell in Inges's care, and hurried towards the door, eager now to be going home. Julitta would be waiting, and although his feelings were still in terrible turmoil, he did know that he was looking forward to seeing her again.

'Join us!' cried Marion, as the physician weaved his way through the throng. Her long teeth gleamed. 'Elene is making cakes, and Henry is fetching another cask of wine.'

'There is water, too,' added Botilbrig, aiming to entice. 'From the well.'

'Really?' Bartholomew hoped it was not the stuff in which Welbyrn had spent the night.

'And Walter the cook has provided some nuts,' added Appletre, bustling up to join them. His plump face was pink with happiness. 'It is a veritable feast! Moreover, I plan to lead a little impromptu singing soon, because Robert has made me precentor again. Please stay.'

'I cannot,' said Bartholomew, edging away.

'Why?' asked Appletre, dismayed. 'There cannot be anything more pressing to do, not now Robert is home. And you deserve some reward for all your efforts.'

'There will not be time.' Bartholomew saw the disappointment on the precentor's face and was sorry. 'But perhaps we can spare a few moments later.'

'Very well,' said Appletre. 'But come via the abbey door – Hagar is going to lock the one that leads to the market, to exclude interlopers. I can see her point: the townsfolk should not see us letting our hair down. Yet we all need to unwind – it has been a trying time.'

'It certainly has,' agreed Bartholomew fervently.

Outside, Langelee was yawning hugely. 'I will collect our bags from Spalling's home, Cynric. You go to the guest house, and start packing for the others. We leave this morning, whether Michael has finished with Robert or not.'

There were no guards on the Abbey Gate, and the monastery appeared to be abandoned as Bartholomew, Michael and Cynric hurried through it. The only people in evidence were Henry and four lay brothers, who were toting barrels of wine towards the hospital.

'Robert said it was too early for claret,' Henry explained with a grin. 'But this is a special occasion, so I defied him and raided the cellars anyway. It will mean trouble later, but the bedesfolk deserve their reward.'

'The whole abbey is invited,' added one of the servants gleefully. 'Monks and lay brethren alike. We all want to hear how the relics defeated Aurifabro.'

'Join us,' urged Henry. 'Much as I enjoyed hearing Inges's account, I would sooner have it from someone less inclined to exaggerate.'

'Perhaps later,' said Bartholomew. 'But surely the monks should be welcoming Robert home, not drinking wine in the hospital?'

'Or even saying prayers for his safe deliverance?' added Michael pointedly.

Henry's wry expression answered Michael's question, and he addressed the rest of his reply to Bartholomew. 'The Abbot will only summon us when he has ensured that his worldly affairs are in order. We will not be needed for a while yet.'

'Have you seen Lullington?' asked Bartholomew, supposing they had better ensure the knight did not slip away before he could be charged with his wife's murder.

'He is with Robert,' replied Henry. 'But *please* have a

cup of wine with us. We have been all doom and gloom since you arrived, and I should like you to see us at our best.'

'We are busy,' said Michael shortly. 'Good day to you.'

Bartholomew shot Henry an apologetic glance as he hurried after Michael. He started to remonstrate with the monk for his bad manners, but Michael waved his protests aside with the curt reminder that they had no time for idle chatter.

They reached the guest house to find William and Clippesby waiting, their faces troubled. William held out a letter, which had arrived at dawn. Michael paled when he saw it bore the University's seal. He snatched it and began to read, while Bartholomew told William and Clippesby all that had happened. He was interrupted by a strangled wail from Michael.

'It is from the Chancellor. He says my Junior Proctor has written Winwick Hall's charter, and plans to present it as a fait accompli on Saturday. There will be a riot for certain, because he does not have the skill or the experience to draw up such a complex document!'

'It has already caused trouble,' said William, thus revealing that he had read the missive, even though it had been addressed to Michael and marked as private. 'There have been three brawls over the matter, which have resulted in several injuries and damage to property.'

'Damn Gynewell!' cried Michael. 'He should not have forced me to come here.'

'We must leave at once.' William hefted his saddlebag over his shoulder – he and Clippesby had put their time to good use, and had packed for Bartholomew and Michael, too.

Michael retrieved the seals, gold and jewels he had hidden. 'We shall – the moment I have returned these to their rightful owner.'

'What about Lullington?' asked Bartholomew.

'And the killer of Joan and Welbyrn?' added Clippesby.

'Henry says Lullington is with Robert, so I shall confront him when I give the Abbot his treasure. And there is nothing we can do about Joan and Welbyrn, because we are out of time.'

'Shall I come with you?' offered Bartholomew. 'You cannot tackle Lullington alone.'

'I am not a dying woman,' said Michael acidly. 'So I doubt Lullington will challenge me, and the Abbot will be there anyway. Be ready to leave the moment I return. And stay away from Henry – I sense danger in that man. Do you hear?'

He left before the others could say whether they had heard or not. Bartholomew slumped on the bed, exhausted. He closed his eyes, but Appletre was leading the revellers in a popular tavern song that involved a repetitive chorus of the kind tipsy people seemed to love, and sleep was impossible. There was laughter, too – the town might be smarting from its humiliation on the Torpe road, but the abbey's residents were in excellent spirits.

'They are very rowdy,' remarked Clippesby. 'It must be the wine. Henry selected a very powerful brew, and no one has had any breakfast.'

Cynric stared out of the window. 'Yet the *defensores* are not drinking powerful wine in the hospital, even though they are the kind of men who will like it most.'

'Yes, they are,' countered William. 'I saw a few enter the place myself.'

'No, I mean the *real* soldiers,' said Cynric. 'The proper ones, not the cowardly brutes who were with Nonton on the Torpe road.' He turned to Bartholomew. 'I have a bad feeling about today, boy. I sense something nasty in the air.'

Bartholomew forced himself to stand up. 'Stay here,' he instructed Clippesby and William. 'Cynric and I will scout around, to see if we can spot anything amiss.'

'Such as what?' demanded William. 'Any plot that might have been brewing has been thwarted by Robert's escape. Moreover, I do not see why we should sit here while Michael hobnobs with the Abbot. We deserve a drink after all our hard work. Come on, Clippesby.'

'No,' said Clippesby. 'Cynric is right: something is wrong.'

'Says who?' asked William scathingly. 'That snail I saw you talking to – the one that Henry stepped on shortly afterwards?'

Clippesby winced. 'Listen! There is not a bird anywhere in the entire precinct. Something horrible *is* about to happen.'

'Bah!' spat William. 'A cup of wine will put paid to these silly fancies. However, if you are too stupid to take my advice, then stay here. I, however, am going to join the fun.'

Cynric stopped and raised a triumphant finger when he and Bartholomew stepped out of the guest-house door, a gesture that said he had been right after all. Bartholomew could see or hear nothing to warrant such a response, and started to ask what he meant, but Cynric waved him to silence. Bartholomew felt ridiculous as they crept along in stealth mode, and hoped no one would see them. No one did, because every building was deserted.

Glancing behind him, he saw William enter the hospital, after which three cheers were raised for the Bishop's Commissioners. Bartholomew was about to remark that they had done nothing to deserve them when Cynric whipped around and bundled him roughly into a doorway. Moments later, two *defensores* walked past, holding Clippesby between them.

'But I do not want to go to the hospital chapel,' the Dominican was objecting. 'It is noisy there. I would rather pray in the church.'

'Perhaps we should let him,' said one to the other nervously. 'He is a saint, after all.'

'We were told that everyone had to be in St Thomas's,' countered the second. 'And I am not disobeying orders. I do not want to end up like Welbyrn. Or Joan, for that matter.'

'What are you saying?' asked Clippesby, bewildered.

'Ignore him, Father,' said the first, scowling at his companion over the Dominican's head. 'He is just blathering. You will enjoy yourself in the hospital – there is wine and nuts.'

When they had gone, Bartholomew regarded Cynric in alarm.

'We had better find out what is happening fast,' whispered the book-bearer. 'Because I have a strong sense that the business with Aurifabro was just the start.'

'The start of what?' asked Bartholomew, struggling to make sense of what he had heard.

'I do not know. That is what we must—'

'Stand still and put your hands in the air,' came a voice suddenly. 'Or these gentlemen will shoot you.'

It was Nonton and several *defensores*, all of whom were armed with bows and swords. Spalling was with them, his face cold and hard as he addressed the book-bearer.

'It was *your* fault that we failed on the Torpe road, Cynric. Aurifabro's wealth would have been mine by now if you had led the charge as I ordered.'

'Would have been *yours*?' echoed Cynric sharply. 'You mean the people's.'

Spalling sneered. 'Large sums of money are bad for the common folk – they spend it all on drink and whores. I never intended to let them keep it.'

'But you said—' began Cynric in a stunned gasp.

'It does not matter now,' interrupted Spalling. 'My so-called army comprised nothing but cowards, so our rebellion is over.' He seemed to have forgotten that he had hardly set a shining example. He turned to Nonton. 'Disarm them. And watch Cynric – he is dangerous.'

'He will not misbehave if he wants his friend alive,' said Nonton, grabbing Bartholomew and shoving a knife against his throat.

The physician flinched from the sour odour of second-hand wine, still struggling to comprehend what was happening. Why had the cellarer thrown in his lot with the abbey's sworn enemy? Meanwhile, Cynric recovered quickly from the shock of seeing his hero in a less than attractive light, and went on the offensive.

'Our people would have defeated Aurifabro had you followed my advice,' he snapped. '*You* lost that fight, not them.' He glared at Nonton. 'And you did not help by running away.'

'Those particular *defensores* are not warriors,' replied Nonton coolly. 'However, these are, so annoy them at your peril. But enough chat. Come with me. And remember that any tricks will result in a dead *medicus*.'

Bartholomew and Cynric were bundled towards the granary, a stalwart structure that stood near the west wall. It had a large door at the front, and a smaller one at the rear. The bulk of its grain had been used the previous winter, although a few mounds of corn remained, along with several heaps of empty sacks and some bales of straw. It had a dry, musty smell, and the dust that was kicked up by the soldiers' feet made Bartholomew cough. Nonton fastened him to one of the wooden pillars that supported the roof, where the hard, tight little knots began to cut off the circulation in his hands. Spalling tied Cynric to another.

'There will be a revolution, Cynric,' said Spalling softly. 'Anyone with eyes can see that it is coming, not just here, but across the whole country. You will have your dream of social justice eventually, so do not take our defeat here too badly.'

'But you will not be part of it,' said Cynric bitterly. 'You encourage others to pour their possessions into the common pot, but you do not do it yourself. You are a hypocrite! You strut around pretending to be one of us, but your clothes are always clean, and you eat like a king.'

'Clippesby saw through you,' said Bartholomew, speaking quickly as Spalling took an angry step towards the Welshman. 'He guessed you would flee at the first sign of trouble.'

'The saint?' asked Spalling uneasily, and his advance faltered. 'Really?'

'Yes,' snarled Cynric. 'He knows that the highway thieves are men under *your* control. He is disgusted, and will have plenty to say when he speaks to the Bishop.'

Cynric was bluffing, because Clippesby had drawn no such conclusions, and would not take them to Gynewell if he had, but Spalling was horrified. His guilty face spoke volumes, and more answers flooded into in Bartholomew's mind.

'So the attacks on our journey to Peterborough were not attempts to rob us,' he surmised. 'They were to prevent the Bishop's Commissioner from reaching his destination. No other travellers were ambushed five times, but your men kept failing, so had to try again and again.'

'But we fought them off with ease,' said Cynric in disdain. 'Just as we did when they tried to kill us by the Dragon Tree. And I know why. It is because *you* were in command, and you are a pathetic warrior who should not be allowed anywhere near a sword.'

'There is nothing wrong with my leadership or my fighting skills,' snapped Spalling, nettled. He glared at Nonton. 'We failed because *you* provided me with inadequate soldiers.'

'It was you who Brother Michael heard cursing in French outside the Swan, too,' Cynric went on. 'You probably intended to stage another ambush, but you lost courage and—'

'I did not lose courage,' objected Spalling, shooting an uneasy glance at Nonton, whose face was a mask of disgust. 'I merely decided that an attack was unnecessary. Michael heard me, which was enough to make him conclude that it was Aurifabro's mercenaries lurking in the dark with malevolent intentions. My objective was achieved without violence.'

'Why are you working with the abbey?' asked Bartholomew, not bothering to point out that Michael had concluded nothing of the kind. 'Its monks excommunicated you.'

'For money, of course,' said Cynric before the rebel could reply for himself. 'They *paid* him to do their bidding. And he is the perfect choice – he has a history of fighting them, so no one suspects they are in cahoots. How could I have been deceived?'

'You played right into my hands.' Spalling seized the opportunity to boast, less to gloat over Cynric than to remind Nonton of how clever he had been. 'You and Langelee are the only ones who can fight, and I neatly deprived Michael of your protection. It should have been easy to dispatch him inside the abbey.'

'And have everyone know that *we* killed the Bishop's Commissioner?' asked Nonton acidly, in response to Spalling's challenging look. 'You are a damned fool if you think that was ever an option! But enough chat. Light the fires, and let us make an end to this business.'

'What fires?' asked Cynric, narrowing his eyes.

'The ones that will dispose of inconvenient bodies,' replied Nonton shortly.

By craning his neck, Bartholomew could see that the *defensores* had prepared several piles of kindling, placed so they would ignite the remaining grain. Spalling crouched down and fiddled with a tinderbox. The moment the first heap began to smoulder, he moved to the second. He was kneeling by the third when Nonton hit him over the head with a cudgel. Bartholomew winced at the sound of smashing bone.

'What did you do that for?' gasped Cynric, shocked. 'He was on your side!'

'He is unpredictable, unreliable and greedy, and I was never comfortable with him as an ally. Do not bother calling for help, by the way. No one will hear you.'

'Wait!' shouted Bartholomew. 'You cannot—'

'Out, quick,' Nonton ordered his men. 'And tell Appletre to sing louder. I doubt anyone will hear screams from the hospital, but one cannot be too careful.'

'Appletre,' said Bartholomew, as the door slammed, and there came the sound of a bar being placed across it. 'I should have guessed that he was involved.'

CHAPTER 14

The granary roof and walls had been well soaked by summer showers, so would take a while to ignite, but the sacks, grain and straw were bone dry. Bartholomew strained desperately against his bonds as smoke billowed towards him, but Nonton had known what he was doing when he had tied the knots, and they held fast. He sagged in defeat.

'No, do not give up,' shouted Cynric urgently. 'Keep trying to fight loose. And while you do, tell me why you suspected Appletre.'

Bartholomew resumed his struggles, although he knew it was hopeless. 'Because of the way he hared off to fetch Yvo when we were on the Torpe road. He knew the Prior would not help, but he insisted on going anyway. It was to consult with his accomplices.'

'Is that all?' Cynric was hurling himself from side to side, frantically trying to tear free.

'No. He offered to go with the *defensores* to collect Pyk, which was unnecessary and odd. And when Spalling's rabble passed him on the road, his invitation to hunt for rotting corpses was meant to ensure they kept going – it was an offer he knew would be refused. Finally, there was his dogged insistence that I join the celebrations in the hospital – to keep me out of the way.'

Henry had insisted, too, he thought but could not

bring himself to say. He coughed as a waft of smoke swirled towards him.

'Do not worry,' came a quiet voice at his side. It was Clippesby. 'I am here.'

'Thank God!' cried Cynric. 'Cut us loose, Father. Do you have a knife?'

'No, of course not,' said Clippesby, startled. 'I never carry one, because—'

'Take the one from my boot. Quickly!'

The Dominican began to do as he was told, at the same time explaining how he came to be there.

'The *defensores* took me to pray in the church, but while we were walking there, I saw you being dragged in here. The moment they left – there is an advantage in being considered a saint, as they did not hesitate when I asked them to leave me alone – I came to rescue you. There is a back door . . . I heard everything Spalling and Nonton said.'

'Never mind that,' hissed Cynric urgently. 'Hurry!'

But Clippesby was not a practical man, and hacking through the ropes took far longer than it should have done. By the time Bartholomew and Cynric were free, the granary was full of smoke. They staggered towards the rear door only to find it blocked by a blazing heap of corn.

'Down,' gasped Bartholomew, dropping to the floor where the air was clearer. 'We will crawl around the walls until we find another way out.'

'There is only one other door, and Nonton just barred it,' gulped Cynric. 'And granaries are not designed to have holes, lest rats come in. We are doomed! The charms I bought from Udela are worthless!'

'Follow me,' said Clippesby, unfazed. 'The mice showed me what to do.'

Bartholomew scrambled after him, noting that the post to which he had been tied was already smouldering. Then he collided with Clippesby, who had stopped and was struggling with a hatch. Bartholomew shoved the friar out of the way, and kicked it with all his might. It flew open. He scrambled out, the others close on his heels, and slammed it shut behind him.

When they were clear of the building, he glanced back. There was no sign of the fire, because it was contained within the thick walls and roof. However, it would not stay that way for long – the flames would bake out the confining dampness and eventually erupt in a blazing inferno. The abbey could doubtless afford to lose it, but fires had a habit of spreading with terrifying speed – the conflagration might even reach the town, given the direction of the wind.

'I will go to the hospital and fetch help,' he said, but Cynric grabbed his arm.

'Nonton or his men will kill you long before you get there.'

'We *must* raise the alarm.' Bartholomew tried to pull away from him. 'The monks and lay brethren will not be part of this plot – it is obvious that they were encouraged into the hospital to keep them out of the way. When they hear the granary is on fire—'

'No!' cried Cynric, intensifying his grip. 'You can see *defensores* patrolling around it from here – the proper ones, not the weaklings. You will never get past them.'

'Can we fight them?'

Cynric shook his head. 'There are too many.'

'What about ringing a bell?' suggested Clippesby. 'Or yelling?'

'No, because Appletre is in there, conducting the singing and urging them to howl as loudly as they can: he will prevent you from making yourself heard. However, I might be able to reach Lady Lullington's window, which is farthest from the patrols. Then I can run downstairs and persuade someone to help me disable the precentor. It will not be easy, though – everyone likes Appletre, and will be reluctant to believe ill of him.'

'The building next to the granary is a stable,' whispered Clippesby worriedly. 'We cannot leave the horses in danger. They must be moved.'

'Then do it, Father – we will never reach Cambridge in time to prevent a riot without them.' Cynric turned to Bartholomew. 'Go to the Abbot's House, and tell Brother Michael what is happening. But be careful: if Nonton or the *defensores* see you, you are dead.'

With Cynric's warning ringing in his ears, Bartholomew began to run. *Defensores* were everywhere, and he chafed whenever he was obliged to duck into a doorway or hide behind a buttress, fretting at the wasted moments.

'Nonton is stupid to have set the granary alight,' he heard one soldier say to another as they passed. Bartholomew held his breath in an agony of tension when they paused so close that he could have reached out and touched them. 'If it catches, it could destroy the whole monastery.'

'So?' asked his crony. 'Who cares?'

'You will, when they spend all their money rebuilding it, and have none left to pay you. Besides, I got a house in town, and it only takes one stray spark . . .'

Desperately, Bartholomew wondered how to turn their concern to his advantage. Should he leap out and urge them to abandon a leader who would almost certainly cheat them? Or would they just shoot him? He suspected they would turn him over to Nonton, who would certainly not let him escape a second time. He clenched his fists in increasing agitation as one produced a flask of wine and both enjoyed several swigs before moving on.

It felt like an age before he reached the Abbot's House. There were no guards and he could hear Michael talking in the solar, so he tore up the stairs and flung open the door. And then stopped in shock.

Michael was sitting in a chair with his hands on his knees, while two archers covered him with crossbows. Appletre was pacing back and forth in front of him, rosy cheeks flushed and his movements jerky and excited. Bartholomew could hear singing from the hospital – a drunken chorus that did not need a conductor, and he was angry with himself for not realising it. There was no sign of Robert.

'Run, Matt!' howled Michael when he saw the physician. 'Now!'

His mind churning in confusion, Bartholomew turned to race back down the steps, but it was already too late. One of the bowmen reacted with formidable speed, and brought him down in a flying tackle. Bartholomew struggled as hard as he could, but two more men came to help, and it was not long before he was overpowered. Then he was dragged back to the solar, and shoved forward so hard that he fell at Michael's feet.

'Stay down,' Appletre barked when he started to stand.

'The granary is on fire,' Bartholomew gasped, as Michael leaned forward to rest a hand on his shoulder, warning him to do as he was told. 'Raise the alarm before—'

'It is not,' said Appletre, glancing out of the window, where nothing looked amiss with the building in question. 'Besides, I shall not care if it is. I never did like it – its acoustics for singing are dreadful.'

He sounded deranged, and Bartholomew regarded him in alarm.

'Nonton lied to you, Appletre,' said Michael. 'He claimed Matt was dead.'

'*Spalling* is dead,' said Bartholomew. 'Nonton murdered him.'

'On my orders.' Appletre bounced up and down on his toes, as excited as a child with a new toy. Bartholomew wondered why he had not seen incipient lunacy in his enthusiasms before. 'Nonton is a loyal soldier, as I keep telling you. He would never betray me.'

'But he did betray you.' Bartholomew understood what Michael had been trying to do and pitched in to help. 'He told me everything. For example, he said that you killed Joan.'

Appletre stared at him. 'Did he? Damn! I thought no one saw me.'

Bartholomew felt his jaw drop. It had been a bluff intended to disconcert, and Appletre's response meant that *he* was the one thrown off balance. Then he glimpsed a wisp of smoke issuing through the granary roof. It would not be long before it burst into flames. He dragged his attention away from it and forced himself to concentrate on the mysteries they had been charged with solving

– Appletre's admission about Joan had answered several questions.

'She was murdered in St Thomas's Chapel,' he said to Michael. 'Where you had gone to give thanks for our safe arrival. It was bright that day, and every time we went from the sunshine into the gloom we were forced to wait for our eyes to adjust.'

'Are you saying he mistook her for me?' Michael regarded him in disbelief.

'Yes – she was tall, fat and wore a billowing robe. And Appletre was sun-blinded as he crept in through the back door.'

'And I suppose we must remember what Clippesby told us,' added Michael, for once overlooking the reference to his girth. 'That she did not usually guard the relics, and had done so that day to impress the Bishop's Commissioners.'

'The stupid woman,' spat Appletre. 'She should not have been there.'

'So it was her fault, was it?' asked Bartholomew coldly. 'Not yours?'

Appletre surged forward angrily, and Bartholomew braced himself for a punch, but the precentor stopped abruptly. 'No. I am not a violent man.'

'You are a fool, Appletre,' said Michael in disdain, while Bartholomew assessed the archers, weighing up his chances of besting them. They were tense and watchful, and he knew he would be shot before he could stand. 'If you kill me, Gynewell will appoint another agent.'

'Not so. His conscience will never permit him to order a second man to his death, and he cannot come himself, because he is having trouble with his Mint.'

'His Mint!' exclaimed Bartholomew in understanding. '*Now* I know what Reginald was doing! He was a cutler, skilled in working with metal. But he was not making knives – he was producing counterfeit coins. I found some that had fallen on his floor.'

'You did what?' asked Appletre dangerously. 'I gave orders to keep everyone out.'

'It was you who sent that instruction to Henry, was it?' pounced Bartholomew. 'With a *defensor* who then rode away to Lincoln? But we did not need to see the money to understand what Reginald was doing – we heard him hammering as he worked with the coining dies.'

He gestured to the table, where the one he had found in Reginald's workshop – the one he had dismissed as an idle curiosity – lay among the other oddments that had been collected and brought to the abbey for 'safe-keeping'.

'And why should Reginald forge money?' sneered Appletre.

'To be taken to Lincoln, which is the reason why Gynewell is not in a position to visit Peterborough.' Bartholomew glanced out of the window again: the smoke was thicker and blacker. Hope surged: someone from the town would see it and raise the alarm. He pressed on with his deductions. 'The Mint is his responsibility, and the King considers counterfeiting a more serious matter than the disappearance of an abbot.'

'We have been told that Nonton and Welbyrn regularly visited Lincoln.' Michael took up the tale. 'One of them must have laid hold of a die and brought it back to Peterborough.'

'Counterfeiting is a capital crime,' Bartholomew went on. 'And Reginald would not have done it willingly. But he was coerced, perhaps on pain of being charged with killing his wife. The strain of his predicament almost certainly contributed to his death.'

'It takes skill to manufacture coins,' added Michael. 'But one man was on hand to explain how it was done – Nonton, who was seconded to work in the Archbishop of York's court for a year. Langelee saw him there.'

'At the Mint,' added Bartholomew. 'York has one, as well as Lincoln. He—'

He broke off as Appletre snatched a knife from one of the archers and advanced with murder in his eyes.

There was little Bartholomew could do to defend himself when he was on the floor with two bows pointed at him. The archers smirked in anticipation of blood.

'Do not do this, Appletre!' cried Michael. 'Think of your immortal soul.'

Appletre stopped abruptly. 'True. I have heard there is not much singing in Hell.'

He dropped the blade and backed away, leaving both scholars and the archers gazing at him in astonishment. And Welbyrn thought *he* had been losing his mind, thought Bartholomew, deftly reaching out to snag the dagger when the archers' bemused attention was on the precentor.

'The granary is smouldering,' Bartholomew said, glancing out of the window yet again. 'You *must* sound the alarm. It could ignite at any moment, and if a spark lands on the hospital, Peterborough will lose its monks, bedesfolk and servants in a single stroke.'

Horror speared through him when he saw the unconcern on the precentor's face.

'Appletre!' cried Michael. 'You cannot risk the abbey for whatever wild scheme—'

'It is not wild,' shouted Appletre. 'Nonton knows what he is doing. Besides, we shall be sent more monks if these die, and I am not averse to having some new basses. It—'

'You are insane!' cried Bartholomew, shocked. 'You—'

'I am not!' screamed Appletre, fists clenching. Then he stepped backwards suddenly, and took a deep breath. When he spoke again, his voice was calm. 'I will not let you aggravate me. As I said, I am not a violent man.'

Bartholomew was far from sure about that, and knew that he and Michael would not be allowed to leave Peterborough alive. With nothing to lose he decided he would have answers, even if getting them did goad the precentor to rage.

'You killed Welbyrn.' Again, it was a guess, but the guilty flash in Appletre's eyes told him he was right. 'He had started to brood about his father, wondering if he might go mad, too. You followed him to St Leonard's and pushed him in the well, leaving him to drown—'

'Stop!' snarled Appletre, while Michael regarded Bartholomew uneasily.

'But it is you who are mad,' Bartholomew pressed on. 'There was no need to harm—'

'There was every need – he kept questioning our decisions, and he wanted to recruit Ramseye, which would have been a disaster. Our almoner may be a sly rogue, but he would never agree to what we intend. And then Welbyrn threatened to tell you everything in exchange for a cure for his creeping insanity.'

'He was not—' began Bartholomew.

'But he thought you would refuse to treat him.' Appletre cut across what the physician started to say. 'So he tried to make friends first. He sent you Lombard slices, but when you were poisoned, he became more unpredictable than ever – the dismay of losing his chance of a remedy was too much for his fragile mind. I had no choice but to kill him.'

'You are despicable,' said Bartholomew in disgust.

'Shoot him,' ordered Appletre, turning to the bowmen.

Bartholomew struggled to his feet as the archers took aim, reluctant to die lying down. He gripped the knife behind his back, but despite his rage against the plump-cheeked little man who danced from foot to foot in front of him, he could not bring himself to lob it. He was a physician, not a killer, and he did not want his last act on Earth to be the taking of a life.

'No!' came an urgent shout from the doorway. 'It will make a mess on my rugs.'

'Robert!' exclaimed Michael, as the Abbot stepped into the solar, resplendent in a clean habit. 'Thank God! I came to talk to you, but this lunatic has been holding me captive and—'

'Do not clamour at me,' snapped the Abbot irritably. 'Well, Appletre? Did you trick them into revealing all they have learned?'

'I believe so,' replied Appletre, smiling smugly at Bartholomew, who saw in that moment that the precentor was not deranged at all, but a cunning manipulator who had deceived him with ease. 'They know about the Mint, so they will have to be eliminated.'

'*You* are involved?' asked Michael, regarding the Abbot in shock.

Robert smiled coldly. 'You do not think Appletre and Nonton could have managed all this alone, do you?'

There was silence in the solar after the Abbot had made his declaration, but it did not last. A drunken cheer from the revellers drifted through the window. Then Lullington walked in, gloriously clad in more robes paid for with his murdered wife's jewels. Michael pointed accusingly at him and started to stand, but Robert snapped his fingers and the archers' bows came up simultaneously. He sat again.

'I am the Bishop's Commissioner,' he said. 'You cannot hold me against my will.'

'Is that so?' murmured Robert, going to his table and beginning to sort through the documents that lay there. He cocked his head. 'Can I hear Kirwell singing?'

Lullington laughed softly. 'Wailing, not singing. The old fool cannot understand why he remains alive after parting with Oxforde's prayer.'

At the mention of Kirwell and the parchment passed to him by a criminal on the gibbet, the last pieces of the puzzle fell into place in Bartholomew's mind. He spoke to Michael.

'Robert was never abducted – he went missing of his own accord. To look for treasure.'

Robert regarded him coldly. 'I did it for my Order. Running an abbey is expensive.'

'It started when Kirwell decided to die and gave

Oxforde's prayer to Robert,' Bartholomew explained to Michael. 'The one he had promised never to show to another person. Except it was not a prayer, was it, Father Abbot?'

Robert smiled. 'Kirwell was almost blind when he was Oxforde's confessor, so he had never read what had been written.'

'It was instructions,' Bartholomew went on, 'which told the reader how to find the money that Oxforde stole during his life of crime.'

'Of course,' breathed Michael. 'That is why there has been a recent rumour that Oxforde gave it to the poor – to stop anyone else from looking. Not that they would have done after all this time, but nothing has been left to chance.'

Robert inclined his silver head. 'It also made Oxforde's cult more popular, thus increasing donations. We could not lose.'

'So that is where you have been?' asked Michael in distaste. 'Not held prisoner by outlaws, but grubbing about for a burglar's hoard?'

'On Aurifabro's land,' elaborated Bartholomew. 'While Spalling and the *defensores* kept him and his mercenaries distracted with spats.'

'You went out with a spade *in person*?' asked Michael, regarding the Abbot askance. 'Most senior churchmen delegate that sort of thing to minions.'

'He does not trust anyone,' said Bartholomew.

'Too right!' muttered Robert. 'There is a fortune at stake.'

'I would have helped you, Father Abbot,' said Appletre reproachfully. 'If I had, Gynewell would not have sent commissioners to make a nuisance of themselves.'

'True,' acknowledged Robert, although he said no more and his silence revealed far more than words: he did not trust his precentor, either.

'So where is this fabled treasure?' asked Michael, while Bartholomew stole an agitated glance towards the granary. Smoke was pouring from it now, and he fancied he could hear the crackle of the flames within. 'Or has a month in the wilderness left you empty handed?'

'Finding it has been more difficult than I anticipated.' Robert turned back to Appletre. 'You failed me this morning. You promised that Aurifabro would be killed or ousted, but he is still in residence, preventing me from conducting a proper search of his estates.'

'Spalling's people crumbled at the first hurdle,' explained Appletre, rolling his eyes. 'And Nonton's idiots ran away. I was on my way to fetch the real *defensores* when I saw you had run into the bedesfolk, at which point it seemed more prudent to let the matter go. You must have thought so, too, or you would not have ordered everyone home.'

A billow of white sailed past the window. 'The granary,' said Bartholomew urgently. 'You will have no abbey to rule if you do not put out the fire.'

'I shall rebuild on a much grander scale once I have Oxforde's hoard,' said Robert. 'And my munificence and vision will be remembered for centuries to come.'

'And your monks?' asked Bartholomew archly. 'They cannot be rebuilt with money.'

Robert did not deign to reply. He glanced at the table. 'Are those my seals and gold?'

'Michael says he found them in Lullington's quarters,' replied Appletre. 'Is it true?'

It was the knight who answered. 'Robert could hardly take them with him, and he is not such a fool as to leave them where Yvo and his devious nephew might have got hold of them. So he gave them to me to mind.'

'You will not profit from poisoning your wife, Lullington,' warned Michael. He sounded as despairing as Bartholomew felt. 'I have already written to the Bishop about it.'

It was satisfying to see the smugness fade from the knight's face.

'What?' demanded Robert, shocked. 'You did away with her?'

'She started asking me awkward questions about your disappearance,' replied Lullington. 'And she was tenacious – she would have found the truth. She was supposed to die quickly, but the potion was defective, and when I saw her corpse . . .'

'There was nothing wrong with the poison.' Bartholomew made no attempt to conceal his contempt. 'It was your ineptitude that sentenced her to a lingering death.'

'Damn!' cried Robert. 'This could ruin everything! The Bishop will come for an explanation and—'

'And you will inform him that there is no truth in Michael's accusation,' the knight flashed back. 'Or I shall tell him exactly what has been going on here.'

Suddenly, Lullington's face contorted in agony, after which he pitched forward and lay still. Appletre was behind him, holding a dagger.

'So much for not being violent,' muttered Michael.

'You believed that, did you?' asked Appletre mildly. He turned to his Abbot, who was scowling as he toed the bleeding body away from his rugs. 'We shall tell the Bishop that Lullington killed himself in a fit of remorse.'

Michael released a sharp bark of mocking laughter. 'Do you really imagine that Gynewell will see nothing suspicious in the deaths of Lullington, his wife, Welbyrn, Reginald, Joan, Spalling *and* us? He will tear your abbey to pieces looking for the culprits.'

'Joan?' asked Robert sharply. 'And Welbyrn? When did this happen?'

'I will explain later,' said Appletre quickly. 'After we have—'

'He killed them both,' interrupted Bartholomew. 'Welbyrn was murdered in cold blood because he was loyal to you: he was the only one who insisted you were still alive—'

'You know why we encouraged people to think you dead, Father Abbot,' said Appletre. 'To see who would take advantage of the situation and thus show themselves to be your enemies. And it worked: Yvo and Ramseye are the two who must be watched.'

'What happened to Welbyrn?' asked Robert flatly.

'He committed suicide,' replied Appletre briskly. 'Like his father. He had become very unpredictable, so it was for the best.'

'Appletre murdered him,' countered Bartholomew. 'And Joan.'

'Ignore him, Father Abbot,' said Appletre irritably. 'He is trying to create a rift between us with his lying accusations. Well, it will not work.'

Robert said nothing, and Bartholomew felt the stirrings of hope. The Abbot would see he had recruited a dangerous accomplice, and would have second thoughts about what he had set in motion. But any spark of optimism died when Robert addressed his precentor.

'If Gynewell does descend on us, I am sure we can devise a tale that will satisfy him. And if not . . . well, I have never liked him. It is time we had a new Bishop.'

There was nothing Bartholomew and Michael could do as they were bundled into a corner and told to stand with their hands on their heads, Bartholomew struggling to keep the knife hidden as he did so. The Abbot became businesslike. He snapped his fingers, and several more *defensores* appeared. He ordered them to toss Lullington's body in the granary.

'Then we can say that *he* started the fire as a way to end his own life,' he explained. 'But first, don these scholars' clothes and make a show of leaving town. Keep your hoods up, so no one can see your faces. When they fail to arrive home, we shall blame their deaths on robbers.'

'You will kill me?' asked Michael reproachfully. 'A fellow Benedictine?'

Robert shrugged. 'Why not? I killed Pyk, and he was a better man than you. He would have been a useful asset with his sharp wits and local knowledge, but he said he wanted nothing to do with Oxforde's treasure. He left me no choice but to tap him on the head.'

Bartholomew stared at him. Pyk had endured a lot more than a 'tap'. Something else became clear, too.

'Aurifabro's shepherd saw you, and raved about it in

his "delirium",' he said. 'But Fletone did not die of mountain fever, and I suspect he was ill far longer than the few hours stipulated by his friends on the basis of his own amateur diagnosis. You poisoned him.'

'I persuaded him to swallow something from Pyk's medical bag,' said Robert, full of arrogant disdain. 'He obliged eagerly, the fool! Of course, it was Reginald's idea.'

Bartholomew supposed that explained how the cutler had known that Fletone had been poisoned, and why he feared the same fate might have befallen him.

'Did you know that Appletre hit Joan over the head with a relic?' asked Michael in a final, desperate attempt to cause trouble. 'A *relic*, Father Abbot, a holy thing.'

'Botilbrig did it,' stated Appletre. 'He always was jealous that she chose you over him.'

Bartholomew was appalled that the bedesman should bear the brunt of Robert's inevitable wrath. 'Where is your conscience, Appletre? How can you sing in a church, knowing that you have committed such terrible crimes?'

'Leave my singing out of it,' snapped Appletre. He turned to Robert and gestured out of the window. 'The townsfolk will see that smoke soon, and come to investigate. We should not be found with prisoners when they do.'

'Then take these two outside and shoot them,' said Robert. He scowled at Michael. 'Call it revenge for you forcing me to buy Aurifabro's damned paten in front of the whole town.'

'Will you use that to pay for it?' asked Appletre, nodding towards the jewels and the gold bar that lay on the table. 'Given that we still do not have Oxforde's treasure?'

'Certainly not,' replied Robert coolly. 'When this is over, I shall make a pilgrimage to Canterbury, to cleanse my soul. I have endured enough privation for the abbey, and I plan to use these to make the journey as pleasant as possible.'

'Then your sins will not be expiated,' warned Michael. 'You—'

'Kill them, and put their corpses with Lullington's,' said the Abbot briskly. 'But do not forget to remove their clothes first.'

'Wait,' said Bartholomew, while Michael began to mutter prayers of contrition, under no illusion about the ruthlessness of the men they were confronting. 'You will never find the treasure, because it is not on Aurifabro's land. You have been looking in the wrong place.'

'Enough,' said Appletre, indicating that the *defensores* were to take their captives away.

'I know where it is,' pressed Bartholomew. 'It is here. In the abbey.'

CHAPTER 15

The solar was silent after Bartholomew made his announcement. Through the window, he saw that the granary roof was alight at last, and that the wind was carrying sparks towards the thatched roof of St Thomas's Hospital. He could hear singing and cheering, and its drunken quality meant the revellers were unlikely to realise the danger they were in until it was too late.

'The physician is lying,' said Appletre. 'He is a stranger, so how can he know more than those of us who have lived here for years? Besides, the treasure cannot be in the abbey or we would have found it.'

Robert ignored him. 'Tell me,' he said to Bartholomew, steel in his voice.

'Why should I? You will kill me the moment you know.'

Robert smiled unpleasantly. 'Yes, but there are many ways to die, and I am sure you would not like your fat friend to pay the price for your reticence.'

'I cannot *tell* you,' said Bartholomew quickly, when one of the bowmen stepped forward with a knife. 'I will have to *show* you. But I shall need Michael's help.'

'Why?' asked Robert suspiciously.

Bartholomew met his glare steadily. 'Because I cannot do it on my own.'

Robert stared at him for a moment, then addressed his precentor. 'Go with them to see whether he is telling

383

the truth. If he is, kill them quickly. If not, make him sorry he tried to play games.'

'Where are you going?' asked Appletre.

'To the hospital, to tell my flock about my abduction. And while I am there, I shall inform my nephew and Yvo – and Henry, because I hate his sickly piety – that they are to have the opportunity to serve God in some of our remoter properties. That will teach them to cross me.'

Robert held the precentor's gaze for a moment, so it was clear that the threat applied to him as well, then strode away, an impressive figure in his fine habit. At a nod from Appletre, the *defensores* shoved Bartholomew and Michael down the stairs, where they met Nonton coming up to make his report. The cellarer was furious when he saw Bartholomew alive, and raised a fist, but Appletre knocked it down.

'Not yet. The Abbot wants him to show us where Oxford hid his hoard.'

Nonton regarded the physician uncertainly. 'Does he know?'

'He claims he does. If he is telling the truth, we are to kill him cleanly. If not . . .'

Bartholomew began walking, so he would not have to look at the gloating anticipation in Nonton's face. Michael came to trot at his side.

'Do you really know, Matt, or are you bluffing?'

'It is in Oxforde's tomb.'

Michael stared at him. 'How in God's name did you deduce that?'

'Because of something Simon the cowherd said – that he had seen Oxforde in his golden grave. I did not understand what he meant at the time—'

'But Simon is addled!' hissed Michael in alarm. 'He was speaking gibberish.'

'Actually, he made perfect sense. Think about it, Brother. What was Oxforde was doing when he was caught?'

Michael frowned. 'Digging by the tomb of a silver-smith, who was alleged to have interred some of his favourite jewellery in the plot next door.'

'Exactly. Why would a successful thief bother with a few baubles that necessitated a lot of hard work? The answer is that he would not: Oxforde was actually hiding what he had already stolen. Then it was decided that he would be buried in the hole he himself had made . . .'

'Because he was so evil it was thought that only hallowed ground could keep him from returning to terrorise the living.' Michael stopped to ponder, but started moving again when an archer prodded him in the back. 'So why did Oxforde write in his "prayer" that it was hidden on land now owned by Aurifabro?'

'That was a ruse, to keep his real hoard safe.'

'It was not much of one. Kirwell kept it secret it for forty-five years.'

'Oxforde reckoned without the sunbeam. Had that not happened, Kirwell would have sold the prayer, and a hunt would have ensued.'

'But Oxforde had been condemned to death. Why did he bother?'

'Because he did not believe the sentence would be carried out. Everyone says he expected a reprieve right up until the noose tightened around his neck. He thought he would be alive to enjoy his treasure, and this was his way of keeping people away from it.'

'I hope to God you are right,' muttered Michael. 'Because I dread to think what will happen to us if you are not.'

'We are dead either way, Brother. So think of a way to escape, because sparks are flying towards the hospital roof. It is not just our lives that are at risk here, but two hundred monks, bedesfolk and abbey servants.'

Appletre's eyebrows shot up in understanding as they entered the cemetery. 'Of course! It is obvious now that I think about it. Fetch spades, Nonton. This pair will dig for us.'

There was a lacklustre cheer from the hospital, which Bartholomew interpreted as meaning that Robert had just walked in. The granary was now well and truly alight, and he could see *defensores* at the gate telling concerned townsfolk that the monks did not need help to extinguish it. He considered yelling a warning, but doubted it would be understood. He glanced up at the hospital roof. How long would it be before it ignited?

'Not there,' snapped Nonton, when in a feeble attempt to win more time, Bartholomew aimed for the hole that Trentham had made for Joan. 'Do not try my patience.'

Bartholomew moved the flowers that covered Oxforde's grave, and at a nod from Nonton he and Michael began to dig. Unfortunately for them, the ground was neither too hard nor too wet, and their progress was alarmingly rapid. One of the guards drew the excavated earth into a pile as they hurled it out, so it could be shovelled back again when they had finished. Clearly the bedeswomen were not to know what had been done to their shrine. Appletre watched, humming under his breath, while

Nonton drank from his flask. Then Bartholomew saw smoke curling from the hospital roof.

'This is madness!' he cried, flinging down his spade and appealing to his captors. 'Some of your choir is in there, Appletre. You cannot condemn them to be burned alive.'

'Robert will not let anything happen to them,' said Appletre, although Bartholomew thought he really was insane if he thought there was an ounce of pity or compassion in the man he had chosen to serve. Robert would be more than happy to be rid of a lot of monks who did not like him and start afresh with new ones.

'Work,' ordered Nonton, prodding the physician with a sword.

Seeing he was wasting his breath, Bartholomew did as he was told, hoping Michael could devise a plan, for his own mind was horribly blank. He dawdled, playing for time, but Nonton guessed what he was doing and lashed out with a kick. Bartholomew staggered, and the knife dropped from his sleeve. Michael pretended to stumble in order to conceal it, and there was a hollow thud as his knees struck the ground. Appletre, Nonton and the *defensores* strained forward eagerly. They had reached Oxforde's coffin.

'Out, Bartholomew,' ordered Nonton. 'Appletre will take over now.'

'Me?' asked the precentor in distaste. 'Why not you?'

'Because I am better at controlling mutinous physicians,' replied Nonton savagely.

Rolling his eyes, Appletre indicated that Bartholomew should be hauled out, and took his place. It did not take him long to clear the remaining soil from the lid, while Michael stood at the far end of the hole, out of the way.

'Look at the number of nails that were used to seal the casket,' the precentor murmured. 'People must have been terrified that Oxforde would escape.'

'Do not bother prising them out,' instructed Nonton. 'Smash the wood.'

'The kitchen is alight!' exclaimed Bartholomew suddenly.

Appletre stood. 'He is right, Nonton. Perhaps we had better raise the alarm and come back to this later, because that is a building I should not like to lose.'

'We are almost there,' argued Nonton. 'A few more moments will make no difference. Break the wood with the edge of the spade. Hurry!'

Avarice and curiosity won out; Appletre turned his attention back to the coffin. He raised the spade and brought it down hard. Nothing happened, so he did it again. Something cracked, and he exchanged an excited grin with Nonton before striking a third time. Bartholomew eased towards Michael and dropped to a crouch, feigning exhaustion. When everyone's eyes were fixed on Appletre, the monk quickly tossed the knife to Bartholomew.

'Use it well,' he murmured. 'Then run. Do not worry about me.'

'No! I cannot leave you to—'

'Run from this place and do not stop until you are safe. Someone must survive to tell the Bishop what really happened, or Robert and his henchmen are going to win. That will be my vengeance. Now go.'

Bartholomew clambered to his feet and braced himself

for a sprint, but one of the *defensores* moved to stand between him and the cemetery gate, his eyes sharp and watchful.

'This is taking too long,' said Nonton impatiently, as Appletre's battering became more exasperated and less efficient. He pointed at Michael. 'You do it.'

Michael made a show of gripping the spade for an almighty swipe, aiming to snag the *defensores*' attention, but the one guarding Bartholomew was too professional to be distracted. He continued to watch his prisoner, even when the wood shattered. Michael bent to rip away the broken pieces, but still the fellow's gaze did not waver. Bartholomew ground his teeth in impotent frustration.

'There is nothing here but bones!' cried Appletre in dismay. 'Bartholomew was lying. Kill him, Nonton. He has made fools of us.'

'The treasure is beneath the coffin,' said Bartholomew quickly, when Nonton raised his sword. 'Obviously.'

'Why obviously?' demanded the cellarer.

'Because Oxforde put the treasure down there himself, of course,' explained Bartholomew acidly. 'It is not going to be on top of his body, is it?'

'Look at the hospital roof,' said one *defensor* anxiously. 'And the kitchen will be also lost unless we do something soon.'

'In a moment.' Nonton was not interested, all his attention on the grave.

'Robert is deranged from living in the wild for weeks on end,' said Bartholomew, fabricating wildly. 'He is no longer rational. You cannot follow his—'

'Enough!' snapped Nonton. 'Shut up, or I will kill you now.'

'Do it,' said Appletre. 'We will have the hoard soon, and he is no longer of use to us.'

Nonton took a step towards Bartholomew, but another cheer from the hospital distracted him. A movement made them both turn – it was Robert leaving the building. Bartholomew frowned in confusion when the Abbot secured the door behind him with a bar. Then his stomach lurched when he recalled Appletre saying that the market-side entrance would also be locked, to exclude gatecrashers from the town.

'He is going to leave them in there,' he breathed, appalled. 'To burn!'

He felt rather than saw Nonton's sword flash towards him, and only just managed to duck away. The watchful *defensor* grabbed his arms and held him while Nonton took aim a second time, but a clod of earth struck the cellarer in the back and made him stagger.

'My apologies,' said Michael. 'Hah! Come and look. We are almost there.'

Nonton nodded that the *defensor* was to keep hold of Bartholomew, and stepped towards the grave. Bones were flying out, along with pieces of shattered coffin, as Appletre worked with manic excitement.

'Christ!' said one soldier uneasily, holding up a piece of lid to show that the inside was scored with scratches. 'Oxforde tried to claw his way out.'

'The Devil raised him,' cried Michael suddenly. 'And anyone touching his grave will be cursed, so we had better run to the chapel to—'

'Superstition,' declared Nonton savagely when the

defensores looked as though they might do it. 'Ignore him. He is just trying to frighten you.'

The soldiers continued to edge away, but surged back when Appletre gave a loud whoop and catapulted to his feet, clutching a handful of glittering metal. He tossed it high into the air with a shriek of delight, and it rained down all around them.

It was now or never. While everyone's attention was on the falling treasure, Bartholomew plunged the knife into his captor's hip. While the fellow screamed in pain, the physician swung a wild punch at Nonton and knocked him cold.

Michael had not been slow to react either, and had dealt Appletre an almighty blow to the chin with the spade. Bartholomew started to run, but the *defensores* were after him in a trice and there were too many to outrun. While three held him down, the one he had wounded hobbled forward, dagger at the ready.

'Look!' yelled Michael, brandishing a fistful of treasure at them. 'Rings, bracelets, brooches! But this is as close as *you* will ever come to it.'

'What do you mean?' demanded the injured *defensor*, swivelling around to look at him just as Bartholomew felt the cold touch of steel against his neck.

'It will be used to rebuild the abbey, and every penny will be needed, because the stables are alight now, too.'

The *defensores* exchanged looks, but the wounded one shook his head. 'You are wrong. Robert will pay us.'

'Yes, but this is more than *pay*,' coaxed Michael. 'This is an opportunity. Take some and leave. You can live lives of luxury with all the women, wine and—'

He flinched back as two soldiers jumped into the grave with him and began stuffing gold into their tunics. Eager not to miss out, their cronies hastened to join them. The wounded man opened his mouth to order them back, but Bartholomew aimed a kick at the damaged hip that sent him sprawling, his face contorted in agony.

Bartholomew scrambled to his feet and tried to haul Michael out of the grave, but the monk was too heavy. Then Clippesby and Cynric appeared. The Dominican was pale and wild-eyed, and Bartholomew suspected he had been watching for some time, helpless to intervene. Cynric was breathing hard, though, indicating that he had only just arrived.

'A *defensor* laid hold of me,' he muttered. 'It took a while to escape the bastard – and I never reached the hospital.'

'Help me!' Bartholomew was tugging with all his might on Michael's arm.

Cynric and Clippesby obliged, and the monk began to rise. The process dislodged the excavated earth, which began to slide back into the tomb, showering down on soldiers and treasure alike. Appletre lay motionless, but the others cursed, although none thought to abandon the hoard in order to escape the avalanche. When Michael reached the top, his scrabbling feet sent more of it cascading downwards.

'Leave them!' shouted Clippesby, when Cynric grabbed a spade and began shovelling for all he was worth, determined to avenge himself on the men who had tried to burn him alive. 'We must save the people in the hospital.'

Bartholomew glanced at the flames that now danced over the roof, and recalled what it had been like in the granary as it had ignited and smoke had seared his lungs. He started towards the chapel, but Michael caught his arm.

'Wait! We need a plan. Robert will order you shot if you just race up to—'

'William is in there,' Bartholomew shouted, trying to shrug him off.

'You will be killed before you are halfway to the door,' gasped Cynric. He was still frantically shovelling soil, drawing furious yells from the *defensores* below.

In an agony of despair, Bartholomew gazed around wildly, looking for anything he might turn to his advantage. His eye lit on the treasure that Appletre had tossed up in his moment of jubilation. Michael had used it to prevent the *defensores* by the grave from killing him, so would the same ploy work on the others? He snatched up the biggest, gaudiest items and ran.

'We found it!' he yelled, waving the jewellery in the air as he tore towards the hospital.

Robert whipped around and barked an order to the *defensores*, but the glitter of gold had caught their attention and they did not shoot. Bartholomew shouted louder: his survival and that of William, the monks, the bedesfolk and the servants depended on him being understood.

'Hurry if you want a share,' he hollered. 'Four of your friends have already left, loaded down with as much as they can carry.'

'They would not dare steal from me,' said Robert coldly. He turned to his men. 'Kill him.'

Bartholomew brandished what he had taken. 'Do you think they would let me take this if they were still here? They knew Robert would not share it. He plans to spend it all on rebuilding his abbey. Why else would he let it burn?'

He felt like screaming when the *defensores* still hesitated. At the end of his tether, he shoved the baubles at the nearest guard. 'Here. There is plenty more in the grave. Help yourself, because Robert will not—'

'*Kill* him,' snarled Robert, exasperated. 'Can you not see that he is lying?'

But the *defensor* who held the treasure was impressed by its weight and quality, and wanted more. He dropped his bow and began to hurry towards the cemetery. Unwilling to miss out, his cronies followed.

'No!' screeched Robert. 'Come back!'

Bartholomew shoved past him and hauled open the hospital door. Immediately, people spilled out, coughing and gagging.

'You locked us in!' gasped William, pointing furiously at Robert. 'And you must have known the roof was smouldering.'

'I did not,' stated Robert. 'I was just coming to—'

'Liar!' shouted Inges. 'We heard you order the *defensores* not to open the door on any account.'

'Lay hold of him, ladies,' ordered Hagar, and her bedeswomen surged forward. 'We shall see what the Bishop says about abbots who leave their flock to roast.'

Robert went down in a flailing melee of arms and legs, still protesting his innocence.

The lesser obedientiaries, quick to understand what was happening, hastened to organise their bewildered

394

brethren. Some were instructed to secure Nonton and the cemetery, while others were directed to fight the fires. Their calm but firm commands soon restored order, and it was not long before the blazes were either doused or under control.

'It is over, Matt,' said Michael, coming to stand next to the physician, who was trying to summon the energy to walk to where Ramseye was dispensing ale to the exhausted but victorious monks, servants and bedesfolk. 'Nonton was stabbed by a *defensor* during the scrabble for the treasure, Appletre suffocated before he could be pulled out of Oxforde's grave, and Robert is under Hagar's watchful eye.'

'I cannot begin to imagine how we will explain all this to the Bishop,' said Clippesby. He had several horses and a goat in his wake, along with Henry.

'I am sure Michael will find a way,' said Henry. 'And if not, I shall do it. I am not afraid to tell the truth about these wicked men.'

'None of this would have happened if you had not buried a felon in your grounds,' said Michael, rather accusingly.

'In that case,' said Henry with a seraphic smile, 'we had better make sure we do not do it again.'

EPILOGUE

Cambridge, three days later

The journey south was uneventful, and with no robbers to repel, Bartholomew did not fall off his horse once. He breathed a sigh of relief when he saw the familiar jumble of towers and spires on the horizon, and was delighted to ride back through Michaelhouse's sturdy gates, despite the immediate accusatory clamour from patients and students who thought he had been gone too long.

When he had seen to the more urgent cases, and the sun was setting in a blaze of orange, he went to the conclave, the room adjoining the hall that was the exclusive domain of the Fellows. They were all there: those who had stayed were keen to hear about their colleagues' adventures, while the travellers were eager to oblige them. Cynric was there, too, serving cakes. Bartholomew took one. It was overcooked, needed salt and tasted vaguely of cabbage, but it was fare he was used to, and there was something comfortingly reassuring about it after the fine tables of Peterborough.

Michael came to slump next to him. 'I should never have gone,' he said bitterly. 'My Junior Proctor not only wrote *and* published Winwick Hall's charter, he gave its founder permission to start building. The place is half finished already, and will open next term.'

'Next term?' asked Bartholomew, startled. 'That *is* fast.'

'Yes, considering these things usually take years – decades, even. It has caused a lot of ill feeling: the other Colleges object to this cuckoo in their midst, the hostels resent its brazen affluence, and the town is angry that they were not consulted.'

'What will you do? Order it demolished?'

'I wish I could, but the founder is a favourite of the King, so Winwick Hall is here to stay. There have already been riots over it, including one last night in which a student was killed. I shall need you to inspect his body tomorrow, then help me find the culprit.'

'It is good to be home,' declared William, just as Bartholomew was wondering whether he might have been wiser to stay away. 'Heresy and wickedness have flourished in my absence, and I shall have to work hard to suppress them again.'

'Do not forget the reason you were sent away in the first place,' warned Michael. 'So watch what you say – unless you want to be dispatched on another journey.'

William closed his mouth abruptly.

'Cambridge may have its drawbacks,' said Clippesby quietly. 'But I would rather live here than anywhere else. At least no one labours under the misapprehension that I am a saint.'

'No,' agreed William sullenly.

'The College cat could scarcely credit such foolery when I told her about it,' Clippesby went on. The animal in question was purring in his lap. 'You see? She is still stunned now.'

'You are not the only one who was perceived as

something he was not,' said Langelee. 'So was Spalling. He had fiery ideas, but he did not really believe in them.'

'He was a villain,' spat Cynric. He did not usually voice his opinions in the hallowed confines of the conclave, where only Fellows ever spoke, but Spalling's perfidy still rankled, and he could not help himself. 'Yet there *will* be a great rebellion one day, when everything he promised will come to pass.'

'I sincerely hope you are wrong,' said Langelee fervently. 'But before we leave the subject of Spalling, I should tell you that I did not know him after all. We got together with dates and places one night, and it turned out that it was another Spalling I met in York. Not him. No wonder he did not look familiar.'

Bartholomew blinked. 'You mean you imposed yourself on a total stranger?'

Langelee shrugged. 'I knew him by the time we realised the mistake.'

William laughed. 'I must remember that one, Master, because it saw you housed and fed most sumptuously.'

'But not as sumptuously as us,' said Michael. 'Those monks knew how to cater to their personal comforts. Of course, those days are over now that most of the obedientiaries are in one kind of trouble or another.'

'Or dead,' added William, rather gleefully. He began to list them. 'Welbyrn the treasurer, drowned in St Leonard's well; Appletre the precentor, smothered in Oxforde's tomb; and Nonton the cellarer, knifed during an unseemly spat over gold. And their helpmeets Spalling and Lullington killed into the bargain.'

'And poor Pyk sacrificed on the altar of their greed,' said Michael. 'Not to mention Lady Lullington and Reginald.'

'But none of them poisoned Matt,' said Clippesby with a guileless smile. 'That was William's doing.'

'It was not deliberate,' insisted the Franciscan, flushing red with mortification. 'I was trying to help.'

'There is a certain irony in the fact that Oxforde's treasure was in their own abbey,' said Langelee, more interested in the hoard than the friar's protestations of innocence – he had listened to them all the way back from Peterborough, because although Bartholomew was prepared to overlook the matter, Michael was not, and had harped on it constantly. 'Robert wasted an entire month digging up Aurifabro's land.'

'Why did Oxforde hide his hoard in St Thomas's cemetery in the first place?' asked William, glad to be discussing something else. 'If he had been pardoned, it would have been very difficult to retrieve.'

'The graveyard only became busy after his death,' explained Michael. 'Before the so-called miracles at his tomb, it was a quiet, secluded place with few visitors. Indeed, it was unfortunate for him that the Sheriff decided to pay his respects to the dead silversmith on the day he was burying his hoard – an encounter that saw him arrested.'

'The stuff he was hiding comprised jewellery that was distinctive,' Bartholomew went on. 'And thus difficult to sell. His plan was to store it for a few years until memories had faded. At least, that is what Kirwell said when I described some of the pieces to him.'

'He thought Oxforde's deception was hilarious,' said William uncompromisingly. 'And he laughed so hard that he died.'

'I think he was laughing at himself,' said Bartholomew,

who had been with the old man when he had cackled himself into his grave. 'For believing a lie all those years.'

'Oxforde was evil,' stated William uncompromisingly. 'He murdered men, women and children in his quest for riches, and I am glad that Henry has promised to bury his bones in a location that only he knows. There will be no more pilgrims praying at his tomb from now on.'

'He was punished for his crimes, though,' added Michael soberly. 'I cannot imagine what it must have been like to be buried alive.'

They sat quietly for a while, contemplating the wages of sin.

'I had a letter from Gynewell this morning,' said Michael eventually. 'He thinks it would be a pity to taint Peterborough by exposing the actions of a few rotten apples.'

'You mean he wants the matter covered up?' asked Bartholomew in distaste.

Michael nodded. 'And he is right. Peterborough is a *good* place, and its monks are decent men. Why should they suffer for what Robert and a few of his obedientiaries did?'

'But the Bishop bundled Robert off to Avignon, to answer for his crimes to the Pope,' said Langelee. 'How can the matter be kept quiet now?'

'That will not be a problem. Robert was found hanged in his cell on the first night of his journey. It was probably suicide, but a tale is circulating that he was killed by outlaws.'

There was another silence, this one longer.

'At least you had some good news,' whispered Cynric to Bartholomew. 'Udela the witch predicted that you would find love.'

'Did she say with whom?' asked Michael, although the book-bearer had not intended his remark for general consumption. 'Matilde or Julitta?'

Bartholomew had seen Julitta that afternoon, and their reunion had been even sweeter than he had hoped. As a result, he was more confused than ever about the possibility of Matilde's return.

'She was vague,' said Cynric, when the physician did not reply. 'But it is something to look forward to, because she is famous for never being wrong. Besides, she did not base her prediction on the magic stones, but on talking to Matilde. They met, see.'

'I am not surprised,' said Bartholomew, with a sigh. 'Everyone did see Matilde except me.'

'I mean in Clare,' explained Cynric. 'Mother Udela visited Suffolk once, where she happened across Matilde. They talked for a long time, and she told Matilde that it was foolish to sit back while the man she loved went hankering after another woman. It was her idea for Matilde to earn herself the fortune she needs to woo you.'

'She needs nothing of the kind,' said Bartholomew, exasperated. 'And I am not *hankering* after Julitta. She—'

He was interrupted by a bellow of manly laughter from Langelee, while the other Fellows exchanged amused glances – it was no secret that she was the first 'patient' the physician had called to see. Michael did not smile, though. He knew Matilde well enough to predict that she would succeed in the task she had set herself, at which point his friend would be faced with a difficult decision.

'What happened to the treasure in the end?' asked

William, more interested in that than in Bartholomew's tangled love life.

'The *defensores* took most of it,' replied Michael, glad, for Bartholomew's sake, to be discussing something else. 'But the rest will be used to build a new church in the marketplace. The abbey will oversee the work.'

'And the monks can be trusted?' asked Langelee doubtfully.

Michael nodded. 'Yes, now Henry is Abbot.'

'Henry,' pounced Batholomew, a little triumphantly. 'You were all wrong about him, and he is the man the Bishop chose to put Peterborough to rights.'

'We were not wrong,' countered Michael haughtily. 'He is aggrevatingly pious, and he is said to have accepted the abbacy with gleeful glee. One of the monks wrote to tell me.'

'He knows the Bishop will be watching his progress, so he will do an adequate job,' said Clippesby, uncharacteristically harsh in his judgement. Bartholomew stared at him in surprise.

'And should he falter, Ramseye and Yvo will keep him in order,' added Michael. 'They are far too bitter about their demotions to grant him any leeway. Peterborough will have a new church, of that I am certain.'

'Does this mean you have decided not to try for the abbacy yourself?' asked Langelee.

Michael sighed. 'I cannot leave Cambridge as long as the trouble with Winwick Hall persists. My University needs me, so I shall stay. For now, at least.'

Bartholomew stood. It was getting late and he was tired.

'You had better not be going to bed,' said William

rather accusingly. 'Not before you have dressed the hand that I burned when I was fighting the fire in the abbey.'

'And you have more patients who want to see you,' added Langelee. He placed a list on the table. 'They include Rougham of Gonville Hall, who says he will forgive you for failing his students at their disputations if you relieve him of a painfully ingrown toenail.'

'And there are two new students who want to study medicine,' said Cynric. 'They are waiting for you in the hall. I told them to return tomorrow, but they refused.'

'Do not stay out too late,' warned Michael. 'I need you to inspect that dead student at first light in the morning.'

'Welcome home, Matt,' said Clippesby with a wry smile. 'It seems it is already business as usual.'

HISTORICAL NOTE

The abbey at Peterborough was founded by Mercian royalty in the 650s. The first church was destroyed in Viking raids, and was not rebuilt until the tenth century when the Benedictines arrived. They remained at Peterborough for almost six hundred years, raising the splendid church (started in 1116 when fire destroyed the old one) that still exists today. After the Dissolution, it was redesignated a cathedral, and visitors threading their way through the modern city are rewarded with the sight of one of the best Norman buildings in the world.

By the mid-fourteenth century, the monastery was one of the richest foundations in the country, although the Black Death hit it hard, reducing its sixty-four monks to thirty-two, even after laymen had been hastily tonsured in an effort to boost numbers. Its Abbot in 1358 was Robert de Ramseye, and a curious incident occurred during his tenure. It was in 1353, when John Gynewell, Bishop of Lincoln, absolved Hugh de Spalling from excommunication. According to the records, Spalling broke the locks on the abbey's doors and gates, fished in its river without a licence, hunted in its woods and felled its trees.

Eight years later, Abbot Robert set off to visit the Papal Court in Avignon, and nothing more was ever heard of him. The monks lived in uncertainty until he was declared dead, which left them free to appoint a successor. This was Henry de Overton, who ruled the community for the next thirty years. Other Peterborough monks in the 1350s included John de Trentham, Thomas Appletre and Richard de Nonton; John de Welbyrn was appointed treasurer in 1351; and Walter was the cook. There was a cellarer in the 1400s named William de Ramseye, whom fellow monks did not like. He part-donated the eagle lectern that still stands in the cathedral, and he was buried in Peterborough after an ecclesiastical career spanning more than fifty years. There was a prior named Yvo in the thirteenth century.

As Peterborough Abbey had been founded by royalty, the King had the right to foist his old retainers on the community, and demand that they be kept for the rest of their lives, sometimes in considerable luxury. These were called corrodians, and one such man was John Lullington. He and his wife lived in style at abbey expense in the 1300s, and he had the right to dine with the abbey's senior officers (obedientiaries).

The abbey had two hospitals. St Leonard's was a foundation for lepers, although leprosy was all but gone from England by the 1350s, and it seems likely that it then became home to bedesmen, perhaps retired abbey servants. In return for bed and board, they recited prayers for the souls of benefactors. Its chapel was said to have had a healing well. In 1362, it had a 'prior' and eight residents. Bedesmen included John Inges, Roger Botilbrig, Philip Kirwell and Simon the cowherd. It was located on the outskirts of the town, on the road named Westgate.

The second hospital, dedicated to St Thomas Becket,

was near the Abbey Gate. It is said that in 1176 a monk named Benedict was in a position to grab himself a few relics from Canterbury before travelling north to take up an appointment as Peterborough's Abbot. These included flagstones from near where Becket was murdered, some of his clothes and vases of his blood. Benedict installed these in the chapel, where pilgrims visited them regularly. It seems that this community was run by women; inmates included Joan Sylle, Hagar Balfowre, Elene Bolton and Marion Raunsfeld.

A market was established outside the Abbey Gate, and not far away was the Swan Inn, mentioned in records dating back to 1338. The original Church of St John the Baptist lay to the east of the monastery, but the market probably caused some resettlement, and in the early 1400s a second church was built in the marketplace – one that still serves Peterborough today. Prominent townsmen in the fourteenth century included Hugh Pyk, Nicholas Piel, Ralph Aurifabro the goldsmith, and Reginald the cutler.

In the early 1300s, a criminal named Lawrence of Oxforde was hanged and buried in St Thomas's churchyard. The authorities were appalled when miracles were said to have occurred at his grave, and quickly sought to suppress the tales. Several monks were excommunicated for encouraging people to visit the site, but the cult was clearly popular. Records show it took three visitations by the Bishop before the business was finally stamped out.

Don't miss Matthew Bartholomew's
twentieth chronicle!

DEATH OF A SCHOLAR

In the summer of 1358 the physician Matthew Bartholomew
returns to Cambridge to learn that his beloved sister is in
mourning after the unexpected death of her husband, Oswald
Stanmore. Aware that his son has no interest in the cloth trade
that made his fortune and reputation, Oswald has left the
business to his widow, but a spate of burglaries in the town
distracts Matthew from supporting Edith in her grief and
attempting to keep the peace between her and her wayward son.

As well as the theft of irreplaceable items from Michaelhouse,
which threatens its very survival, a new foundation, Winwick Hall,
is causing consternation amongst Matthew's colleagues.
The founder is an impatient man determined that his name will
grace the University's most prestigious college. He has used his
wealth to rush the construction of the hall, and his appointed
Fellows have infiltrated the charitable Guild founded by
Stanmore, in order to gain the support of Cambridge's most
influential citizens on Winwick's behalf.

A perfect storm between the older establishments and the
brash newcomers is brewing when the murder of a leading
member of the Guild is soon followed by the death of one
of Winwick's senior Fellows. Assisting Brother Michael in
investigating these fatalities leads Matthew into a web of
suspicion, where conspiracy theories are rife but facts are
scarce and where the pressure from the problems of his
college and his family sets him on a path that could endanger
his own future . . .

Out now